ADAM

RESURRECTED

BOOKS BY YORAM KANIUK
PUBLISHED BY GROVE PRESS

Adam Resurrected
Commander of the *Exodus*

ADAM
RESURRECTED

YORAM KANIUK

TRANSLATED FROM THE HEBREW BY SEYMOUR SIMCKES

GROVE PRESS
New York

Published simultaneously in Canada
Printed in the United States of America

Library of Congress Cataloging-in-Publication Data
Kaniuk, Yoram.
[Adam ben kelev. English]
Adam ressurected / Yoram Kaniuk ; translated from the Hebrew
by Seymour Simckes.
p. cm.

ISBN-13: 978-0-8021-3689-3
1. Holocaust survivors—Israel—Fiction. I. Simckes, Seymour. II. Title.
PJ5054.K326 A6713 2000
892.4'36—dc21   99-056655

Design by Harry Ford

Grove Press
an imprint of Grove/Atlantic, Inc.
841 Broadway
New York, NY 10003
Distributed by Publishers Group West
www.groveatlantic.com

09 10 11 12   10 9 8 7 6 5 4 3 2

T O

MIRANDA KANIUK

Elazar the son of Ya-ir said: God must have made up His mind irrevocably against the Jewish People, his former loved ones, for if He had continued to show us a friendly face or if He were angry for just a short while, He would not have been absent, so totally absent, during the Great Destruction.

JOSEPHUS, *The Jewish War*

A man is a god in ruins.

EMERSON

CONTENTS

ADAM
RESURRECTED

1

THE CLOWN

SHE TAPS HIS DOOR with dainty fingers. Her hair, drawn back, is fine silver, and her face smooth silk. She wears a light summer dress, a flower print—obviously a recent purchase—with a wide sailor's tie around her neck. She looks as though she has just stepped out of a faded photograph. "Adam, Adam!" she calls, at once correcting herself, "Mr. Stein," mumbling in addition, "It's time, Adam . . . I'm very sorry." And, in fact, the landlady of the pension *is* very sorry.

She clasps her neck with her delicate white hands woven with bluish veins and, for a moment, seems to be swooning, the victim of a strangler. Only yesterday she was almost choked to death and now she is greeting the dawn, and this door, and about to greet her charming would-be murderer with pride, her heart beating like a young girl's on a first date. Earlier, when she hadn't yet thoroughly wakened and was still half slumbering, the morning appeared lovely. But once she had actually risen, she remembered and understood. She touches her own throat now and hates it, knowing that her fate will be decided in just a short while.

Though awake an hour ago, Adam pretends he is still asleep, like a child who thinks he's concealed if he shuts his eyes. Except that Adam's lids are slightly ajar, so he is able to catch the movements of shadows across his walls, shadows of cars. Through his not quite meshed lashes he sees himself spread over the worn, faded wallpaper. Instead of stereotyped flowers, he sees his own image multiplied a thousand times. He knows the landlady must now be clasping her neck. He senses her hands fondling her own throat, tender and stretched forward. He isn't worried about last night, he isn't worried that her neck remains superfluous in the world. He knows how to achieve happiness and knows that he knows how. However, he also understands the essence of finality. That everything must come to an end. And God is no more precise than myself, thinks he.

The cedars outside cast silhouettes, now and again, where his face is multiplied across the walls. They seem to be sailing, sailing to the corner of the room and out of sight. At the sound of Mrs. Edelson's slight voice on the other side of the door, at the sound of her whispering to herself, he opens his eyes. He even hears the thoughts of her heart.

With the look of someone just waking, Adam rises from his bed, commences dressing. Now that he is on his feet, he can see through the window a tall cypress that resembles the Grand Inquisitor's miter. This past night he dreamed of the *auto-da-fé*. For some reason, since he settled in Israel, he has hardly ever dreamed the events of his own life; instead he dreams events of centuries ago, concerning persons whose fate has only the remotest connection with his own. At night his own life is censored, while in its place he sees public bonfires. Last night the Grand Inquisitor was burning a certain book. It seemed to Adam that the name of the book was *Faust*. Despite his feeling that the book, to a great degree, deserved to burn, the business pained him. The Inquisitor, with his black conical hat, though true to his name, was after all burning *Faust*.

Today breaks like a blitzkrieg. From the street, voices climb into his room. The noise of cars rushing downtown jumbles with the usual clanging of the milkman's bottles. Somebody shouts: "Mrs. Epstein, your paper!" Then a newspaper whizzes through the air and bang! is on the porch, while across the street a child is howling. Adam can hear the landlady breathing on the other side of the door. He is certain this refined woman is now peeking through the keyhole. He sticks his wet face over the edge of the old-fashiond little sink whose faucets shriek and gurgle, and cries out toward the door: "The sun's countenance is pitch black, Ruthie, and clouds cloud the heart."

She blushes, poor thing, and her head, which was close to the keyhole, bumps the door. He almost bursts out laughing, but this morning has brought with it a hazy realization that Mrs. Edelson deserves different treatment, so he nips his laughter in the bud, transforming it into a loud gargle.

"Adam, what are you really thinking about?" says Mrs. Edelson in German.

"Nothing at all, Ruthie. I simply wanted to know if I am still handsome in the morning."

"You are, Adam," and again she blushes, that woman out of a faded photograph.

A prolonged silence as he finishes washing. Then Mrs. Edelson giggles just a bit.

"It's early in the morning and already we're romantic," she says, half embarrassed, while he brushes his shirt with a silver-handled brush. Adam adores the landlady's German, a language which, in his own words, "uplifts you to the height of heights and flogs you with horsewhips!"

Ruthie still speaks the German of her youth. Every day since his arrival in Israel, he has renewed his acquaintance with that beautiful ancient tongue which, here, has not gone sour in the past twenty years. When Ruthie spoke, he saw the mysterious beauty of an old book, of a bookcase of old books, of a picture from the house of his parents. Through the words of Mrs. Edelson, the pension landlady, he heard the voice of his mother and Uncle Franz-Josef and his father.

He had, however, a complaint against the body of this dainty elderly woman. How was her body able to preserve its luster of youth, its resilience, its infallibly smooth skin—the body of a woman past childbearing? How was this possible?

"How old are you, Ruthie?" he shouts suddenly.

"Fifty, Adam. Don't laugh, just today I turned exactly fifty!"

"*Glückauf!*" says he and lowers his head into the sink. The nerve of her! With poetic license yet! As lovely as a virgin. A warm body, silver hair drawn back. When she stood naked before him, he couldn't take his eyes off her. Not a single wrinkle in her whole body. What passion intact! As though her body had been frozen years ago and now had suddenly thawed.

Right now, though, he is in a hurry. He puts on his fancy blue shirt, smooths out his jacket, carefully shining its gold buttons, every one of which has the emblem of Herr Von Hamdung stamped on it, the very Von Hamdung whose lovely mansion in Berlin Adam inherited. He dons his black felt hat, manufactured by A. N. Fischer, Berlin, with its round brim curled slightly upward, and is ready to go. But when he opens the door, Mrs. Edelson loses her balance. She didn't have time enough to retreat, though she was peeking through the keyhole, and the door, flinging open, strikes her hard. A faint cry slips out of her pursed mouth. He smiles. "That's the way you scream, my silk-stockinged woman?" and his polite penetrating precise glance swerves toward her slender neck and stalls there.

That swan, he says to himself. He sees the explanation for this morning in her neck. In her neck he sees his humiliation. Yet he knows that you cannot place the blame on another person. I am the man who has dug for himself all the pits into which he has fallen. He feels somehow relieved.

"Ready, Adam?"

He bows in front of her. He is inviting her to dance a waltz. She debates with herself whether or not to tell him, whether or not to remind him where they are. However, she herself prefers to forget, so she lets the matter pass.

"Well, let's go," says he. But amid the soft music which has begun to play in her heart, amid the light steps of the dance, she distinctly hears the voice of the Yemenite maid of the Goldstein family in the house across the way. The maid yells: "Matti, Jules, to school, hurry up!" And Ruthie raises her arm, waits for Adam to hook his in hers, and then, her face plaster white, she leads him along the corridor.

"So, my doll, let's go?"

She smiles against her will, and he skips a bit, shifting the weight of his body forward, and after a few seconds of walking she is no longer leading him, he is leading her. And in her own house! She traces a shy finger across the expensive cloth of his coat and her mouth opens for a moment. She looks frightened, and he cries out: "Horse-cloth! Cobwebs!"

Somebody shouts from the room they are just passing: "How about a little quiet? This is a pension, not a train station!"

Adam strikes his finger against his mouth, shrugs his shoulders like a boy caught in some mischief, and pulls her along— disgraced like himself. They descend the steps as one person, their breath mingling. Her gossamer gait makes her realize that, unquestionably, time has stopped somehow and exists no longer.

Nonetheless, beyond the minds and hearts of Mrs. Edelson and Adam Stein, the new day sweeps across the quiet little street. No longer dripping with dew or cloaked in morning mist, the day is already aflame with its sun proud above the tall apartment houses in the east. A Tel Aviv autumn morning bursts over the eucalyptus trees that dance by the Yarkon River, and for a fleeting moment, before the fine fog has evaporated and while the day is still very young, it is possible to imagine the Yarkon as a wide river whose far bank is not visible to the naked eye.

Downstairs in the hall stand the suitcases, side by side. Five suitcases made of high-quality leather, Prussian blue, with gleaming ivory handles. Each suitcase is about four inches taller than the one beyond it, so from the top of the staircase they look like an additional flight of stairs descending right into the carpet. Or, in Adam's words, "an addendum to a grotesque stage." He examines his luggage as though he were witnessing his entire life stretched out before him. He no longer reflects on Mrs. Edelson's neck or her young flexible body, nor does he imagine any more dog bowls or other painful sights. He witnesses seas and oceans. He envisions silver, money, and power. He is strong and handsome, and his suitcases are a passport to splendor. Last night, after the incident occurred and he had fallen asleep, Mrs. Edelson packed his belongings. The time she spent packing she also spent crying, and among his clothes he will find her tears, frozen in the shape of her body, a reminder of the graceful neck which he strangled with a joy almost indistinguishable from the passion of youth. And she? She who arranged every sock, every shirt, every undershirt, every tie? She is looking at the five suitcases like somebody seeing them for the last time.

She understands, as a woman, that you pay a price for every item. Now that she is unable to cry any more, she knows that her tears will accompany him. She will remain here, among the cypresses and the eucalypti, alongside the river, rich now with the illumination of the rising sun. And the days will run on. Run on—and she get older, and her limber body become a question mark.

She starts biting her fingernails, and her bitten fingernails sing: "Adam is leaving . . . Adam is leaving . . ." She yearns for childish comforts. If she could, she would jump rope. Instead, silence. A crackling silence. Adam raises his eyes and his eyes photograph the room which, together with Ruthie's German and her lovely body, from the time of his arrival here a few months ago, has poured into him the peaceful feeling that a child has on returning home.

Wasn't it here, in the presence of this old outmoded furniture, that he called out, a few months ago, to his father? Wasn't it here, one night, while standing in front of the pitch-black window as Ruthie was pouring brandy into two red goblets, that he cried out to his father because suddenly, in the opaque window, he saw his own reflection staring back at him and he was older than his father had ever been? At that time he said to Mrs. Edelson: "Ruthie, look, I called out my father's name. My father's gone. I'm fifty-three. My father died when he was forty-eight. Today I could be *his* father!" And he burst out laughing. Now, for a moment, he remembers something else: Klein, Herr Klein, Herr Commandant Klein, standing at the entrance to the concentration camp and examining the new arrivals with empty eyes. And there stood he, Adam, among the other creatures, Adam with his handsome green suitcase in his hand as if he were traveling on a vacation, surrounded by a fence with a sign saying WORK LIBERATES. And suddenly Herr Klein was shouting: "Hey, that's Adam Stein!" And in his voice you could hear the tune of admiration, intense admiration. Adam almost expected Herr Klein to ask him for his autograph, but Herr Klein did not ask him for his autograph—instead, he granted him his life. An autograph he did not ask for, I ate on all fours, from the dog dish, with Rex the cur.

Here in Ruthie's room his former days came back. For instance, the picture, framed in gold, of those horses standing in an Olympian pose beside the royal palace in Vienna. And the magnificent red chariot of Empress Maria Theresa. And, a red-cheeked girl taking care of geese and, under her, written in Gothic letters, *Gesundheit*. And the portrait of a young woman, her face white and drenched with the sorrow of youth, her hair drawn back and adorned with a diamond pin—obviously Mrs. Edelson herself, Ruthie, in the days of her youth. Through an act of grace or a miracle, her body was still young. Yes, everything was preserved: her elegant diction *à la* Schiller, Jean Paul, Wassermann, the furniture, the chest of drawers, the paintings,

the white ceramic plates decorated with blue designs . . . the
poster of a 1911-model Maxwell roadster with its gearshift outside the driver's compartment and the spokes of its wheels
golden. All of these stared at him during that single outcry to his
father, stared at him with a gorgeous emptiness that warned him
of their non-existence. As though everything present before him
were a star long ago extinguished, as though the images he was
seeing amounted to dead light, the emanations of a star that had
ceased shining a thousand years past, even though the earth was
still receiving its defunct rays.

Yes, including his childhood, which disappeared like smoke
in the presence of Herr Commandant Klein but reappeared, in
compressed form, in the well-preserved body of Mrs. Edelson,
preserved just for him—as though the curtain had fallen but the
play was continuing. Because, as in the case of the star, the end
was tied to the beginning; and the beginning was still breathing
and alive. Here, in particular, at the source of the Yarkon. The
Berlin of his youth was right here, and more alive here than
there.

The sharp ring of the doorbell rescues them from their
thoughts. It brings the terrible silence to an end. The door
swings open and two young men come in. The door bangs behind
them.

To Mrs. Edelson the two young men look like a pair of
agents, agents of evil, she says to herself, agents of the Devil.
They hardly look at her. Courteously, but unmistakably, they
indicate to Adam that it's time to go. Adam examines them with
a smile. Slowly he recognizes them. He rushes over to the suitcases, grabs the smallest one, lays it down on its side, opens it
and rummages through it. He takes out a shirt, two ties, a wine-
colored leather case which holds his electric shaver, and some
plasticine, but the tears of Mrs. Edelson he keeps inside the suitcase. He ransacks his belongings as if looking for something he
has lost, and drops them one by one on the rug. His face shows
apathy. To the two men watching him he might be a tired and

bored Rothschild making a rough estimate of his fortune. They nod, as if to say, We know what you're up to. They do know, and Mrs. Edelson, for that reason, shows them her amazement, doesn't disguise her annoyance. For the occasion itself is bitter enough on its own, with its own inevitable ceremony of finality, and doesn't need any extra realizations contributed by them. The plasticine lying on the carpet hints to them: I'm not an easy catch. The men observe the movements of Adam's hands. The movements are amazing, so exact and so quick. One of them says: "What grace. In another minute he'll be pulling pigeons past the gold buttons of his sleeve. . . ."

The other man's head says yes. He reads the tags attached to that suitcase. Grand Hotel, Zürich; Plaza, New York; George V, Paris. From the oh so elegant tags, to Adam's lovely suit, to his hat. The two men nod. Mrs. Edelson tries to be practical; she is, after all, the landlady. She's had the boardinghouse for fifteen years, and this is the first time that an incident like this involving her has happened in her house. Her evasive glance passes from the two men to Adam and then back again to the two men. Adam is laughing in order to postpone the whole business, she tells herself. But he is shrugging his shoulders now, not only because there is no way to escape the bitter end signaled by the eyes of the agents but because, somewhere in his mysterious heart, he is in fact welcoming that end.

He remembers the ecstasy on the face of Professor Schweizer —still a typical student of the University of Heidelberg of a thousand years ago—while he clarified to him how the criminal must rejoice in his punishment because that is his highest goal and therefore his secret desire . . . *and here I'm toying with these two fools!* He locks the suitcase and stands erect. A quick glance toward Ruthie. Afterward, resolute, he steps off.

The door seems to swing open on its own accord, and while the doorway frames him, a grayish halo, a reflection of the lintel, clings to him. In the eyes of the two men he appears too tame and, consequently, they are confused. In fact, to a great extent, they even share his pain, but they reserve their thoughts for themselves. He appreciates this and respects them.

Mrs. Edelson draws near to Adam, stands up on her toes— her head extended, her mouth practically touching his Adam's apple. As if she were dabbing his face with cotton, she gently smooths his face. His larynx is the boundary of her vision, the source of her trembling, her landscape of life and death. She feels her way toward his mouth; like the wings of a butterfly kissing the air, her fingers hover and barely touch his clean-shaven face. Adam suddenly says: "You've got the touch of toothpaste!" And she hears the voice of the clown.

His face is serious. Stern. He must cross the threshold under his own power. But he remains standing in the doorway like a statue, like somebody no longer able to function on his own. The presence of the two strangers brings out his hidden nature which gives him orders and doesn't allow him any games of free will.

Meanwhile her butterfly fingers model the shape of his face. She feels his beauty and it makes her sad. Always he reminds her of the autumn evening mist of her childhood. His thick gray hair, his chiseled features, his solid manly chin. Each black eye an ellipse within an ellipse, like rings of a spreading wave. His eyebrows somewhat curly, his nose straight and not too short. What spirituality in his face, and also what unashamed sensual-ity! The face of a philosopher and a lover, of an incorrigible romantic and a murderer. She recognizes all this and her fingers search for the secret meanings of the lines in his face—did he actually try to strangle her? It is already hard for her to believe it. She stretches herself, almost floating in the air, and with all the intensity of her preserved youth she brings her thin lips to his and penetrates him. Then, choking with tears, she runs up the staircase to her room and disappears.

Adam wipes the wetness off his lips and prepares for his exit —*his* exit. For he wants his departure to be appropriate and gracious. All of a sudden, manners are important to him. Mean-while these two men are waiting for some sort of cue. He makes a gesture with his hand and they pick up the suitcases.

"Have you already got the guitar and the typewriter?"

"Yes, Adam."

The door slams behind him. He enters the station wagon which has been waiting for him outside and, not looking to the left or the right, he waits. The driver starts the engine, the engine growls, and they're on their way. Then, suddenly, as if from a single blow, his body sinks down strengthless, his face hidden in the floor of the car, its expression dull. Like a dog that's just been beaten.

Across the windows of the car fly autumn scenes. A torn sign which amounts to DON'T TALK—KEEP YOUR MIND ON YOUR DRIVING. And sand, sand, and more sand, right down to the sea. Trees praying, their faces toward the east, toward the mountain that once had a temple. A cypress, brown from the sand. A small empty gas station, and two women sitting in Oriental fashion and laughing. A child chasing a kite, green orchards, yellow autumn oranges, fields, and an old Arab house whose blue paint is peeling. Piazzas and lovely oval arcs for roofs. Once, as he notices a packing-house in an orchard, the arcs and the domes make him imagine the superb figure of an Oriental potentate. He doesn't know that in this very place, sixteen years ago, a fierce battle took place. At present the orchards are at peace and a pleasant autumn wind traipses through the leaves, toying with them.

"Why did you try to kill her?" The young man has a cordial smile on his face. The ice is broken.

Adam purses up his face, and assumes a look of innocence and amazement for his interrogator. "I didn't try to."

"Yes, you did. You tried to kill her."

"Really? Who?"

"Mrs. Edelson, the landlady of the boardinghouse."

"Ruthie?" Adam fumbles in his pocket. One of them hands him a cigarette. The other lights it.

"That's right! Her!"

"Her?" The lit cigarette flickers.

The other fellow smiles and extinguishes the match on the car floor. "Yes!"

"Really?"

"Don't play innocent, Adam." And he adds, for a jest which he considers particularly witty, "After you gave her a share of this world, you wanted to give her a share of the world to come." And he lights a cigarette for himself. Adam notes the self-confidence of this creature of the law, this man who only follows instructions and is satisfied that he's an instrument of the Supreme Moral Code because he enjoys his work. Adam scrutinizes him for a long while and doesn't say a word. He lowers his eyes and suddenly starts pissing in his pants. The urine streams down his leg and drenches the floor. One of the men bursts out laughing and slaps his shoulder. But Adam stares at the piss, and a cold hatred burgeons in his eyes.

The two men return to their conversation. The landscape outside the windows keeps changing. Adam knows the route, because he has taken it twice before, in this very same car. After a while, as they are passing a grove of giant eucalyptus trees, he says in a whisper: "You're lying, I didn't try to."

The fellow gives him a prosecuting look and shoots out his words: "You *did* try to! And what's worse—you almost succeeded. It was a close call. . . ." He puts out his cigarette with his foot, scratches his right forearm with the little finger of his left hand and, as though all his compassion has dwindled to zero, he confronts Adam with a smile which hangs there in front of him like a frightening object, as if the whole matter were decided once and for all. Adam tries to stand up and bangs his head against the roof of the car. The knock hurts. "Oh, what a joke," he says, "I don't remember a thing. . . ."

Sand in an hourglass, that's the most precise way to describe it, thinks Adam. See how the green is devoured and disappears. Fewer trees, groves, fields, orchards. Instead a group of white storks standing near an Arab house that is about to collapse, on which somebody has written in bright red on the wall: THOU SHALT NOT COMMIT ADULTERY. The left side of the road gets more and more gray, accumulates more and more pot-holes. Beyond a tree that has painted itself brown to match the sorrow of the wasteland, yellow desert sands merge with desolate limestone hills and, farther on, the white mountains of Hebron and, farther still, mountains of violet. The sky is the color of a lemon, its sun boundless and bright. So, in this desert decorated with Bedouin shacks and Bedouin tents and a military car raising clouds of dust, far off in the distance Beer-Sheva can be seen. In a little while the car will burst upon the Hotel Oasis, which is still asleep. The Tourist Camel is sprawled outside the big tent and chewing its cud. The Bedouin in charge of the Tourist Office is smoking from a hookah and watching the cars fly by, his face covered with the blankness of boredom. Right next door is the gas station. The white houses of the new city are plaster casts. The streets absorb the heat of the sun, but they don't reach any of the houses yet.

They drive through the city. There's the Well of Father Abraham on the left, and two Bedouins laughing, their mouths filled with gold. Farther on, the desert begins. And, suddenly, a few acacia trees that look like unshaven savages. A few inns. Broom brush. More broom brush. And wasteland. Mountains of chalk, limestone, sand—but unlike the sand of the beach, hardened fissured stony sand. The tents of the quarry men are already behind, and the car is racing past the ravines and wadis that cut-split-cleave across the desert. Mountains everywhere. Greenish, yet without a spot of vegetation. Green from the sun. Plus red mountains. And black mountains of basalt. Carved by some giant with one swipe of his hand. Next comes the loess of the plains. Dust fills the station wagon in clouds, and suddenly the desert hides itself.

In the distance, high on a mountain, impressive yet desolate, a solitary structure. Perhaps a small factory. Or a Border Patrol station. Or a relic from another world. You can actually feel the miracle of creation here, in the presence of the white mountains of Arad, in the presence of this chain of mountains that divides a dead sea from a dead desert. God's own autograph: Here is where I performed the creation, where I celebrated the drunken ceremony of hallelujah! Consequently, everything here is desiccated, desecrated, disjointed, berserk, forever banished from everybody and everything, yet also sublime and beautiful, as beautiful as an eagle, its beauty dreadful, primordial. They whiz past Arad, the lovely small new town, climb the mountain, and reach the sign:

MRS. SEIZLING'S

INSTITUTE FOR REHABILITATION AND THERAPY

ARAD, ISRAEL

The sign is in three languages: Hebrew, English, and French. Adam scrapes the dust off his feet and says in a joking voice: "A false tooth in a lion's mouth . . ."

"What?"

"It's your house. Your Institute. Have you ever seen a lion with plastic balls?"

"Adam!" The fellow laughs. "Cut it out . . ."

They stop in front of the big gate.

"Haven't you planted a single tree here yet?"

"We did. *You* even planted some. But it takes a long while for them to grow."

One of the men jumps out of the car, rings the bell, and waits.

A little window opens and the head of an aged Kurdi peeps out. He brings his hand to his forehead as a sign of greeting, locks the window again, and opens the gate. He has a beautiful gray beard and his little eyes keep blinking under his knitted eyebrows. An extinguished cigarette butt dangles from his lip. Once the chain is removed and the gate open, the car moves forward into the courtyard. The Kurdi discovers Adam and for a minute the expression on his face changes. "Mr. Stein! Welcome to our humble abode!" He actually kneels upon the sand of the courtyard. This extra little desert in the courtyard is too much for Adam—the smile of the old Kurdi, the enormous courtyard, the white chalk paths, the dust, they all get on his nerves. Already he is preparing himself for his . . . entrance? his re-entrance? He no longer knows how to label his coming.

He raises his eyes and through the car window sees the big house. Three stories stretch up like the features of a hostile, glistening-white giant. Tiny windows, gray supports of rein-forced concrete, a flat roof with a gigantic water tank on it plus some bulging elevator compartments. The building is enormous, but within its surroundings is puny.

No connection whatsoever exists between this huge white sun-drenched house and the sand, the scorching wind, or anything else around it. The house mocks, perhaps despises, its surround-ings. But in the presence of the vast courtyard this tall gawky building becomes a dwarf, a comma that someone has intro-duced into the long intricate sentence of sand and limestone and loess and chalk which all reach as far as the horizon. And on the other side of the house, wherever you look, you see only hills: brown ones, yellow ones, white ones, blue ones, golden ones—forever and ever—until Doomsday.

"Well, now, Adam," The man's voice interrupts his thoughts. "How does it feel to be back home?" His eyes are smiling at Adam. The car stops at the front door of the house.

"In the end the hangman's rope catches its thief," says Adam. He gets out of the car, stretches, adjusts his shirt, puts on the hat which he previously has removed, and steps into the house. The men follow him with the suitcases.

Adam points toward the long corridor. "I'll take a quick look at the recreation room. Wait for me."

"Okay, Adam," says one of them with a speck of sarcasm in his voice. "Dr. Gross is expecting you, don't spend too much time there or he'll get nervous and take it out on us."

Adam steps down the hall. The black carpets glow softly. The air-conditioner chills everything and slows down his gait. Hidden loudspeakers blare out a fast-clip tango. Says Adam to himself, A king doesn't hasten to sign in before the Inquisitor. Outside, a wild sandstorm is in the making. Through the high windows he can see clouds of sand leaping everywhere as if filled with hate. Already the sun has turned from white to red. And he is all by himself in the long corridor. With the sand hitting the windows. Each door has a number on it, and is locked. As he moves, the carpet swallows his steps. When he reaches the first radiator (and in a little while, once winter begins, these radiators will warm him in the cold nights) he looks all around like a professional thief. The moment he is sure that nobody is anywhere in sight, he draws out from a secret compartment underneath the radiator a bottle wrapped in rags. He removes the rags and, seized by a sudden joyous impulse, hugs the bottle. Then, addressing his bottle, *his* bottle, his *life,* he gasps: "Dewar's—the best whiskey! You're still here? That bastard Dr. Gross didn't find you!" He pops the cork, takes a few gulps. Then he recorks the bottle, wraps it up, and returns it to its place. The whiskey burns his chest. Now he is much happier, his body has regained its spring. He reaches the bulletin board, which is drenched with dim fluorescent light. "The nursery celebration of the Feast of Tabernacles is coming! No charge!" "Canadian transistor, excellent condition." "Greetings to everybody from Solomon Kramer of New York—I'm feeling fine, I miss you!" "Next Thursday, a movie: *African Queen* with Humphrey Bogart and Katharine Hepburn." While I was gone, who was in charge of selecting the films? Who? Arthur?

Adam is in a hurry now, he has no time to waste. The whiskey has invigorated him. He can hear conversations going on behind this door. A variety of sounds converging and mixing. There are a lot of people on the other side of the door. Their voices reach him all garbled, but there is a carefree quality to some of the sounds. A tiny sign is stuck on the door: RECREATION ROOM. Adam straightens his jacket, adjusts his hat slightly, and enters.

The recreation room is really humming. Somebody is playing the piano. Others are seated at tables and painting with gouache colors. Several women at a round table are looking at various foreign weeklies and monthlies. Adam stands in the doorway and, so far, nobody has noticed him. In the middle of the room, on top of a very large table, an electric train is racing. A frightening black metallic engine is pulling a lot of shiny cars. Bridges draw up and down, code signals flash, the train crosses mountains and valleys made of tin and plastic and enters a tunnel. Adam watches and his eye turns into a camera, a moving camera. There goes the train, from mountains to darkness. Darkness. Darkness. And now he himself is cramped inside the transport train. And a Hassidic Rebbe is singing the Yiddish song about "Rebbe Elimelech." Through a crack he is able to see cows mooing in a pasture. Handsome fat Polish cows—that makes it even worse. Outside, cows are actually mooing. In the sun, under trees, with somebody looking after them. Is that possible? The train which has suddenly turned into an actual train now encounters another train emerging out of his other past, and the two almost collide, but in the nick of time someone pulls the right switch, and the trains continue side by side.

Around the table are standing ten or so men with serious faces. They are concentrating on the path of the train, on the signposts, on the jumping flag men, on the bridges going up and going down. Two of them are working the switches. The rest are spectators, they give advice, get excited and scream. On their heads they wear conductors' caps. And that same Arthur Fine who obviously has taken Adam's place, who in Adam's absence has been choosing films and doing, God knows, a hundred other things he should not have been doing, is now the leader of the group. Alert and tense, he controls his switch. Short-statured, sharp-nosed, and green-eyed. He is so preoccupied with the train's journey that he doesn't notice Adam. But Adam knows that Arthur will be the first to discover him, so Adam stands in the doorway and waits. Gradually he senses how his unacknowl-

edged figure is upsetting the peace of mind of the chief conductor more and more, until finally Arthur's green eyes rise and fish
out from the doorway the gorgeous shirt and the wide-brimmed
black hat—and then Arthur's hand starts to tremble. His eyes
blink. He tries his best to continue the game. But he is begging
for some miracle to bar the others from noticing this sight. He
doesn't want Adam Stein around. Adam Stein will ruin the
calmness that has prevailed here for many months. Adam Stein
will upset the balance of things in his own favor, and Arthur will
again be shoved into a corner. He knows this. At one and the
same time, he is scared and excited. He steps on a pedal as hard
as he can and at once the pulley which controls a bridge swings
around and the train again zooms into a tunnel—but everybody
has already noticed Adam. The silence which has pervaded the
murky atmosphere of the open doorway now lurks inside the
room, then they rush over to Adam, welcome him, slap him on
the back. Arthur Fine is left all by himself at the train table. The
engine shoots fiery sparks as the train whizzes on, but Arthur's
eyes take in what's happening. His face is transformed, a veil of
sorrow falls over it, cold sweat breaks out on his forehead. He is
about to weep, his existence is shrinking. He grabs the edge of
the large table, making it tremble so much that the train skids off
its tracks. Ffffft! The engine struggles as hard as it can. Over-
heated, overworked, it gives off sparks. But the train refuses to
budge. Once off the track, the wheels don't move. Says Adam to
himself, That Conductor of the Mournful Countenance! In spite
of the great reception he is getting, he still keeps one eye on the
man there at the table, and that eye envelops Arthur, plagues
him, lances and spears him, yet at the same time also pities him.

As the tumult subsides, Adam rapidly looks around the
group, rendering them perfectly silent, and then, still keeping
Arthur Fine in view, and with a smile that endows his face with
the expression of that universally beloved figure, the professional swindler, he speaks in the voice of authority. "Look," he
says, "I'm glad you're all still here. But I must inform you that

this time I've come in a different capacity. In other words, I wasn't brought here, I came here myself. Of my own free will I entered. I was asked by the Bureau of Health to conduct a study of what's going on in this Institute. I want the world to know, I want the whole world to know in detail, the therapies performed by the nymphomaniacs and other maniacs who run Mrs. Seizling's fake sanctuary, I want—"

"Who authorized you to do this research?" chokes Arthur. The train isn't budging from its place. Arthur knows this question will cost him plenty. Adam's eye is ripping him to pieces already, he's dying and suffering his death agony.

Adam raises his eyes and smiles. "The Prime Minister, Arthur!"

"I see," mumbles Arthur. "The Prime Minister."

"He invited me to his place, we drank Courvoisier, and he said to me . . . By the way, he really has a fantastic office—blue telephones!" He knows very well that this is expected of him: they have been waiting for him to say something of this sort. He might have said that God Himself sent him, or that it was his job to design the five-year plan for the city of Arad. But, standing there, his black eyes smiling, he is convinced that in order to be a plausible fraud you must not only stick to your story but must also be careful not to make it too fancy.

A short woman approaches him, sucking her thumb. He gently taps her thumb and she is left open-mouthed, two gold teeth peering through her lips. "Adam, did you know that Columbus was a Jew?"

"Yes, Mrs. Lipovitz, he was definitely a Jew, both a Jew and more. As a general rule, to tell the truth," he goes on, his eyes mesmerizing the crowd—even at the concentration camp he was able to interrupt any activity going on and say what he had to say, not to mention those days when he had his own circus and thousands of people used to cheer anything that came out of his mouth—"both a Jew, Mrs. Lipovitz, and more, but, as a matter of fact, it means little, very little. I don't trust the Italians any more than I have to, they are enlightened and yet they invented the ghetto. In northern Nigeria they'll amputate your legs and set fire to your guts, but there they don't talk about the enlightenment. Bootlickers, that's what the Italians were, yet now they're confident that everything will turn out all right."

They ask him when he is going to start giving his classes, the courses which he conducts for the Institute and which everybody looks forward to. He promises that he'll commence classes very soon. Someone (Mr. Faigelbloom, who at one time was a clerk in the Leumi Bank at Rehovot) sidles up close to his ear and whispers: "Look, I got two hundred and sixty lira, what's worth investing in?"

"American Tel and Tel," pontificates Adam. His left eye is still playing on Arthur. The engine hasn't budged. From the apertures on top pour out sparks. The whole contraption shakes and hums, but the train will not move. "American Tel and Tel, it went up two and a third percent last month—give me the money. . . ." Faigelbloom hands over the money that he's pulled out of his jacket pocket, Adam counts the bills and sticks them in his pocket. All eyes—black eyes, blue eyes, gray eyes, miserable eyes—are fixed on his fingers, astonished at their professional pace. Whatever Adam Stein does amazes them.

A few years ago, before Mrs. Seizling's Institute was founded and when the hospital was still in Jaffa, Adam was brought to Dr. Gross for the first time and noticed a lovely Arab saber hanging on the wall, right beside a gold-framed portrait of Dr. Freud. The beautiful saber was made of silver metal and adorned with multi-colored marble. Its noble wild desert-like appearance excited him and he stretched out his hand and started to finger it.

Dr. Gross will never forget how he himself sat down and watched Adam, whose eyes were shut tight. Adam went on feeling—in fact, it was his hands that actually told the story while his mouth only mouthed, blindly and endlessly, the words and names like a dummy. Ojeh al-Khafir, El Arish, a street in a white city, a seashore, a mosque with a coffeehouse alongside it, then all of a sudden tumult, noise, and two Arabs fighting—and Adam screamed across to Dr. Gross: "The owner of the saber killed the wrong man!" Dr. Gross paled, took a deep breath, and watched while Adam traveled eastward and reached Aden, the area of the Persian Gulf, Birobidzhan, the silver mountains, the lofty mountains of Persia itself. And all at once Adam shouted in English: "The Sultan is dead, long live His Majesty King George the Fifth!" Dr. Gross's father had served in the Turkish army, then in 1915 joined the British police force, risen to the rank of officer, and wandered to every single place Adam had mentioned.

Pleased, Dr. Gross began to smile. Suddenly, Adam was no longer talking, but grinding his teeth and looking all around him. What was happening? Something was blocking him, a certain word was stuck in his throat and wouldn't come out. It was a trial and tribulation to him. Finally he spoke: "Ruth. I cannot explain why, but that's the word which wants to come out of my mouth, Ruth."

"What happened to you, Adam?" Yanked from those fantastic deserts, Dr. Gross returned to his office, where the portrait of Dr. Freud recalled his own atmosphere of permanent gloom which refused to compromise with the primitive world concealed in the minds of his patients. "Adam, what happened to you?"

"I have no idea," said Adam. "Ruth. That was my daughter's name. She is the one I'm looking for here, don't you know? She's the one I betrayed. But that sword is yours, what does it have to do with my daughter?" Dr. Gross had no idea either. Apparently there was no connection whatsoever. Who was Ruth? Dr. Gross racked his brains and couldn't figure it out. Later on, he found out from his mother that his father had married an English-woman before marrying her, a certain Miss Jeanne Parker, who came to Israel on a British archeological expedition, made a dig near Janeen, fell in love with the young Gross and actually married him. The old men of the ancient town used to call her

"Ruth the Moabite" and behind her back would shake their heads in anger: "Gross joined the Turkish army, donned a turban, and married a Christian woman." She couldn't take all the whispering and fled to London. That was when father Gross wedded the woman who was to be the mother of Dr. Gross. This saber—his mother told him with eyes red from longing and from an old wound that never healed—was a present from that Christian woman, from that "Ruth."

Adam has stuffed Faigelbloom's money into his pocket, but Arthur is still trying, without any luck, to get the engine working again when the door opens and in steps Jenny Grey. She wears a white uniform that looks cold and stiff, all starched and ironed. Her hair is carefully combed, and her lovely face is an oval of reproach before the blinking eyes of the crowd. Her cold eyes are fixed upon Adam. The room goes silent. He feels her presence, but doesn't turn his face toward her. He knows who can plunge this room into such a deep freeze. Nonetheless, he won't acknowledge her existence, not yet. Everything must proceed according to a specified order, it is necessary to follow the rules, and she is the first person to understand and appreciate this fact. Of course! Scared stiff of her, and only her, the patients stare at Jenny. They know that Adam and she, they know that she—that she what? That she's in love with him? That marble statue? He's just exploiting her. He's just playing around. No, he loves her. And she loves him. But she isn't used to being in love. A nurse in a hospital doesn't fall in love with a man who is incurable. She's such a scarecrow. Yet beautiful! Marble. Coldness. Hate. She loves him because she hates him. No, she hates him because she loves him. Is there anybody there who doesn't know that Jenny has been waiting for him? For the past two months she has been praying for his return.

Chit-chat. The fear suppressing the group finally opens their mouths and forces out clipped, snatched words. Adam can read them like an open book. His back to Jenny, he steps over to the table with the electric train on it. So there she is, my lovely one, my diabolical one, let me show her my back. All eyes race from Jenny to Adam, who is heading for the table.

Arthur sees him coming. Immediately he rushes around the table, trying all the pedals, pressing all the buttons, whacking the train itself with hate as a last straw, but the engine doesn't stir from its spot. The tracks give off an electric gurgling, overtaxed. The engine emits sparks, snorting like a monster. The train hums. The electric current shakes it, seeking some outlet, like lightning stuck between heaven and earth. Arthur gives up. He stands there like a student who has flunked, his arms outstretched on either side like a scarecrow; shame and suffering trace the shallows of his cheeks, and his thin nose looks like the beak of an eagle. Adam refuses to face him. He knows everyone is watching him, measuring each step he takes. As casually as can be, he lifts the engine, holds it up to the light, turns a small screw at the bottom, and puts the engine down again. Then slightly yanks the red cord hanging from the watchtower overlooking the entrance to the tunnel, softly kicks one leg of the table, and immediately, without waiting for any results, heads toward Jenny, still pretending he hasn't seen her though he's almost on top of her. The moment he actually reaches her and extends a hand of greeting, that very moment, as if it were planned or destined that way, the train starts to move.

Arthur, who has gone blank from fear, is aroused by the trembling of the train. His face expressionless, his body awkwardly bent forward, he caresses the table, biting into the green felt covering. Afterward he straightens, his eyes streaming tears, and wanders into a corner of the room—the others, still fixed in their places, alternately switching their attention from him to Adam. From a clothes hanger, Arthur takes a faded army shirt, green with gold buttons for decoration, and puts it on. He plops a crumpled shabby lackluster watchman's hat on his head, straps a child's trumpet to his neck, stands at attention, salutes; during his salute the tears in his eyes dry and his face readjusts itself, so that a certain quietude already begins to engulf him as he exits into the corridor.

Through the open doorway they can see him marching with vigor, perhaps even with joy. As though the spirit of merrymaking has suddenly seized him and he is blowing a march on his trumpet for himself, accompanied by the other instruments of the concealed background music. Everyone is dazzled by the chocolate soldier trumpeting his own disgrace until he disappears around a corner.

Adam weaves his arm through Jenny's. She grants him a smile now because she knows that this little ceremony took place for her and her alone. They enter the corridor together, while back in that room the silence breaks, noise erupts, voices intersect, the train goes its own way, sparks flashing from the engine's face, and everyone knows that Adam Stein is indeed home.

The corridors of the Institute for Rehabilitation and Therapy are unlike the musty zigzagging corridors of the former hospital in Jaffa, which no longer exists. In Jaffa the odor of the past invaded everything. The walls always gave you the impression that they were regretting times gone by, meditating on foreign nations and conquerors. Who knows?—maybe in this very hall stood King Solomon (who perhaps rebuilt and renovated it) while waiting for his Queen to emerge from the waves. And maybe also Ibrahim-Pasha the Cruel, who ordered a pyramid of skulls constructed in his own honor; and Napoleon, who slaughtered his sick *en masse* (two thousand to be exact); and short-tempered Abu-Naboot, the ruler of Jaffa, who walked the streets lashing people, who made love on the rooftops of the city to Maria Mabalin, the daughter of Constable Philip; and their son Sampad, the husband of Jezebel, that beautiful and adored woman from far-off Armenia. Down these damp corridors they all walked, along with history, along with the land of Israel, along with the city that Adam—the first man on earth—built, the city where the righteous Noah was interred, a city upon whose rocks the Greeks bound Andromeda, who, according to legend, became a star. And lo, above this city conquered by a thousand armies but not by a single individual, that star still hangs.

Whereas, in Mrs. Seizling's Institute for Rehabilitation and Therapy everything is brand new, shiny. Perhaps also inhuman, with its fluorescent illumination, background music, constant air-conditioning, square corners, white paint, black carpets that sponge the noise of footsteps, with its windows, hundreds of them, one after another, just below the ceiling, its lighting from invisible bulbs, its music from hidden loudspeakers, its doors with no knobs, its radiators concealed in white compartments camouflaged by matching white walls, its ceiling which you don't even notice because of the way the lights are arranged to give you the impression that the ceiling is transparent and the illumination passes right through it. The whole place looks as though it has been designed by a computer to have no connection whatsoever with any human past, any human location, any human feeling. It just happens to exist: cool, cute, comfortable. A sterilized, unimaginative, undistinguished bulk. Yet, by not getting on your nerves, it cures your depression. While, outside, on the other side of the thick walls, a savage sandstorm rages. Out there, desolate hills of rock stare at this synthetic sanctuary, and the wind attacks thorn bushes and wild serrated wadis. Out there a white sun is groaning above a white desert not far from a white new city without trees, without grass. However, for promenading Adam, the tumult is totally stanched, the storm on the other side of the walls is dead, Arthur's tooting bugle has long ago been drowned by shmaltzy violins playing "Tea for Two."

Adam and Jenny do not exchange a single word. They are still suffering the effects of the impact of their meeting. Besides, it is Jenny's duty to take Adam to Dr. Gross. Gross purposely delegated her to fetch him. He knows everything, that doctor. "Please bring him to me," he told her and set his solitary self down in his big white room, on his "white toilet seat," as she called it, and "sniggered sourly." She despised him at that minute, but kept her mouth shut and sought out Adam. In the recreation room, as soon as she saw him, everything flew out the window: protocol, rules, possibilities, impossibilities, every single thing. She castrated Gross with an imaginary hatchet and enjoyed doing it.

"Don't squeeze, Adam," she says, and her smile stretches her mouth and widens her whole face. She feels like a paper tigress, like a fly-trap that has snared itself. She suddenly has gained self-confidence, the soft music emerging from the concealed loudspeakers sounds to her like a military band that will one day lead her to her secret dream. A quiet, gentle march—like the rhythm of scraping sandpaper. Of course, all she really wants is for her man, her handsome man, to stop walking, press her against the wall, squeeze her, bring his mouth to hers, and with his tongue fish inside her as if she were an open sea, an ocean of pleasure, yes, she, the vulture.

They stop in front of a door. On it a little plastic card says: RECEPTION AND CLASSIFICATION: DR. NATHAN GROSS. Adam pretends to be reading the card for the first time. He scrutinizes the lettering of the words, the small black print engraved on yellow plastic. Jenny is at his side, her face practically touching the white door. He bends his head and brushes the bare surface of her neck with his mouth. Jenny doesn't move her face even an inch. His nimble evasive hand reaches out for her, slips under her blouse and massages her until she begins to purr. Her face is so close to the door that she cannot read the blurred sign. His hand goes quickly up and down her body, from her loins to her breasts and back again to her loins, then down to her thighs. Once there, his fingers pinch her tender white flesh so hard that her head, which is close to the door, bangs into the little sign and a voice from the other side pipes up: "Come in!"

Jenny, her head stinging, is so startled by that voice that she almost lets out a scream. She actually jumps backward and Adam Stein laughs. Immediately Jenny looks in all directions to see if anybody has seen. Her face all flustered and blushing.

Adam watches her, protected by his shield of laughter, and waits. He is absolutely certain that now her attitude will change, that laughter will rise up inside her, her face light up, and he, gazing upon her lovely countenance, will see her embarrassment snake its way across her bright face. Only then will his peace of mind return. Jenny says: "Adam, that wasn't nice." But she's already laughing, laughing at her own words—and she is again the woman he has been anxiously waiting for, a woman who needs to be shown a whip. "Come in!" repeats the voice on the other side, a little louder.

Adam stares at every part of Jenny's face, each expression of desire, of passion, her flashing eyes and feverish mouth. While Jenny, on the alert again, is looking to all sides, checking. Then she seizes the hand that pinched her flesh and licks the taste of her own body off his fingers. Her chilly eyes implore him—what else? that was his intention—and he delves into her eyes to discover there an extraordinary mixture of victory and defeat, desire and guilt. And he says: "We're back together again, my good woman. . . ."

"Yes, Adam. Touch me."

And he touches her gently, caresses her face, but the moment they embrace and he has a vision of her beautiful panting figure, he knocks on the door again and shouts: "It's me, Adam Stein."

"Come on in already, for crying out loud!"

Adam opens the door and stomps into the room. Jenny remains in the half-open doorway, offended, in suspense. Adam won't invite her in and, of course, neither will Dr. Gross. She gathers up her loose hair, straightens her skirt with an authoritative sweep of her hand, and mumbles something to herself.

Long-faced, fat-bodied, self-satisfied, Dr. Nathan Gross with his black eyes and yellowish hair that requires a bit of brushing every little while to hide the flourishing bald spot—jumbo-sized Dr. Gross, who moves like an awkward goon, sits there behind his huge desk and smiles at Adam.

Adam gets himself ready, struggling as hard as he can against

the shadows already encompassing and draining him, leaving
him only a jot of strength. With one eye he catches a glimpse of
Jenny still standing in the corridor, planted like a scarecrow on
the black carpet and looking in, completely at a loss. Then,
boom, something unexpected happens. Gross coughs and Jenny
discovers a young boy smoking in the hallway. She turns on him,
her face transfigured, and in a furious voice orders him to stop
smoking in the hall. The frightened boy doesn't know what to do
with his hands. Shivering, he drops the cigarette on his right
shoe and crushes it with his left. For a second or so, the cigarette
butt sits on his shoe. He looks all around and then sprints away.
Jenny keeps her angry eye on him, picks up the crushed butt and
puts it into her blouse pocket. She takes out a handkerchief from
another pocket and rubs the carpet. Adam bursts out laughing
and Gross gazes at him and says: "Why don't you close the
door, Adam?"

Adam doesn't answer. At the sound of Dr. Gross's commanding voice, he feels his muscles become tense, as though he were
an animal sensing an approaching danger. In this room he has
no capacity for self-control. He knows this. How many times
has he shrieked in here and banged the wall with his clenched
fists? He shrivels up because he has no place to flee to. None
whatsoever. He cannot stand erect as he did earlier. Dr. Gross
knows Adam Stein's habits, therefore he never argues with him
over minor matters. He gets up from his desk, his gawky body
stooped slightly forward, treks over to the door with heavy steps
and arms loose, and slams the door himself. On his way back to
his desk, he hears Adam say in a new voice, loud and perhaps
also emotional: "Are you still so tactful, Doctor?"

Dr. Gross waits till he is at his ease in his armchair, then he
leans forward, relaxes, spreads his hands across the desk, and
says: "Adam, you son of a bitch, go to hell!"

"Why?" chuckles Adam, getting more and more wound up.

"Why?" Gross sits up straight for a moment, tilts a pair of
penetrating eyes at his friend. "Because, Adam, maybe you'll

learn some manners there."

"Nope, never, not a chance." Adam tries to inject some composure into his words. "It's me, Grossie baby. I won't learn! Your eyes work, don't they? I'm back, Grossie boy, did you miss me?" He tries to smile. "This time I was conveyed here as a result of the complaints of that landlady, Mrs. Ruth Edelson, which were all a pack of lies! Ah, what's the use pretending? Didn't I want to strangle her? I did. By the way, her name is Ruth, just like your mother."

"Not my mother, Adam. My father's first wife. And, to be precise, her name was Jeanne Parker."

"Your father was hip, but you're square." And Adam paces up and down with his hands clasped. "Listen carefully, Grossie boy. That she was the landlady of the house is immaterial, right? I could have been sent here by your wife or your first mother. It would make no difference! What is the significance of an old virgin in this story of ours?"

"This story of yours, Adam. It's all yours!"

"Ours, Gross. Ours. Yours and mine—we're two sides of the same story. Don't forget who I am. I was *there,*" and he emphasizes the word *there* and stares at Gross and pauses. "I know that one kills human beings and not thin air, and you can't slaughter a child that doesn't exist, that's missing. Every coin has two sides, yours and mine, don't evade that. Even if Ruth Edelson had never existed, wouldn't you still be waiting for me here? Answer me that!"

Dr. Gross leans back deep in his armchair and waits. Adam quickens the pace of his speech, his voice thickens, the veins of his neck suddenly bulge.

"Look here, Grossie, how about cutting out this bureaucratic nonsense?" He feels as if the ground, *his* ground, that stretch of floor which he is standing on or trying to stand on, and trying not to slip off of, to which he is hooking his body with his last spark of consciousness which is leaking bit by bit—this very ground is being pulled from under him. He feels that any minute he will start spinning like a top, and he says in a half-gruff, half-shaky voice: "Start writing already! My name, age, marital status, business, my number, the number on my arm, and my passport, write it down already, you know all the facts anyway, send me to my room and let's end this stupid farce. Me you have to classify? My only hope is that my room has been repainted. Your painters always do a messy job. There's a terrific plastic paint on the market now, you don't have to plaster rooms any more, all you do nowadays is slap on a plastic that looks just like wood paneling, write that down, Grossie baby, *plastic,* not *plaster!* In Jaffa—remember, Sigmund?—in Jaffa I used to see spiders climbing up the walls and you, Doctor Nathan Sigmund Gross, you said that that was just an alchoholic hallucination. Yes, that was your decision, my little God. But in the end I proved to you—and believe me, what with my empathy for your predicament and my great sympathy for your first mother, it pained me, but I proved that those spiders were real, and their webs were real. Plus the mice, those gigantic mice, historic creatures from the time of Father Abraham. And you said: *No more than one mouse, maybe just one mouse! And even that one mouse is nothing but an illusion.* Remember? I explained to you at the time that it was in fact just one mouse that passed my eyes but, because of my hallucinatory vision, the poor thing dropped dead, so the worst part of it was the funeral which his friends, a hundred other mice, arranged for him. And these mice, they didn't know the first thing about hallucinations. . . ."

Adam sees that Dr. Gross doesn't think his words warrant a proper reply. This hurts him, disturbs him. His voice gets rough again, hoarse, urgent: "Grossie, my boy, my tiny divinity, cut out your smart-aleck silence and say something."

"Adam, how many times have you been here?"

Adam looks at him. If he were able to, if he possessed the necessary strength and daring and self-pity, he would start laughing—and not just for a while. "How many times? Five. Six. Three times in Jaffa. Or maybe twice. I don't remember just now. But this is my second time here in the sanctuary of that noble *grande dame,* Mrs. Seizling. I'm tired, send me to my room."

And now, like a peeled onion, Adam shows what he really is with no shell to protect him, no wise-guy wit, no clowning genius, no Dorian Gray pose for the nurse Jenny—a weary exhausted man with a wrinkled face, with grooves crossing his cheeks, his forehead deeply lined, his body shrunken, and his entire existence humiliated.

"Send me to my room. . . ."

"No, Adam." Dr. Gross attempts to give his voice a touch of affection, of charm. "You must understand why. Really, try to answer my questions, it's important!" Dr. Gross's eyes are fixed on a diagram hanging on one of the white walls, protected by shiny plastic.

"I don't understand," whispers Adam, "I don't understand. The only thing I do know for sure is that you always used to stand here, in the doorway, striking matches and counting me off. And that you're not such a successful God. How many matches have you struck here, my dear little Grossie? But down deep—" at this point Adam's face somewhat overcomes defeat and exhaustion to smile a bit—"down deep, what the hell do you care about me? I'm a big boy now. I wasn't born yesterday."

"I don't understand." Dr. Gross thinks out loud, not for the benefit of Adam Stein, who, though bowed by depression, is trying his best to sound comic and satirical, but for the benefit of the diplomas suspended on either side of the diagram, one from the University of Jerusalem and one from the University of Vienna. For the benefit of Dr. Freud's portrait, which is very nicely framed in black. For the benefit of the bookcase with its editions bound in magnificent leather, inside which lurk thousands upon thousands of questions—and, maybe, even some answers. "I don't understand why we haven't figured out how to help you yet. Why? You are indeed an intelligent man, mature, who wasn't born yesterday, who understands his situation thoroughly, and yet again yesterday you tried—"

"Look, Gross." Adam shoots out his words. He has to hurry
before he is exterminated by the eyes of the Inquisitor. "You're
a nice guy, maybe even a very nice guy. A good man. It's not for
nothing that you were appointed head of this Institute. I could
even stretch it a bit further, without overstepping good taste in
the least, and say with all my heart—but also with a certain
predilection for generalizations—that you are one of the last
good guys left on earth. However, in some circumstances you
are ludicrous. Like most good guys, you've been blessed with
your fitting share of folly. Commandant Klein used to call it
ardent liberalism. Such ardent types are so wise that their wisdom includes a good deal of folly, but where I was it was ridiculous to believe in the sun, or a kind word. In a world dispos-
sessed of miracles, *you* still believe in miracles. And what's even
worse, you not only believe in miracles, but, like all the other
good guys, you rely on them. In the final tally of justice, you
introduce not just the possibility of miracles but the fact of miracles. And that amounts to hypocrisy. That amounts also to
nerve. That is actually a cruel distortion of the laws of existence.
And therefore also a crime. I have given you my best years. For
you I was a locus for medical experiments, psychological, therapeutic—call them what you will—and you failed, because the
miracle which was supposed to happen didn't happen. And now,
having failed, you dare come to me and ask me why. Whereas,
actually, you've already decided to dump me in Hell. So what
are you waiting for?"

"How do you figure all this out, Adam?"

"Don't forget, Doctor, that I can read you like an open book.
In your face I can read that this morning you had two hard-
boiled eggs and toast. In your face I can read that last night you
argued with your wife over the question of your lodging. In your
eyes I read that this morning your car had a flat tire and you
walked on foot from the bus station to the gas station, and there
you called the Institute and asked for somebody to pick you up

in a car. And in your face I read that you have decided to put me
in Hell. That's fine with me, but what's the meaning of your
word 'miracle'? What does 'miraculous' mean, Grossie baby?
The failure was yours, not mine. It was your job to rescue, not
mine. It was my destiny to fail, that's my side of the story. But
this Institute is yours. You have a big budget, a nice car, a
house, perfect labs, an excellent team of doctors, scientific literature, the latest discoveries, universities. What do I have? Myself.
And I'm sick, I'm a clown and I'm about to die, I'm dying. Bit
by bit. And you haven't done anything to baffle the wheel, to
stay this death. I could do it, but don't want to; you're obligated
to do it, but can't. Let me go to my room, Sigmund, I am weary
and I am about to die. Very soon. It's a question of time, and
what's time between you and me? Smash your Doxa watch and
go hang yourself on a tree, except there isn't any tree around
here. Then use a telephone pole. Your cure has been a total flop,
Grossie, my boy."

Dr. Nathan Gross has ceased inspecting the sad eyes of Freud
and the ornate signature on his Viennese diploma and is now
looking again at Adam. The smile struggling through his eyelashes reminds Adam of the desert sun rising in a window of the
Institute, rising among the barren mountains, among the white
cliffs, among the brambles. A crate of iniquity. A box of terror.
Cosmic folly committing suicide through suffocation, through
tears. A mosquito become a jackal, a peaceful doe that is nothing but a joke that packs a horror. Like the glass eye which
Adam imagined set in the face of the lion, the plastic-testicled
lion. One time Adam thought, I'm going to hunt tigers in the
desert. Paper tigers, tigers of blood. Bedouins, camels, and
broom brush, singed dead tree stumps. And, suddenly, a house
for men with blue numbers on their arms. A striptease of torture. Stripping, stripping, trampling, smashing, spitting on that
Gross—that know-nothing. You must learn how to suffer. No,
you must learn to be worthy of suffering. In order to be worthy
of suffering, you must cultivate the sign of Cain on your fore-

head. And Dr. Gross was born in Israel when it was Palestine, in the Old City of Jerusalem, in a small house behind an Armenian church. A funny man, he throws me into Hell while Jenny extinguishes cigarettes in the hall. I am exhausted. Let me die in peace.

Tears gather in Dr. Gross's eyes, to the point of ludicrousness, of disgust, even pardon, because the Doctor is now so completely revealed that it is possible for Adam to freeze all his hatred against him and keep silent until the sun comes out to melt the ice. Damn these tears, they're ruining Adam's top-notch performance, even if Adam was perhaps dragged into the act against his will. Gross smiles, though it is difficult for him, and declares in a fractured voice: "I'm sorry, Adam. With all my heart, Adam, I'm sorry."

Where Adam stands, on his left a yellow sun gazes through a window. He is alone with that sun. Surrounded by Mrs. Seizling's freezing air-conditioning, he is cut off from the sun, but its power still reaches him. Mercilessly it beats down upon gigantic stretches of sand and loess, upon cliffs and gorges, upon the beauty extending as far as the Dead Sea, upon the mountains of Edom that mark the horizon blue. He has almost lost, by now, his vision and his hearing. He has definitely lost his confidence. He can just make out an unintelligible soft humming, strange yet familiar, the voice of Aunt Gretchen announcing: "Coffee is ready!" He is nowhere. The numbers on his arm have been transformed into freckles. He is quoting some passage out of Fichte or a poem by Heine and is almost blind. Dr. Gross's face looks to him like a white negative against the bright windowpane. It is pale, its lovely eyes spinning in their sockets. They blink. Adam's body is perspiring. Simultaneously he is hot and cold. He would like to beg his body's forgiveness before it collapses in a minute. "Go ahead, Adam," concludes Dr. Gross, and sinks back. "See you later. . . ."

Adam doesn't hear the words, but he catches the tone, the quality, the lilt. He turns about and starts walking. He falls

down, gets up, his face soiled. He stretches, straightens, and
feels foolish. He knows he'd like to drop down on all fours and
bark. Herr Commandant Klein would split his sides laughing.
But even this pleasure is denied him. The war has come to an
end. Klein is Weiss nowadays, and Adam is no longer able to
crawl. Weiss now lives in a small room in Berlin, and if it were
not for that letter from Adam's missing daughter, Adam never
would have reached this cursed land. This country of Grosses.

Jenny is not in the hall any more. Soft music pipes from un-
seen loudspeakers: "When you say no, what do you mean?" He
tramps toward his new room, his new living quarters, toward his
new life which will peter out in a jiffy. Rescue and death are
around the proverbial corner. In some spot of his brain that is
still pumping, he knows that for him suffering is the only way.
Nobody expects anything else from him. They won't attempt to
cure him, they'll let him die. Actually, they are doing me a favor,
he tells himself. Yet feels somewhat guilty, as though he had
denied them a privilege, their privilege to cure him.

Adam Stein is on his way to die in his new room in Arad, in
the desert, under the sun, near the Dead Sea, near the Bedouin
caravans, in the synthetic house of Madam Seizling. No hope
exists in this desert. Somehow, the dead live and die, eating the
best of foods. One big feast that gives you the chills. "Father!"
he cries, and the music swallows his cry. "You're older than me,
my son. You're older."

The carpet swallows the cry. Here everything has been arranged so that a certain dullness sponges any pain of his, shrinks
him, vetoes his very existence. Gross has his own little ideas and
you can't blame him for that. Failure is not a final verdict; in
fact, a lot of greatness attaches to failure. Yes, he knows that.
Weren't his own father and his father's father and his father's
father's father each a member of a certain weird tribe classified
by the non-Jews as *Yids?*

As his last strength pours out of him like blood, like water
from a shattered reservoir, he plucks up his final courage in

order to tell himself: "Even amid this destruction they won't correct me. I shall be my own master. Dr. Nathan Sigmund Gross shan't feed me from a spoon any more!"

Dr. Gross, sunk in his armchair, ponders his mad patient and says to himself: "Twice here, four times in Jaffa, three years. We haven't benefited him, he's absolutely right. It was our duty to save him, he had no obligations at all, he is a swindler, he is shrewder than I, shrewder than himself, than Jenny. He comes, fixes the engine, devastates Arthur, fondles Jenny, accuses me, reads me like an open book, yet this same man tried to strangle an old woman. Yes, I must remember that. He's not a genius, but a strangler, a murderer, a psychopathic killer, a miserable madman, an impostor. Inside his own heart he has purchased for himself a gravesite and he is heading right for it, non-stop. He's a corpse pretending he's alive still, and I'm supposed to reverse the wheel that's taking him around to his death, but how? There's no way. I have to write in my book, in my journal, in my student notebooks, in a letter to Sigmund: There's no way. We failed. In a hundred years we'll know what to do with Adam Stein, with those like him. Now there is no way except to admit failure. And I, God of Medicine, make that admission." And Gross salutes like a disciplined soldier who has been trounced, and he smiles to himself—whether with bitterness, humor, or despair, remains unclear.

2

MRS. SEIZLING

ONE BRIGHT hot unforgettable day in the summer of 1960 a dwarfish woman with a coarse wide fleshy face and eyes like the eyes of a mouse skidded, as it were, into Lod airport terminal. She wore a faded dress—a flower print—and a brimless straw hat. Nobody was there to welcome her, nor did the customs officers spread a red carpet at her feet or conduct her to the room set aside for VIP's. They combed through her suitcases, sent her back and forth from one official to the next, found lots of irregularities in her papers, and by the time she exited to the concrete surface outside the terminal and stood with her back to the wonderful posters of Israel in the windows of the Government Tourist Office, she was physically a wet rag—but her spirit was undaunted.

The first few days of her visit she spent on guided tours. She lodged in the Hotel Dan, which in her eyes was an architectural

flop. The rusty and neglected beach at the foot of the hotel had
no magical effect on her because a Tel Aviv beach is not a capti-
vating sight. However, Mrs. Seizling hadn't come to Israel looking for beauty and charm, she'd come looking for a purpose to
her life. She paid no heed, therefore, to faults of such little con-
sequence.

She rented a car and was driven all over the land by a driver
named Jonah Benvenisti. On account of his blond hair, he reminded her of her sister Zelda's boy who had died not long ago
from infantile paralysis. So she was clearly fond of this swarthy
slender driver whose nose spread across his face as if it had been
left too long in the frying pan, who kept whistling for her benefit,
throughout the trip, one of the symphonies of Beethoven, a
composer who, as far as Mrs. Seizling's knowledge went, was
deaf, born in Bonn, and either he himself played at Carnegie
Hall or his works were played there — she herself adored Cole
Porter and Gershwin, though Fred Astaire and Joseph Cotten
were her favorites — but in memory of her late nephew she forgave Jonah Benvenisti and didn't complain. And Jonah Benvenisti described to her the halcyon days of Israel. He told her
about the pioneers and about the conquest of the desert and
about the Jewish National Fund that had planted all the trees,
though she heard later from Adam that this organization had
"laid waste the wasteland." He showed her the caves of prophets, the rock of Father Abraham, the tree of Simeon the Mac-
cabee, the caves of the Zealots, the mountainside where were
buried Joshua the son of Nun, Caleb the son of Jephunneh,
Jephtha the Gileadite, Mother Sarah, and three kings. He
showed her the path taken by Jesus' family on its way to Nazareth. He showed her Jacob's broken ladder, the stone he laid
under his head for a pillow, Kibbutz Exodus—but the crowning
glory of the entire tour was when, at a certain guest-house in the
north, he pointed out to her the woman who was made love to
by Ari the son of Canaan among the rocks of Galilee.

She talked with practically nobody else, she simply devoted

herself totally to the merrymaking pitter-patter of her nephew who had died of infantile paralysis and who now was singing the praises of Israel, top to bottom, from Galilee to the Negev, and whistling Beethoven, and expressing rather complicated opinions about current events, Vietnam, President Eisenhower, the black question in the Southern states.

The doorman at the Hotel Dan, since she made no special requests, didn't even bother to raise his splendid silvery eyebrows when she scampered past him on her way to or from the car. For him—as for every other native of the land—Mrs. Rebecca Seizling was just another nameless tourist from Cleveland, Ohio, who was white and Jewish, one of the 130,148 Jewish tourists who would stay in Israel for approximately 10.8 days on the average, who would spend $20.60 a day, buy mementoes, art objects, religious items, jewelry and other products, drink 124 cups of coffee, and complain about the impoliteness of the waiters. On the other side of the coin, however, Mrs. Seizling would be among the 53.4 percent of American Jewish tourists who would consider Israeli restaurant food satisfactory, and easily among the 2.9 percent of white Western tourists who hadn't anticipated much and would therefore not fall into the 5.5 percent who *had* anticipated and were disappointed. She would smoke American cigarettes (Marlboro) and ultimately join the 18.5 percent who on the last day of their stay would discover the flea market in Jaffa and buy there two Persian necklaces, a copper Arabic incense bird, and a Yemenite ring. And at the hotel, in the gift shop, her eyes would get greedy and she'd buy, despite her revulsion, a blue-green plate made of beaten copper with the gravesite of Mother Rachel in its center—for a relative, or some acquaintance, or just for no reason at all. Moreover, she'd be among the 22 percent of American Jewish tourists who within five years would be back visiting Israel again.

One day, after she had toured the length and, wherever possible, breadth of the country, Mrs. Seizling rummaged through her purse and fished out the telephone number of a certain official in the Prime Minister's Office named Zuter, somebody her friend Shaindy had asked her to look up. "You see, he's a distant relative," Shaindy had explained, "and I've never even met him, but, you see, his father . . . and that makes him my uncle—and a relative is a relative, no matter what, right? So why not send him regards from the family over here?" This official named Zuter, the moment he heard Mrs. Seizling's voice on the telephone, developed a migraine. On the one hand, why should he bother with the company of an American tourist who was bound to be boring? Yet, on the other, family was family, and this woman claimed that she was a good friend of his relatives in Cleveland, and if someday he should be sent on a mission outside of Israel and arrive in Cleveland, wouldn't this hospitality of his be remembered then to his credit? So that's how it came about that, on account of etiquette (to use a euphemism), Zuter the official invited Mrs. Seizling to a social gathering scheduled for the following day in the house of the said official, in the capital city of Jerusalem.

Zuter the official performed his civil service in the Office of the Prime Minister, and Mrs. Seizling wondered what they did in the Prime Minister's Office which they didn't do in other offices. Upon arriving at this office to pick him up, she found a hundred other civil servants just like Zuter who (let it be said on his behalf) were doing no more than he was doing, though it must also be said that, surely, it was absolutely impossible to do any less than he was doing.

At the party in Zuter the official's house, during a cordial conversation that shifted to the general subject of outside contributions to and collections for the State of Israel—namely, the Jewish National Fund and the like—as well as the particular activities of American Jews in Israel, this Mrs. Seizling, the dwarfish woman with the coarse fat face and the faded clothes and the straw hat, spoke up boldly and said that, in her opinion, everybody had to invest in this country. "Because of our unfortunate

brethren," she said, "because of those poor creatures who escaped the European holocaust and Arab ghettos and came here,
or were brought here, to the land of Israel which God Almighty
has intended for his own people Israel." The guests around her
laughed, raised their drinks, and toasted her health and good
nature, but she caught the mockery in their voices and said, in a
blasting voice and with an expression on her face to match her
fierce mood: "Have a little respect for those who give you your
daily bread!" As she spoke, she saw the faces of the various
junior officials go thunderstruck, flabbergasted. So she beat her
sunken chest, a gesture in which one of the officials saw an exact
replica of the behavior of Cheetah in a Tarzan movie; unable to
control himself, he broke up and his laughter made a clean
sweep of the embarrassment that had existed just a moment ago
when her angry words first knocked them in the face.

Mrs. Seizling, though, didn't give up so easily. She demanded
that this official Zuter—her only connection, she said, with the
government—assist her to donate money to this country "which,
in such a short time, has become the apple of my eye." Since
Zuter the official realized that he was dealing with a lunatic sent
by his relatives just to plague him, he agreed to hand over per-
sonally to the Prime Minister any check she would now care to
write out. Everybody chuckled good-humoredly, but as the
glasses in their hands wobbled and the ice cubes clattered, Mrs.
Seizling sat herself down in an armchair, opened up her big
purse, drew out a brown checkbook, asked somebody for a pen
—having left her own Waterman at her Tel Aviv hotel—and
wrote: "For the management of Israel, exactly six million dollars and no cents." She pulled a small signet box from her purse,
removed the seal, pressed it against the circular ink-pad, blew on
it, and stamped it down alongside her signature: "Rebecca Seizling, Inc."

Everyone took a peek at the check, blinked, and laughed.
Then Zuter the official stuck the check in his pocket, left Mrs.
Seizling, and didn't see her again till the party ended.

Mrs. Seizling returned to Tel Aviv, while Zuter the official, at the stroke of a single check, was no longer an anonymous figure sitting couped up every day in a tiny room on the second floor of the Prime Minister's Office; he was now the focal point for laughter and fun in Jerusalem.

He'd go from party to party, from house to house, telling the tale of Mrs. Rebecca Seizling, Inc.—how she'd rung him up, how she'd come to his house and said that everybody had to do something for "our unfortunate brethren." As soon as Zuter the official thought the right moment had come, when the entire bunch was laughing, he'd pull out the crumpled check and pass it around from hand to hand until everybody was shrieking with laughter and having an even better time than before, slapping him on the back and, incidentally, learning his name; for the first time in his life, Zuter the official had made a splash and become a social figure. In short, Mrs. Seizling had practically pulled him out of the grave, rescued him from Hell, from the oblivion at the bottom of the civil-service ladder, and Zuter, of course, knew this in his heart and thought of sending her a bouquet of flowers as a token of his appreciation, but never did. He realized that while his name was on everyone's lips—who knows!—perhaps he would be assigned a job commensurate with his talents. Hadn't he already Hebraicized his name, learned how to dress in accordance with the fashion and even how to speak only in hints and signs and quotation marks, with an occasional clearing of the throat? Wouldn't he soon be famous . . . be rich . . . ? Who knows!

In the capital city of Jerusalem, at social gatherings of officials, in their offices, at their committee meetings, in the Parliament cafeteria, and in every department of the administration, it wasn't very long before all that anybody had to do was say, with a serious face, "Mrs. Rebecca Seizling, Inc.," and everybody would burst out laughing.

Yet, what saved Adam Stein and Dr. Gross and Arthur Fine and Miles Davis and Wolfovitz the Circumciser and many others was the fact or the miracle that a girl named Ruth Lichtenstein was invited to one of these parties. Ruth listened to the whole story, giggled along with everybody else, and when the crucial moment arrived for the check to start passing from hand to hand she peeked at it and her face made a double-take of astonishment: hearing the name had had no particular effect on her, but seeing the signature suddenly activated, in a corner of her memory, the image of an evening with her relatives in Cleveland where much had been said concerning a certain "marvel" named Mrs. Seizling. Yes, she remembered the name now, and also how she'd been driven to the outskirts of the city and shown the miserable house in which the richest woman in America was living, a woman who owned steel corporations and perfume-manufacturing companies, who had thousands of shares in cigarettes, herds of cattle in Nebraska, and a rubber-tire factory in Akron, Ohio—in other words, an empire. Nonetheless, she lived in a wretched old wooden house with fire-escapes climbing up its sides and, on top, a broken pole flying a white flag as though it were declaring some truce. A truce with whom? "The woman was declaring a truce with God," one of the Lichtenstein relatives had joked. Now she remembered it all.

Ruth Lichtenstein was a close friend of Zuter the official, at one time there had even been some talk between them about getting married, so with a minimum of coaxing she managed to wangle the check out of him—for one day only. At the Office of the Ministry of Finance, where she worked, she knocked on the Minister's door and, after a quick explanation, she pulled the check from her purse and dangled it before the eyes of the Minister. His face changed colors like a chameleon, he talked simultaneously into six telephones, and, before you knew it, six shiny black official government limousines were zooming toward the Hotel Dan in Tel Aviv.

Mrs. Seizling had a smile all ready for them; she'd known they would be coming. She was willing to overlook the fact that nearly a month had passed from the day she arrived in Israel to the moment when these public figures set foot in the Hotel Dan and made ingratiating faces before her. In the time she'd been in the country she had come to know its ways and, besides, her heart was determined to rescue her soul and find a purpose to her life. Also, in the interval between the party at the civil servant Zuter's house and the moment when the mouth of the doorman at the Hotel Dan gaped open and he rushed to tell the hotel manager the walloping news that the lady in 222 was not just some ordinary lady but . . . well, between then and now, a decisive encounter had taken place, transforming the life of Mrs. Seizling.

A week earlier, merely a week, Mrs. Seizling had met the elder of the Schwester twins.

The day she met that Schwester twin a heat wave commenced. Fatigued birds were seen circling and hovering in the unbearably hot air of Tel Aviv. People lost the little patience they'd had to begin with and cursed one another. Mrs. Seizling sat in a café on Ibn-Gabirol Street, sweltering in the heat, with her eyes fixed in amazement on a woman about sixty whose upper lip was crowned with a slight mustache. The woman sat at a small table, dressed in woolen attire, her face as fresh as a daisy, and was drinking a steaming cup of tea with obvious pleasure. Mrs. Seizling, who was exhausted and practically dehydrated from the heat, leaned toward the woman and spoke in a voice that hadn't a touch of shyness in it but rather a touch of provocation.

"Excuse me, madam, am I disturbing you?"

"No, not at all, not in the least."

"May I ask you something?"

"Please do. That's why I am here, in order to answer questions." The woman sipped from her cup of steaming tea, looking at Mrs. Seizling with inquisitive and eager eyes.

"How are you able to sit here in the heat of the day and look so fresh? Do forgive me, but how . . . *how* are you able to wear a woolen outfit on a day like this and drink hot tea without sweating?"

The Schwester twin tilted a pair of big bright eyes at her, smiled, moved over to Mrs. Seizling's table, her cup of steaming tea wobbling in its saucer, and said with utmost seriousness: "It is all a matter of faith."

"Faith?" Mrs. Seizling tried to understand, it being crucial that she comprehend. Tel Aviv, from here, seemed to be swimming in deep waters, entirely submerged, without solidity or existence, feverish, foggy, cacophonous.

"It all depends upon what you're thinking," continued the woman with the small mustache, while sipping her hot tea. "Take me, for example. I, madam, am thinking about God."

"Eh?"

"Day and night, He is in my mind." And once she began talking, the Schwester sister didn't stop. The encounter between these two was a stroke of fate, as though some angel had prophesied it. The two women turned each other on. After ten minutes a friendship had already taken shape, after a half-hour their hearts were on each other's sleeves and no barrier whatsoever stood between them. The Schwester sister even told Mrs. Seizling about her twin—who was younger than she by two minutes and forty-one seconds—openly complaining to Mrs. Seizling that her younger sister didn't take the matter of God with proper seriousness. God, of course, meant love, and forgetting about one's body, and concentrating perfectly. Yes, she did have an "idea," she had been thinking this one idea for years. From the time her late husband passed away and left her a small but dependable boardinghouse. At this point the Schwester twin's mustache trembled and her eyes kindled with the fire of prophecy, a sight that didn't go unnoticed by Mrs. Seizling, who was like a little girl suddenly discovering flavor, sweetness, and joy for the first time. A few years ago, for instance, the elder Schwester sister had traveled to Africa. She wished to reach the spot said to be the genuine Paradise. She wanted to see it with her own eyes. She had been seeking a future for her life, something to uplift her soul, when in a dream she saw an angel who advised her to go to Africa. She was already fifty-two years old, in her prime years. Her sister, younger by two minutes and forty-one seconds, refused to accompany her. So, alone she traveled, and alone she reached a small town in Kenya, where she was directed to the mountain which the children called "The Lost Paradise." She stayed at a small inn, and in the night, while she tried to sleep, insects bit her ravenously; all night she tossed in agony and couldn't get to sleep. "For at that time," she explained to Mrs. Seizling, "faith had not yet been revealed to me." She lay on her infested mattress, her body a prey to insects that were sucking her blood. She decided she had to do something the following day to protect her body. So the next morning she went to a hardware store and bought six empty tin cans. All day she wandered through the place called "The Lost Paradise." At night she filled the cans with kerosene, arranged them around her mattress, and put a match to each one. In the flickering sextuple light she fell asleep. And, in fact, got a few hours of sweet slumber out of this trick. Then the Schwester sister was wakened by a weird tapping sound. Tick-tick-tick. Like drops of rain falling on a tin roof. She opened her eyes, but couldn't see anything wrong. The six tins of kerosene were smoking passionately. All of a sudden, she felt a sting, and another sting, and yet another. At last her eyes stared at the explanation of the mystery: an endless caravan of insects, giant African insects, was climbing up one wall of the room and crawling across the ceiling. The moment each insect reached the spot on the ceiling directly above her mattress, in the center of the six smoking tins, it let go and dived straight for her—her face, her hands, her legs, her whole body. . . .

At that point, in the midst of her stupor, while her body was still groaning from the pain of the stings, she saw the significance which transcended the event itself: the creatures were coming to her, bypassing her roadblock and outwitting her human ingenuity, because of a gigantic love, a profound love, for her body. No man had ever really loved the body of the Schwester sister. She knew this; she didn't lie to herself. But now, look! these insects were making love to her with ecstatic desire for her body, sucking her very marrow. And on account of their love, she too, in a miraculous fashion, through suffering, learned how to return love to them. She spoke to them, looked fondly on her multitude of lovers stepping up the walls and then across the ceiling and finally thrusting themselves into her perspiring body, showering her with stings and passion. She yearned to love them to the very limit of her capacity, their love having heightened the perception which had been dimly lurking inside her for many years, that only through love can one arrive at the core of things, that only if one knows how to love properly will all the answers be granted in good time. There on that stinking mattress in a Kenyan inn, in the jungle, in the heart of the world, near the spot where Adam, the first man, once dwelt, there she discovered that faith was her soul's cure, or, in other words, that it was her mission to bring about, through some action as yet unknown to her, the reappearance of God. . . .

"And the miracle of this land is God's miracle," she told Mrs. Seizling, who was listening intensely. "Right here God revealed Himself. Right here faith was designed, here His words were articulated—no, not here on Ibn-Gabirol Street," and she laughed a bit and sipped her cooling tea, "not here, but there, under the sun, in the desert, among the cliffs, among the crevices, along the vast stretches of sand—a place that has no corners," getting more excited, "no corners, no make-up, no subtle colors. Everything cruel, shrill, totalitarian. From Elat upward I've hiked, I've tramped all around there. His spirit is still alive there, there you feel it, the roar of His might, His giant proportions, His cruelty, His essence . . . in the caves, the cracks," and with her wrinkled hand that had a red ring adorning its little finger, the Schwester twin was beating the top of the table, "there all is vacant, stale, severe, intense, yet gorgeous."

Her face suddenly exposed the craving of her soul, and Mrs. Seizling's eyes, gazing at that soulful face, filled with tears. "And there, in the wasteland," continued the Schwester twin in a whisper, as though she were revealing some secret, "there in the wastes, among the hills of gravel, loess, and sand, among the glorious forms carved into the tall and everlasting cliffs, there spoke God, there out of the craters of dead volcanoes, out of the intricacies of canyons, from the circuits of the eagle, there He spoke, there revealed Himself, the God Who is the glory of the desert. The prophets went out there, there the nation was conceived, from there have come its unity, its laws, its rhythms, its nationhood, its genes. There it learned its lesson of morality, strength, and sensitivity, and there—there the Covenant with Abraham shall be re-enacted."

Mrs. Seizling, feeling that her blood was draining away from her brain, stretched out her hands, spread them across the table, lowered her head onto them, and burst into sobs. The Schwester twin, her eyes focused on some apparition, on some divine halo hovering upon the surface of the desert, smoothed the hair of the old American woman and added: "And, my good woman, what do you think these prophets were? College professors? Government officials? Tourist agents? I'll tell you what they were!" At this point her voice got loud and hoarse. "Uncompromising men, weird men, of a kind that this land has always stoned to death. But God has loved them. Spoken with them. Not with the politicians, not with the kings—but with the psychotics has He spoken. They are the salt of the earth."

Mrs. Seizling calmed down somewhat. She sat up and wiped away her tears. What words! Yes, for this, in order to hear such words, had she come to this land. She signaled to the weary waitress and ordered iced coffee, plus ice cream with whipped cream on it. No, she wasn't afraid that she'd gain weight. Her eyes swung back to the Schwester twin, whose soul was soaring now in a far-off world. "Believe me, madam," said the Schwester twin from the depths of her majestic vision, "the desert is God's palace. There you can actually feel Him, sense His power. In the presence of those wadis, the blasphemous babble of my younger sister dries up, out of utter shame. God is alive there, existing and breathing, inside the cracks, along the routes of flying hawks, in the spread of eagles' wings, through the peristalsis of snakes, in the incredible heat, in the endless whiteness veering off into nowhere. And He will again reveal Himself to and speak to the insane! They comprehend, they are sensitive, they shall see Him. Who are they, though, these madmen of ours? Tell me!"

Mrs. Seizling didn't know. Sipping her iced coffee through a yellowish straw, she saw eagles, huge eagles, wheeling over the gloomy heat-struck houses of Tel Aviv and blotting them out.

"I'll tell you. All of us who came back, who returned to this place." A crafty mischievous little smile sparkled in her eyes, as though she had just cracked an intriguing joke which nobody had ever heard before. For the moment, Mrs. Seizling had a vision of Perry Mason solving the murder of the Third Triplet.

"We were a nation," said the Schwester twin, "a nation that betrayed its God. And we paid the highest price possible—we became smoke and ashes. My brother-in-law's son was eight years old when they buried him alive. And what remains, what's left? Wretched, nerve-racked, hopeless sticks. Are they beautiful? I don't know. Beautiful grotesques. Human beings who have been halved, quartered—the Rabinowitzes, the Spiegel family, the English teacher Mrs. Spring, all of us. During the day we may be complaining, yawning, making money, building houses, scrambling around as fast as we can, but at night we are insomniacs in our spacious houses, our modern apartments, our magnificent cars, at night we dream nightmares and shriek, for Satan has tattooed our forearms with blue numbers. Do you know, my dear Mrs. Seizling, why these cries, these shrieks, are heard in this land in the dead of night? All those numbers screaming and crying because they have no idea of the why or the wherefore or the how or the how long or the when or the whereto of it all? They cry because there is no escape. The insult scorches. The knowledge, the final realization that they were simply raw material in the most advanced factory of Europe, under a sky inhabited by a God in exile, by a Stranger, this information drives us crazy. Such humiliation! So we have turned this country into the largest insane asylum on earth. I tell you that out of these, out of the lunatics who weep in the night, will emerge somebody who will enter a wadi among the rocks and be received by God in friendship and spoken to. And those words, those words they will exchange, shall cure him. If I only had a million dollars! Of course I'm exaggerating, because who of us has a million dollars? I have a net income of six hundred liras a month from the boardinghouse my husband left me, and with this I have to support my sister and send some wreaths once in a while to the cemetery, and prices are rising. But if I had the money, a lot of money, I'd build there, in the desert . . ."

Mrs. Seizling was a practical woman who knew what she wanted. The words of the Schwester twin sank into what Mrs. Seizling called her "IBM,"—namely, her brain. Her heart knew how to avoid a collision with her head. Yes, she was moved by what she had heard, but Mrs. Seizling was not one of those women who live by their feelings alone, whose only function is to have emotions. She listened, digested, knowing that her whole life, that all her actions up to now, amounted to zero, and now, in the evening of her days, she was being given a chance to perform something great. She listened, pondered, meditated, then realized what she must do.

The Minister of Finance and his underlings sat on one side of the table and drummed their fingers. Mrs. Seizling spoke: "These six million are a drop in the bucket. I'll build industrial centers and border settlements for you. But, first, I wish to build a mental hospital. A modern institute, in the desert. I'll tell you where and you'll get me the permits. I don't need either your advice or your assistance. You hurried here? You rushed the whole way? You're a nervous people. But when I'm involved in anything, then, by God, there are no tricks."

And they: "But, Mrs. Seizling, we need industrial development in industrial areas, and there are also the problems of settling immigrants and of security. We need tanks, tractors. . . ."

"That's what you need?" She had learned fast. "I am a novice in a new order and you don't even realize that you are members of it too. All Israel are members. You'll do what I want and say amen, because I'm doubling my offer. Twelve million! Six million for the institute and six million for graft. That's my offer. You have no choice. The clever Jews immigrated to America or died in Europe. The fools and the heroes are still here. During the day they play muscle men and soldiers, and at night they weep. I'll cure them. Twelve million is plenty of cash. Even my six would be a nice addition to your foreign capital reserves. But twelve million in ready cash!"

The Minister of Finance swallowed the gnat and the camel! The deal was signed, sealed, and delivered. With six million in his hands for himself and another six million for the economy, the Minister of Finance returned to his office to conduct state affairs. "It's all for the best," he told the Prime Minister as they sat together in the evening, over tea and dominoes.

Mrs. Seizling was not a woman who did just half a job. Once the agreement was concluded, she asked the Schwester twin to accompany her on a tour of the Negev. They stayed a few days in Beer-Sheva and went on to Shivta and Mitspe Ramon. In jeeps supplied by the army, they circled the vicinity of Dimona, drove to the Gaza Strip, penetrated deep into the Negev, crossed the desert, and reached Elat. In Mrs. Seizling's eyes, the most appropriate location of them all (and, for the Schwester twin, absolutely psychedelic) was the heights above the new city of Arad, close to the mound of the ancient Arad and just a stone's throw from its old temple. The Schwester twin and Mrs. Seizling were mesmerized by the Arad landscape, by the sight of the Dead Sea opposite the white mountains and canyons and ravines, by the desert stretching westward. The wildness, the harsh beauty, the brand-new houses of the lovely small town, the pure dry air—all this infected the two old women, and at the same moment they stretched themselves out on the ground and sang in unison, "And this is what stood by our forefathers and us," a song from the Passover ritual for which they both knew the same melody. Kneeling in the sand, their eyes waterfalls of tears and their voices thin and chirping, they sang and trembled. Off in the distance, birds, flocks of birds, perhaps eagles, perhaps hawks, were circling around some remote prey down in a deep gorge, while here, on this spot which had soaked up their tears, The Institute for Rehabilitation and Therapy was, in a sense, being built.

Mrs. Seizling turned to the office of Ilon, Tamir, Gat, & Shoshan, Inc., and commissioned them to design the Institute. In effect, she bore the expenses of the entire office for a whole year. The architects Gat and Ilon even traveled outside of Israel to explore the total range of possibilities, studying many hospitals, hotels, and various institutes in Switzerland, England, America and Sweden. The building permit was issued, and one bright day the construction of the Institute was begun.

When finally completed, the gigantic edifice was one of the most *avant-garde* structures in Israel. Three proud stories high, and a fourth below ground level. No detail escaped Mrs. Seizling's eyes; she gave her opinion on every item, each door, each handle. It would be difficult to say of this building that it was a thing of beauty and a joy forever. Quite the opposite. Many complained that "functionalism" was invading every fine spot in the land, and they asked, if so much money was available, why wasn't a more beautiful edifice constructed? Nonetheless, Mrs. Seizling set before her eyes the vision of the Schwester twin and, believing that it was the tragic fate of the Jewish people to have no time to spare for beauty or aesthetics while they were shrieking at night in terror, she demanded of Ilon, Tamir, etc., efficiency instead of aesthetics, good doorknobs instead of a hyperconcern for ornamentation. She even considered this enormous ugly building a symbol, a symbol of a nation hastening to set up house for a transient generation in a place where you must strike roots upside down, a location to which old people were coming in order to be born anew in the womb of their ancient mother whose loins were clogged with holy dust. Mrs. Seizling was for comfortable bathrooms, up-to-date air-conditioning, game rooms, lecture halls, laboratories, a nice dining hall, a modern kitchen, and she got all this from the architects Ilon, Tamir, Gat, and Shoshan, Inc. She wasn't particularly interested in the shape of the building, for the two of them, she and the Schwester twin, knew perfectly well that, following the Day of Judgment, God would wear a new form for everybody.

She had playing fields laid out, and established a wine cellar. She hired an excellent team of doctors, therapists, male and female nurses, division heads, air-conditioning and heating mechanics. She had a garage built and populated it with four station wagons, two ordinary stick-shift Chevrolets, a small Simca, one Deux Chevaux, and a few jeeps for desert travel. An up-to-date infirmary was set up in which it was possible to perform the most complicated operations. The six million became ten and a half and she moved around like a tank in battle and truly nobody could stop her. After two years there stood opposite the growing town of Arad a modern palace whose ugliness was quite impressive.

"God is no aesthete," said Mrs. Seizling, quoting the Schwester twin and Adam Stein, whose personality fascinated her when she met him in the old hospital at Jaffa. "Actually, God despises the beauty of Western civilization, of the non-Jewish world, and we are his favorites. We are a footstool at his feet."

"He didn't die of shame," said Adam, "when his little children expired into smoke. He adores the relentless unflinching desert because its magnificence argues the opposite of beauty, because the desert is a spitting image of himself."

"A hundred years from now," said the Schwester twin, "we'll mourn over that ugliness, search for antiques, collect portraits, arrange flowers. Today our business is to rescue as many as possible from the slaughter. Though they are already slaughtered. Yes, their bodies have reached this land, but their souls are still in the furnaces."

3

THE SWINDLER

ADAM STEIN leaves the office of Dr. Nathan Gross and creeps along the corridor. Fat Manny Berger, his head lolling on his shoulder, is fast asleep in his wheelchair. Spittle oozes from his mouth. Adam halts at a radiator, pulls a bottle of French brandy from behind it, and examines the label: "Biscuit." He uncorks the bottle, takes a swig, and returns the bottle to its place. Through a door with two red bulbs shining above it bursts a bald male nurse in white. In his hand he carries a bunch of keys that make a terrific racket. Soft music sweeps across the walls and sinks into the carpets. Beyond the small high windows, white hills sparkle against a red sky. Drops of blood. By the dozen. As many drops as there are windows subject to fluorescent illumination. Outside, the desert is burning and white, though from here it looks tame and, consequently, appealing. The two of them, guard and inmate, march side by side. The Displaced Person

and the SS Man. *I and Commandant Klein.* Definitions scare
Adam. This house is called the Institute for Rehabilitation and
Therapy. Before he was appointed camp director, Commandant
Klein belonged to a medical establishment that went under
the name *Reichsarbeitsgemeinschaft Heil—und Pflegeanstalten*
(The National Coordinating Agency for Therapeutic and Medi-
cal Establishments).

The nurse—Jacob Shapiro, a native of Tiberias, bald, dressed
in a white uniform—accompanies Adam Stein, unaware that he,
Shapiro, has become, for the moment, another person. Shapiro
stops, opens a door that is no different from all the other doors
facing the corridor, and waits. Adam squints into the unfamiliar
room, a room in which in the old days they would have locked
him up as in a prison. He would like to enter and relax. The
blood inside his head is pounding. Any minute he will lose all
contact with Shapiro the nurse and with the Institute, and return
to Commandant Klein. Suddenly Jenny appears, like a ghost.
Where did she pop up from, that spook? *Get thee to the desert,
make love to a rock, give birth to an eagle.* He laughs to himself,
but his face is murky. I'm dying. My life is spilling out, drop by
drop, into the final measuring cup. The soap is practically finished. Yet he smiles to himself. His face ashen. Jenny and the
nurse Shapiro are having a whispered conversation: the SS's are
whispering their poison. In a minute the doors will open and that
odor, that terrible stench, will scorch his nostrils. But it makes
sense that in the presence of Jenny's face, that lovely face, he
should remember Kleg, the German soldier. Kleg used to watch
while Adam Stein entertained the Jews on their way to the furnaces. Once, when Kleg was invited to join the act, he refused.
He was the only one who, any time, any place, ever refused.
Everybody else was happy to take part, oh so jubilant! The compensation of food and drink was too great a temptation, too
good a deal: A fifth of Schnapps. Five cigarettes, good ones,
gold-tipped—ah, that marvelous fragrance of tobacco, so mas-
culine. A quarter-pound of blood-sausage and bread. And once

they even distributed duck legs. You remember, Shapiro? Shapiro doesn't remember, he was born in Tiberias. Jenny was born in Rishon Le-Zion. At the sight of her face, the remnants of his pride stir and he dismisses her with a rudeness that startles even himself:

"Tell her that I'm tired!"

"Speak to me directly!" Jenny shoots out her words arrogantly. Poor thing.

"Tell her to go away, I have no strength."

"Say it to *me*."

"I-I-I—I'm tired, Jenny." He tries to chuckle. "Go. I'm exhausted. I'll be Klein. You know who that is?"

"Yes." She knows. She heard.

"So go, go, go on." He sings:

> *"Just with our fists we'll smash the foe,*
> *We with our eyes so cold, so cold,*
> *We with our hearts of hate*
> *And our eyes of blue."*

"What kind of a song is that?" asks Jenny.

He heard it someplace. Maybe when he was a kid. Maybe in the circus. Maybe in that other place, Klein's? Jenny is about to say something else when he laughs and spits out a challenge: "You sycophant!" The nurse Shapiro signals for her to leave. Against her will, she obeys. And Adam, Adam despises as well as admires her, precisely because she obeyed. He admires her for her submissiveness, but despises her for her love. Has she again recalled the rules? The house rules? At the sound of any instruction, she becomes a tame animal. He turns to Shapiro, as though they were in cahoots together, and just as Jenny disappears around a bend in the corridor, just as her beautiful, quite beautiful, body shrinks out of sight, he calls out in her direction: "Do you know what that is? A book of rules with a nice ass!" Shapiro takes a last look at those buttocks and bursts out laughing. The idiot!

Adam enters the room. Shapiro hangs towels on the racks of the blue porcelain bathroom, checks the bell, checks the suitcases arranged along the wall, folds the bedspread, goes back to the door, and stands there.

Adam notices his twin, Herbert Stein, sitting on the windowsill. Since he attempted to throttle the pension landlady, they haven't seen each other, a fact which didn't bother either one of them very much. Now, though, Herbert would like to strike up a conversation. Adam's twin, who was a philosophy student in Heidelberg and studied under Professor Maritain and under old man Ludwig, the author of *The Lucky Columns,* somebody who will never acknowledge the bitter truth that Adam Stein, his twin, was a circus clown who became the lowest of the low, namely, "the Jew who made Klein laugh," the Jew who performed there, twisted his nose and prestidigitated, and all this in front of his proud wife, Gretchen. "But, Herbert, my brother, we remained alive on account of my clowning and not on account of your being a famous Hegelian. . . ." Adam is tense, his body one taut bow; soon he will hear the keys in Shapiro's hands clank and the door slam, soon the swish of the lock and the background music in the hallway will vanish and just the two of them will be left, he and Herbert, and then he can die. Meanwhile Herbert is still on the windowsill, as the white of the Dead Sea flickers in the distance and signals crooked images with its rays.

Herbert speaks: "Adam Stein, you amaze me. You're miserable, very miserable. And to think that we two are caught in one body. It's weird, really weird. And sad. Above all, sad."

Adam clenches his fist. How ridiculous he is, this perpetual student sitting on the windowsill. "Get down from the window, you beast of prey. You're driving me crazy."

"Me?" Herbert bursts into such laughter that it shakes the mountains of Judah, the desert, the ancient Dead Sea, the salt flats, Lot's wife, the Essenes, Elijah. "That makes two of us. If you're crazy, so am I."

His teeth are blackened from too much smoking and too much drinking. Herbert is not as handsome as Adam, and Adam is proud of this fact. Adam is, to quote Jenny, "a Dorian Gray who will get old all at once." One day old age will jump on him, devour him, lick him.

"Though I'm hooked to this window, brother Adam, I'm still just a ghost."

"And I am sick."

"Yes, you are sick."

"You're sick too."

"No, not me."

"Yes!" Adam's teeth chatter. Lock that door already. Shapiro studies him. That bald ball-less bastard! Fifth Columnist! *Judenrat!*

"They're locking you in now," says his twin.

"I know," whispers Adam.

"And why are they locking you in?"

"Why are they locking me in? Because I am a danger to society. I who was once the beauty of the land, the salt of the earth, I who was once so famous, who had ten bank accounts in Switzerland alone. I who . . ." But his words go dry and his mouth clamps shut. He is a coil in tension. The door slams now, he hears the key turning the lock. The carpet swallows Shapiro's footsteps. For a moment his eyes are on the verge of tears, but he will not weep in front of that clown sitting over there in the window. He drops onto all fours and starts crawling across the room, and the twin shouts: "Again? Back at that again? You're no longer 'there' any more!"

"Shut up!"

He proceeds to his suitcases. They're empty. Jenny has already emptied them, hung some things in the closets and put others away in drawers. His brother, his twin, whispers with a venom that suits him so well against the incredible desert background: "Hep, hep, hep, hep, hep!"

Adam pays no attention. He gropes around. His eyes blind,

his agony sharp, his terror huge. He grabs his guitar case and hugs it with affection, with gratitude. He crawls to the middle of the room, removes the guitar from its case, and begins strumming. His tempo is slow, in time to the beat of his heart, tom-tom-tom-totom, picks up pace, picks up volume, goes wild as Adam's hands lose all contact with his own body, with his brain. His hands strike hard, they invent rhythms which come from nowhere. "The anthropology of primeval forests," the twin is quick to say. Adam's twin knows how to be a kill-joy, how to deflate any situation with a few hermetic words, with a sentence that sounds as though it has been said a hundred times, some heartless dry sentence. Meanwhile, Adam is in a train, the clown is traveling east, east, tom-tototom-tom-totom-totom-totom, and the train speeds on. Where to? To his Aunt Lipson? No, to Commandant Klein. He'll have a great time. He remembers a bar in Berlin where a naked black woman danced, her body graced with the nimbleness of a cat. Totom-tom-tom. As the sealed train traveled on, the cows outside in the fields mooed and the sun shone and the trees were green, while inside, in the packed train, the old Rabbi died. From what? From shame. Totom. Then, all of a sudden, Adam's twin has a fit of exhausting nervous laughter, and just as suddenly Adam himself knows he cannot take any more and must beat up his brother, but what can he beat him with? He'll whack him with the guitar! His twin, though, leaps from the window snappily, eluding him, till they wrestle. Adam is hurt, wounded. Herbert hit him, of course, but who will believe it? Will anybody believe it? Gross? That eunuch who called the spiders in Jaffa hallucinations? Some experts I have here! On account of them I'm croaking. Whom are you hitting? Yourself? Blood streams from his forehead. He jogs around the room. Herbert escapes him, that bastard. Adam extends a trembling puzzled hand to his forehead, to his eyes. That redness, the redness of the blood, affects him, startles him. He drops to the floor and returns to his guitar, strumming on it. Then, without a single drop of strength left, he lets go of it and lowers his head into the womb of the dark case, like a child trying to get back inside his mother, and slams the lid. His head is hidden. From within that dark case rumbles a wail, the wail of a wounded animal. "You're screaming for nothing," says his twin, but he is no longer laughing. His face is sad. "Adam, you have nobody to cry to. Father is dead, Mother's dead, we are orphans." Adam hears this comment and laughs. Inside the case he laughs and howls. "We are orphans!" The combination of these words amuses him. He has no wife and no children any more; he may have Jenny, but he himself is nothing but the twin of a perpetual student and an orphan.

Jenny, Jenny Grey, lovely Jenny, "the rulebook with the nice ass," the vulture, the brainless charmer, rises early in the morning (precisely at 6:30), treats herself to a cold bath, brushes her teeth, which are whiter than the toothpaste, and now, dressed in a smoothly starched uniform, she steps toward Adam's room. If not for the fact that the carpet drowns each click of her gait, she would sound like a disciplined soldier on parade. Nate the nurse has informed her that he heard laughs and sobs coming out of Adam's room, but when he looked through the transom Adam said everything was okay and he should take it easy, yet Adam still lay there on the floor. Jenny has no ears now for such distressing news, she's all excited and imagines herself, for the moment, to be a small child. She is thinking about him, his beautiful face, his silver sideburns. She is fantasizing about his body, about the classes he will soon, of course, be giving. It amuses her that this living corpse which is perishing every minute, which is getting closer and closer to total death, this man whom they have written off as a hopeless case, an incurable, will be at it again, in a few days' time, running the whole Institute for Rehabilitation and Therapy without a single rebuke from anybody. Certainly not from me! she says to herself. And the others? They'll fall into his trap. That swindler.

On reaching the door, she realizes it's locked. She fishes in her

pocket, pulls out the key, and enters. There, sprawled on the
floor, obviously having slept in his clothes (the nurse Nate will
get it from her!), is her heart's choice, the master of her joy—
his head, his handsome head, caught inside a guitar case. She
stoops, opens the guitar case, and liberates his head. His face is
white or, more correctly, yellow-white, the color of a heat wave.
At the secret fold where his lips meet, a lizardlike pattern of
congealed blood stretches, and on his brow looms a blue bruise
surrounded by an intricate system of bloodstains. Jenny dashes
to the nurse Shapiro, who, doing his part, runs to the doctor on
duty. Meanwhile Jenny, with great difficulty, drags Adam over
to the bed, lifts him onto it, takes off his shoes, and, after some
consideration, pulls a small comb out of her pocket and begins
combing his hair. She gets pleasure out of combing his hair even
while the closed eyes of his unconscious face are staring at her.

But the pleasure, the numbing of her senses almost to the
point of fainting which seizes her whenever she combs his hair
(or his eyebrows at times, and once, ah, once even the curly
white hair of his chest), this delight is abruptly interrupted, for
two doctors barge into the room. She stands by the window and
observes them, their professionalism, their humanitarianism that
lacks all compassion. They go over his medical record in gruff
ungraceful voices, in dry precise language, and as they talk, they
examine him, rub his temples, wipe away the blood.

"High blood pressure. Irregular pulse." They give each other
numerical messages: "149 . . . 52 . . ."

On the other side of the window, the morning is already burning hot, and here in the room it is so cold. Roly-poly Dr. Nachwalter, with the face that reminds her of a film actor whose
name she has forgotten but who usually plays a monster, is in-
forming his colleague of the many operations Adam Stein has
already undergone. She cocks her ear, eager to catch the story
again. She loves to hear them praise Adam as though they were
talking about some mythical hero. They are talking of him as if
he were a phenomenon so exceptional, so special, that he

couldn't be measured on any human scale, whereas she, on the contrary, knows that he is a faker.

"It is quite common for a man to damage his body with his own hands," explains Dr. Nachwalter in his soft, controlled, matter-of-fact voice, "but in Adam's case . . . Well, in the beginning he managed to give himself a malignant stomach ulcer. Afterward he impaired his vision and we had to operate. I'd say that his body has spat out—if I may use such a vulgar expression—about ten organs. And every one of these ailments and diseases came upon him simply by the strength of his own will. This man decides to have a certain sickness and after a little while that very sickness actually attacks him. What an amazing gift for self-destruction . . ."

The young doctor is still trying to locate Adam's pulse.

Jenny ponders about this faker of hers. On many an occasion he has repeated to her, in detail and with great enjoyment, how a certain rascal had lodged in his body and was dying there only gradually. How that rascal, his twin brother Herbert, decided that Adam had to fall terribly sick, unbearably sick, until his soul broke loose from his corpse. One time he claimed that in about two weeks he would suffer a hemorrhage, that suddenly, without any incision, the big toe of his left foot would spurt blood and the ensuing hemorrhage would be impossible to stop. Two weeks later Adam lay down on his bed and concentrated on this one matter as though hypnotized, as though he had turned into a cocoon that would any minute burst into a butterfly. Finally, blood jetted from under the nail of his toe. The doctors labored for hours trying to stanch the bleeding, not a single one of them understanding how the toe could hemorrhage this way. It stopped at last, only after Adam was left with almost no blood in his system.

Dr. Nachwalter injects a serum. The faces of both doctors are solemn. Jenny, gazing at her beloved's tormented visage, notices, to her surprise, that his right eye opens for a second, blinks, winks, and then swoons again shut. She pretends she hasn't seen a thing, and tries to forget that wink. Her confidence in his swindling powers doesn't preclude her worrying now about his fate, and the mumbling of the doctors, which sounds like the voices of Catholic priests at their devotions, terrifies her, prophesies doom, blinds her vision, while outside a desert day burns white and yellow and mournfully desolate. During the Latin-like mumbo-jumbo, Adam quickly, secretly, jerks his hand out and tries to pull her white uniform. No longer able to control herself, she bursts out laughing, against her will. The doctors stare at her with fury. Dr. Nachwalter says with the cruelty of a sworn humanist addressing a cannibal in the heart of the jungle: "I am sure that Jenny is capable of looking after him, isn't that so?" And the young doctor mutters: "An inexplicable attack . . . his pulse is getting stronger . . . we'll have to analyze his urine . . ."

"Yes, Miss Jenny can look after that too," says Dr. Nachwalter. "She's an expert when it comes to Adam, she knows him thoroughly, isn't that so?" His contempt, the contempt which a courteous restrained man of science feels for an over-passionate romantic, hangs thick in his voice.

The doctors pack up their various bits of apparatus and exit; she is left behind, alone with the faker.

"Adam . . . Adam . . ."

He is unconscious, he doesn't reply. Jenny is no longer certain —perhaps that wink was just her imagination, perhaps her uniform wasn't yanked by anything except her desiring heart.

"Say something, come on!"

He doesn't budge. His mouth is locked. His face is a white death-mask. She takes a small transistor radio from her pocket and plays with the knob until she hits the voice of the morning newscaster. Jenny adores the news program. She loves to hear that reserved voice coming out of nowhere, a voice that knows everything but reveals just the circumference, omitting the secret center of the matter. That controlled voice which talks about some terrible storm and about two infiltrators who were killed last night while attempting to set fire to the fields of Ein-Gev. These facts, spoken in excellent Hebrew, with pleasing emphasis upon all the crucial vowels and consonants, give her the feeling of belonging to some mysterious inaccessible enterprise. As though she were a party to some mystical creation, to the ocean storm, to the infiltrators in the night, and even to the fields ablaze up there in the north. Everything is okay, Adam, the world follows its usual ways, the same things are said and done.

"Those lovely eyes," thinks Adam to himself. Though he seems to be still in a coma, his closed eyes follow her, fish her out of the news. As soon as the news and the weather forecast end, somebody starts singing, the radio makes some idiotic far-off voice sound beautiful. He won't, not Adam, do her the honor yet, he won't grant her the peace she wants. For the present, let him just meditate about her, undisturbed, and observe her evil ways. He has to come to some decision concerning her. Can he return to her as if nothing had happened, does he want to, is he at all interested in that? After all, in her eyes it's a fact that only a few days ago he attempted to throttle his landlady! Has he forgotten what he found out about Jenny the first time he saw her, when he inquired about her and they practically threw stones at him out of hate for her! They told him that from the moment she came to the old hospital in Jaffa she was more strict than anybody else on the staff. Hell itself was less obnoxious to her than a person who broke the slightest regulation. "Even in a prison for child-killers they aren't that strict," Arthur once told him in a moment of frankness. They despised her not only for her callousness, not only for her hostile attitude toward anybody who dared to smoke in the corridor or failed in the most minor way to conform to rules; on top of all that, they despised her for her beauty.

When he was still a student and, to support himself, played the violin in a silent movie house in Berlin, he met his wife, Gretchen, his beautiful delicate wife, that funny woman who came to watch each time he entertained the Jews of Commandant Klein, who went to her own death without knowing that that was where she was heading. In those student days he used to stand behind the screen onto which the film was being projected, and he'd play whatever he felt like playing. One time she appeared there behind the screen, stood beside him, and watched the shadows of the silent film, the pale images, reversed, pinched on the sides and almost obliterated in the middle —and that's how they came to know each other.

Jenny. A pearl in a dunghill. Adam's regret is that when you look straight at her for any length of time (which is the regular, lustful custom of Dr. Gross) you discover that her beauty, her magnificent version of beauty, has one weak spot.

Jenny is a cold cruel stunning beauty, a knockout. Her eyes are black, her eyebrows as if formed by a razor. Her brow is high and narrow, her nose straight except for a slight turn upward where you can see, if you stand close, two dark spots that look needled there. Her black hair is smoothly drawn back, her chin not pointed but horizontal, her cheeks sunken as though all her wisdom teeth had been removed. Her neck is long and she has a faint down of hair on her arms, a down that arouses affection. Her body is slim, almost boyish, its curves so cautious that you are amazed by the sight of her modest, trembling womanhood. The presence of this cold woman rekindles the childhood days of Adam's romanticism, the days when a girl would cover what a girl of today reveals.

There is a classic perfection to Jenny's appearance, a certain balance that you find only in some ancient works of genius. Therefore—or, possibly, nonetheless—her beauty harbors a serious flaw. What exactly is that flaw? (Jenny is listening now to folk music. Somebody is singing about the disappointed love of some Yugoslavian peasant. Who cares about it? thinks Adam. Yet, in fact, it does matter. Why is that? Are we all brothers?) With his eyelids clamped tight, Adam speculates that perhaps the flaw of Jenny's beauty is the absence of any flaw. In other words, what is terrible and also marvelous about Jenny's beauty is its very perfection. In Adam Stein's judgment—that famous comedian who studied, in his youth, aesthetics and philosophy at Heidelberg—beauty, any beauty, demands some blemish, requires some detraction. A beauty built on absolute symmetry is not true beauty. Genuine beauty—at least, that was what Adam learned—must approach ugliness. "Anybody who studies beauty is devoted to death," said August von Platen. In short, the opposite of beauty could not possibly be ugliness. Yet here, in her face, in her body, in Jenny's whole being, is an example that robs all the authorities of their authority, that turns everything upside-down. Jenny, with her compass-drawn nostrils, her eyes equidistant from her nose—to the thousandth millimeter, he is certain—Jenny with those two absolutely matching halves of her face, this Jenny is beautiful despite her symmetry, despite her almost inhuman perfection. And her beauty proclaims that by its very nature it cannot conform to the rules; consequently it acquires a fault: being inexplicable, it becomes also cold, terrifying, confounding.

The patients go wild when they see her, they drop their lit cigarettes on the carpet, frightened by the coldness blowing from her. They wish she were ugly, or that her beauty were more human.

This Jenny whom everybody fears, who upholds each regulation and sub-regulation and sub-sub-regulation, who is alarmed by any deviation, however slight, from accepted procedures, this Jenny whose nostrils are machine-made and whose every step and movement is preconceived, this Jenny, when it comes to Adam, is another person altogether.

When they first met, in the old hospital in Jaffa, he took her hand in his, stared into her face for a long while, and then burst out laughing. Thrown off-balance, she stared back at him with fierce eyes and said: "What are you laughing at? You're a rude man!"

"And you're a whore," answered Adam then, in a quiet confident voice. "I know you, you'd sell everything you have in exchange for the pain that pleasure might inflict upon you. You've known only one man and don't even realize that. What do you know about your father? That he's dead? I also know that he died. You'd sell everything for a cigarette's worth of disgust. You're sicker than all the patients in this building and one day you'll fall on your knees before Satan and weep, but he'll be too good for you. You're strict with everybody because you're afraid. And what are you afraid of? Yourself? What depths of hatred I fathom in your face!"

She slapped his face. She blanched, her eyes flashing a wild flamenco, and burst into an hysterical howl. It was a difficult job to pull her away from him. After a week of agitation which she herself didn't quite understand, she came to a decision. She asked the permission of the head doctor—at that time Dr. Zikhroni, of blessed memory—and took Adam, on her own responsibility, to her mother, a widow who lived in the settlement of Rishon Le-Zion.

Throughout the trip they didn't exchange a single word. In silence they approached the small white house with its red roof smothered by a cluster of bougainvillea. Jenny's mother turned out to be a petite woman who still preserved some of her beauty among the wrinkles and cracks in her face, and still had a portion of her early liveliness and childishness. First she told him about Mr. Charminsky, who had pursued and taught her to drink white wine with fish meals. Then she offered Adam a glass of tea ("Does the gentleman take loose sugar or lump?") with cookies.

Jenny sat quiet and pensive. Suddenly she set her glass down with a bang and said in anger: "Mother, tell me about Father. The whole story. I want to know. Right now!"

The old woman gave Jenny a long look and her eyes grew moist. She took a lengthy sip from her tea and smiled, and her smile stayed on her face as she spoke. "When I buried him, I had nothing left. Not even you. You were always making fun of me. Yasha might have become a poet, but instead he worked in the fields of some Mr. Levitan. And died of malaria. Even in his sickness he was handsome. When you were ten, in the winter— it's interesting that you forgot, how could you forget?—it was very cold out, we lived in a shack and"—Adam felt that once she spat everything out, now that she was able to speak, it would be better for her afterward—"we shivered from the cold. It was a terrible winter. Even some snow fell here, here in the south. That was just the beginning. Then came fierce hail. You got out of your bed, which was drenched because of the leak in the roof. And you came in to us. I had been sleeping, but suddenly I woke up and saw him and saw you, saw him with you, and he was drunk or asleep, I don't know which. Perhaps he was actually dreaming—he had such fantastic dreams, he could have been a poet. I didn't say a word. He was crying and crying. I remember I wanted to bury myself alive, but it was too cold to get out of bed. He cried and embraced you and cried and was asleep and was drunk. We used to drink cognac in those days to fight the cold. Later, when you were asleep, he woke up sober and thought I was sleeping and kissed me as if it were our first kiss. And his tears fell upon me and I loved him. The next day we even went to see a silent film, our first movie since we came to this country. . . ."

Adam mulled over the story. Over Yasha. Jenny. She forgot. Her father was dead, so he too no longer remembered. That's what the mother thought, that old toothless woman who was once, was once . . . So, until she met Adam, Jenny hadn't kissed a single man, though she was already twenty-five and lovely, the loveliest woman he had ever seen. She had preserved her virginity not on account of any principle, but out of indifference.

Adam knew that his calling her a whore had actually pleased her. She had taken him to her mother not in order to reveal a secret but to become a partner to a secret. He aroused her. The word "whore" fascinated her. Until she met him, she was a virgin—as far as she knew, anyway—but she adored the label he

had stuck on her. And, for some reason, she was sure that he
knew it. And if he did know it, he could read her like a book, he
could penetrate her to the core, he was just like a god. The way
Father was once, but Father was dead, and Father labored in
the fields of some Levitan, his son started a construction business and one daughter married an engineer and settled in the
development town of Herzlia. In a villa. That's what her mother
said. And all because of Father, who paved the way for them,
who paved the way to gold—who died. At that point she recalled a childhood incident, the time they took her to the Old
City of Jerusalem and as they were walking along Via Dolorosa,
that path of suffering, she suddenly felt terrific pains in her belly
and sobbed. And when she told Uncle Joseph, who was an ex-
cursion guide and a man with a sense of humor, he said: "You
must be giving birth to the Messiah."

But now Jenny is listening to a duet about the flowers of Gil-
boa, sung to the accompaniment of a guitar. Busy with her own
thoughts and unaware of Adam's, she is telling herself that she
knows she is completely in love with him. She is actually not
ashamed of this fact. Rather she is proud of it, proud of her
strength and her love. *He'll never marry me,* she reminds herself
once again. *He's sick, sick beyond recovery, beyond life. He is a
fraud and he's dying.* But whenever he is released from the Institute and sent out into the great world, she sinks into a lethargy,
as though she herself were dying, as though she were a bear
hibernating in winter. She does all her assignments without a
smile. She sleeps alone in her bed without even a dream. But the
moment he is back at the Institute, she revives like spring. She
abets him in his swindling, knowing that in doing so she is help-
ing him to die, yet she is unable to stop herself. She knows she is
in love not merely with his life, his body, his frauds, but also
with the death implicit in every step of his, every word issuing
from his mouth. If not for the fact of death, she would fear life,
the life that would continue away from her. But since such a life
is unlikely in the body of a dying person proceeding to his death

with so much determination, she loves his death as well. And Adam appreciates this more than anything else. She is waiting for him not just in his room or in the recreation room or the dining room or outside among the shrubs, but also at the very end of the road, at the limit of the path he is treading. There she stands, his vulture, a piece of the longed-for conclusion.

When she heard of Adam's return to their building, the elder Schwester twin trembled all over. She was living in the Institute, together with her younger sister, younger by two minutes and forty-one seconds ("It was fate!" she once told herself, muttering the words like a prayer)—living there in accordance with the last will and testament of Mrs. Seizling, who had passed away but whose body (and this was truly a frightful scandal) still lay in a freezing Cleveland morgue while attorneys of countless clients were disputing the right to her corpse. Her will stated that she wanted to be buried at the Institute, in the courtyard and, furthermore, "close to the spot where God will reveal Himself." Her relatives claimed, and with considerable justification, that this final clause made the entire passage suspect. A case of this sort on the lips of the lawyers in the Cleveland office of Judge Jonathan R. Gilhoney sounded weird, outlandish. Lawyers who had always dealt in business contracts and deeds were now disputing the legal meaning of the Revelation of God. Is such a term definable in modern times, or is it perhaps only pertinent to a former age? As long as these lawyers kept wrangling, as long as their dissatisfied clients—the children and relatives of Mrs. Seizling—kept harping on "the temporary madness of our mother" or "our distinguished relative," so long did Judge Jonathan R. Gilhoney have to listen to this mockery which had dragged on for almost a year, and just as long did Mrs. Seizling's poor corpse have to lie in that cold morgue. Mrs. Seizling had left a considerable amount for the maintenance of the Institute, but for the Schwester twins she had made a separate provision, bequeathing to these two a set-up that probably matched the one arranged for that famous couple in Paradise.

Having gathered some pretty flowers, the elder Schwester twin is now standing in the doorway of Adam's room, together with Miles Davis, Wolfovitz the Circumciser, and others, and in her mind's ear she already catches the footsteps of the coming Messiah. For, from the moment Mrs. Seizling and the Schwester twin met Adam Stein, hadn't they known perfectly well that he had been destined to perform the great task? They didn't say so openly, they merely exchanged glances and burst into peals of joy and rapture. On that day Adam accepted the assignment of realizing their great dream, and despite the entreaties of Dr. Gross and Jenny, he never disclosed his judgment of the entire matter. Mrs. Seizling believed that she and the Schwester twin had anointed him the way the prophets used to anoint the King of Israel. She was convinced that from that instant the "glad tidings" were poured into him and consequently he was nothing less than the agent of the nation, whether he knew it or not. And at times, when the spirit seized him, he would stand by the window facing the desert, blanch suddenly, turn his eyes to the Schwester twin, and gasp: "I am not entirely sure, but I have the odd feeling that . . . I can hear . . . Him coming" The Schwester twin would get excited, dash to her room, wake up her sister (who, most of the time, was thinking about movie actors and other such stuff), and with a sense of sanctity the two of them would quickly don their wedding gowns of white silk and lace and set crowns of plastic flowers on their heads.

Adam would then retract, to her great distress: "False alarm! Not yet!" And she'd say: "The chaff has not yet been sifted, the path to Revelation not yet purified, Satan has begun his offensive, his demons have set up new obstacles." And Adam would calm her with: "We will overcome, my sweet Schwester, through patience, for His footsteps are audible, and come He will! The Great Day is near! It may tarry, nevertheless it will arrive. According to every calculation, it is around the corner!"

And, lo and behold, yesterday Adam was back, the man who

would herald the Redemption, the man who would stand amid rocks and hear the word of God. In a dream she had three days ago, an angel came and sat at the edge of her bed and patted her two big toes. He even tickled her a bit, and when she laughed, he told her: "Rachel, Rachel, Adam is coming back. The Great Day is close." The next day she was informed that Adam was indeed back.

So, with flowers in her hands, the Schwester twin now kneels outside Adam's door, singing and weeping. "A waterfall!" says Miles Davis. "She and her God! God is nothing. This whole world of yours is nothing but a drop in the bucket of existence. And what's so special about this miserable globe? Or the Chosen People? Or God Himself? Where was He all these years?"

"He went to buy some cigarettes," says lame Nathan Aharoni, laughing.

At the doorway many are standing, they have come to see Adam, having heard he was sick again. Eyes shut, Adam keeps his ear tuned to the tumult outside his door, discounting the usual background music of that air-conditioned corridor. He is depressed. His body aches and he knows that Jenny is debating whether to open the door for them.

"Soon our agony will touch His footstool," prays the Schwester twin, loud enough for him to hear, "and the gates will split open and God will show His face to the sun-struck, to the ones with blue on their arms, numbered by Satan, and you, Adam, will stand, and you will listen, and you will comprehend, and you will proclaim, and you will rescue, and you will usher in the Redemption."

Me? The clown? The impostor? God, it's a good thing you don't exist, that you died long ago, for if that were not the case I'd certainly be punished for all this terrible innocence. "Eiiiii!" Adam's cry rips open his locked mouth; at the sound of it, they all freeze. Miles calls out: "Jenny, what are they doing to him?" And with hate in their eyes they stare at the Schwester twin, who hasn't heard a thing, whose face is shining from the rays of her inner vision as she murmurs words of gratitude to Heaven.

Jenny swings open the door, knocking down the holy Schwester twin, who is at the point of suffering the ancient birth pangs of Revelation, and she races down the corridor. They make way for her, then peek inside.

"Take away the pain!" he screams at them, knotted in agony. "Kill me!" His mouth is foaming, twisted, shrieking, but his left eye, half open, is peeping and joking. Miles sees this and smiles, despite his momentary shock. How can this man cry in pain with one eye and with his other laugh like a wise guy?

Jenny is helter-skeltering down the hall and Wolfovitz the Circumciser says in a whisper, as though just to himself: "Fire! Fire!" and he guffaws for a moment, but it dies out almost immediately. Roused now from her swoon of devotion, the Schwester twin studies Jenny as she runs down the corridor. "That Lilith! That chaff!" But, on the other hand, she knows that the path to Redemption is strewn with many a Lilith, many an Ashmodai, many a Jenny. The Schwester twin has a little mustache with a small cleft in the middle. She once told Adam that, in her opinion, men love a woman who has a faint mustache to beautify her face. "Not a real mustache!" she said in the bass voice of a man, adding immediately, with a sweet-sweet smile and a tiny voice: "A wee mustachio."

The younger Schwester twin, who has no sign of a mustache above her upper lip, claimed, on the contrary, that the real cause of her older sister's widowhood—and consequently her notion of Revelation, which wouldn't ever have arisen if she hadn't become a widow and traveled to Africa and discovered how the African insects loved her—the cause of her widowhood was that very mustache. "Believe me," she said or rather sang, "that mustache made her a widow! Her husband, Jacob-Nathan, was a good man and maybe you could say that he loved his wife. But one thing he hated, and that was her mustache." The younger twin giggled as she told how once, during Passover, the deceased man, that dearest of men, was a little, you know, tipsy—I mean, completely drunk—and he babbled about a certain kiss, about the time he once kissed his wife and suddenly thought he was kissing his father on the lips and just as suddenly he felt as though he were a balloon that had lost all its air, you understand . . . they were in bed and she was hungry for a child. My sister. But her husband was a modest and humble man, and every morning, before going to his small haberdashery shop, he'd leave behind some hint in the house so that the miracle might take place while he was gone: an open razor on the table, or the latest shaving device for women, a beautiful unique colorful apparatus, on the bureau beside the bed; when that didn't work, the wretched man left shaving creams and razor blades, even an electric shaver that he bought off a recent immigrant in Tel Aviv, he left them everywhere, in the storeroom, in the refrigerator, in her purse, in the medicine cabinet. One time he actually left razor blades inside the cake dough and she baked the cake with the pack of Gillettes inside. This business gradually wore him down, it filled him with anger and sorrow, pain and resentment, said the younger twin. But as for the wife, she wouldn't talk about the matter. It was a closed subject! Because she came to the conclusion that her husband was teasing her for fun, and that in the depths of his heart he loved her little mustache, like everybody else. "Whereas that man," ended the younger twin in a voice that mimicked the turnings of a snake, "finally died because she didn't shave her mustache."

And now everybody makes way for Jenny, who is retracing her steps in the company of Dr. Nachwalter. The door stays halfway open after they enter. You can peek in and see what's happening.

Dr. Nachwalter injects another serum. Blood is gushing from Adam Stein's foot. Jenny stands at the head of the bed and mulls. Everything is weird in her eyes: the crowd in the doorway, Adam's joke on her, the doctor, her own almost involuntary meditations, the storm in her heart. She wants to climb into bed, to become a little girl, to caress his face, his body. Above her thoughts she hears the doctor leaving. Hears the elder Schwester twin traipsing back to her room. Everybody brings in flowers and bonbons and get-well cards and heart-warming post-cards and places them on the bureau. They stare at Adam, nod, and exit the way they came in. And Jenny experiences that anarchic love which confounds her whenever Adam is back, back for her and for his death, which are one and the same, that love which knows only lust. She senses how that anarchy packs her with the carefree abandon of a crushed sinner. And she wishes to utter horrible things, words that are forbidden. To cry and divulge the secrets of her soul.

The bark was loud and clear and dreadful, its echoes suffocating the house. Even through the background music, the bark was terrifyingly distinct.

"What's that?" She knows that the question was addressed to her, for they are the only ones left in the room. "What's that barking?" he asks once again.

"What barking?" She is still way out somewhere, far off, longing, self-startled, abashed. Her eyes flash. She knows how pretty she must be now. But he won't look, that bastard.

"Is that a dog? What's a dog doing here all of a sudden?"

Yes, Jenny has heard the question, why shouldn't she have heard it? Wasn't she standing right beside him? And wasn't she craving for him, at his side, in his room, opposite the tame desert in the window. But something was happening to her and she wasn't quite sure what it was. Suddenly she wakes from her reverie and her body contracts, her muscles shiver, and without knowing why or how, she feels compelled to sing. Jenny, my dear, it's an easy thing to drop the jaw and to sing. So she begins to sing, as though to herself, off somewhere, yet within earshot of his roaring question: Why have they brought dogs in here? What nerve! And to do it on purpose, that's even worse, that's swinish! He'll protest! According to Mrs. Seizling's will—oh, that bastard Gross wants to torture him, he brought the dogs in for Adam's sole benefit, because Gross knows something about dogs, about Adam's life which was one long nightmare: his entire life amounted to one frightful year of three hundred and sixty-five stinking barking lice-ridden dogs eating from the bowl, from the ground, tearing their food apart in the company of the famous clown Out-Stein! Out-Jew, *Judenraus* Stein.

Herbert breaks into laughter from his window seat. Jenny hears nothing. She neither sees Adam Stein burst into tears nor hears Herbert laugh. Jenny stands like a wax statue. Stands and sings. What is Jenny singing? Jenny is singing a love song. And why is Jenny singing a love song? God has all the answers. Why doesn't she hear Herbert laughing and Adam wailing and the dog barking? Because Jenny is singing a song of love.

> *Your eyes overflow green,*
> *Like two emeralds their sheen.*
> *My heart needs a rest,*
> *You are far from my nest.*
> *My heart sews a dream*
> *In which my hope may gleam*
> *In longing for the green*
> *Of your eyes of emerald sheen.*

Adam is enraged, his muscles are tense, his mouth contorted. He roars: "Where is that dog? And you, stop grinding your teeth, stop clattering. What do you think you're doing? Singing?" He is frightened, the barks terrorize him. But Jenny is caught up in the ticking tango and doesn't hear him.

Only when she suddenly realizes that she is singing does she stop and see, to her surprise, that Adam is standing in the middle of the room, screaming. He's talking to me, she says to herself.

"You woke up, Adam. How do you feel?"

"Fine. In pain. When will you learn to sing?"

She blushes. "I didn't know I was singing. What's happened?"

"A dog. Gross has brought a dog in here. To kill me."

"I didn't hear a thing."

"You were busy with your imitations. Go tell Gross that there's no room here for dogs."

"Go yourself, Adam."

"What's the matter, Jenny mine?" His voice changes, begs. His face opens, glows with a tenderness which takes her by surprise.

She smiles, against her will. "I took care of you. You had a mild attack."

"I saw everything. I wasn't asleep."

"But you didn't say anything."

"I had nothing to say."

She brings her hand close to his face, wanting to soothe it. He grabs her with both his hands, draws her mouth to his, and whispers into her dry lips: "I will kiss you, child, but first of all get these dogs out of here."

"That's a bad start, Adam."

"I won't run away from you, child."

He about-faces, takes two steps, rips open the closet, removes a suit of clothes. Before her eyes, he takes off his pajamas and puts on his suit. As he stomps toward the door, she runs after him.

"You hear?"

The dog's howl nails him. He stands for a moment riveted to the carpet. His face blanches. His eyes open as far as they can go. His pupils are spinning.

"I hear."

"It's a disgrace. I'm telling you, it's a disgrace."

"Adam, you're sick. You're weak. They gave you an injection a while ago. Your foot is bandaged. Lie down. I'll fix things—"

"You?"

And he runs toward the barking.

4

THE BARKING

ALONG A LIGHTED CORRIDOR, dreaming of a woman stuck in a morgue. It's a shame, he thinks to himself, but doesn't look anywhere for her rescue, or the dream of a rescue for the lady of the house, our darling Madam Seizling, who lies frozen because of those clever lawyers. He hears more barks, they call to him. Remember? In '43 Gretchen was no longer the same petite woman whom you once met behind the movie screen, that time she came to see pictures in reverse and found you instead. She loved you. You played your instrument and Charlie Chaplin toddled on his cane. Or perhaps it was Harold Lloyd or W. C. Fields. In any case, some genius who taught you how to make a whole audience laugh without your smiling even once. Oh, those tricks of yours! "Genius," they said. Even to your face. Commandant Klein altered your fate and proclaimed, "This man stays!" on account of your conjuring, your magic, your incredible guesswork, that eighth, ninth, tenth sense of yours, but not on account of your intellect. Such touching humanity! Your wife died. Your first daughter died. Only Ruth, your second daughter, was compelled to escape, to save herself. And because of her you forsook a nice mansion in Berlin which came your way thanks to that humanitarian Klein. Get thee to the dog, he barketh for thee. When Commandant Klein used to fetch Rex's portion—bones with a little meat on them—he'd set the bowl on the floor and seat himself in the lovely armchair he'd taken from the Wolf residence in Warsaw right after the days when the Wolfs would invite him as a guest of their group and buy tickets for him to every performance in Berlin: *Saint Joan, The Taming of the Shrew, The Threepenny Opera* with Lotte Lenya (a great performance!). Yes, he came to their house afterward and lugged off the armchair. He always loved comfortable armchairs. Who can blame him for that? Who doesn't love comfortable armchairs? As soon as Commandant Klein had placed himself in that easy chair, he'd call for Fräulein Klopfer, set her pleasant little fanny on his knee, her fanny that stretched tight her perfectly clean skirt of khaki-colored silk, and he'd fondle her roughly and call for you. And you, *à la* contract, came on all fours and crawled around with a smile on your face (that was part of the contract too). On all fours you crawled over to Rex, rubbed against him, nose to nose, and the humanitarian Commandant and Fräulein Klopfer laughed. They laughed partly because Rex's nose had been trained to hate, so that any Jew who came near him got the same treatment, fangs! vivisection! But not you! *You,* Rex forgave. *You,* he was even fond of, in spite of the fact that he had to share his meals with you. The two of you, on all fours, used to tear the meat off the bones. Fräulein Klopfer had an extremely fair complexion, gray eyes, and lovely short blond hair. After the war she must have opened a small store in Berlin or Munich. You never met her again. But she was always talking about the shop she would someday open. She adored thinking about her adding machine, her wrapping paper, her multicolored ribbons. If she ever chanced to bump into you, her face would certainly light up, she'd greet you nicely. You went through a lot together. That awful stench night and day. And later on the wandering, after Commandant Klein kept his word and, through him, you acquired money and a house. The marvelous mansion of Von Hamdung, including his wardrobe, the suits with the gold buttons, and the seventeenth-century medallions. You ought to look her up some time and kiss her gray eyes. She saw you as you really are! A genius?

That dog is still barking. I'll cut his throat. Why? Isn't that too vulgar a way to commit suicide? My death I am going to arrange in a much more elegant fashion. I've learned something from Commandant Klein.

A dog is a domesticated savage. A dog both loves and hates human beings. A dog can be trained so that he cannot shake off his training, but he hates it nonetheless. Sad-eyed stupidity, that's a dog. Boundless loyalty, that's a dog. The focus of compassion, with wisdom, on occasion, in the eyes, that's a dog. You can kill people without grief—just ask Commandant Klein—but when the British bombed Frankfurt and hit the SPCA building, wiping out nearly a hundred dogs, the mothers of Frankfurt wept, women whose own sons came back from the war maimed and blind.

In a world that lacks all meaning because it lacks the fear of death and has only the fear of life—yes, most people fear the wrong things—a dog is the height of meaning.

Dr. Gross's revenge, is that also a dog?

It's a dog that's barking at Adam Stein, and Adam, to the bottom of his soul, is terrified, saith Adam to himself.

On his way, Adam pulls out of its hiding place his bottle of gin (Beefeater), takes a swallow, and puts the bottle back, feeling somewhat relieved, then rushes in the direction of the barking, past closed doors. The barks keep running alongside him until, finally, he reaches the door behind which the barks are so clear, so close, they resound like bells.

He stands there with his face against the door, listening. Tom-totom-tom, tototom goes his heart. Inside, total darkness. And those growls. Adam, who is able to distinguish semitones and quarter-tones when it comes to the howling of dogs, senses the panic soaking into the terrified dog in that room, terrified on account of Adam's coming. The frightened animal's growls are intelligible to him. If he wanted to, Adam could answer back, growl for growl. Didn't he used to converse, with Rex, like two friends, over the meat bowl? Commandant Klein poisoned Rex the day the Americans arrived. That's what he told Adam when they met afterward. Commandant Klein was Dr. Weiss then, Professor of Semitic Languages from Berlin who had been deported to Treblinka during the war. So he claimed. He was of Jewish stock—Adam ordained him a Jew, official identity papers included. Tit for tat, one good turn deserves another. But Klein/Weiss was frightened, just like the dog on the other side of the door here. After he furnished his modest flat, he never left it. Except for Adam's visits, he didn't see a single soul. Adam delivered a small ration to him each day and he sat studying Semitic languages. Adam was of the opinion that his knowledge of Akkadian and Ugaritic was enough to assure him a chair at a university in South America or even Israel. He was once going to suggest this as a compensation for his self-hatred, for his being not just a Jew but a living Jew. Here was a German doomed to live out the rest of his life as a Jew! And for someone like Commandant Klein to know from experience what it means to be a Jew . . . Commandant Klein, alias Dr. Weiss, used to carry a mortar shell around with him. Adam didn't know why. This shell, which had been shot at the approaching Americans but for some reason hadn't left the mortar, he used as a hammer. He'd bang nails in with it whenever he wasn't studying Semitic languages or hosting Adam—for about ten minutes each day—in his humble room. Adam would bring him his daily ration of coins packed in an American rubber contraceptive—such was the lot portioned out to somebody who used to set Fräulein

Klopfer on his lap to help him enjoy the sight of the two dogs, Adam and Rex, gnawing on the same bone. Two noses, one bone. So, his free time he'd spend banging nails into the wall of his room and hanging up small pieces of paper that contained queer sentences in Ugaritic, Akkadian, Phoenician, Hebrew, Assyrian, and Babylonian. Yes, he'd knock in those nails with that shell of his. And Adam would laugh. On one occasion the landlady of the house came into the room just as Herr Klein—read Weiss—was whacking a nail into the wall with his shell, and she fainted. So any time the two of them wanted a good laugh, they'd shout for her to come in and Commandant Klein, read Weiss, would smack a nail with that shell and she'd faint. And they'd laugh. Until he left for Israel, Adam set aside ten minutes each day for delivering his ration inside a rubber condom. After that, who knows what happened to Commandant Klein, alias Dr. Weiss, without his daily portion?

The thick darkness thins somewhat, gradually his view clears. It is already possible to make out a few objects in the room: a chair, a window, a cabinet, a chain. The dog is chained to the wall at the left of the window. You cannot tell what kind of dog it is because it is completely covered with a sheet, except for a big hole where the dog's face must be, through which he obviously looks.

Goldin, the nurse, approaches the door carrying a tray, and on the tray is a plate that clatters back and forth, and on the plate is some bread and meat. Goldin gently pushes Adam aside, tosses the food into the room, screws up his face on account of the stench, and exits. Adam is unaware of the stench. He is immune now because years ago he became thoroughly accustomed to it. Goldin has never been a dog, but Adam was. Adam now peers in through the observation window. The dog has not budged from his spot. He growls, claws some of the paint off the wall. Then ups, still bound in his sheet and by the loudly rattling chain, reaches the food, tilts his face, barks, paws his meal, drags it under the sheet, and goes back to his corner of the room.

Now that Adam Stein's eyes are used to the dark, he is able to make out the dog's eyes staring at him from the hole in the sheet, that filthy sheet which harbors a frightened dog. Why is it so scared? Once, in Jaffa, they gave mescalin to a certain dog and the dog lost its identity. For a moment it turned into the spitting sketch of a cat trying to catch its own tail. What a riot! It crawled around on its belly, emitted a caterwaul, leaped off the roof, and was killed.

"Why are you hiding under that sheet? What's your name?"

The sheet barks like an earthquake.

Jenny, who has been standing quietly beside him, stretches out her hand and pats his shoulder. But Adam cannot take his eyes off the dog, off the sheet.

"Who are you?" Adam is upset. He senses that something is askew; his nose catches some anomaly. The stench here is a bit irregular, it has a human edge to it, and lacks the sweetness of a dog's odor.

Then it hits him. No doubt about it, this dog is nothing less than a monster in dog's clothing: it may stand on four legs and bark, but its eyes, those eyes are almost human.

"Come, Adam, come, let's get away from here!" Jenny tries to pull him along. She's afraid for him. Torment is in his face.

"No."

The monster sticks its nose through the aperture in the foul sheet and wails at him again. Are you too telling me to go away, dog? Why? I'm just as sad as you. Adam's quick ear, or heart, catches another melody. The monster transmits again, and Adam, with his ability to read words that are never spoken and to guess secrets, deciphers in that howl a certain quality which he classifies in his mind as childhood rebellion. The signal is as simple as that: a child rebelling. In his rebellion, the child doesn't choose the way to his goal, he has no bad conscience. It's a game that has gone wildly out of control, dropped all its rules. He donned a mask which he can no longer remove.

This message baffles and frightens Adam Stein. He is pre-

pared for anything except a monster whose basic posture is imposture. Has someone managed to escape even further than
himself? Is that the surprise and the revenge of Gross the eunuch? Was it he who brought into the walls of the Institute
somebody whose gift of escape, whose gift of deception, whose
gift of pretense that has become second nature, is superior to
Adam's own?

The dog, meanwhile, is quaking, bundled up in his dark corner, unaware that Adam Stein has labeled him a monster. Adam
slams the observation window and turns toward his own room.
Amazingly enough, his pains are gone. Temporarily recovered
once more. The lovely Lilith at his heels is forgotten. He returns
to his room, slams the door in Jenny's face, in the whole world's
face. He combs through his belongings. Takes out his guitar.
Strums "The Trout" by Schubert. The music instills in him a
certain sense of security. Whenever his mother would hum "The
Trout," he knew that his parents still loved each other and he felt
safe. Even in a fierce lightning storm. He stares at a few of his
belongings. His plasticine. Tomorrow he'll do some modeling.
He'll model a head. He loves working with plasticine, loves its
stickiness, as if it were mud, loves the way it penetrates under
his fingernails like dirt. Herbert is gone, vanished. At present
Adam's mind is peaceful. The beat of his heart regular. The man
has recovered. For a day. For two days. The path to Hell is
strewn with such recoveries. He sings, sings the words to "The
Trout" in the old-fashioned German of the pension landlady
who was out of step with her times and wanted to be strangled
by Germany's greatest clown. Yes, that was her wish! No doubt
about it. In the mitosis of time he spins off toward a grandfather
of his who didn't know the meaning of becoming a dog. He lived
inside a narrow ghetto and adored his Creator. Who burned
them. What a joke.

They no longer lock Adam's door now when he leaves his
room. He is like all the others in the pension of Mrs. Seizling

under the management of Dr. Nathan Gross, Chief Executioner.
Adam enters the kitchen. The polished starched mammoth
kitchen. The noon meal is in tumultuous progress in the dining
hall. Everyone is seated around small tables covered with clean
green tablecloths and pitchers of cold water, salt and pepper,
mustard, anchovies, chili sauce, lemon juice, vinegar, and olive
oil. Pierre Lotti, the chef, is preparing chocolate mousse for the
evening meal; he neither hears nor understands what Adam is
saying, yet hands him precisely the candies Adam wants. "Here,
take!" and he holds out the candies, mumbles something under
his thin mustache, and continues his task, which demands considerable expertise and maximum concentration: *Mousse au
chocolat à la Arad.*

Before proceeding on to the observation window, to the dog
who calls for him, before turning in the direction of the monster
and executing him with candies, Adam must eat. Even those
whose lives are temporary are obliged to have a meal. It's a
biological tragedy. He knowsknowsknows. Herbert, leave me
alone! The candies are for the monster. Oh, that's my problem.
Maybe now you'll manage to disappear for a while. Nobody will
laugh! They will?

The big dining hall is painted a dainty yellow and hung with
flamboyant chandeliers. Loudspeakers hidden in the walls play
soft music. Waitresses dash around the tables, serving nothing
but the best. The fragrances intoxicate: fried onions and wonderful sauces mingle with the odor of carnations placed in blue-
and-white vases in all parts of the enormous room. Four persons
to a table. Quadruplets, always quadruplets, that was the decree
of Mrs. Seizling, she whose body is still cold-stiff in a Cleveland
morgue. ("What would happen if there was a power failure in
Cleveland?" Arthur once asked.)

Adam sits down beside the elder Schwester twin. They all say
hello and smile at him. He waves to his friends, to those who ask
him how he feels. He thanks them for the flowers they brought
him, for the cards. A woman seated next to Arthur has one hand

raised in the air; with her left hand she eats, with her right she
upholds the sky. Mr. Zuckerman, who is sitting beside Wolfovitz
the Circumciser, has many enemies, such as Handsome Rube.
Mr. Zuckerman looks around suspiciously and then, as if he
were performing an act of magic, he rapidly transfers his fork
from his right hand to his left. That is the signal they were waiting for, those secret agents scattered throughout the house, some
of whom were planted by Mrs. Seizling, who was herself nothing
but a tool of the CIA and the FBI.

The doctors' table blurts out laughing. Apparently one of
them, perhaps Dr. Fabricant, just told a risqué joke, forgetting
that he'd already told it a hundred and one times. But a new
doctor is there, so they laugh. Out of politeness, it seems. The
two tables set aside for guests are filled with gorgeously dressed
people enjoying the air-conditioning, the excellent food, the superb wine, the music, the service. Few are lucky enough to be
invited to a meal at the Institute for Rehabilitation and Therapy.
You have to wait your turn. First come the aristocracy of Beer-
Sheva—the atomic-reactor people, the scientists—then, defense
personnel, engineers, old-timers from Arad, and finally ordinary
guests. The thick blinds block out the desert, neutralize the
white mountains, the heat wave, the wind, the hawks, the eagles.

A young boy wearing a black shirt and a squashed hat, who
suffers from depression, is concealing his yellow-handled dinner knife under Arthur's plate. Mrs. Tamir, who remembers
Adam from Camp Auchhausen, is assisting the young boy with
his meal. The guests pay no attention to Mrs. Tamir. They are
embarrassed to watch. They're hungry, they've been looking forward a long time to this invitation to taste Pierre Lotti's special-
ties, and one's appetite is something that can be spoiled. In
shrewd anticipation, they've been eating less and less for an entire week. Mrs. Tamir dips a beautifully engraved spoon against
an absolutely empty soup plate under the very noses of the jocu-
lar doctors and the dodging curvacious Moroccan waitresses
who were hired precisely for their gift of evasiveness. As Mrs.

Tamir feeds the young boy from the bare white bone-china plate, the boy swallows the air with obvious ennui. He hasn't the courage to eat by himself. He's nineteen. He wept an entire year non-stop until he was practically dehydrated. Now he no longer cries, but nobody knows why. This pallid dependent of Mrs. Tamir, a woman who lost her child "over there," must always be fed. But she loves her assignment. As Dr. Gross says, it's half her cure. At night they feed him intravenously; for the present he just swallows the air half-heartedly. Meanwhile, Adam eats feverishly, anxious to finish and get back to the barking.

Pierre approaches Adam and asks if he'd like to try some wine. Adam tastes it, smacks his lips, and says "Mmmmmmmmmm" appreciatively. Pierre gestures with his finger and the waitresses pour the wine into lovely long-stemmed goblets.

Pierre Lotti's reputation is already international. *The New York Times* once published an article in which its correspondent claimed that the meal he had at the Institute was one of the finest meals he had ever had in his life, adding that Pierre Lotti's cuisine was the best in all Israel and perhaps even in the entire Mediterranean area. And that precisely had been the aim of the late personage whose corpse still lay frozen in a Cleveland morgue, who had wanted—so much wanted—perfection in every aspect of the Institute.

Some years ago, when the Institute was in the design stage, Mrs. Seizling went with the Schwester twin to the hospital in Jaffa to talk with Dr. Gross, who was to be the director of her Institute. While Mrs. Seizling was conversing with the doctors, under the supervision of Dr. Gross, asking all kinds of questions whose answers might aid her in planning for the Institute, supper was served. One of the young doctors, a recent immigrant from France named Josien Levi, toasted the French Revolution. It was the 14th of July, Bastille Day, the 170th anniversary of that event. To Mrs. Seizling, the French Revolution meant the idiotic and cruel take-over by the communists, who had demolished the royal house of George III and sent the entire nobility, male and female, to the electric chair. She also recalled that, in the wake of this business, Joseph Stalin had climbed the ladder to power and destroyed the Jews. So Mrs. Seizling winced at the words the young French immigrant was spouting, she blanched and her whole body shook, until Dr. Josien Levi explained. It happened that Mrs. Seizling, ever since childhood, had been open to new ideas and glad to "live and learn"; therefore, when it became clear to her that she had never understood the first thing about the profound revolution that had brought democracy into existence, under the considerable influence of the ideas of George Washington and Thomas Jefferson—*her* Washington and *her* Jefferson, he said, flattering her enormously—she replied with a lavish toast to the culture of France and the Great Revolution, and the Schwester twin applauded hysterically and kissed her on the forehead.

Almost immediately, however, this talk about Liberty, Equality, and Fraternity showed itself to be mere lip-service. In the dining hall for the patients she discovered the gap between the menu and those fine slogans. The food was wretchedly stale, constantly circled by clouds of flies. Even the water wasn't fresh. The olives were fermented, the potatoes burnt, the meat so tough you could hardly chew it.

That day she made up her mind that in her Institute the food would be superb, the cook French, and the doctors would eat with the patients—in compliance with the three doctrines of the Revolution: Liberty to select healthy and tasty food from a varied menu, Equality between doctors and patients, and Fraternity between France and Israel. On her way back to America she stopped in Paris and sought for her chef. At last she came up with Pierre Lotti. Pierre, who had a wife and a daughter, was reputed to be a magician in the kitchen, a knight of the kitchen magicians, even the King Arthur of the kitchen table, and a man of learning and imagination, both an artisan and an artist. In short, everything that Mrs. Seizling desired. Pierre was chef at the Cluny Restaurant, but his wife had recently developed a bad

case of asthma and the doctors advised that she convalesce in the
Atlas Mountains. When Mrs. Seizling found him, he was pains-
takingly arranging the details of the trip and utterly depressed.
For some reason, he couldn't resign himself to the harsh decree.
North Africa—with all its advantages—lacked the cosmopolitan
vitality, the city life, which he loved. Mrs. Seizling's offer, on the
other hand, was interesting. (1) He admired Israel and Moshe
Dayan on account of the Sinai Campaign of not long before, and
what fascinated his fertile imagination most was the consciousness of a mission which seemed to be ingrained in the Jewish
people. (2) The climate of Arad was excellent for asthma patients, and some even said that for this illness there was no place
like it in the whole world. Arad was a new city—in the process
of being built—and though Pierre adored weary sated cities like
Paris, he sometimes dreamed about pioneers, about conquering
the desert, about Gaza, about the Wild West, about howling
jackals, about a certain wondrous yet terrifying virginity. Arad,
from this point of view, was fine. Israel wasn't big, you could go
to Tel Aviv whenever you liked. To be close to a genuine European city and yet roughing it in the wilderness as a pioneer!

Pierre Lotti not only took well to the Institute, he became
devoted to it. His work there was much more exciting than he
had expected. He set up a small laboratory for himself and in-
vestigated Eastern cooking. He even planted a little herb garden,
making experiments with the local spices, attempting to fit them
into French cuisine. His secret wish was to write a book one day
titled *French Cooking in the East,* or *Eastern Ways of Cooking
After the Classical French Manner,* or *Pragmatic Cooking: A
French Cook in the Wilderness.* But meanwhile, until he had
time for such a book (he never decided which of the three to
write), he cooked dishes that Israel hadn't ever tasted before.
The word spread throughout the surrounding cities—Ashdod,
Ashkalon, Gedera, Rehovot—and then to Tel Aviv and Haifa.
People waited on pins and needles for a week-end invitation to
the Hospital, or Sanitarium as they called it among themselves,

in order not to have to say in plain Hebrew that "I, the chief engineer of group so-and-so, with degrees in science from Cambridge and M.I.T., am praying for an invitation to spend a weekend in a madhouse built by a woman who was madder than the patients in whose mad honor the madhouse was set up far out in the desert, in the middle of nowhere, near a wild new development town named Arad. Switzerland? Safed? Nahariya? No! A madhouse, my dear friends, but one where an exquisite *soufflé* Rothschild will follow a meal of rich *consommé aux quenelles,* a light jellied eel, desert quail in champagne sauce, a crisp light salad and the finest of French cheeses, all accompanied by the most appropriate of local wines.

As far as Pierre Lotti is concerned, Adam Stein is "a man of the great world," a gourmets' gourmet, the only one who truly appreciates his cuisine, his "pearls cast before swine and fools."

So Adam samples the wine, expressing his judgment with a nod, has a whispered conversation with Pierre, and squeezes the candies in his hand. On to that room! To that louse! To destruction! To the monster! "The roast duck with wine sauce was superb—yes, absolutely, though maybe it needed a touch of souring . . . no, no, no, no, but, actually, three bay leaves would have—no, you're right, Pierre, aniseed would be better in this case, some aniseed from your own garden, fresh fragrant aniseed, well ground, with lemon, onion, a pinch of sugar, and mustard, ahhh! And you, my dear Schwester, what's your opinion?"

She's furious. Yesterday she prayed outside Adam's room, and here he is busying himself with trivia. "God is waiting out there in the desert and you're wasting your time eating abominations! The fate of the world is about to be sealed and you—"

"Yesterday, when I was in a coma, I heard a weird sound, a murmur."

"A murmur?" All excited, she hangs on his every word. "What, what, what?"

"Just a noise. I don't know what it was. If it comes back

again tonight and Herbert sits on the windowsill, I'll ask. Maybe these are the sounds we want. His footsteps?"

She hides her face and sinks into a pleasant reverie. Her soul is on tenterhooks. God, how long must she wait? How long? The young boy gets up now from his place, finished with his meal. Mrs. Tamir leads him by the hand. While somebody sings in a corner of the room, sings to himself, quietly. Is he humming? Is he praying? Perhaps, perhaps.

Adam gets up, his fist full of candies, and leaves the dining room, just as the mousse is about to be served to the magnificently dressed guests from Beer-Sheva who are ready now for their dessert.

Adam is at the door. Candies in his hand. He looks all around, opens the observation window, and spills the candies, the kind that made his daughter so happy, onto the dark floor, where they wait for—for whom? whom? whom? For the dog, for the dog to take them. Adam stands there, examining his whereabouts and holding out his hand, but who will eat from his hand? Huh, huh, huh! Go on, maybe you're a monster, but I've seen sights that would make you faint just looking at them. For example, a chimney, a smoking chimney. Smoking smoke and smoking Lotta. European civilization at its peak. Take your hat off to the victors. Your hat? Who had a hat in that place? Rex had a hat. Came the holiday of Purim, and Commandant Klein decided that Rex should masquerade. How did he know it was time for Purim? From the underground radio of the Allies. That bastard, he listened in to them. He wanted to have his cake and eat it too, so he found out it was Purim. And we had to dress Rex in white underwear and striped pajamas and paint black circles around his eyes and make a fire in preparation for the sacrifice of the ancient Hebrew. But at that point, at that point Fräulein Klopfer intervened, so Rex's Jewishness lasted for only an hour and he became again our good friend, our first-rate Aryan dog Rex. *Heil!* Yes, a chimney. Hoo-hoo-hoo! Who are you? A smokestacked barge—oh! Where's your cargo? Where

you from, chum? From far away, where dogs do play, with
knapsacks and sticks, hoping to get their licks, and come to the
land of Israel. Hail! Oh, my tender monster, I'm going to open
up all the gates for you—the Gate of Pity, the Gate of Dung, the
Gate of Lions. The Gate of Zion. Through these gates, my virgin
Zion, come right in. Adam's heart has a good laugh. Everything
is harum-scarum. A child's world of higgledy-piggledy. When
the hospital was in Jaffa, Adam used to eavesdrop on the city
kids. Those little Jews who had no idea what sort of miracle had
saved them. One day they would conquer all of Israel, the entire
East, the whole world. They would raise their flag and rule the
Universe. All because of that satanic promise: "For you and
your children." But where are these children? Where is that
pledge? Shhh, here come some immigrants. Hoo-hoo-hoo, who
are you? Di-di-aspora Jews, on a chimneyed ship, a life-or-death
trip, sailing from Diaspora. Ha-ha! Monster, take a candy and
drop dead. What am I doing here? Idiot, you lost out on Pierre
Lotti's mousse and Pierre Lotti's mousse is inspired poetry. Like
solemn mass, or Monteverdi, or even Muzak's "Moonlight in
Vermont." My dear lady in your Cleveland freezer, how are
you? No ants? What a lucky land, it has refrigerators without
ants.

The dog, the monster, hasn't budged from its spot under the
sheet. Adam slams the observation window and stomps off. He
debates: Should he go away or go back? The room barks again.
He dashes back to the window and peeks in. The candies are
still where they were. Yet the dog barked. This last bark, then,
served some special purpose. Adam attempts to analyze the
monster's logic. If it had eaten the candies and not wanted to see
my face in the window, it wouldn't have barked. But it barked
without having eaten the candies. If that's the case, you can in-
terpret the matter this way: It knew I was waiting anxiously. It
liked my being here. It wanted me to know that it won't submit
to my will—it won't eat the candy—and in order for me to
know that, it barked. For a monster, that was almost self-
abasement.

And now? The sheet is throbbing. The dog is trembling. The monster is scared. Adam is scared too. Says Adam to himself: Get out of here before it's too late. He edges away. He mutters: "It's just a lousy mutt." And he doesn't know, or he knows quite well but pretends that he doesn't, that when he leaves (but not *because* he has left—on the contrary, it would be the monster's way of preventing his leaving) the dog will crawl over and snatch the candies in his paws, take them into a corner, under his sheet, and squeeze them with all four paws which are black from offal and filth.

Adam goes to Dr. Gross's office, the man who had this dog brought in for the express purpose of breaking Adam down. Dr. Gross holds out his hand and says hello. He doesn't ask why Adam has come. He sits in his armchair, on his "toilet seat," as if all this while he has been waiting for Adam Stein to honor him with his presence. And Dr. Gross unfolds all his own problems before Adam. From his point of view—i.e., from Dr. Gross's vantage point—the fact that Adam slept with his head in the guitar case in his last attack is a terrific problem. Someone just arrived from Boston, a thorough adherent of Watson's methods, would like to give you a few tests, similar to Rorschach's but along a different line. As a matter of fact, we ourselves have some brand-new medicines now.

"I'm just a patient, Grossie boy, do what you want with me. By the way, can't you see that I'm smiling?"

"You have tears in your eyes, Adam. You're lying."

"You're lying."

"Those are tears. I can see them. The light's coming from behind my back. I can see them perfectly."

"It's just water. I drank some water a moment ago."

"Oh, with your eyes? Adam Stein, that's pretty poor. I expect better from you."

Adam smiles at Dr. Gross. "I'm ready, Grossie boy, always ready and willing. If experiments are your thing, then let's have experiments right to the very end. Despite all your flops. I'll be the marker on your grave, your memorial of shame, the Wizard of Oz in the sanctuary of Mrs. Seizling, may she freeze in peace. Experiment some more. Watson, Rorschach, Freud, Jung, LSD, Mexican cactus roots, mescalin, Dr. Aronson, Dr. Samit, Dr. Weiss, partial hypnosis, total hypnosis, Benzedrine pills. Try! But before you'll ever cure me, you'll turn into sick patients yourself, all of you. Even so, for your efforts you deserve a medal. As a matter of fact, there's a factory in Cleveland that is manufacturing such medals this very moment. Out of frozen blood. Eh?"

That evening Jenny and Miles Davis come to Adam's room, Miles carrying a small suitcase which he deposits in a corner. Arthur waits outside. On the other side of the door. Adam says: "Tell him to come in! It's okay!"

Miles says: "He's waiting for an invitation."

"From whom—me?" laughs Adam.

"You know Arthur," Miles confirms.

Miles exits and re-enters pushing Arthur. Arthur is embarrassed, he shrugs his shoulders, squints his eye. His thin nose quivers. He takes a breath. One nostril has excess moisture in it, a dull red stream which swarms down. Arthur inhales it back inside his head. He'll be sick again tomorrow—sinus trouble. In Adam's room, though, he calms down. He takes his small child's trumpet out of his coat pocket, hangs it on his neck, and waits. "What comes next? Do we play on our instruments?"

"Before we start, does anybody know anything about the dog in Room 285?"

No, Jenny know nothing, though Miles is certain that Jenny actually does know. Of course she knows. But for some reason is holding her tongue. Whereas Miles himself is the one who knows nothing. Arthur, naturally, knows everything. It's a sea-dog from Australia, in the kangaroo family, a cross between a Belgian wolf-dog and a kangaroo, a dangerous breed. And Adam, on his part, knows that it's a monster.

So Jenny knows absolutely nothing. Well, that is, she does know, and there's no law against her knowing, but for the past few days her overwhelming feelings of failure have compelled her to be alert and try her hardest to outwit any enemy. And that monster is an enemy. She can sense it in her bones. Adam chops the wall and blood spurts from his hand. He shouts: "It's against every rule in the book to bring into this Institute any monsters, wild boars, dogs, elephants, tortoises, schizophrenic lions, or bats. It's written in black and white in Mrs. Seizling's will." He hasn't ever read that will, but anyway that frozen stiff woman isn't about to revive and either erase anything or write down what she never wrote in her lifetime. The karate blow that he handed the wall has calmed him. Jenny stops knitting her red scarf, gets up, and kisses the blood, which makes her lips, for the moment, as red as the scarf she is knitting.

"Disgusting," he says.

"What's disgusting?" Jenny wants to know.

"You!"

"Oh, that's already encouraging, Adam."

Adam gets his guitar from the cabinet, and tunes it. "A kangaroo-dog. What idiots!"

Miles is the conductor for these music sessions. Two years ago, when Miles first established these nights of music, they had a terrific problem. Miles was a better trumpeter than Arthur, who used to blow his child's horn to scare away the bats. If only there were some, thought Miles. If only there really were bats. There's something melancholy about a bat's face. In any case, what could they do? Adam kept strumming his guitar until they finally found a solution, or, more correctly, a way out, which didn't embarrass any one of them, which they all accepted nicely. The key lay in what Miles called (who else but Miles? he knew what he was talking about) Arthur's "gigantic musical talents." Let Arthur learn to play the drum. And Arthur learned. Arthur, go blow your horn as much as you please, any day, any season, but come eventide, when we gather in the inner sanctum to play our music, to inspire ourselves, to dissolve into jazz, oh then, Arthur, you're at the drums, Miles at the trumpet, and Adam Stein at the guitar. And Jenny? Jenny sits in a corner holding two knitting needles that look like two of Cupid's arrows which have accomplished their mission, her face frozen in an expression of deep inner peace, as deep as her love and as meek as her love.

Miles has a swarthy thin face, a small precise mouth, a nose wider than average. And always, night and day, a pair of dark sun-glasses conceals his eyes.

"Okay, boys." In this room, at this hour, the language is always English. When it's time to play music, Miles can't talk Hebrew. "Okay, boys. 'Lullaby of Birdland'!"

Miles and Handsome Rube are among the few patients at the Institute without blue numbers on their arms. Nobody knows why Dr. Gross admitted them. He must have had his reasons. Maybe he simply wanted to break the monotony a bit. After all, there are good grounds for arguing that this building was founded not only to initiate conversations with God. In addition to such profound and metaphysical motives on Mrs. Seizling's part, one other purpose always existed: the attempt to *cure* unfortunate, uncared-for, disturbed wretches.

Between breaths, as he blows his horn, Miles screams: "Splendid, man, splendid!"

Jenny loves these nights. Desert nights with pale moonlight for clothing, caught and diminished by the size of the window. And the white mountains, the pervading gleam and stillness.

During the break Miles tells his tale of New York. That's where his heart is at. Here, he's just passing through. In a little while his secret agents will release his papers, he'll leave this railway station and start on his way home. To New York. There, in Minton Playhouse, in the black world. A lone Israeli. He used to live above a nightclub and wash dishes nights. In the next room would be playing Charlie Parker, Miles Davis, Jo Jo Johnson. He can remember the tender strumming of blind Lenny Tristano and Budd Paul's shriek of "Coocooricoo!" after each seance, the man who thought he was a rooster. And Max Roach and Tony Scott the clarinetist. One time he heard Billie Holiday—Lady Day—in her long white shroud of a dress, with

a white rose stuck in her hair, as she half sang, half said: "God
lives in a lonely place."

Her face was shining. Shining black. And she sang: "Don't
ever explain nothing, fire don't explain itself." Her eyes were
pitch black, endlessly lonely exploring eyes. Her white teeth
flashed, her eyes spun sideways, her eyebrows stretched as far as
they could go—half theatrical, half genuine. Truth itself. "Like
God's tear" shouted blind Lenny Tristano, who never saw her
but sensed everything some other way. The tense atmosphere
above her head gave away what she was all about, the shuddering
waves of air around her gave away her sadness. And I lived
upstairs, room number 30. Address: 161 West 117th Street, the
black belt. I learned to play. It was crucial to me. I had to. They
made fun of me. I had no past. When I was a kid, I dreamed of
playing, but never did. In Harlem, though, among the whores
and police officers and jazz musicians and hashish pushers, I
washed dishes at night and during the day I practiced. Lovely
Billie Holiday sang for me, just me, in my honor. "For my little
Israeli," she said, and half sang, half spoke. She yanked the
words from her heart, and as they passed through her lips her
teeth cooled the flames so the world got passion on the rocks.

They're playing "Making Whoopie" now and Miles craves for
the good old days. Hector's Cafeteria. The train to Coney Island. Hot dogs. He recalls the little girl he kissed in Coney Island one winter, among the garbage cans. Under her fur coat she
was naked. He remembers the musical Automat in the big store
on 42nd Street right below the movie house for zany films. Outside, there were crazy mirrors that distorted your shape; in one
you were as fat as Hardy and in the other as skinny as Laurel.
To this store there once came the Creature from Mars. Miles
giggles. He's sure, or at least he thinks he's sure, that he saw it.
It had two plastic arms, antennae looming out of its faceless
head. It teeth were transistors, it legs coils of rubber, its eyes
windows with tiny adding machines set deep inside. And this
creature from Mars approached the music box which was play-

ing "How much is that doggie in the window?" and said in a
metallic voice, "What's a nice girl like you doing in a place like
this?"

Suddenly, in the middle of "Making Whoopee," Adam leaps
up, drops his guitar, ruining the peace and the beauty and the
memories and the red scarf and the brotherly get-together,
leaves the room, slams the door behind him, and runs. Shouting
to himself: "Damn it, I must know. Is it a monster? Win or
lose!"

In his anxiety, his hands perspire. Mice nibble at his heart.
His blood spills. He is moving across his own blood, a carpet of
blood. His legs labor like bars of lead. The corridor music-
machine plays a schmaltzy rendition of *Scheherazade* with a
hundred violins—a hundred ducks extend their necks to him
and get slaughtered, their fat is tasty and thick, good for whatever ails you. That homicidal monster, that bastard Gross, that
eunuch! He reaches the door. Room 285. Another person with
no blue number on his arm. It's some prank! How do you know?
Maybe they rescued this dog from the crematorium. And what
about you, didn't they save you from there? Commandant Klein
himself—i.e., Dr. Weiss—pulled you out! Who brings him coins
now in a rubber condom? He laughs for a moment.

He lifts the observation window and at once, in front of this
window, all the shrewdness by which he has managed his life
withers, ends. The candies he tossed into the room earlier are
still there. In the same disgusting spot. The monster hasn't accepted them, hasn't swallowed them. What a shame, what a rot-
ten shame! He cries into the room: "Monster, I can be just as
brutal as you." The tone of entreaty which he catches in his own
scrambled voice perplexes him. So Adam Stein drops his voice
to a whisper: "Crawl out of that filthy empyrean of yours. Show
me who you are. Do you have horns? What kind of a dog are
you? Dog? You don't have the eyes of a dog." To tell the truth
—thinks Adam to himself—they are dog eyes, but with a monstrous or human edge to them. The rubber face of Adam Stein,

the great clown of the famous Adam's Circus (Come to Adam's Circus and see the seven wonders of the world, all in one tent! Sixty horses, elephants that stand on their trunks, jesters! The greatest clowns on earth. As for trapeze—the most daring, most dangerous leap in history! Seventy feet into fire! Bicycles gliding across ropes. Bears dancing *Swan Lake*. George the Conjuror and his Disappearing Act. The notorious Indian hypnotist Jal-Haj Hamoni and his terrifying trip into the past, encountering relatives who died a century ago! A fluorescent cemetery with phosphorus skeletons, plus X-ray photos of dead spooks! A cricket over three feet long, skiing into a pool consisting of disembodied shrieks! The wonders of the world! The best of sights and marvels! All for one German mark! Come one and all, to the circus of the know-it-all professor and greatest clown that ever was, Dr Adam Wolfgang Stein!!!!!)—the rubber face of this genius was framed in the observation window, illuminated by the crap in that room. Longing. Until, without realizing it and without any prior preparation—for someone like him, that was out of the question—he inflates his left cheek and his tongue clicks (monkey see, monkey do, yoo-hoo-hoo) two songs of Schubert. Clickety-clackety. While he twists his nose to the left, flaring his nostrils and making his right ear hop up and down. In vain. His clowning has no effect whatsoever. The monster has no sense of humor. All it does, under its sheet, is tremble. Is that really its only reaction to a performance by the best clown of Germany? No, something else: its eyes, they gleam through the hold in the sheet. As though glazed with tears. Adam slams the observation window and trudges off to one of his many whiskey caches which never get discovered, takes out a bottle of Canadian whiskey, and drinks. "Bronfman," he announces in a big voice, "I salute you, Brother Bronfman. You're the Prince of Whiskey. By the Canadian waters of whiskey, there you sit and weep at the remembrance of thirsty, forever thirsty Adam Stein. You manufacture whiskey and you make big contributions to Israel, but have you ever seen a Jewish drunkard? I've never seen one.

Commandant Klein's very own complaint! According to Klein,
that was the crux of the Jewish Problem. Yet the little *Führer—*
*mein Führer, heil!—*never caught the subtle irony of it."

Under the serenity of the background music, Adam sits upon
the charming soft carpet selected by Mrs. Seizling herself, may
she indeed freeze in peace. Somewhere over the rainbow blue-
birds fly. His fingers dance around the neck of the bottle. Far off,
a rainbow. Birds, birds. Cows on the other side of the barbed
wire. Dr. Weiss, I've brought you a thousand teeth. *Heil!* The
younger Schwester twin rushes toward him. She doesn't notice
him. Her face is shining. She has a cord in her hand and the cord
drags along the carpet a wooden horse on wheels. When she
does finally notice Adam, she is startled, but there is no way to
avoid a meeting—so let him see, so what? Her face again lights
up.

"Adam, again? Is that nice? Drinking like that? Isn't it suicide? Well, it must be all right," she answers her own question
and smiles. For a brief moment she is confused. Then once more
she repeats her question that doesn't sound like a question:
"Drinking again . . . "

"That's right, Sister Schwester," Adam comments. "You have
good eyes. Penetrating. I'd say almost prophetic."

She tries to hide the wooden horse from him. It's hers! He
mustn't see it! He's bound to misunderstand. Her older sister
will find out and scold. Yet she cannot take her eyes off that
pallid noble face. Her tender soul is plagued by the fact that this
elegant-mannered, this so wise, man is sprawled on the floor
drinking whiskey. What would her mother say? Obviously she'd
weep, and hide her inaudible tears in her palms.

Now he addresses the monster, which has paid as much attention to the candies as Adam has to the younger Schwester twin:
"I'm the boss around here!"

"Yes!" she answers. "You always can do just as you please."

"Because I'm smart. I'm clever. I'm brilliant. I can read them
all like a book, you included. Hold it, you've just come from

your room," and he places his hand on the horse, fingers it, smiling. "I'll tell you what you were doing there! You sat in the
bathroom, sat there a long while."

"Please, Adam——"

"Hush, child. You sat there, that's a fact."

She brightens. Her eyes sparkle.

"You sat and didn't feel so well. Were you sick? Your intestines! Again, your intestines. The doctors will kill you one day.
Anyway, it wasn't fun sitting in the bathroom all that time.
Without a door. And your holy sister scolded you, that sacred
lass whose putrid body and unfortunate mustache were loved by
those bugs. So you got dressed and, in the process, tore your
dress. You panicked and grabbed the wooden horse, and the
moment your sister wasn't looking you ran away. That horse is
good to you, it loves you."

She giggles. "Where were you? Under the bed?" He knows
everything. She looks adoringly at the horse.

"I was right here, sweetheart. Right by this door. Inside is the
hangout of a certain monster that I'm not able to psyche out. It
barks like a dog."

"Adam . . ." She blushes now, stooping over him. From his
seated position on the carpet, he notes the absurd, unfortunate,
inexplicable—though of course significant—fact that the
younger Schwester twin is wearing under her dress a man's
woolen underwear. He has to laugh. That only baffles her all the
more. But she keeps talking, perhaps to overcome her confusion: "When will you start your courses? The last time you were
at the Institute, your course on the politics of the Middle East
was extremely fascinating. Everybody said so. Do you think
you'll start soon? I prayed every day that you'd come back. Did
you really strangle that old woman?"

"Dear younger Schwester twin, you have lovely eyes and you
wear your father's underwear, may he rest in peace, that saint,
but what you've just said isn't nice." He raises his voice, for no
reason, merely to frighten her. She *is* frightened. She straightens

herself, moves back a bit. "I ask you, who gave you permission to pray that I'd come back? I was free. I had it good. Maybe it was your prayers that brought me back here. In any case, tell me, is it ever nice to pray for somebody to go to jail who's happy where he is, on the outside?"

"You're right, it wasn't nice." Her voice is still shaky, but she wants to apologize. "Every night before going to bed I'd say to my sister, I'd tell her—you're right, it wasn't nice of me—I'd tell my sister, 'You'll see him again, Adam will be back.' Actually, as far as I was concerned, I was more interested in your giving those courses and livening up the Institute and driving the doctors crazy than in your talking to God. I even asked my sister, 'What can God tell us in our day and age?' God's place was in the Bible, and that was before air-conditioning. God doesn't fit into our stereophonic systems, our nuclear panics, our technology and all the things that I myself don't even understand. I'm sick of hearing my sister talk about her God as though he were still living in a cave now and everybody rode on donkeys, as though our plastic flowers, hers and mine, were actually for God. Together with our white dresses. Don't tell me that an intelligent man like you really thinks that God is going to show up! Is he?" He enjoys the way she loses her confidence, the way her statement becomes a question.

"Of course he will reveal himself. Of course!"

"You're just like her!" She's outraged. Her body shivers from anger. What a scandal! Adam, a man, a swindler who sells wooden nickels, actually believes her sister's lunacies! Mrs. Seizling is one thing—it makes sense for her to believe—but a handsome man like Adam Stein? "You're both awful. You think you can pluck God off of Mount Sinai or wherever the Hell he is and transport him here? He's happy where he is. He has what he wants there. He can die there in peace. Know why he doesn't hear a thing? He's deaf. I agree with Wolfovitz the Circumciser, whose daughter's head was mangled in that cellar. God's a product of the Sinai Desert and that's where he stays. Consequently, as Wolfovitz says, God couldn't hear Wolfovitz the Circumciser's daughter crying in a cellar when her head was being squashed."

Adam stares back at her; she's gained stature in his eyes. "Thanks, little Schwester, you're a good guy. The whiskey's great. Sitting here is great. Relaxing. Makes you feel warm, like you were at the peak of meditation and the trough of desire. With just one shot of whiskey, or two, at most three. Bronfman the Jew makes his whiskey in Canada, other Jews make Judaism, Christianity, modern capitalism, modern medicine, socialism, communism, the New Deal, atomic physics, the Bomb, liberalism in Soviet economic planning; Bronfman makes his whiskey while other Jews make a Jewish state in the desert alongside a mute God, a state with an idiotic economy and a superb army, MIG 15, 17, 19, 21, the cure for infantile paralysis, ecumenical councils, inroads into freedom and slavery; Bronfman makes his Canadian whiskey and the profits go toward the corruption of Israel—airless hotels on the seashore, whores on the road to Haifa and Tel Aviv with Herzl above their heads saying, Where there's a will there's a way! Cheers, Bronfman! And as for you, my lovely one, my little Schwester, about face!" For a second the Satanic idea occurs to him that all he has to do is stand up, pull her to him, and lick her ugly face, and she's bound to grow a mustache. Instead he gives his command and she obeys, scared stiff, scared yet respectful.

"About face!" and she about faces. The horse sits on the carpet, its small black eyes gazing at him with a glazed expression, for they are in fact made of glass. He snatches up the horse in his hand without her noticing. "Now, forward march!" She starts moving. The cord goes taut, tauter, tautest, till down she trips and Adam has a good laugh. She gets up, adjusts her dress. As far as Adam can see, her woolen underwear is the same kind his father wore. More frightened, she is unable to speak. He lets go of the horse and orders: "No stopping! Forward march! Left right, left right, left right . . ."

Stunned by his commands, she obeys.

"Now, old girl, run!"

And she runs down the hall. The music whispers: "Hey, Simona, from Dimona!"

"Left right, left right, faster, run with your right, leap with your left, right left, lift your feet! Faster!" Just as she disappears around a bend in the corridor, he hears the dog barking behind the door, a terrifying bark that tears right through him. At once his face is no longer laughing, but wears an expression of intolerable agony. He drops the bottle, drops Bronfman and his Canadian whiskey, stands up, approaches the door, practically rips out the observation window, and stares in at the monster that is barking his head off.

The gloom slowly disperses. Violin in hand, he stands and plays. Camp Auchhausen was not one of the big camps, he once explained to Dr. Gross. In camp Auchhausen you could feel a certain humanity, see a distinct spark of the classical liberalism of the Europe which exists no more. So claimed Adam. It's hard to kill people when you know them all by name, when you know what their occupations were before the war and where they were born. Adam fixes his attention on the monster. The sheet, the monster's only clothing, moves a bit. The candies are still in the same spot. Will the dog creep over to those candies? That's the $100 question. The question of his life and death. During those Auchhausen days there were no candies at all. He played, clowned around, wagged his ear, made his nostrils do a jig, at first just for Klein, but afterward, as Klein's Jews began trekking to the showers in order to wash up and refresh themselves before going on to their so-called work camps, he played for them too. And that reassured them. Once reassured, always reassured, said Commandant Klein, whose birthday was the sixth of May, 1895, under the sign of Taurus, the very day and sign, it so happened, of Adam Stein's birth. Commandant Klein was born in Stuttgart and Adam Stein in Berlin. Adam's father and grandfather were born in Trenopol, Galicia, his great-grandfather in

Germany, and his great-great-grandfather in Cologne, where Adam's ancestors had settled in the time of the Roman legions, before any Christians set foot in Germany. Yes, both Adam Stein and Commandant Klein were born under the sign of Taurus, though Klein's father was a bastard, born nobody knows where.

That minute's walk from the huge room to the showers, that insubstantial passage in time and space—about equal to the present distance of the dog from the candies—was something harshly real. In that mere transition hung a hint of humanity. This is what he was trying to tell Dr. Gross—that Commandant Klein wanted with all his heart for them to die in peace, complete peace, without any complications, no tears, no foreknowledge, and consequently no unnecessary suffering. This single fact was worth a thousand witnesses testifying to Commandant Klein's nobility. In order that "they" might die in peace, he grabbed the great clown Adam and authorized him to survive. So when the Spiegels came by—are you listening, monster?— Adam smiled and played. Mrs. Spiegel said: "Adam, where are we going?" but the officer didn't wait for Adam's reply. "To another camp," he said. "In the meantime, wash up. Work is salvation, but first comes cleanliness. If you want a sound mind, you need a sound body." And they believed him, on account of Adam. Even when his wife Gretchen appeared, pulling along little Lotta, he still played, all smiles. And his smile told them that everything was kosher. Nothing disturbed Commandant Klein as much as the dread that they might die screaming. There was something unaesthetic, unclean, about the shrieks of the dying who want to go on living. Therefore, Franz Wolfgang Stein played and joked. Klein said: "It must be done quietly," and shot Hans Glaubsmid, the SS man, for raping the young girl from Lvov. In front of everybody, he shot him down. Only for the sake of peace and quiet. Fräulein Klopfer believed what Commandant Klein told her, that the rapist Glaubsmid had been executed because a work-leader was defiled by screwing around with the factory's raw material. She felt—and Adam agreed with her—that the rule was basically sound and the matter properly handled.

Of course, Adam Wolfgang Amadeus Johann Christian Philipp Emanuel Stein knew the issue was more complicated, that it was really a question of the culture and personal humanity of that noble man. On account of whom modern Germany gained the common expression: "Mechanical murder's fine, but a rape's a crime!"

"Come, monster, draw nigh," whispers Adam to the dog. Whereupon, as if by magic, the embodied sheet begins its approach to the candies. Closer and closer it comes, until it snatches the candies with a paw that looks just like a hand (or perhaps a foot, eh, monster?), hoarding them, growling, and retreating.

"Eat!"

The animal answers with a bark.

"I was a dog once. Rex was once a dog. We all were dogs once."

Adam is running down the hall again. Past doors, hundreds of locked doors, behind each one a blue number. You poor dog, you took my candies. Soon you'll be eating from my hand. You're lucky, but not me. You're a creature that is able to bark at God and man, even at Adam, Adam Stein. You can die without knowing that you're doing it, you can die with a clear conscience, without committing a sin. That's why they never locked you up in the ovens.

Adam bumps into Wolfovitz the Circumciser. No, no, he hasn't seen Jenny. Where can she be? Who knows? Maybe she's dead. Two male nurses pass by. They don't know anything either. One of them nods. "The pretty one? She's gone."

"Where?"

"She must have gone to your room, Adam. Yes, to your room. Maybe she's licking your bathtub clean for you!" Laughs, vanishes.

Nobody has seen Jenny. What was that sign on Commandant Klein's desk? *"When you need them, they're not around. When you don't need them, they sob."* He needs her, his Jenny. He must get the key to Room 285 from her.

On his way, Adam meets Lord Nelson, who is also, in an emergency, Theodore Herzl. Who gave Adam money the day Adam arrived, to invest in American Tel & Tel.

"Any results?"

"Everything's going to turn out all right, My Lord Admiral. Yes, sir! The stocks are bullish. In a few days the profits will really be something!"

A passing woman stops for a moment. "I told you Columbus was a Jew."

Green-eyed Lord Nelson, the man with a beautifully trimmed beard, gives his judgment: "The important thing is that he was a human being and that he discovered America. That is the issue. The Jews had no place to go when Spain kicked them out, so Columbus came along and showed them the way to the New World. That's the key thing. How many people are there, all told, anyway?"

"Not many!" decides the woman.

The others nod in agreement.

"But there are man-eating actors," says somebody.

"And the world will end someday."

"Never, it'll never come to an end."

"It will."

"The European market is in great danger, they're manufacturing too many cars. After they manufacture a million of them, they'll buy them all up and start killing each other off. Then there won't be a single consumer left, because they'll all have cars already, and the dead ones won't travel anywhere, they'll just stand in line with all the other unemployed."

"The age of the Desert!"

"The age of the Flood!"

"The age of the Sun!"

"The age of Formica!"

"The age of Enamel!"

"The age of Fluorescence!"

"The age of Muzak!"

"The age of Espresso!"

"The age of Hashish!"

"The age of Nothing-at-all!"

Adam sneaks off while they're still arguing. He takes his own route, or his route takes him. Vertigo. No time to lose. These maniacs are driving him crazy.

Take for example the case of Jenny Grey, the maiden in love, tall, young, pretty, the diligent worker, hated by all, including herself. Jenny loves Adam the way she loves inflexible commandments. One time, when she was in charge of the elevator, a sick old man came over and asked her permission to go up to the infirmary. She refused to allow him inside because the elevator was full and a sign on the wall stipulated that only twelve persons could ride in this elevator at any one time. Though he begged, though she knew beyond a doubt that the man was in agony, she slammed the elevator door in his face. No, he didn't die, though he might have. "Is that being a nurse?" yelled Adam in his fury. "You call yourself a sister of mercy?"

She smiled. "There's no other way, Adam. The rules are wiser than we are. If we break just one, the tiniest one of them, we break the whole system. It's not my job to ask why these laws were written or who wrote them, it's not my job to wonder if these laws are intelligent or foolish. It's my job merely to obey them—reason or no reason. If a law is on the books, I must obey it."

"One of these days you're going to die from a misprint," he told her. He wanted to say that Commandant Klein and she, despite certain obvious differences, were quite alike. But as soon as he said that she had no heart, she almost collapsed.

"For you, Adam, I'd break all the rules."

"Commandant Klein also broke all the rules for me. Every

Himmler had his Jew. Himmler himself said so. But, actually, I'm no sample of a Jew."

Adam stands outside Jenny's door. He hesitates for a moment. Just for a moment. Then enters.

Room 26, in Mrs. Seizling's plan, was designated as "The Tent of Meeting," but everybody in the Institute calls it Compromise Hall. The elder Schwester twin requested that a hall be set aside for devotion and thanksgiving, and that was done—but in the meantime, since God hasn't yet shown His face, the hall is used as an extra cultural-activities room; however, on those days when not many activities are scheduled, when arts and crafts and classes generally are on the wane, they add a second compromise to the first and give the hall over to Jenny. There Jenny conducts what she calls occupational therapy.

Twenty women, some old, some young, some in between, are seated one behind the other in four rows as straight as ruled lines, and in front of each woman stands a loom with threads of many colors.

Wearing a starched white uniform and a tightly fastened white head band, with an ominously long knitting needle for a baton, Jenny, that kind-hearted lass, that Toscanini in a white uniform, that Ibn-Toscanini, is conducting an orchestra of looms from the top of a footstool. Boldly, baldly, but not badly! "I said your left hand! Now right, and again right. Two loops and then switch to the left and reverse the bar and pedal. One two three, now right hand, two loops to the left, raise the bar, keep the beat. Right right, then left, switch, loop, release, now from on top, sideways, like a letter opener, I said from on top! And right, right, loop, finish the line, take out a red button from your baskets. Without looking. The second on the right, among the top row of buttons, don't look, donkeys! Keep your right hand always on the bar, yes, to the right and two loops to the left . . ."

And forty hands, forty hands below rolled-up sleeves, forty sweating hands work as though they belonged to one person. A ballet, a ballet of degradation. Twenty wretched prisoners obeying orders blindly. And those eyes, those lackluster, dead, yet obsessive eyes that almost never blink, those exhausted bodies, those ears cocked to catch every order, throb with fear, silencing fear.

Jenny claimed: "That's the way to achieve Nirvana. Their bodies function like precise first-class watches. So for a while their bodies are absolutely free, free from worries, free from all anxiety." And, amazingly enough, Dr. Gross agreed with her.

There she stands. The Statue of Liberty with a reverse meaning. An exclamation point *à la* Auchhausen. Her arm outstretched, her knitting needle stiff, but her eyes everywhere, on the twenty looms, the forty hands, the forty eyes, the fear, the slightest error. Nothing escapes the lighthouse sweep of her vision.

The second time in his life that Adam saw Jenny, she was lording over a similar situation. At Jaffa, at the old hospital. Then as now, he shuddered in the presence of the tension moored in her body like a coiled spring, like a loaded pistol. Except that at that time he shuddered in awe. In awe of her ability to be simultaneously human and bestial. He honored her because, as a dog eating from Commandant Klein's dog bowl, he had learned to respect the whip and pay homage to the victor. It was easy to pick the winner between Adam Sebastian Stein playing his instrument and Fräulein Klopfer writing her reports. And Jenny? Jenny was an inspiration to him. Here in the middle of the desert, by a new town that was being constructed without humor and perhaps even without wisdom, here where the shriek of the desert was jailed in sterilized corridors, here Jenny represented the race of conquerors, and he admired that. They have guts, their blue numbers can be rubbed off. At night they may weep, but in the daytime they stomp across any limitation, across the wasteland, taming everything, omitting any fun, any beauty, any charm. Masters are never pretty, never aesthetic types. Consequently, they have a future, even a past, a remote past, right on the spot where they have discovered a sanctuary

that belongs to them, that belongs to Jenny and Jenny's grandmother who resided here nearly two millennia ago.

He trembles before this finely sculpted statue aloft on a footstool, this immortal block of ice. Powerful, yet holding back its
strength. He beholds an absurd and ugly military stride, but who
can refrain from clapping? Everything is at attention, the flag,
her eyes. Though the anthem is a miserable song with empty
words, you jump to attention. Muscles taut. Involuntarily, you
salute. That's what Jenny does to you.

Jenny notices Adam in the doorway, yet doesn't interrupt her
orders, her poetry of pride. Jenny the great poetess, the Sappho
of Arad. He wants to shout: *Heil, Hitler!* Would it be worth it,
though? To play the conquered before the conqueror?

The moment those forty eyes discover him standing in the
doorway, Adam reconsiders. He approaches Jenny and whispers
something in her ear. She continues the performance, her eagle
eyes maintaining their bead on their prey, twenty items of
quarry. But she signals with her face that she cannot do as he
asks. So again he whispers into her ear. He helps her off the
footstool while the women work as though the orders were still
coming. Then, bang! they stop. Twenty left hands about to make
the third loop to the left, twenty right hands about to turn the
bar, suspended between the top of the loom and the threads.
"I'll be back in two minutes!" She spits the information at her
frightened flock. "Don't budge from your places. I pity anybody
who does. I'll be right back." And, together with Adam, she
exits in a flash.

At first, no hand moves. Though the door has already closed,
each woman is like a can of packaged panic. But gradually, like
branches catching fire, they start fidgeting. Shifting their heads,
breaking loose from that "all together now." A hand falls, yet,
wow! the ceiling doesn't bash their heads in. They get up, look at
each other, initially nervous, scared, then with a shame that
quickly becomes mischievous. And, all at once, there's havoc.
Total tumult. As though they had just gone from Hell to

Heaven, to the land of perfect happiness. They start giggling, whispering, looking out the windows, listening to the sounds outdoors. They shed their fears, they rebel—a tired rebellion.

Jenny and Adam are arguing in the hall. He cannot persuade her. "You want a key, Adam, and a beautiful evening suit? So get it yourself. You have a suit in your closet. It doesn't have to be any particular suit. I have to go back to my women. What's with a key all of a sudden?"

"Please, Jenny, you must help me." Oh, naturally, always, but this time even Jenny understands that there's a limit. He wants a particular key in Jenny's apron, the one that opens every single door in the Institute. In addition, he wants Jenny to pick the best suit from the storeroom for him. She, however, has a good excuse for not doing it: from the moment he returned to the Institute some while ago . . . "you've insulted me, annoyed me, and we've never been alone together, you always pretend you're asleep."

"I only insult people I love. Have you ever seen me insult someone I don't love?"

"You don't love anybody."

"Yes, I do—*you*."

"Nobody."

As he casts a thorny glance at her, his eyes penetrate her lovely thighs. Savoring somebody without self-respect, somebody who is a carpet to his own desires. God, she is so easy. We are all easy. Everything is simple. Press the button and out comes your free sample. Open sesame! Get the picture?

"You know, Jenny, that I am unable to control myself. A tidal wave is always after me. What can I do? Down deep, where it really counts, though, you understand, where one's being is most sensitive, the tides of love rage. I wasn't strangling the old woman, if you really want to know—it was you I was strangling."

Now a slight smile spreads her mouth open. Bull's-eye, you bastard!

"You and you alone, Jenny. I thought of you. Suddenly—it's the truth—I thought to myself, Jenny is screwing around with a young doctor. I went crazy. Couldn't. And therefore. A young doctor, handsome, a man, and me with the old mummy in the parlor, drinking vermouth. Hell on earth! We drank, you understand. Nothing special, just drinking vermouth, and conversing in the German of our parents, and we were old, and all of a sudden you, with the young doctor. It was impossible to reason any more, or govern myself, so I got on top of her and for a moment she was you and I throttled and throttled you for betraying me. Then when I returned here—and wasn't that why I strangled her, in order to come back to you?—when I was back, that other feeling, that insane throb of hatred, strangled my love and I was all, you know, wait a minute, you haven't any idea . . ."

And Jenny fondles his hair like someone who not only is no longer sure she is in the right but doesn't care any more one way or the other. Her slender, so womanly finger grazes across his lips and up his nose.

"Want some whiskey?"

"No, sweetheart, just love."

"Liar!"

"I'm not lying."

"Both love and J&B, okay?"

"Canadian whiskey's best."

I have her where I want her now, says Adam Stein to himself, *but whiskey, as they say, is whiskey!*

She blurts into a short-lived laugh, and he faces her with a sudden whisper: "Come, child, let's get out of here. I'll drink up all your juices. I'm crazy. You shall tickle me and we shall go places. I'll do the traveling, the adventuring over your maddening body."

She laughs. Her laughter is ominous and grating in the corridor, where the music now plays softly.

"Come, child, let's sit quietly. Come, child, let's cry."

The carpet swallows her ugly laughter that rings with a rusty hysteria.

"But why, why can't you get it yourself? They wouldn't refuse you. Why should they?"

"I have an important appointment, Jenny. A very important one. You must give me both the key and the suit."

"Tell me, Adam." She is truly baffled. "Why is it that when you can do something without any difficulty whatsoever, you have to pretend that you are obliged to go through crooked channels and deceptions and tricks? They would give you a suit from the storeroom without any complications."

Adam answers impatiently. "And you? You who claim all day and all night that you lovelovelove, that your love is overwhelming, and you write me sugary letters, why can't you simply do what I ask you to? A trifle like this?"

"You mean, why don't I want to. If I wanted to, I could."

"Exactly. Now hurry up."

"Do you remember that woman at the Jaffa hospital, Mrs. Friedland? She once wanted an abortion even though she wasn't pregnant."

No, he has no time for chit-chat. He must make a social call on that monster, that dog, and find out what's what. He is driven to it, it's the most important thing in his life. And he doesn't even know why.

"My pretty one," and he pets her starched back, "come on, now. As they say in the movies, on the double!"

She trains her eye on Adam and raises her hand in a salute, with a big smile on her face. "Right, General! An order's an order!" They walk off, she first, he following. So why, he asks himself, why did he have to make a dirty sign behind her back and laugh when she swung her face around to him, she having missed that vulgar gesture?

They quicken their pace. In precise unison. And reach the storeroom. Jenny removes the magnificent suit of Baron Von Hamdung with the gold buttons adorning its jacket. As she hands him the suit and the key to Room 285, Jenny can't help admiring this man for having managed to be devious even in this situation where there was no need for deviousness.

Once the door is slammed and he stands amid the stench and gloom, in the presence of the dog lying muffled in a sheet, he experiences at last, after all the running and anticipation, a certain exaltation. He is wearing a gorgeous suit, a handkerchief gleaming from its jacket pocket—a patron of the arts. A patron of the opera. Any minute the curtain will rise and Pavlova will dance, two glissades and a grandiose *tour-jeté* into the center of the stage, where she'll smile at him. He'll wave his handkerchief and Diaghilev, from behind the scenes, will scrutinize him through gold binoculars; subsequently, in a certain pleasant restaurant, they'll nibble on frogs' legs. Adam crosses the room with a gait of self-confidence and composure. With one pull, he opens the window blind, and the powerful desert light floods the room. Only now does he actually see how filthy and repulsive the room is, how much urine and dung there is. His nose rebels. In such situations it doesn't pay to pretend. Yet he actually doesn't have to pretend, for in fact the odor doesn't bother him that much. My dear Baron, how far you have fallen! Von Hamdung's buttons in a public lavatory.

The dog rumbles under the sheet. He is chained to the wall and the links make a racket. But oddly enough, the last link, the one attached to the wall, is unlocked. The dog could free himself. Besides, the link at his neck—or, more correctly, the link connected to the strap around his neck—is unfastened. With a twist of his head he could be free. Who are you? A monster? A dog?

He knows the dog is no dog. He knows it. He knows that it's not even a monster. In his bones he knows it. He approaches. He tries to get a better look. He says: "Who are you? What are you?" The dog shakes. The sheet goes up and down. The dog clears his throat. What starts as a barely audible gasp turns into a heavy growl. Is this a dog on the prowl? With me as the quarry? Adam focuses his eyes. Cold sweat on his forehead. He fears that he may be losing his chance. Instead of striking while the iron is hot, he's playing footsy with silly questions. Eyes fixed on the sheet, ears fixed on each growl, each bark, each breath, he paces back and forth. Then halts in front of the sheet, hands on hips, and inhales as deeply as his chest permits, straightening himself like some kind of animal—a dog, say, on his hind legs—and starts barking loudly at the monster, at the sheet. Adam knows the business of barking. He was actually able to fool Rex: he used to copy the bark of a bitch in heat or a starving mutt, and Rex would dash over to him and search behind him for the dog that had barked. Frightened shadowed eyes peer underneath the sheet as Adam barks now. Adam barks and the dog stops growling. And Adam says in a bored voice, "You don't scare me, dog. Anybody can bark!"

Adam hunts for something to sit on and finds, after a few steps, a ripped lopsided footstool.

"I still don't know who you are. You keep hiding from me. Maybe you're a dog. Maybe you're a monster. Maybe you understand my language. Maybe you don't. I have no idea. So, if you do understand, kindly nod your head."

The sheet doesn't stir.

"You took the candies, didn't you? You ate them. Who do you think brought those candies?"

No answer.

Adam gets up and stands by the window. The desert stretches everywhere. The skies are white, not blue, and the mountains too are white. From his vantage point, he can see a ravine cutting through the desert, weaving its deep way out of sight. An abyss of silence and emptiness, surrounded by mountains shaped like Purim *Hamantaschen*—all sizes, all types, round, single-pointed, double-pointed, triple-pointed—with a caravan of camels in the distance. In the camouflage of mist, the hoofs of the camels do not seem to be touching the ground. They perform a ballet, a delicate yet solid dance. Where are they headed? Edom, Moab, the Dead Sea, as far as Masada, and then south along the ancient Dead Sea route and the Nabatean route, to Gaza. Far off, lo! a miracle, the clouds are forming. It is fall, late fall. Soon winter will arrive.

A commotion under the sheet. A definite bark. Not a growl, not a clearing of the throat. What's this creature up to? It's frightened. Me too, so am I, like a fool. Who are you? Who am I? We both must find out. Jenny's an idiot, she doesn't count. Next to the dog, she's nothing.

"Listen to me!" he says, still facing the desert. "You're not the only one—do you hear? There are others. Me, for instance." Adam digs into his coat pockets and comes up with a package of Kents that has been there for a long time. He lights a cigarette with a shaky hand and blows out smoke. "Listen to me, dog, take me for an example. A con man, a freak—in other words, something of a monster? Weird, out of the ordinary, capricious. In short, a genius. But with a fly in the ointment, a curse. A person with a great voice goes into opera. A mathematical genius makes discoveries, figures out formulas. Likewise a physicist. But me? My great, my amazing, gifts were marginal; they marked me for the circus, in the company of the fattest lady in the world, the man with six fingers, the child with two heads. There I was the 'genius.' Nonetheless—and for that very reason—I'm in this Institute. I've swindled myself and now I am wretched. I'm a dead man. I'm privileged to be the one and only genius here, yet I'm about to die—the victim of my own great gift. That's the truth. Like you, I tried to escape, but you'll see, believe me, you won't make it. Never, not a chance. Because we are in an Institute of a woman who is lying right now in a refrigerator. And that's sad."

All of a sudden, with a tenderness that smooths every tortured line on his face and sweetens his voice to the point where it is unrecognizable, he whispers: "Did they beat you?" The sheet shifts. "Did they beat you? Were they brutal, those sadists? What did they do to you? Electric shock? Cold bandages? Insulin? Shock treatment? Cures they haven't got, but tortures they do. Those fools! Look, dog. I've been thinking about you. From the moment I heard your first bark, I've been thinking. Something tells me that you're more than a dog, or less than a dog. I'll tell you what. You're a human being even if you are a dog. You're the only one I can talk to in this lousy synthetic place. And yet you've managed to remain a dog. That's a big deal. You're not a phoney. The others are all phoney. I can smell a phoney a mile away. It's something I acquired from a very expert teacher in this business of smelling, called *Sturmführer Rex.* "Look," and again he faces the desert, "you must know me. It's boring, it's no fun dying alone, it's not right!"

The dog crouches under the sheet. What could he have understood? Isn't he a dog? But if he's a mutt, why does he have such human eyes? And if he's human, why does he have the eyes of a dog? Adam stretches out his hand and tries to grab the sheet. The sheet jumps, the chain rattles and creaks, there's a growl and the sheet edges a bit backward. Adam is bushed. His words have all dried up in his mouth. He's thirsty for a drop of whiskey or some brandy, vodka, gin, arak, wine, even cider or beer.

Shame will always loom between me and all that I could have become. I protest against my fate, against my crackpot honors. Wait, look, come here, Adam, look beyond your thoughts, beyond your failures. See: the sheet is stirring somewhat. The dog, the dog is actually approaching you, Adam.

Adam has won, though he's not ready to accept such a victory, not yet. What is he doing now? He is retreating. The dog is moving forward and he backward. Despite his gorgeous suit and his knack for imposture, despite the handkerchief bulging from his pocket and Baron Von Hamdung's gold buttons, he is retreating. He stares at the insect crawling toward him under the sheet. Through that hole he sees those eyes. They are fixed on him. He tries to identify their color, but their expression, their watery glaze, puzzles him, disturbs him. Something isn't right. As though he were looking into a mirror. The best of mirrors, he tells himself, angry and scared, yet compelled to look into that mirror without lowering his eyes. With courage. But where will he find such courage?

"Come on, dog. Come on, you monster."

And then, through the hole in the sheet, a mouth gapes open. The monster, the dog, the thing, extends its jaw. Before Adam manages to figure out what is happening, the thing, the dog, the monster, leaps forward and bites his hand and immediately retreats to its spot in the corner, where out of its mouth undulates a growl that turns into a bark, the worrisome bark of a wounded animal. The room fills with wailing. The whole Institute must be hearing it.

Adam is stunned. He raises his hand and examines it, distinguishing the teeth marks that have lacerated his skin and penetrated deep into his flesh. Slender streams of blood emerge as though from some gushing well. He sticks his injured red hand into a pocket of his gorgeous suit. He hears steps coming down the corridor. Shapiro and another male nurse bursts into the room.

"What did that 'barking case' do to you?"

Adam feels the blood pouring down his clothes, over his body, and gazes at the dog bundled up in the corner. The dog is trembling and howling. His wail sounds human, so childlike. Pity him. To hell with the blood. That crying! Children after their mother has already disappeared through the camp gate and their own turn has not yet come. They are naked in the big hall while Fräulein Klopfer is still checking her list.

"Nothing!" he says. And adds: "He didn't do a thing. I gave him a spanking and he cried. That's all."

"Bad animal!" utters the second nurse in a whisper. The first one is bald. The second has blue eyes and curly black hair. A cross-breed, thinks Adam vaguely.

"He barked," says Adam. "And I barked, too, we both barked at each other."

And he understood you?" says Shapiro, having a good laugh.

"It's a code language, dear boy." Adam tries to smile, but his hand aches. The blood is drenching his suit, his body. He doesn't feel well. Air!

As the door opens, the figure of the dog is clear as day, draped in that sheet and growling, howling: the picture of panic.

"You've got to get out of here now."

"But nothing has happened."

"What about next time!" Shapiro urges.

Hand hidden deep in his pocket, Adam Stein heads out of the room, then turns around, facing the dog, and emits a slight bark. The sheet jumps. Shapiro laughs. Says Adam, "I told him a joke!" His face is white. Shapiro pulls Adam by the arm. "All right, come on already. My God, does it stink here!" The moment Adam actually reaches the doorway and the music of Mrs. Seizling's indefatigable corridor, he looks back and with absolute clarity sees the dog's head under the sheet, as if head and sheet were one: the dog, the monster, nods and the taut sheet goes up and down, up and down.

Excited, Adam whispers softly, with the perfect grace of a man of the great world, a patron of the opera, a graduate of Heidelberg University, a child of enlightened liberalism: "I'll be back, you poor thing, I'll be back."

And at that very moment the door shuts in Adam's face and Adam notices that the bald nurse has witnessed this tender scene and is smiling to himself. To Adam that is unbearable. In a berserk rage, he falls upon the nurse, beating him with his fists, with his blood-soaked hand. Finally Shapiro and the "cross-breed" overcome Adam. Screaming, spitting blood, cursing. They gang up on him. He is dying and they know nothing of politeness. Doctors come running. Heads pop through the observation windows that bang open. They overcome Adam, bind him to a stretcher, and carry him to his room. He beats the air as the straps tying him down cut into his hands, and his mouth foams with blood and spittle, and his closed eyes revolve inward to watch his own death and vivisection.

5

RUTH

ADAM STEIN ARRIVED at the port of Haifa in the blazing end of
the summer of 1958. In Berlin, where he was born, he had been
living a life of ease, as comfortable and carefree as a vegetable,
since his return from the Camp. He had few obligations. Except
for his daily visit to Dr. Weiss, alias Commandant Klein, bearing
that rubber condom filled with coins, there was nothing much
left for him to do. But even that was too much. He had a lovely
house encircled by poplars and lindens. A maid came every day
to clean his house and cook his meals. His parlor, which he had
bought with all its furniture and odds-and-ends from Baron Von
Hamdung, was crammed full of books, beautiful pictures, orna-
mented chandeliers, ancient carpets, Oriental vases, easy chairs
upholstered in reddish-brown leather. A massive white Mercedes, in perfect condition, was parked in his garage and was
looked after by a courteous young chauffeur in a gray uniform.

Adam lacked nothing. Berlin was in the midst of its miraculous economic recovery, and Adam in the midst of his own bank accounts. He had no worries to plague him. There was no dog around. Just a canary bird in a gilded cage. When he returned from the Camp, following Commandant Klein's promise of escape and compensation—that had been the original agreement, and the German kept his word, just as, alas, had Adam, who had entertained everybody on that last trek, playing a violin and making funny faces—he won his court case and received full payment for the circus he had owned before the war. The circus had continued in operation during all the war years, and on its tours through the occupied countries it was a big hit. It even went under the same name: Adam's Circus. After entertaining the victorious Germans and the occupied allied countries, it was also a hit with the British and the Americans. At its sale it was worth (so stated the court judgment) half a million American dollars. And that entire sum was paid to Adam. Adam was wise enough to invest his money in the miracle of recovery, and after a short while his fortune had tripled. Then he took his money out of circulation, deposited it in Swiss banks and savings accounts, and lived in high style off the interest. Subsequently he had no interest whatsoever in the stock columns.

Nor did he return to the circus. He even refused to appear on television or radio. Hugo Wolf, an old friend, tried to persuade him to appear in the new theaters, to open a satirical nightclub, to play in a movie, to rejoin the circus, but Adam refused. Once in a while he'd meet some professors from the Institute for Research into Supernatural Phenomena, which was based in Hamburg though partly financed by the famous research team of an American university. These men were studying those inexplicable powers he was blessed with—powers which now, for the first time in his life, were no longer instruments of cheap and vulgar entertainment but would one day shed light upon the structure of man's mind and its unknown possibilities.

They tested Adam's card expertise—his ability to guess any

number or picture without looking, or to see right through a card. They confirmed his power to read a book through its cover and to sense with his eyes shut the history of an object by handling it.

Once they took him to an isolated house in the forest and seated him in the enormous library of Dr. Joachim Von Albending, an eccentric man who had sat hidden in his house all his days, never leaving it, never allowing anybody to come inside, and who just recently had died. In the library were hundreds of manuscripts of sagas and romances and religious poems and stories of knights, all written by German authors of the twelfth and thirteenth centuries—manuscripts that had never been published and of which there were no known copies. Except for the executor of the will and three professors who were named in Dr. Joachim Von Albending's will as the inheritors of this library on behalf of the university where they taught, nobody had set foot in the room where Adam was now seated—other than the Doctor himself, of course. But now, there sits Adam, opposite the three professors, the executor, the representative of the law firm Vogel & Strauss, a representative of the University of Cologne, and three research scholars from the Institute for Research into Supernatural Phenomena. Adam's eyes pass over the embossed bindings and he says to one of the professors: "Pick any book, any one you want. You don't have to point to it or even look at it in any special way. Glance at them all and just decide on one. Have you chosen it? Good." Then he turns to a second professor and asks him to pick a page. Any number. From 10 to 150. Simply a page number. "Have you chosen one? Wonderful." Then he turns to a third. "Pick two lines, from three to twenty. Two lines. Easy, no?" And then Adam tenses the muscles of his brow and puts on the face of a thinker, a theoretician, somebody who's trying to find a connection with, and corroboration from, mysterious external forces. That's all he does, put on a face. And finally he says: "The lines read, 'And Prince Willsberg lifteth his blood-soiled arm and crieth in broken voice and sunken spirit, Caitiff! How may I leave, whilst my lady is yet holden captive by you?' "

The professors then do as he bids. Professor A takes out a book wrapped in spiderwebs and dust, a book that hasn't been touched in many a year, and opens it. Professor B says: "Page ninety." Professor C says, "Line thirteen." Enough said: the clown-prophet was right, word for word. Not knowing what to make of it, they laugh and decide he was pulling their legs. What else could they think? Yet their laughter didn't help them.

Oh no, Adam did not return to the circus. He sits in his well-lit parlor, browsing through the many books left behind by Baron Von Hamdung (who, though sitting now in a cell, will one day be released and fit right into the miracle of recovery, but in the meantime Adam has paid him in hard cash and nobody can come to him with any complaints), smoking fragrant cigars or American cigarettes, and feeling himself not at all alien or new to the place, unaware of the fact that now, for the first time in a thousand years, Berlin is at last free of Jews, *Jüdenrein*. He sits amid sarcophagi, cabinets, and books. Records—Scarlatti, Monteverdi, the Bachs (John Sebastian, John Christian, Philipp Emanuel), and also Handel, Mozart, and the final quartets of Beethoven. No further. As for paintings, miniatures and reproductions—up to the Renaissance. Giotto, Cimabue, Fra Angelico, yes, but not Leonardo, he had too much turmoil. As for books: Goethe, Heine, Schiller, Jean Paul. No further. Adam Stein, then, is seated in a sarcophagus, free of Jews, surrounded by records of sweet music, old books, unremembered spiderwebs, ancient paintings, numerous archeology texts, whatever is dead, passed from the world, philosophies that can no longer be deciphered, literatures that were beautiful to a bygone age. He has no job. He is rich. Magic? What about a miracle? The miracle is that the miracle is not a miracle. So Adam lives off whatever is deceased, whatever has been demolished, *Jüdenrein, Humor-rein, Liebenrein.*

* * *

Adam would certainly have sat there hidden inside his lovely parlor till the day he died if not for the information he was given one day—namely, that his daughter Ruth, his first-born, who was taken from him and his wife on May 3, 1938, the day that Adam's Circus was declared *Jüdenrein,* who thereafter disappeared completely, who they thought had died in Dachau because somebody actually saw her there, this daughter was alive and living in Israel.

The information shocked him deeply. He had seen his wife, Gretchen, and his daughter Lotta on their last trek. They smiled, knowing that they were safe. Was it possible at that time to comfort them? And jeopardize everything? His whole purpose was to blot out the fear of death. Death itself he could not prevent, nobody could have brought death to a halt, but the dread of it he could dispel for them. Commandant Klein didn't hate Jews any more than the average butcher hates his cows or the average hangman those he hangs. Instead he tried to be helpful. He located Adam, set him up in the corridor, so that during the entire procession Germany's greatest clown would be right up front clowning. After all, if such a person were around, things couldn't be so bad. So Adam didn't address his wife or child, and to the very end they walked with trust and peace in their hearts. Only two years later, when he found himself in neutral Switzerland, did he begin to have longings for Gretchen and Lotta. But by refusing to acknowledge his longings, he saved himself from the shame which was his greatest fear, the shame of guilt. Adam refused to admit his crime, he loathed the way some of his friends would parade their guilt, though in some cavern of his mind he recognized the fact that they had the right to be guilty, whereas he did not.

He said to himself, Palestine is nothing but a joke. Refugees, escapees, bits and pieces of humanity, chaff tossed in the wind, they cannot establish a homeland for themselves and are not worthy, perhaps, of having one. Berlin received him with open arms. His neighbors and acquaintances were glad to have in their de-

veloping city, in a little house surrounded by trees, the greatest
clown Germany had ever possessed, a clown who had chosen to
return to their midst from the furnaces which they themselves
had manufactured for him. He was sort of an insurance policy
against Hell, in case there was anything more terrible than the
things they had created with their own hands. They wrote essays
about him, interviewed him for magazines, showered him with
medals of distinction and tokens of affection, and he recipro-
cated in kind, according to their deserts. From his chosen sarcophagus, from his remote world amid deceased music, he
smiled at their lives, and sometimes he even attended their parties and, along with them, gnashed his teeth at Germany's dis-
memberment.

However, when he learned that his daughter was alive, his
house of cards buckled and collapsed. Everything was mud-
dled, no longer understood. He sat wrapped in his thoughts, asking questions that the sarcophagi could not answer. Even Dr.
Weiss—that sworn humanist, that pious fool who had saved
Adam's life, who had kept his word and was now being kept
alive by Adam—did not know what to reply. And Adam was
exposed to feelings entirely new to him. Feelings of the present
tense and not of sarcophagi. He started to miss someone whose
face he had forgotten and who probably, after more than twenty
years, no longer looked the same. He sent Ruth a letter at the
address he had received. He told her about himself, her mother,
her sister. He wrote that all the while he was watching them step
toward their death, they smiled with joy, so they were certainly
happy where they now were. When he didn't receive an answer,
he wrote again. He wrote that God kept quiet. That the good
world had died in 1933. That Europe, Christianity, Judaism,
Myth, Greece, Scripture, St. Augustine, Civilization, Culture, the
Roman Empire, Humanism—everything was ended in one day.
Again he received no answer. He wrote that while he was living
in a sarcophagus he became estranged from the Messianic vision,
from the Jewish madness, from the incomprehensibility woven

during more than a thousand years into a compendium of pining
and expectation that finally brought about the creation in the East
of a nation of Blue Numbers. He wrote that he was separated
from all this and was lodged in a coffin, and since he had once
been a dog he was no longer a Jew, no longer even German. And
that he was her father, and that she ought to write him. If she
wrote, maybe he'd understand. That he had neither right nor
obligation. He was just a vegetable. A stone. We're a people, not
a state. Judaism doesn't know of any regular state, it knows only
of a nation. God and his people, both have sinned. No answer
arrived, and Adam began to show signs of distress. Once, at a
party which the municipality of Berlin arranged in honor of the
author Hermann Scheling, who had just won an award for his
book *Ikon Named Anne Frank,* Adam stood up and declaimed
at length in a weird language that nobody understood. When his
astonished hosts asked him what language it was, he said he
didn't know. A famous scholar who was present at the celebration, Wolfgang Goering (no relation), later explained that
Adam had recited to them the book of Job in Esperanto. What
puzzled the scholar most of all was the fact that the book of Job,
as far as he knew, had never been translated into Esperanto.
Adam swore he had no idea how the book or the language
"came to him," for he knew neither, and then he suddenly
jumped up and screamed: "A letter has just arrived for me, an
important letter has just arrived for me, and I'm wasting my
time here over nothing." He ran as fast as he could to his house
and indeed a letter was waiting there for him.

He ripped open the envelope, spread out the letter, and read.
His heart shuddered. It was from Israel. A Jewish stamp, in Hebrew, Arabic, English, come to a city that was *Jüdenrein.* A
miracle.

Dear Mr. Stein,

*My German isn't good enough to write in and my English
is not of the best, consequently please forgive all the many*

mistakes and the bad grammar. I am your daughter Ruth's husband. This morning at 5:30, I took her to the Hadassah hospital in Jerusalem, in order that she might give birth to my son or my daughter. I prefer a daughter, though Ruth wants a son. When I was back home, I searched through her papers (on the way to the hospital she asked me to find some documents and bring them to her, her immigration papers and other credentials, she wanted to have them by her bed, I don't know why) and I found your letters.

She never said a word about these letters, and I'm stunned. Today I discover that my son or my daughter has a grandfather. Amazing! Tomorrow I will no longer be just my father's son but also my son's father, and the fact that, for me, you were born on the very same day causes me great joy. It's hard for me to explain. I know that Ruth never answered your letters. At the bottom of one of the letters she wrote in her green Parker: "Father, I'll never talk to you. It's impossible. Not because you write that you were a scoundrel but because I wasn't there to guide you." Forgive me for writing this down for you. But anything's better than silence, which must certainly be painful to you. That's the way Ruth is. But as I held your letters in front of me, I thought to myself that you ought to know all this. Why? I don't know. I understand that you were separated a long time ago. That you don't know a thing about her. Therefore I'll give you a brief summary. If it won't help, it certainly won't harm. Ruth came to the Land in 1945. She arrived in a blockade-runner. Once here, she tied a small gold crucifix around her neck and swore that her children would be Christian. That way they'd be safer. She was determined, and she used strong language: for example, she told her friends in the youth movement that she would erase the covenant of circumcision—that cursed covenant—from her children's flesh, and would plan for them a way of life in the world that didn't cherish the circumcised. Permit me to boast in front of you—after all, you are my father-in-law—and tell you that thanks to our

*marriage she became a totally different person. She overcame
the terrible fears that were attacking her, and when she became
pregnant she took the crucifix from her neck and rejoiced over
her pregnancy, even though two years ago she swore to me that
she wouldn't bring Jewish children into the world. She was very
sick. Some claim that "they" made experiments on her body.
She refuses to talk about this subject. Dr. Klein, who took care
of her in Jerusalem, says that she went through Hell and was
already "beyond death," so beyond that death was for her almost an understatement. That's what Dr. Klein said, and here
in Jerusalem he's considered a first-rate doctor.*

*Let me summarize, in conclusion: Today you are a grand-
father. From what I've been saying you can obviously understand that Ruth has changed, and therefore, in the opinion and
name of Joseph Graetz, who is your son-in-law, you have a
home in Israel. If you want to come, come. I'm convinced that
if Ruth saw you face to face, she'd forgive. And if not, from
reading your letters I deduce that you could stay with us even
without forgiveness.*

Yours, in friendship,
Joseph Graetz

Adam grumbled over the last lines of the letter. He hadn't
ever asked anybody to forgive him. Nobody was entitled to forgive him. But in less than two months Adam was in the port of
Haifa.

From the day he arrived, he felt at peace and didn't know
why. He wasn't a stranger: in his eyes the East was neither too
oppressive nor too exotic. Everyone welcomed him. He understood why, felt he understood. He was in no hurry to reach
Ruth. He thought he should postpone his coming. Perhaps he
was afraid, he didn't know for certain. He settled himself in a
lovely pension on Mount Carmel, run by the Deutsch family, an
old German house surrounded by tall shady pine trees, in a
pleasant room whose old chests-of-drawers reminded him of his

parents' house. He toured throughout the country. Explored the holy places. Went up to Safed and was delighted by the gnarled crooked streets of the mystic city. He visited Tel Aviv and the Negev, went down to Elat and bathed in the clear waters of the Red Sea. Once, without knowing how it happened, while he sat in a cab taking him from Galilee to the Deutsch pension, he emitted a tiny bark at the driver's back. And the driver burst into an enormous guffaw and, coughing, said: "You people with your sense of humor!" not explaining what he meant by "you people." However, one day, as he was browsing through the Carmel market in Tel Aviv, Adam found the unambiguous meaning of that "you people." He was walking among the stands of vegetables, fruits, and clothes, among the blood-drenched butcher shops, among the multitude of people and sounds, when two kids came up to him and tried to sell him a camera. In explaining to the boys that he had no intention of purchasing a camera, he attempted to use the little Hebrew he had picked up by then (the pension landlady, Mrs. Esther Deutsch, claimed that during his two-month stay in Israel he had learned more Hebrew than she had since she immigrated to Israel in 1934) and in the process he stumbled and stepped on the bare brown foot of one of the kids. The boy turned to his friend and said: "Let's bugger this soap."

Adam caught the gist of the remark, though the expression "soap" was new to him. What made him remember and think about the phrase "you people" was the use of the word "soap." It amazed him how many meanings this word had in Israel. He pondered the origin of soap in Sidon, the development of its use throughout the world, and the word itself, which in the camps, under the influence of his commandant, had acquired a mystical new import. Men are soap, they hold people in their hands, clean innocent sterilized people. Oh, that sterilization. Those cultivated rules of the game. Oh, the latent terror of the fact that today you can say *I scrubbed him good,* meaning *I finished him off*. And any paleface who looks like a refugee is a piece of soap. And soap has no body or muscles. Soap is what they made out of us. And here? Street boys call him a bar of soap right to his face. So nonchalantly, so easily. To give him a good scrubbing, a good soaping. Once upon a time there was a man who became a bar of soap. There was a soap that once had been Gretchen, Lotta, and Spiegel family. On the store shelf, wrapped in yellow paper with olive leaves on it, you will find the Rabinowitz family: perfumed soap. Robert, the first-born, has perhaps a pinch of lavender. The second son, Peter, who was also named Simon, is perfumed with daphne. And little Deborah —a strange perfume, ah, fruit blossoms, maybe citrus? To scrub soap—can you really scrub soap? He was soap personified and saponified, ambling through the markets in order not to have to face Ruth. The former Ruth Stein who was turned into a pillar of soap but escaped and became a golden crucifix. That's fate. The sign of circumcision she can erase with a knife, but what about the soap? Someone had to play an instrument, make the procession laugh, no? Otherwise all Hell would have broken loose, with knives in people's backs and bullets flying everywhere. And that's a dirty business. My Commandant Klein liked order and cleanliness. Soap. *If I am a bar of soap in the country of sanctuary, then I have come home,* said Adam with tears standing in his eyes. To come back a hero? No, it's possible to come back just as soap. For only such degradation would rescue some of the dignity I never had but nonetheless destroyed with my own hands. And that was how Herr Stein, Adam Frankenstein Stein, the admired and honored citizen of the new and different Berlin, turned into a willing piece of soap, a bar of soap in a nation of soap bars. What else was possible for a piece of soap? It must be, at one and the same time, cruel and hopeless, despairing and strong.

When Adam Frankenstein Stein went up to Jerusalem, he rented a lovely little room in the Mittelman pension in Rehavia. The owners of the pension were very excited to have Adam Stein. They treated him as if he were their child. After a festive dinner in their dwelling, Mr. Mittelman set the record player on a card table in the living room, and the three of them drank chilled vermouth and danced in turns, first Adam with Mrs. Mittelman, then Mr. Mittelman with Mrs. Mittelman, and late in the night, after they had laughed to the full, Adam even asked Mr. Mittelman to dance, and the man and his wife both laughed. Since the time they were youngsters and went to see Adam's Circus in Dresden, they hadn't laughed like this. In the days of Palestine, you understand, humor wasn't quite the thing. People were serious, life was serious, the Mandate was serious, then came the troubles with the terrorists and the war, and naturally the rationing—all those things. When could anybody laugh? The man of soap, though, laughed. All the men of soap. It was a goodly and pleasing thing for men of soap to sit all together.

Late that night he took leave of the merry landlady and landlord and went away. In front of the large hotel, he got into a cab and handed the driver an address.

"There's shooting there at night, you know," said the driver. "They've shot Abu-Tor before."

"And that's where they live?"

"Yes, it's the address you gave me. If I were you I'd wait till tomorrow. Those Jordanians don't play favorites. You'll catch a bullet yet. That house is in a pretty lousy location! Right on the border. Listen to me . . ." They had arrived. Adam held out a bill and the driver left in a hurry.

Adam stood in an empty silent street. In the deep of night. Thick-leaved trees. Stone houses. In the distance the gilded domes of the Old City. Soon, day would break.

All of a sudden a burst of bullets, from nowhere, from everywhere, simultaneously. The biting chirrup of the bullets, the whistle of their flight, the striking of targets were perfectly clear. Adam searched for the number of the house. Unafraid. His fears had all died. He had been thinking for a long while about a little girl coming to ask him something. Daddy, who has more money, God or you? Daddy, who do you like better, Mommy or God? Is the world ever going to end? How much is a lot? Is a little more than a lot? Why is Lotta crying? Mommy killed her. I'll bury you with the ants in the back yard. Robert killed an ant. Me too. And Mommy too. Daddy, why isn't my wee-wee like yours? The shooting, the whistle of sniping in the thick of the night. Once there was a child. Once there was a Ruth. They are shooting at you, Ruth. They are killing your ants, Ruth. He'd defend her. He'd protect her. Would she have a son or a daughter, the young mother? Would there be a crucifix around the child's neck? Adam found the house. Sprinted up the three flights at a gallop. The shooting stopped. Nobody was stirring. The house was still. Were they asleep? Were they tossing from side to side? On the third floor he saw the small letters of the nameplate: RUTH AND JOSEPH GRAETZ. He stood staring at the words, wanting to ring the bell. But instead, like a true comedian, like the owner of the best circus in Germany, he spread his arms as if crucified and screened Ruth's door from the bullets. He wouldn't allow her to become smoke, like Lotta. Like Gretchen. Like me. You men of all times and all generations who have turned into smoke, unite! You have nothing to lose but your soap. Your only soap, Herr Adam Superman Stein.

He heard laughter coming from the downstairs doorway. A couple, a young boy and girl. It sounded as though they were singing. Were they just coming back from a party? And what about the baby? Was it at the grandfather's? You have one grandfather and another grandfather. And the two grandfathers will never meet. Parallel grandfathers, one soap and the other not soap, can never meet.

Adam was panic-stricken. The couple was almost at the top of the stairs. Ruth and Joseph? Have they returned from the battle drunk? Laughing? They'll see me, Ruth will cry. Her tears will be precious. Today they'll be precious. For what reason? Why is there smoke, Daddy, and why isn't the smoke on fire any more? What are people made of? Does God sleep at night? When will Elijah the Prophet come? Did Elijah the Prophet know

Jesus? Was Jesus born a million years ago? Today's his birthday. Today they light up a tree. Why don't you? You do? Yes
and no? Oh, your tree isn't a tree. You don't light up a tree. The
Stoll family really has a tree.

Adam galloped up the spiral staircase to the roof, burst
through the creaking wood door. There was still some shooting
going on. Jerusalem spread out before his eyes. The golden
domes glittered in the light of the full moon. The house was
surrounded by heavy-faced trees. Odd cypresses such as he had
never seen before. Like priests in cassock and pointed miter.
The young couple went into one of the apartments. The door
slammed. Adam didn't know what apartment they had entered.
He raced down the staircase and fled from the house. Through
the empty streets he fled. Fled, hoping he wouldn't see anybody.
He reached the pension at six in the morning as the landlord was
lighting the gas oven. Said the landlord: *"Gut Morgen,* Herr
Stein, did you sleep well?"

"Yes," answered Adam. *"Ich liebe die Ferne, alles ist licht
und glanz."* ("I love wide open spaces, everything is brilliant
with light.")

The next day he did not return to the Graetz family's lodgings.
He began to feel a pressure in his chest, in his throat, in his
pharynx. He couldn't swallow. This morning, after he returned
from Ruth and Joseph's house fleeing through the empty streets
of Jerusalem, he had begun to feel afraid. He hadn't felt such a
dread from the time Commandant Klein took him as his dog to
the day he reached Jerusalem, the eternal city, the city of the
Forefathers, Zion, the city of the Yevusi. He didn't love it—too
glorious a city. It hadn't been totally destroyed and then rebuilt
as a synthetic sanctuary on the model of Berlin. Here they had
built one city on top of another, layer upon layer, from the time
of King David. And even David he didn't like. Something in
David's story depressed him. Saul was a man after his own
heart. But Saul was betrayed. And didn't live in Jerusalem.

Adam Stein goes to a newspaper agency in Jerusalem and has

an ad published in three papers, as follows:

"Would Ruth Graetz (formerly Stein) please come to Pen-sion Mittelman, Ussishkin Street, Jerusalem. Any hour of the day or night. It's for her own benefit. A friend of the family."

Then he sat down and waited. In two days she was knocking on the door to his room. When he said, "Come in!" she came inside. She sat opposite him and asked him to light the cigarette shaking in her mouth. She was lovely, her hair chestnut, her eyes gray, her nose slight, and a certain grief in her face. He knew that her trembling would pass, that a wise woman was sitting in front of him. He could have fallen in love with her. He could even have killed her. He could certainly have understood her. She had a bold presence and she vanquished his room. With confident movements she switched the position of a chair, dragging it to the end of the room and sitting down. She looked at him a long while, glanced at his suitcases, "measured" him. She opened the old green blind all the way, and the sun leaped into the room. You could hear cats howling in the yard. She wanted to throw some scraps to them, but didn't budge from her place.

They talked. At first, words, words, words. *Those cigarettes are really good. Made in Israel? A nice pension. Yes, my son is growing up. He's already laughing. He looks a bit like me. A bit like his father. About in the middle. A cross. The Galilee is pretty. Haifa's great. The landscape is enchanting. Really good cigarettes. Summer nights are chilly. We wear vests. In Tel Aviv you sweat. Yes. But in Tel Aviv you have the beach. And life-guards. The boardwalk stinks. It's neglected. The army? No. But Joseph was a soldier.* Adam is amazed. She isn't saying a thing. Her eyes speak, yet what's the story about? What's the song about? I'm no longer her father. That ended twenty years ago. They've taken a corpse out of the earth and transported him to the Mittelman pension. She's a strange girl, lovely, a bit cold, bold, kind. *Yes, of course there's an ashtray! Here, yuh, it's three-thirty in the afternoon.*

I learned Hebrew out of a book. Gut Morgen—good morn-

ing, good evening—Guten Abend, let me introduce Mr. . . .
I'm glad to meet Mr. . . . (She smiles. Beneath her pain and
anxiety, she smiles. I fish the smile out, I'm a swindler. I came
for love, and I try to buy it. To give something. A sorry swindle.) *I'm coming, thanks—Danke, ich komme. Is your watch
working? Regards to Father, Mother, your sister, your brother,
your brother-in-law. It's late, it's early, my watch has stopped!
Stopped? I have plenty of time, I haven't any time, the rainy season is here, it's raining already, rain is falling, take an umbrella,
wear a raincoat, it's pouring out, the rain has stopped, the sky is
clearing, Succoth is a gorgeous holiday, the wind is changing direction, a storm is breaking, the wind is coming from the north*

from the south
from the east
from the west
from the sea
hot
cold
moderate

Waiter, please wash this oilcloth again. I'd like black bread

white bread
old bread
fresh bread
biscuits
toast
salt
pepper

*Me . . . yes, another cigarette. Does the child cry? At night.
And you nurse him? It's beautiful. It's healthy and good. Am I
funny? I used to be. This ashtray? Black and White. I prefer
Dewar's, or J&B. Oh, I just remembered one other thing: Do you
have any sour cream? Haben Sie sauer Sahne? Yes? I was
younger once. Is that funny? In Jerusalem the air is pleasant.
This window? No, there's hardly any noise. Rehavia, is a quiet
spot.*

Ah, the godly glory of humiliation, thought the "soap" now. Meanwhile Ruth gets up from her chair, paces back and forth, goes to the window, takes a deep breath and says: "Father . . ." He feels the need to flee for his life, that he is disgusting. She seems to him a cheap actress, a vile faker. Father? I'm a dog. A little restraint, *Mademoiselle*. Father? Who's your father? Run away. Escape, it's a C movie. In a back street. Miserable. Talentless. He is flabbergasted. "Get up, get up!" She is kneeling now. The vulgar actress. Melodramatic. He wanted to shout: Maestro, the music!

"I love you . . . Father . . . and forgive . . . Father . . ."

Get up, you actress, you worthless thing, it's a cheap act. *I'm* a stranger. *You're* a stranger. He runs his hand over his coat, grabs a cigarette, lights it with a shaky hand, weeping—a terrible sight. He opens the door, about to leave, to bolt. In the doorway stands a tall youth with a serious face. He is wearing a blue vest and a gray felt hat, oh so gray.

The young man goes pale. He scans the girl, who is bent over on her knees, and shouts in a frozen threatening voice: "Get out, Iris!" She gets up, her face white like the boy's, crosses past Adam, looks at him for a moment, makes up her mind, and rushes out. From the corridor, from beyond the utility closet, he can hear her voice. Is she laughing? Crying? He can't tell.

"That was Iris," says the young man. "My name is Joseph, Joseph Graetz."

"Pleased to meet you. Why . . . ? Who is she . . . ?"

"She is a friend of Ruth's, Mr. Stein." Joseph keeps looking at him, tries to smile.

Adam sees this and attempts to evaluate the possibilities contained in this moment.

"Let's go to her now," say Joseph.

"Yes, let's go."

And the tall youth with the gentle face and the heavy body takes Adam by the arm and leads him with firmness, yet with tenderness. And Adam senses for the first time in years, in gen-

erations, in a jubilee, that he no longer is and never again will be
his own master.

Adam Stein and Joseph Graetz are treading on stony ground.
From the station to a path with stones and thorns. Adam
doesn't know where he is going, or why he is going there. Is
there, though, any need to know? At the end of the road will be
Ruth. Another Ruth. He has already lost two Ruths. When they
enter a cemetery, he isn't surprised at all. Night has fallen. The
cemetery is wrapped in shadows and secrecy. The tombs sprout
up from the darkness and flicker among the trees, among the
rocks. Adam is pondering his feeling of security. In the Camp,
among the black bunks and barracks, he used to feel safe because he knew where he was, where he stood. The bunks were
designed by architects who had studied with him in the university. They came from the same culture: the culture which made
Adam Stein also made the Camp. In the Carmel market, with its
heat waves, its barefoot boy who called him soap. Adam knew
he didn't understand anything, that it was impossible for him to
understand. Now, in this cemetery, everything is simple and
comprehensible. His feet are treading a gravel path and he is at
peace. Where is he going? He doesn't know and doesn't care to
know. They pass an old Jew immersed in prayer. A magnificent
time of night. If I had been allowed to pray, would I have? He
had no answer to that.

The watchman, carrying a sooty oil lamp in one hand and a
cigarette in the other, asks them for a light. Adam hands him a
pack of Kent cigarettes. The watchman thanks him, fondles the
pack with lust in his fingers, and disappears among the graves.

"There she is," says Joseph, his voice calm. You can see no
emotion in him. No music. Don't stop, don't. Why have we
stopped? Let's go on. On, on. All around. But never once say,
There she is. Let's walk till we faint, till we lose our senses, and
never get there.

"Here's where I buried her," say Joseph. He seats himself on
a tombstone and points to a mound of loose earth in which a

small sign is stuck like a flag:

RUTH GRAETZ
BORN IN BERLIN, MAY 4, 1929
DIED IN JERUSALEM, APRIL 24, 1958

"Now make her laugh. You're funny, aren't you?" said Joseph.

Adam stares at him. He can't understand, but the words ring
a distant bell in his ears. Now/you/must/make/her/laugh
. . . Klein's command! Herr Stein, your life for your clowning. A clown can pass through fire and not get burned. He'll give
up his life. He'll return. And there's always Switzerland and savings accounts. The circus will be yours. So now be a clown, entertain! Rex, don't bark, this man is your brother. You're a
purebred and he's a mongrel. Who will win out, the pure Jew or
the pure dog? The pure dog lost because the pure Jew was much
more popular. Rex, the kingdom of Rexes. Rex and the Knights
of the Round Table. The culture of Rexes in the seventeeth century. Rex-Luther is after the pure Jew and burns people, Rex-
Faust and Rex-Mephisto. Rex from Weimar is researching the
nature of color. Rex the Jew, the father of elegant language, who
called himself Heine (but we know very well that his name is Rex),
was received by the back door. The Rexes actually write beautiful music. They have music in their hands and power in their
heads. The *Führer* has a Rex. But Rex has no *Führer*. And
here? The ones who haven't, have; and the ones who have,
haven't.

"You'll make her laugh. She told me you were a clown." His
voice is strong. There's no escape. Adam knows it. Here, too,
you have a version of *Jüdenrein:* no non-Jews are buried here.
Not here. *Jawohl, mein* . . . He will obey the order. He has no
right not to obey the order. And he desires no escape, because
there isn't any. He sits down on a tombstone. Jerusalem gleams
in the distance. A blaze of colors. A blaze of shadows. A blaze
of winds. Autumn. Many years have passed since he worked at

the only occupation he ever had. But he will do his job faith-
fully. Of course, Joseph counted on that. He expected it. Adam
takes off his shoes, pulls off one sock and stretches it over the
top of his head, dirties his face with the loose earth between the
graves, rolls up the cuffs of his pants, undoes the buttons of his
coat, and then redoes them immediately but with the loop of the
third button now holding the fifth button. After a few minutes,
with the perfect seriousness that comes from a wide experience,
from a rooted tradition of clowning, Adam Stein transforms
himself into a circus clown. Just like that. With no aids. No
make-up. Everything extempore. His face distorts. His eyes
dance with mischief. One ear skips. Both nostrils shiver. Gradually he begins to live the moment. Ruth is an enormous audience. Everything else is gone. The alignment of delicate light
hovering over the towers of Jerusalem disappears. Adam spouts
small monologues. His tongue goes silly. But he remembers the
routine. The old words come back to him, his mouth delivers
them with more and more confidence. Young woman, *Fräulein,*
here, give me your hand. Your ring! Yes, your ring—which I
now have in my hand—was given to you by a man about forty
whom you scarred on his left cheek, who works as a waiter in
the Vienna Coffeehouse, Wilhelm Strauss by name. The fellow
has serious intentions and, though he's already had two loves in
his life, is still a virgin . . . and here before you is Monsieur
Maurice Chevalier singing "Erica!" and now, ladies and gentlemen and whatnot, right before you is Marlene Dietrich singing
"The Blue Angel" in the bedroom of the Jew Roosevelt. Who
formerly went under the name Rooseveltzweig. And his wife, Mrs.
Sadie Cohen. As for money, here is an endless flow of Jewish
silver. Here is a portrait of God in Heaven looking down on
Commandant Klein while he is doing his bookkeeping, after
everybody has had his cut. Isn't it funny?

   At this point, Adam retreated to the days when it was possible
to tell other kinds of stories. To divine, to handle watches, fountain pens, fur coats, hats. He sang. Made jokes. Joseph Graetz,

who hadn't been laughing, now laughed. In Adam's ears his laughter increased a thousandfold. The great hall of Vienna was laughing wildly and cheering and applauding. The opera house of Prague was about to split its sides from laughing too hard or collapse from all the bravos. Always on the move, he travels here, there, everywhere. He sends his wife a telegram at the birth of their daughter: DULCINEA MY BELOVED MY NOBLE DULCINEA STOP KISS MY FIRST-BORN'S ASS STOP RETURNING IN A WEEK STOP NURSE TILL THEN STOP WHEN I'M BACK WE'LL SWITCH STOP YOUR LOVER.

The laughter keeps mounting. Ruth hears nothing. She's used to it. But through the thick fog he sees the ring of his admirers, his fans. These are the beggars of the cemetery, who grow and live here like mushrooms. Always bleary-eyed, drowsy, yawning, dark mouths open like split hoofs, their jaws appallingly wide. They circle him, wakened by his screaming, and celebrate. Joseph Graetz, surprised by their sudden coming, stares at them in astonishment. But all their laughing and shouting is drowned by the voice of Adam, by the many voices of the clown.

Their look is hostile as they make a racket with their tin boxes of charity. *The emptier the can, the more noise it makes.* It is cold out. Windy. The treetops with their clerical hats are showing courtesy to a clown. The circle gets smaller and tighter around Adam and Joseph. And Adam, Adam drops on all fours and begins to kiss the loose soil of his daughter's grave. He will buy a tombstone. Or else will himself be one, frozen there on the mound of earth. His mouth is wet with sweat, his body weary, his face ashen. The lame and the halt, with their faces of fear, keep shaking their tin boxes: *clink, clink, clink,* charity prevents death. Joseph is scared. The laughter of the beggars exposes gold teeth. And mouths that are toothless. Dark caverns. Stench and grotesquery. The beggars see that the two men are shocked, and laugh. And laugh. And laugh. Money! Money! *Geld! Geld!*

"Adam, let's run!"

"I can't."

"What's wrong?"

"I don't know."

"Come on, let's go."

"My body refuses. I cannot. Go yourself."

"No."

"Yes."

"I cannot." It is God's doing. Adam wants to laugh. Recalls Rex. Rex was, Rex is, Rex will always be. You will come from dust and to dust you will always return. Good old dust. They both stink. The usual odor. Soon they will be smoke. Smoke has no color, just odor.

Joseph goes. He breaks the circle of beggars. Adam crawls after him. The beggars are disappointed. It was such a nice performance. The man was funny. Now he is no longer funny. He's crawling. An insect. "Demon!" screams a fat old woman and scampers away in panic. "Demon! Bug! Monster!" They themselves are frightened. What a joke! He looks up at them from below. How ugly! Before, they were terrifying; now they are scared. So, like a boy and his dog, Joseph and Adam leave the cemetery, the dog wearing a long thin tie that drags in the dirt, in the gravel. The paupers panic and flee. The moon sinks into a corner of the sky.

6

A CHILD

THE FUTURE IS FIXED, inflexible. Only the past changes. The past is established not by locks but by binoculars. You stand and look back: if I were to bang my head against a wall, my past would shift accordingly. I'd be sprawled in a garden of lilies and drinking champagne from the armpit of a young nymph. One side of the coin is always better than the other. I was in the dog's room. He nodded his head, I got excited. Why? Because I wanted to get excited and nobody can tell me, can tell Adam Stein, what he should do and what he shouldn't. The dog was excited, too. That was very clear, obvious. The idiotic nurse, that bastard, saw and smiled. I killed him. Or maybe I just injured him. Anyway, a terrific struggle broke out and now I am in my room. "Hello, my Herbert." In the window again. Sitting.

"Hello!"

"Ah. That's really quite nice of you. I'd almost say it was an act of friendship. Friend, brother, give me your hand, I want to vomit you out of me."

"Just lie down and don't move. When are you going to stop this comic routine?"

"Soon, brother. The end is approaching. The real end. It winks at the finish of the road. There are many endings, all serious, sad, barren, just one beginning. All ends have one origin. And that, my dear brother, my beloved twin, is God's irony. God is not, as many think, at the beginning of the road, at creation, at initial primordial stages, but at conclusions. There he waits. Like Klein with his roll book and his scrupulous records and his accounts of the causes of death. Like a gravedigger. Like Dr. Gross. With a cane. With a submachine gun. With pins. Satan pushes you on your way and there is only one direction. Later the road branches—though you're still heading toward the same end, the same Person. So be it. What time is it?"

"The right time, the moment of grace."

"Thanks, brother."

"Don't mention it."

We awaken from our swoon, my Herbert, my infant. There's ingratitude for you. If I had continued to sleep, you would have slept also. Tell me, were you a good student in Heidelberg? A regular Hegel! Drowned in plenty of German Romanticism. I remember something, then. So tell me, how did it happen that I went off to become a clown and abandoned you? Jenny will come soon. She'll ask for something. To the dog I cannot go, or maybe I should? But not now. Let him wait. The monster! I bark at him like a regular Rex, he barks back like a Jew. There is nothing funnier than a barking Jew. Hegel would have made a dialectical issue out of it. Outside, rain is falling. Over the desert. Pouring. Rain striking the desert is a beautiful sight. Apparently I've been sick for many days. Maybe a week, maybe a month. It's winter already. The sun is missing, obviously it's gone blind. The white mountains drink the rain. The wadis will burst their banks and perhaps sweep a truck or two along with them. Jenny's ass is also a mountain, a range of cheeks, waiting for the first rain of the season. I am healthy, strong, I want to live. And I am the first rain of the season. If only for a while. When I am through, I will die. Herbert, you are free. Liberated. To you I wouldn't have brought coins in a rubber prophylactic, I'll tell you what I would have brought you: you, I guess, I would have brought a fart in a rubber condom.

Let's add up the score between Adam Stein and the monster: 0 to 0. Nothing has happened. He bit me, I barked at him. Stalemate. So you're up, Adam, on your feet. Now get dressed. What should you wear? Gray pants. A knitted brown shirt *à la* Von Hamdung—*Heil, mein Führer!* Moccasins, a sweater. Brush your hair. Jenny isn't around. Long live the absence of my Jenny. Tonight I must . . . no doubt about that . . . why didn't you take . . . ah, it's a complicated business. She'll want to get married, and marriage to a corpse poses some sticky physical problems. Like: who's going to pay for the tombstone? Should it be in the shape of a rubber condom or a dog? I'm coming, Mr. Monster.

The dog is sprawled in his corner. The window is shut. The door opens easily. Yes, the dog is sprawled in his corner. The state of neglect here is appalling. As it always was. Adam opens the window. The stench remains unchanged. He stumbles over the tin plate, which makes a racket. The dog growls, but doesn't bark. Adam sits on the couch. Watches the sheet. From the hole in the sheet, the eyes peer. Adam puts his hand in his pocket, a chance gesture, and he feels an object. What is it? He pulls the item out of his pocket. A small transistor radio. A very powerful Japanese transistor radio. How did I get it? Apparently I bought it once and forgot about it. In Berlin? Somewhere along my travels in the world. Attached to the leather case are a small screwdriver and a tiny sack containing two spare batteries. The dog is no longer growling. Adam examines the thing and, all of a sudden, removes the screwdriver, places the two batteries on his lap, opens the radio, and proceeds to dismantle it. The dog watches, amazed. Minuscule parts. Coils. Blue batteries with red letters on them. If a monster sees a transistor radio, a monster will eat a transistor radio. The monster will then play music with its belly, and I'll control the buttons. Switch the current. Automatically. I have my own monster that plays music right from his stomach. Just press this button and you'll hear Schubert.

Adam has finished tinkering with the radio and now reassembles it. The Yarkon Bridge Trio is through singing "The Construction Workers' Love Song" and at once you hear the calm, deep voice of the announcer: "The Prime Minister and the Minister of Defense made a tour today somewhere in the south and saw exercises of the armored division. . . ." And out of the rumble of chains and the shouting of commands which merged in the terrible heat of the wind blowing down there, however far away or nearby, comes the voice of the Prime Minister addressing the dog and Adam through the small Japanese cockroach that shines in the flimsy light of the cloudy winter day. " . . . I am happy to be here . . . among members of the armored corps who have been models in their work . . . I thank the commander of the armored forces and his team of officers. . . . We will purchase . . . develop . . . assemble . . . exploit our technical know-how, expand it, strengthen it . . . and we will win."

This victory, this future victory of the commander of the armored forces with all his tanks, what meaning does it have in this small stinking room?

The dog didn't nod his head; consequently Adam, ashamed, left. But soon he is back. This time he has not only the transistor radio with him. This time he has brought along his electric shaver.

The room is silent as ever. As smelly as ever. And the monster is sitting there in the window, against the background of the white mountains of Judah, against the sere winter sky. Adam takes out his electric shaver. Looks for a wall socket, finds one, inserts the plug, and begins to shave. In front of the monster.

Let it see. And under the sheet, it actually is peeking. Its back goes up and down. Maybe it is excited? My good dog. My Rex, look, Daddy is shaving . . . and what is Daddy shaving? Daddy is shaving a shaved face! The mad whirl of the machine shakes his hand and he sinks into a sweet lethargy that muffles any reactions, that caresses and makes no demands, that soothes the mind, and . . . Look, look, look, look, Mr. Stein, Mr. Stein, look! Mr. Stein looks. Through his sheath of slumber, his sheath of exhaustion, he sees how the dog is nodding his head under the sheet: up down, down up.

"I've come from outer space," he says and yanks the plug of the electric shaver out of the wall socket. "Also, my name is not Father Abraham." He puts the shaver in its case. "I am comfortable." He gets bolder. "Dog! Monster! Don't be glad that I'm here. I'm sick, no less than you. So don't be so glad."

And this time—no, no, I don't want it, I'm afraid. Dog, stay underneath. Don't do it. Don't reveal yourself. Don't cause mayhem. Remain mysterious, unknown, odd. No! Oh, no! The dog casts the sheet off his head (it's that electric shaver's fault, I'll smash it!) and shrinks into a corner. Shivering. Then Adam realizes that all along he knew what he now knows. That's how they all looked, just like that, with those sunken bleary dog-like frightened eyes, those sunken cheeks, that thin tubercular body, those dark rings around those pure innocent virgin eyes, and that nose narrow and trembling. Despair in their nostrils. An animal in a trap. Children stepping into the final solution. With the eyes that the God of Israel has set aside for the children of his nation, in order, perhaps, to slander himself. But these are not those eyes, these are Junker eyes, blue. With hair that hasn't been to a barber in many months, maybe even years. Yes, he knows the answer. A child, a dog; a dog, a child. A child that is not a child, and a dog that is not a dog. Yes, the way his mouth secretly shivers points already to a premature maturity, an appalling old age, a stubble field on the face of an infant. The mouth crumpled, the expression wrenched. Large flowers.

Klein's flower gardens. The flowers that Fräulein Klopfer looked
after with such devotion. By the fence. A gigantic tree for shade.
A chinaberry tree. Flowers grew along the fence in the shade of
the chinaberry tree. These flowers had a unique sense of humor,
like their creator. They flourished because he gave them permission. Here Adam is reminded of the flowers. Because of those
eyes flourishing under the sheet like blue flowers. Because of
that face with its barking mouth. That innocence frozen into two
blue pools, that ugliness which suddenly turns beautiful, the
wakening into bright light, into contact, in the presence of Adam
Stein, who is nothing but a cadaver on a vacation.

A tear forms in his eye. A tear of disappointment. A hunted
animal is staring at Adam. A dog. A child that is an animal.
Something frightfully ugly, yet beautifully ugly. And he, he knows
neither what to give, nor what to say, nor how to rescue. For he
himself is seeking a savior.

Adam gapes at the child. How old is he? Twelve? Twenty?
The dog dumbfounds him. The feeling of compassion which for
a moment surged in him gives way to envy. Envy of the young
boy, the child, the monster, who has managed to outwit the
world, Adam, Jenny, Dr. Gross. Adam whispers to him:
"Thanks!" Yes. Then the tone of his voice shifts and anger
bursts through the slit of his clenched teeth. He shoots out his
words with the staccato rhythm of thunder: "Listen, dog, don't
dare depend on me. Don't rely on me. Understand who I am. I
am a broken reed. I will snap before your eyes and you will fall
down. Stumble. Smash your teeth. Lose your dog features and
be miserable. Like a saint. A pit of terror. Everything is a lie.
The radio, the batteries. There was no need to change the batteries, the batteries were good. And as for shaving, I'd already
shaved before I visited you. It was a lie. All lies. I was escaping
from outer space. I had plastic antennae. With a color TV in my
kidneys. I had taped the conversations between my navel and
my ass. And in addition to everything else, I am God. Weary
God."

The dog swerves his watery azure Aryan eyes toward Adam. The dog quakes. The poor dog perspires, despite the air-conditioning. With a horrible kind of humiliation, the dog crawls back to his sheet. A cheated savage. He seizes the sheet in his fingers, his claws, crumples one end, inserts it in his mouth and sucks on it. And, as though the act has granted him a certain momentary fragile security, he crawls over to the couch—with the end of the sheet still in his mouth—reaches out for the radio and is about to pet it. Then, the moment his hand touches the side of the black radio, his body stops trembling. Adam stares at the sudden silence.

"Did they torture you?" He must know this.

The dog doesn't reply. The dog isn't even listening. It isn't just his fingers that are patting now the quivering rough leather side of the radio; his whole being, his entire twisted body from azure eyes to feet, is concentrated in those fingers, partners in the act of petting. Then, unexpectedly, Adam shudders wtih the memory of the delicate fingers of the pension landlady.

"I strangled an old woman!" he says and blurts into laughter. "I'm writing a study of this hospital. They don't fool me, the doctors are scared of me. I have connections."

The dog keeps sucking the sheet and patting the radio.

"Listen, child. If I ask you a question which you want to answer but are unable to because you cannot speak, nod your head. If yes, down and up. If no, right and left."

The dog, his whole existence centered on the radio, answers nothing. That is, at first he answers nothing. Then something stirs him—as though some invisible ray of light has penetrated and danced into his brain—and his head starts to shift, first right and left and then, reversing its meaning and direction, the movement abandons the subconscious depths of negation and becomes a nod going up and down.

"They tortured you?"

To the right and to the left. Hands caressing. Eyes gaping at the knobs, at the buckle, at the numbers on the dial.

"You're a diplomat, child. You lie, but nobody lies to Adam Stein! Tell me, when they brought you here, did you pass through the big iron gate?"

Up and down goes the dog's head.

Now Adam is eager, excited. "And was the gate suspended over you like a disaster? Sealed from the other side? And you were inside, jailed? In jail, in jail. In the refined synthetic sanctuary of Mrs. Seizling, who is being refrigerated. Afterward you walked through endlessly long corridors where idiotic music, hidden melodies, emanated from the walls as though the world were blind. And sick. Did you notice? The doors, hundreds of them, had no handles. Hundreds of missing handles and little windows. And did you notice the black carpets? Going from hall to hall, through the phosphorescent light? And *you* never tried to choke an old woman! Who had the right to treat you so evilly? Who? The man who was guiding you, Shapiro? Or that bastard Gross? When Shapiro dragged you along, was he carrying a big bunch of keys? They rattled. I recognize the ring. And you were miserable in the corridors. With the keys playing a march for you, and that bastard opening door after door. You kept passing through halls, corridors, doors . . ."

The child lifts, then lowers his eyes. Then raises his head again, his expression showing shame, amazement, incomprehension. His head swings right and left. But Adam is no longer watching him. Adam hates himself. He suffers. He is jealous.

"Look!" His voice is now almost a scream. His stomach aches. The light in the window terrifies him. He gets up and slams the shutter. The dog cowers in a corner. The dog senses a betrayal. Adam stands opposite him, old and wrinkled. He looks his age again, without any trimmings. His forehead is like a plowed field, with sweat pouring down the grooves. "Look, child." He extends his arms as if he wanted to embrace the entire room. In the window sits Herbert, and Herbert says: "What are you doing, my baby? Are you showing off in front of a dog? You're a sick man and a liar. You'd sell your mother for a worn-out penny!"

"Child!" Adam chases away the image mocking him from the windowsill. "One day I'm going to bring you the keys. That cold fish Gross, I'll thread the keys through his nostrils. Talking about love—what does he know about love? How dare he ask me why he has failed with me! He's as dry as old paper. I'm going to bring you the keys."

Adam now approaches him, grabs him by an arm, by a leg. The dog tries to bite Adam's trembling hand. "You hear me, you little tag, you?" The dog is unable to bite; Adam notices this and giggles for a moment. "Be a man, march through the corridors with the keys in your hand and open door after door. From your room to the gate. A hundred doors. A hundred keys. And finally, on the other side of the last gate, you'll be left with one key in your hand. You'll be free in the desert. Away from everything. Broken through to the other side, the safe side. And you'll take that final key and cast it over the house, over this synthetic sanctuary, and everything will go up in white smoke."

Laughs Herbert: "See how you've let him down!"

"I know." Adam tries to add something. His voice is hoarse, exhausted, sad.

"What have you done to him? Fool, you've deceived him. He smells the deception."

And the child crawls away, hopeless, sad-eyed. He nears the wall and howls. Wriggling toward the chain and wailing. At the sight of the sobbing dog, Adam has a fit of uncontrollable laughter. Adam panics. He gathers up his belongings. Bolts from the room. The door slams. The dog creeps under the sheet, wraps himself in it, and starts barking. The sound of this barking accompanies Adam as he rushes down the corridor. Adam stops to swig a few mouthfuls from his secret bottle. But that doesn't help him very much. His head aches, his stomach aches, his body burns. He is haunted by that barking. He can no longer laugh. And no longer cry.

Something is going to happen this morning. The stench of the future is in the air. Adam pities history, for it must always prove and justify the existence of the present, thinks Adam in his great agony. It's been a few days since he came back from the battle-field, from the bad defeat. The doctors again looked after him. Said there was no hope, shrugged their shoulders, realized he was dying. Instead, he recovered. As always. For the time being. However, in a short while he will plug up his body and die properly for them, those half-asses, in their very arms. How does a person become a clown, a madman, and a dog? How? Mother wasn't. Mother was a woman. With two flashing brown eyes, silver hair. Thin body. Father was a baker. But Grandfather— Grandfather, when I knew him, used to travel in a carriage. As the man in charge of orchards. Strawberry beds. Pear orchards. Apple orchards. He would sleep under the canopy of heaven. A Hassid was he, who ate just fruits and bread, except on Friday night, when he would return home and have his only hot meal of the week. As a young man he came to Israel. Here he married the virgin Hiah Rosen and took her back with him to Poland. So in our veins flows the land of Israel. My grandmother was born in Jerusalem. And me, I was born in the lap of Commandant Klein and shall die in the lap of Commandant Klein, and in the meantime, ho!—in the meantime, I will sell paper bridges with forged deeds. Bridges in the sky, on the moon. And everybody will purchase one. A faker always wins. Truth-tellers die young. Jenny will be here soon. This time I am ready for her. Am I in love? Old Adam is not in love. He loves an idea he once had whose realization would have been the crowning glory of a full life—in other words, to grow old like his grandfather or his fa-ther. It was a nice idea. But the necessity had arisen to kill both the idea and the person who had the idea. Bang, bang. Child, don't shoot. I'm a hero. *Herr Reichsführer* Stolz! Hats off to him. With his hands he yanked out gold teeth. If a piece of soap shoots at Adam, Adam shoots back at the soap. If a dog eats Adam, Adam eats the dog too.

The moment she comes, he changes the expression on his face, putting on the look of embarrassed dejection which she

adores. There is no need for any great effort. She softens immediately. The landlady of the pension was softer but less trusting.
This one, this Jenny, to the entire world she pretends to be
tough. That obviously helps her digestion, thinks he. Poor thing,
she suffers from indigestion. He knows enough to tell her that
the landlady of the pension gave him no happiness. And she
smiles. He tells her he spent some time with the dog. To this she
has no answer.

"Why is he here, Jenny? You know that he's a child? You
think he's a child? He's a dog! I'll tell you something funny. Mrs.
Elsa Klein once came with her son Hans Klein to visit Commandant Klein. That was a happy day in my life. The cook diligently
prepared delicacies in honor of the distinguished guests—roast
goose—and we, Rex and me, ate our fill. They all sat at the table,
we at their feet. The boy didn't laugh at the sight of me. I was
stooped over the dish at the foot of the table, eating away. He
gave me a somewhat puzzled look. His father told him that he
ought to laugh, but he refused to laugh. Elsa, on the contrary,
was laughing without anybody telling her that she ought to
laugh. She remembered that she had once seen me in the circus
and had laughed then, at the circus, so very hard that she—if I
may excuse her expression and Hans not consider it a breach of
manners—pissed in her panties. With me on all fours next to
Rex, she naturally was reminded of what had happened earlier. I
wanted to tell her that at that time I wasn't a dog. But that she
was one, that Klein was, that Hans was. But I didn't say anything, I smiled. I was bent over. Cramped on all fours. I wanted
to bark, so I barked. The bark cheered her up enormously. She
cried from laughing so much, and dried her eyes with a handkerchief that you could have wrung out afterward and filled up a
glass—all because she once saw me at the circus and broke up
laughing.

"But Rex is a thoroughbred, I said, with Hans in mind. I
didn't want his education to lack anything, to be spoiled. And, in
truth, the lady showered me with a look of gratitude. *Thank you*

was written in her eyes. She threw me another bone. With my teeth I tore off the bit of cartilage and the two fibers of meat that were left on the bone, and swallowed them. Rex, jealous, wagged his tail. But the woman wouldn't pay him any attention. The bone, I recall, was stamped with the imprint of her lipstick. Even that I licked. When Commandant Klein left for a moment to receive the daily report from the officer who was waiting impatiently for him in an adjoining room, I rejoiced and lay my head in her lap. Hans was startled, shocked, frightened. I pitied him. I could have stood up, but didn't. I wanted to grant her total satisfaction. She came by train. She had traveled forty hours from Cologne. She wanted to enjoy herself. I knew it as soon as I saw her face. She was starving for a little pleasure. She actually fondled my hair and I rolled myself up at her feet and moaned. Later on we sat in Klein's room and listened to a record of Mozart's Requiem. She wept from excess joy and sadness. We drank superb Italian port. The air outside was foul. It was summer then and the odor was unbearable. The smoke spread across the camp, but didn't leave it. Even so, the Requiem was lovely. During the night Klein was called for. They came to tell him that a new transport had arrived. He cursed and scolded, but went. The trouble, as I tried to explain to her so she wouldn't be hurt, was that sometimes the tracks had to be used for military trains carrying soldiers and arms to the east, so the transport trains were delayed and, therefore, you see, in the middle of the night . . .

"In the middle of the night I came near her bed. Klein, who had been back for some time, was snoring in a corner of the bed. She was sad, so sad. I sat at the foot of the bed and she patted my head, rubbed my scalp, and her tears dropped onto me. She whispered to me that she could no longer take it. She wanted to laugh, but here it was sad, sad, sad, and the stench . . . I calmed her. Climbed into bed and lay at her side. She had a full body, overflowing. Klein was snoring. 'Port always puts him to sleep,' she said, 'my poor darling, he works too hard.' Then she

made love to the *dog* and was able to laugh again. She had slept
with the *dog* because she had wanted to laugh. That was in '44.
'So little humor is left in Germany,' she said. She was laughing,
Klein was snoring. I was the first *dog* in her life, as she told me. I
aroused pleasant and somewhat plaintive associations in her.
She'd once had a dog of her own who was poisoned—it was a
sad story, but I've forgotten the details—so it was a relief to her.
The night was hot, the stench horrible. I was used to it, she
wasn't."

Jenny loves listening. Adam knows that Jenny is attentive.
Not just enjoyment flashes from her eyes, something deeper than
that. Jenny feels guilty. Though born in Israel, she experiences a
supreme sense of guilt whenever she hears stories of this sort.
Because she wasn't there. If she had been, everything would certainly have been different. Ruth too thought that if she had been
with her father . . . It's an outstanding female trait, apparently. A woman always thinks that her presence would have
constituted a rescue. An influence. A lesson. For that reason, all
those who have tried to reform the world have slept with
women.

Adam stares at her and draws out her gaze like an experienced fisherman. He approaches Jenny, who has shrunk into a
corner on account of the story. He kisses her brow, her hair. She
is in good spirits now. He kisses her lips, unstitches her mouth.
She swims backward, her hands supporting her body while it
almost stumbles as it moves. Her mouth is wide open.

"Adam, what are you doing?"

"I'm licking your teeth."

"Ah, so that's what you're doing!" Her voice is festive, a hint
of childish mischief plays in it. "Listen, sweetheart, wait here a
moment, I'll be right back." And she nearly runs out. A certain
strange and perhaps sinful warmth is choking her. The dog
kicks, the dog bites, and the night is lovable, my good child.
God, it was so nice of you to create me. Adam smiles and awaits
her return.

When she is back, he closes the window and sits naked on his bed. She loves looking at his body. "You certified nest of lice!" he told her once. She didn't know what he was hinting at, and he never clarified it. She takes off her uniform and sits beside him. From a drawer she takes a black comb. In the pale light coming from the window she starts to comb his hair. The two of them are silent next to each other. Jenny and Adam. Herbert is sitting, as usual, in the window. The combing gives Herbert the idea that people who become addicted to a familiar routine are bound not to accept their fate. But nobody minds what Herbert may think. Not today. Not now. Go away, go, you bore me, mutters Adam. Herbert laughs. Inaudibly. Jenny hasn't seen him at all. The two of them, Adam and Jenny, are silent. She combs his hair, he watches her. They look like robots, or perhaps angels.

Jenny finishes. She returns the comb to the bureau and, with a delicate gesture, closes the drawer and faces Adam. He extends his damp narrow silken hands, fills his palms with her firm breasts, and brings them close to him. Behind Herbert, beyond the pale window, rages the last of the rain, the sand, the lightning, and the wind. Black clouds rush westward, swooping one on top of another like beasts of prey, merging into a gigantic black creation, wrapping in a heavy shadow the white mountains and the dark wadis. A ray of sunlight, penetrating the clouds, illuminates the fierce downpour of rain like an artificial searchlight. Adam drops to his knees opposite her—*the routine, still the routine!* screams Herbert—and kisses her nipples. She barely feels the touch of his lips. He half contacts, half hovers. A shudder passes up her spine and she watches lethargically, with plaintive joy, the progress of his sex towards her. His hands release her breasts and slip along her backside; then he joins her to him and with joy she takes his sex in her hand, the crux of his life, and kisses him, crying. The tears drop on his sex, and he is impressed again, all over again, as if it were for the first time. And that is a stroke of magic more amazing than the thrust of love. The tears dissolve his years. That's how he feels. And when he realizes that, after all, he is only a bold youth about to stir and conquer and storm the world, he pulls Jenny into bed and makes love to her. Violently, the way she wants. In an insane pace, pulling her hair, beating her body. That's her nature. And that's what he'll become for her sake. He always knew how to adjust himself like a chameleon. From Heidelberg on, it was the law of his life. A man's a man, he'd whisper to himself with the satisfaction of a boy sowing his wild oats. And the moment of ecstasy will obliterate all dread and turmoil from her heart. She will have peace. From the reservoirs of violent passion, peace will come dragging into her.

Adam, Adam Stein, the man of quick transitions, the acrobat, the sorcerer of leaps, that man she knows. Yes or no? Tomorrow or yesterday? To slumber or wake, die or live, turn left or right? From one extreme to another. Herbert's Heidelberg professor stood in the railroad station when Herbert was taken to Auchhausen. Imagine that, Jenny! He looked at me. I remember how he removed his glasses, wiped them, and smiled at me. The platform was bustling with sub-humanity on its way to extermination. And he was smiling. He had a good smile. Bright, cultured. Afterward he put his glasses back on and nodded. Through his eyes I saw sub-mankind. This man, in his day, advanced European liberalism with his brilliant and beautiful articles, was a prolific contributor to the journals. Later on, when I returned to Germany, I found in a lavatory in Hamburg a bundle of papers and among them were pages from his latest book (the one just before *Democracy as Human Conformity and Social Obedience in an Era of Rosy Hopes Which Can No Longer Go Unrealized, Munich,* 1951) and in the chapter dealing with sub-humanity I discovered a perfect description of myself, with all my symptoms: nervousness and excessive cleverness, a talent for business, lack of self-respect, impure blood, membership in secret international organizations, group guilt, ambition to dominate, hatred of Northern races, physical inferi-

ority, spiritual blemishes, terrible indigestion. Blood which carries eighteen infectious diseases liable to exterminate an entire
population in a relatively brief period. In short, if you take a
single Adam Stein and place him beside a well of water in a
forest, among trees, upon pure beautiful soil that has no bound-
aries, that stretches endlessly on its own power, stretching with
the knowledge that it bears good tidings in its blood, and you let
that Adam Stein sit down by that well from which Aryan cows
suckle and Aryan potatoes and other Aryan vegetables are irri-
gated—all Aryan means of existence will be polluted! A sub-
human has only one job, purpose, function: to facilitate his own
death. There's also an ironic side to this business. You take a
filthy animal like a pig and make fat out of him, and from the
fat, soap, and with the soap you wash the biggest pig of all, the
pig of pigs, who is creation's glory. Whereas, on the other hand,
you take a sub-human, melt down the gold in his teeth—which
is worth, according to statistics, 0.05 German marks on the average—expropriate his clothes (that's another fifty pennies)—
and then the bone marrow? With that dirty tainted murky
Jewish marrow you manufacture soap; stir in some lavender and
you've got scented soap. "With blood, sweat, and tears . . ."
    But why ponder these things? It's a dead issue. Gone. The
world is new. Jenny has marvelous breasts. There is no more
soap in Auchhausen. In Auchhausen there is a museum and,
next to it, a German military camp. This time we will beat the
Communists and save the world. Adam is a man of instant
transformations: from soap to distinguished citizen, from distinguished citizen to a strangler of an old woman, to a dog, to a
rapist. From the genius of the circus to a swindler, from swindler
to a madman in love, from a madman to the person who would
bring Mr. Weiss his weekly portion of coins in a rubber condom.
From a Heidelberg aesthete (Herbert!) to a dog in a cemetery.
From lying in bed with Jenny to standing in the middle of the
room. Hup! There he is. On his feet. Humming a merry tune.
And Jenny, that bargain, who knows the heart of her pig, is also

on her feet. She's not hung up on illusions of love, on hints of love, on the quaffing of images that have no end. The ceremony of love is over. Next comes a different ceremony and discipline. Clothes on. Yes, madam; no, sir. *Jawohl,* Fräulein Sub-human!

"You're sub-human yourself."

"You have the body of a sub-human."

"You're skinny and your skin is like an old man's."

"I *am* an old man."

"That's very good."

"You're lying."

And the two of them laugh and continue dressing.

"Listen, Jenny, nobody has the right to be more than me. Not you, not the dog."

"More what?" She gropes in the dark, feeling her way, then stretches her nylons over her legs, one foot raised and placed on the bed. It's a lovely leg and a single ray of light is dancing on her knee.

"Crazy! He's crazier than me."

"You're not crazy, you're sick."

"I'm crazy, you're sick. That dog is superior to me. You understand? No. He succeeded where I failed. I'll break him in two."

"Adam, I think I have the right to say that—"

"You've said it a hundred times."

"What?" She tries to smile.

"That you love me."

"How did you know what I was going to say?"

"I read you, child. So cut out the nonsense now. You love old man Adam Stein? Why? God has all the answers. I'm somebody else, I'm Rex Wolfgang Adameus Stein, or Pure Adam, or Pure Pig, or Mr. Sub-human, or a man with an empty conscience, or somebody half-dead half-alive, or, at most, God's agent in the middle of the Negev."

"Adam, don't. It's important that you know, that you know it, really know it. I actually . . . and it makes no difference why

. . . but I do. Really. And I always will. Always. With my whole heart."

"You're a whore and I use you. And you'd do anything for me, and I can get rid of you the way I'd get rid of a fly."

"You're cruel."

"If only I were. I need a drink. I'm thirsty. My body's exhausted. You drained me. The pension landlady was a quiet type. Fucking her was like fucking butter. Fucking you is like fucking a motorcycle."

"Adam!" She tries to be angry, offended, insulted, but bursts out laughing.

"That's what saves everything. A sense of humor. Commandant Klein was smart enough to know that. You can weed out more sub-humans in a day through a combination of Zyklon-B and humor than with just Zyklon-B alone."

Suddenly he seizes her in his arms and fixes his gaze on the observation window in the door. He shakes her and keeps facing the door. She waits. He stares at the door. She understands. Smiles. He understands that she understands, and also smiles.

"Forgive me, Jenny. Go now, now go. I must—why? I don't know—be alone. With my thoughts, with Herbert, with the dog."

"I'm going. Yes, I'm going. What was her name?"

"Whose name?"

"The one you tried to choke."

"Ruth."

"Like your daughter."

"Yes, like my daughter, like Dr. Gross's stepmother."

"Goodbye, Adam."

"See you."

In the corridor, amid the music of "If you love me the way I love you," she thinks that it would be worthwhile and necessary —if she only had the chance—to seize the day by the horns, as they say. I must escape. Where to? I must save myself. I must— if only it were worthwhile—I absolutely must rescue the honor of love. He should behave like a man, stop trampling on me.

Yet, on the other hand, it's fun. And never boring. And in the situation of love there's no place for any talk of honor. Is anything less honorable than love? Therefore she flees for her life. *Goodbye, Jenny.* She knows what he's whispering to himself as he locks the door after her. Evening has fallen. Today he won't eat, he won't go to the dining hall. Won't allow the nurses to feed him. He rummages through his suitcases and from one of them digs up a huge old doll, a dog with ears askew, one eye out, and its mouth ripped. He's ashamed to admit that he found this dog in Baron Von Hamdung's house and brought it along with him as a gift for Ruth. When he packed the dog he had forgotten that Ruth had left him when she was a baby and now was a woman. However, he had never unpacked it. The landlady Ruthie refused to accept any "symbols," so he hadn't ever taken the doll out of the suitcase. Now he places the dog on a chair, grabs his guitar, tunes it, seats himself on his bed of prostitution, and plays for the dog. He plays the Kreutzer Sonata and the Andante from Bach's Second Violin Concerto. His eyes are elated. Outside, beyond the window, the sand is wildly spinning. The sky is dark. Rain gushes upon the desert. Adam drowses. The glass eye of the dog watches the storm.

All of a sudden lightning hits the house. Darkness prevails. And the silence after the thunder sounds like the terrified barking of a dog locked in a room. Adam is dreaming that the doll is barking. He's glad that the doll is barking. In his dream he is standing by a lake out of which escapes a smothered whine. In his dream he realizes the weird fact that the dog's bark emerging from the lake duplicates the doll's bark, and the barks cross each other until they superimpose as one. The barking in the dream somehow reminds him of a howling child. A child standing by the railroad station. Father and Mother took the train. Herbert's professor, the one whose book I found in the Hamburg men's room, wipes his glasses with a perfectly clean handkerchief and reflects on sub-humanity.

The child cries, howls. Doesn't bark. Plain *ei-ei-ei-ei*. Yet the Professor is frightened. The howl of a sub-human child can muddy any mood. He hurries home. His wife has prepared Viennese Schnitzel *à la* Holstein with the best anchovies from liberated thousand-year-Reich Poland.

THE GREAT ARSONIST

ARTHUR FINE is wearing his parade outfit with the gray army hat. Is it German? Polish? Or maybe it's a sergeant's uniform in the underground Eskimo army that's fighting against the ice-cream industry? Impossible to know. He steps firmly, head up, eyes forward. With a stupendous effort, he flattens out the lines of his brow. In his hand he holds his toy trumpet, which is attached to his neck by a golden cord. The bugle's blasts of joy smother for the moment—and perhaps it's just as well—the unceasing buzz of music.

Arthur is dressed in army parade uniform because he is scared. Whenever he is choked and shaken by dreadful fears, he transforms himself into the soldier on parade, blowing his bugle and wearing his peculiar costume. Today Arthur has been thinking about Mrs. Seizling. About her frozen body. Frozen like a fish in a Cleveland morgue. In his mind's eye he saw her eyes that

were nothing but ice cubes, though they were staring wide open.
He asked for a glass of whiskey on the rocks and somebody put
Mrs. Seizling's eye or her navel or her Adam's apple in his drink.
The sight pained him. He is afraid of death, of the inevitable
nothingness. He wants to live forever. That was why he played
God for a long while and the therapist Dr. Jacobi yelled at him.
The bugle is telling the story now and any attentive ear with the
slightest good will, with the slightest heart, can make it out
clearly. Who has a heart here? The frozen heart of Madam Seizling was a heart! Dr. Jacobi yelled at him: "You're not God. Get
down on your knees!" Three male nurses then seized him and
forced him to bend his knees. And that bastard Dr. Jacobi proclaimed: "You are not God! I am God."

Many days have passed since Dr. Jacobi forced him to bow
down, yet the vision of Mrs. Seizling's corpse still fouls his
mood. "I won't die," blasts the children's bugle in the synthetic
corridor. "I won't die. I'll live. Even though I'm not God, I
won't die. Whoever isn't dead won't die. Whoever is dead will
die. The dead die forever. The living can go on living. You have
to be willing, it's worth a try. There's hope, if only a dark horse.
I know what's what. It's a cheap bugle I'm blowing. For children. It was bought on Allenby Street in Tel Aviv for the absurdly
low price of forty cents. And who bought it for me? Adam Stein
bought it for me. So Miles and he would have someone else to
play with. A trio. They wanted a trio. That old bastard. That
swindler . . ."

Through the high windows in the corridor a bright lovely day
gazes at him. Above the Institute for Rehabilitation and Therapy hangs a clear azure sky. The air is somewhat sour. A cool
east wind is blowing now from the desert.

Arthur Fine releases the trumpet, which hangs across his
chest on a gold cord, and halts in front of the door to Room 26.
Arthur tries to make up his mind. His face registers worry. He
knows very well that he doesn't have to enter; it's up to him. He
knows that he ought to control himself, to tell himself a few

encouraging words and return to his room. To rest. To escape. I'm an adult. But amid the beatings of his mind, his hand somehow, on its own, rises and clings to the door and he is suddenly inside. In Room 26. In the Tabernacle, which is the compromise room where, at set times, Jenny gives her occupational-therapy classes, but today she isn't. Today Adam Stein is teaching. His lesson! His course! That impostor. What does he know? The philosophy of clowning. But political science? And with a salary. You pay. He pays. She pays. And I pay.

From the doorway Arthur sees Adam facing thirty people seated at fifteen small tables. He counts them. Thirty. All the people—among them Miles, Wolfovitz the Circumciser, the Schwester sisters, Handsome Rube, Naomi Davidovitz, Mrs. Tamir, and the Melancholic Kid are gazing at a little platform on which Adam is sitting by a square wooden table painted black and covered with an embroidered yellow tablecloth. On the table are a full bottle of whiskey and a glass. Behind it is a blackboard. A guitar is hanging from the back of his chair. On the blackboard is written in white chalk:

Acting and drama group. History of the theatre from the 18th century to the present. Classification of European and American styles of acting. Chinese and Japanese theatre. Children's theatre and puppet theatre.

ADAM STEIN
Dramaturge

Adam Stein the dramaturge is now taking a long swallow from the glass in front of him and thirty people sit waiting for dramaturgy. "The obliteration of sub-humanity is a zoological dramaturgy," he says. "Sub-humans act best on fire. Theatre is a cult, and in a cult the person who offers a sacrifice gets louder applause than the person who is offered as a sacrifice. The butcher merits the praise, not the butchered." Arthur's eye wanders from Adam to the audience and back again to Adam, jumping like a yo-yo. He knows that his head is jumping like a yo-yo. And that his uniform will be laughed at.

Adam invites him in: "Come in, Arthur, maybe you'll manage to learn something." But he doesn't budge, doesn't flinch. A target for everybody present. Ashamed of himself. Confused.

"Sit down already, Arthur." Adam is still polite, courteous.

"Is it really all right, Adam?"

Arthur twitches. Adam senses it. He's hooked a whopper of a fish today. The fishing season has begun nicely this year. . . .

"It's okay—of course it's okay. Now sit down."

"When do I register? Everyone else must have signed up already."

"There's one more place available. You can register now."

The younger Schwester sister gets up from her seat and comes over to him. In the meantime he sits down at the table and his eyes gape at the blackboard. She stands above him, pulls a notebook and pencil from her pocket, straightens her back.

"Your name?"

"What, you don't know, Schwester?"

Looks of contempt, looks of disgust. Adam overcomes effortlessly, quietly, the general ill-will.

"We maintain a certain procedure here, Master Arthur. What is your name?"

"You said it yourself."

Everybody bursts out laughing. Like a bunch of wild children. Their eyes almost shout for joy and swerve toward Arthur. The orchestra has cracked up with laughter. Laughter. Laughter. His head rumbles. He regrets having said what he did.

"I said what?" butts in the Schwester twin, and she gives Adam a knowing smile as Adam nods in understanding, in fondness, in an expression of boundless trust.

Arthur insists. He is sorry, but it is impossible for him not to be stubborn, just as it was impossible for him not to enter. "You yourself, Schwester, said, 'Arthur, what's your name?' That's just what you said."

"Right. So now, what's your name?"

"Arthur!" His voice is shattered. What is left for him to do?

"Arthur what?" She won't leave him alone.

"Fine."

"Ah, Arthur Fine." She registers his name as slowly as possible. The seconds drag. Adam drinks whiskey. The others watch in silence. Arthur has a lasso of contempt around him. Where can he go? Where can he escape?

"My name is Arthur Fine. In charge of ocean transport. An officer, the rank of colonel."

"I know."

"So," booms Adam's voice, "now everything's been cleared up. And clarity is a good thing. For what we are actually trying to do is place the world in a corner so we can survey it clearly, with greater seriousness, and be able to recognize and understand its foundations and consequently our own. All of us here are undefined, whether we're watchmakers, goldsmiths, soldiers, or idiots. But ants and beetles don't see any differences among us. In their eyes, we are all—including watchmakers and goldsmiths —members of the trampling nation, as much as Albert Schweitzer and the Pope are members. Yes, as far as the ants are concerned, these men are also just tramplers. Right. . . . Theatre is an unrespected institution. Adults dress up as if they were children and pretend. Theatre, as everybody knows, is the outcome of a storm in which we sometimes have to cast the ship into the sea in order to save the cargo. Theatre isn't just an act. If it were, the audience would perform and the actors watch. But, on the other hand, acting is theatre. So now we reach the realization, which makes almost no sense, that in the theatre there are not two sides to a coin, because no side can match or contradict the other side. It may be that in order to arrive at the truth one must lie, yet it is impossible to arrive at a lie by telling the truth. And if it is possible, then woe to that truth. Now let's establish some laws. Good acting is a good thing. There's no disputing that. The problem before the researcher is: the conceptualization of dramatic discipline whose nature constitutes, in the most complete manner, the basic support and center of staged events—through an irrational system of ethics or a supra-psychological multi-dimensional effort—namely, the absolute reversal of daily existence as it expresses itself in the street, in the coffeehouse, in place after place, so as to dislodge the stage itself and let it become valuable in its own right even without actors acting on it.

"A dog barks. But a dog barking on a stage is no longer a dog. And what about the barking? Or, for instance, my drinking? Here, I am raising my hand, bringing the glass to my mouth —am I drinking? I pretend that I'm drinking. You must watch the process and also, simultaneously, close your eyes to it." Adam Stein the dramaturge turns his face aside for the moment. His twin, Herbert Stein, is seated beside the blackboard, legs crossed like a Bedouin, and smiling. "You think you're smart. But you're not. You're ridiculous, not funny. You're a thief, a trickster. You're playing with fire. I'll smash you." Herbert vanishes. Adam looks around for the sneaking figure of his twin and then turns to face his impatient class, who were writing in their notebooks every word he spoke, but now have nothing to do. In the middle of drinking and not drinking. Adam continues: "In order to drink whiskey—*on the stage*—in accordance with the acting style that I call the categorical style, your task is to pay no attention to the words themselves, not to think of 'whis-key,' but to think of that sharp ultra-fine sourishness, that magnificent maddening intoxicating hated-loved essence bubbling in that glass, and contract your spiritual diaphragm—that is, the notion of the diaphragm—and at this point *I,* at least, believe that I am actually drinking. But what benefit do I derive from this? The audience doesn't understand. Nor the critics. Whereas, on the other hand, I can, when I want, actually drink and the audience will think that I am just pretending and not drinking at all. But to drink, to taste the joy of drinking, and at the same time convince the audience that I'm really drinking as part of my

role, the role of someone to whom the director and the playwright assigned the job of drinking, oh, that's a . . . for that
you must . . . that's the point . . ."

The younger Schwester writes everything down. The old
virgin writes in a way that Adam calls powerful, as though she
were engraving in stone. In cuneiform. Courage, my dear! You
don't understand? Me neither. But at least I can formulate
things nicely. She cannot hear my inner thoughts because they
are hidden, and that's how it should be. Miles is also writing.
Adam doubletalks, but charmingly. Arthur pities himself. He is
pondering his very presence here, a presence which was forced
upon him by a second self, by a wild impulse that he cannot
control. He ponders his attraction to Adam, the way he behaves
like a moth in front of a candle that will erase him, exterminate
him, cremate him. He who was destined for great things. The
empty words, the whiskey Adam is gulping, the screech of the
pencils—they all repeat to Arthur, for the hundredth time, for
the thousandth time, the story of his failure, the story of his
collapse, the crux of his worthlessness.

Me me me Arthur (while Adam says: The stage has three
walls, the fourth is the audience) I'm the one who sees them
marching. In black. Black flags. Black hats. Blue eyes. Swasti-
kas. Black shouts across the distance of a thousand years, and
afterward long years in a forest. Dark, mute. What happened? I
do not know. I don't recall a thing. I don't remember, Doctor.
The commander, Mr. Henry Samit, of the Eleventh Division, of
the American liberation forces, he, my master, didn't know what
had happened to me. I simply forgot. A blank blackboard.

It's been four years, three years, I don't know exactly, and I
don't remember a thing. Camps? Isn't a number tattooed on my
arm? Yet I do not remember. Total amnesia. But then came the
relief-lief-lief. And we reached Palestine-tine-tine. The land of
sunshine. The Irgun and the Stern gang were killing the British
in the streets. It was hot. People were strange. Children
screamed at the cinema. They built white houses with flat roofs.

Planted too many trees. Had a symphonic orchestra without sufficient financial backing. Factories going bankrupt. Hens laying enormous eggs. Fatless milk. American butter. They manufacture loads of khaki. Youngsters are throwing hand-grenades on the descendants of William Shakespeare. ("William Shakespeare wasn't William Shakespeare at all," says Adam and they write it down. "He wasn't even Bacon or Marlowe. His plays were machine-made. He willed a bed to his wife.") And they wind up being hanged. And Arthur—Arthur got his first job. Later, when the storm was over. As a government official. Not in the British government. In the Hebrew, the Israeli, government. After a thousand years. In a state that had just established itself on its own feet and proclaimed austerity measures, and its inhabitants were chewing leather belts and eating ration books and cursing the enthusiasm with which they had exchanged their lentil soup for a flag. And all this passed, too. Contributions poured in and they were able to plan programs. Roads were paved. And in the meantime Arthur had a job. At a big table, with a green tablecloth. Behind him hung a portrait of Herzl standing on a bridge watching the water slowly converting itself; his beard was so lovely. On Arthur's big table was a strip of white cardboard: THE IDEA IS NOT RESPONSIBLE, THOSE WHO BELIEVE IN IT ARE.

Adam is now holding on to the system of vague truths. I recognize it from the days when I was a government official. At every single meeting they spoke like that. "Tel Aviv lives with her back to the sea." I know that style. And everybody copies it down. Truth is truth and not its opposite. Good theatre is not good drama. In a comedy we laugh at the ways of life of a citizen. In a tragedy we are shocked by his fate. Jason can be returning from Creon's palace and yet convince us, through his acting, that he has just come back from a folk-dance in Beer-Sheva. A certain actress played Medea as if she were the Bette Davis of a neighborhood of new immigrants from Iraq. Shakespeare for the poor. A good playwright is somebody who writes

a good play. Words, words, words. The world is swarming with
storekeepers who have Ph.D's. And with swindlers like Adam
who are doctors that carry their mark of fakery, their storekeep-
er's trait, with pride.

And me, what did I carry off? A wife. Yes. Why? I was in
love. Adam talks talks talks. And I recall that a daughter was
born to me, a little monkey. And the fact that I succeeded. That
I climbed the ladder of officialdom, as they say. From the
seventh to the second rung. I ascended. There was no end to my
progress. Nobody could stop me. I was in a great hurry. What
did I want to become? A king? A mosquito. A king's mosquito.
The Prime Minister's clerk. The King of the Portfolios alongside
a mosquito. And then, after I had risen from seventh to second
place, I began to hear the voices.

On account of them Arthur locked himself up in his room and
started to burn papers. Burn what? The God of officials knows
all the answers. Because, after all, somewhere, sometime, there
were forests and black shirts and a blocked past: wherein the
blind and the deaf died and were reborn with blue numbers on
their arms. How did it happen? He didn't know. Arthur, the
senior official of the government, simply shut his blinds and his
curtains and sat in his room burning papers. Tons of papers.

Legal documents, political documents, confiscations of property, papers with thirteen copies, the carbon paper itself, folio
paper, quarto paper, newspaper and ordinary paper, thick pa-
per, thin paper. Papers for direct taxes and papers for indirect
taxes. Secret papers and elaborate classified dossiers. Receipts
for gasoline, restaurant receipts, building certificates, land certificates, death certificates, marriage certificates. Travel tickets,
grocery bills, butcher-shop bills, all the documents of his daughters, Hannah's papers from nursery to kindergarten ("worthy of
entering primary school") and Rena's papers from primary
school to second grade ("improving in all subjects, especially
cleanliness, attention, diligence, and conduct"). All these papers
made a nice bonfire. In the middle of the room. The documents

crumpled in a tight fist. And then I wrote—Arthur smiles to himself: Adam has reached Stanislavsky, the rifle suspended above the mantelpiece in the first act must go off in the third— and then I wrote an article. In that article I tried to prove in a completely scientific fashion that it was possible to cremate a man's body without leaving a relic of any sort behind. I wrote the article after I had burned the bookcases, the table, the chairs, after the walls were black from smoke. And when the newspapers refused to publish the article on the grounds that it was unjustly and unambiguously anti-Semitic, Arthur Fine made a personal demonstration against the evening paper whose editor had written him a particularly vulgar rejection. He wore the costume of an old Boy Scout, with a Purim soldier's hat, and even bought a toy drum that he suspended from his neck with a golden cord and beat wildly. And that was how, as he used to tell the various therapists who worked with him over the years, he transformed himself wittingly into the chocolate soldier craving demonstrations and parades. In Prague, his home town, lovely picturesque Prague whose houses and palaces were graven very deeply into the flesh of his memory, in that Prague whose only power was in its smile, its generosity, its culture, superb parades used to take place. Where in the world will you see such ruddy-cheeked soldiers today, marching in such spectacular uniforms? And one day, after he had set fire to all the papers and documents and portraits, to most of his books, his furniture, his wastepaper basket, after he had fumigated and exorcised through fire the demons in all their habitations, he placed his six-year-old daughter on his knee and said: "Answer Father. Yes?" She answered yes and crumpled up his nose. To this day he remembers with a touch of sadness her twisting of his nose, the precise way she used to squeeze it, and the laughter which poured out of her at the sight of his squashed nose, the laughter of ringing bells.

"If I told you that water burns, would you believe me?"

"Of course, Daddy. But water doesn't burn."

"But if I said it did, does it?"

"Of course it does, Daddy."

"And if I told you," he whispered, "if I told you that fire can never burn, that if I command it not to, it will obey me, would you still believe me?"

"You can command imps and spooks," she said coquettishly, her face afire.

"Yes, imps and spooks."

"And then fire won't burn?"

"It won't burn.

She believed him.

"Then come, child."

He took his beloved daughter by the hand—with tenderness he took her hand, for he loved her—and together they went down into the cellar. The cellar was aglow from the small brick oven that was exploding flames as red as Ashmodai's tongue, the oven he had built to aid him in his task of burning the papers, the books, the furniture. He stood by the fire, his face reddened by the flames, and ordered his daughter to stretch out her hand and enter the fire. She was frightened, but nevertheless stretched out her hand. Her eyes were streaming tears. But Daddy said to do it, Daddy commanded her! And she would then see the spooks. The ones who put coins under her pillow when she lost her two upper front teeth, the ones she read about in books, the imps that Edith Newman saw when she and her mother went hiking in the woods one night, the night they slept in a tent after a picnic. Her hand shivered, but she brought it closer to the flames. And then she lowered her hand into the fire, and her cries, the cries she made, her cries . . . to this day he can still hear them.

Arthur covers his face; tears stand in a corner of one eye, both corners. She had a cat. She had a cat and she called it Pansy. Nobody knew why she called the cat Pansy. The child claimed that the cat named itself. The cat was on fire, and the odor of its scorched corpse, the stench of its burned fur, was appalling. So too the scream of the child. Adam bursts out laughing. He's already drunk half the bottle; that means class is half over. For every amount of whiskey an equal quantity of dramaturgy. He is explaining the difference between a clown and a comedian who loves sorrow and lives off it. He goes on talking, and maybe this time he's not just prattling, thinks Arthur, who sanctified his small daughter's hand—after all, Adam had indeed been a circus clown and famous. Why did that Nazi save him? And who rescued me? And why did I burn my daughter's hand? Did I do it to avenge my fate? To get revenge against the unknown person who saved me? That would be the revenge of a sick child. And am I not a sick child? Of course I am a sick child. Very sick. "Arthur, what do you think about when you cover up your face? About hatred?" laughs Adam. But he continues with Stanislavsky.

I remember now how my wife abandoned me. At that time I had been taken to the hospital in Jaffa. Gross was one of the doctors. That bastard knew how to lick asses and he rose. Now he has everything, everything except Jenny. Jenny belongs to Adam. After a year of insulin, therapists, analysts, electric shock, my condition improved and I was released from the Jaffa hospital. I went down to Elat. The city of freedom, they told me. I wanted to make a fresh start. I worked in the womb of Mother Earth, in the copper mines of Timna. A bearded beatnik miner. I who struggled up the ladder of officialdom and was about to become the Prime Minister or Chief of Staff with a car into the bargain plus midday meals signing documents and a darling redhead for a secretary—when suddenly came the spooks and I had to exorcise them.

So all the varieties of Dr. Gross were unable to disclose what had happened to me from 1940 to 1945. A dark passageway. A mysterious hidden road from Prague to Israel. And what occurred on that road? All Arthur remembered was forests, nothing more. Forests, trees, and voices that kept screeching in his ears. He had come from the elegant sculptured streets of Prague, where every telephone pole was a work of art. But here you had

Tel Arad, Ein Bokek, Ein Yehav, and wastelands. The very names of the places terrified him. I was uprooted and flung through the air into the desert. Into the source. *The miracle will happen here,* he thought as he brought tourists to the Nabatean town of Shivta, to Beer-Ora, to the Gaza border, to the amazing ravines and canyons ripped out of the desert. And mountains ablaze with brazen colors, looking like insanity itself. And Mitzpah-Rimon, the ancient route to the Dead Sea, the route of bandits, smugglers, and spices. In Elat he worked as a bartender in the Tall Tale nightclub. At three in the morning, when he finished his tasks, he went to sleep on the shore. One day, or one night, an "old-fashioned" night of superb martinis, beautiful Beatrice stepped into the circle of his life. Beatrice was Dutch. She fell in love with him and they lived together for a whole year. On the beach they lived. Between the Tall Tale and the sea. In winter they set up a tent; afterward they built a mat hut. Early each morning they would jump into the water for a swim. They loved getting rid of their hangovers by swimming. Then they drank Arak, ate green olives and salty cheese, salty goat cheese that they bought from the Bedouins. "Theatre which tries to sell itself," says the dramaturge at this very moment and his bottle is just about empty, "is mere trumpery, the material of cheap propaganda that totally camouflages its propaganda, and this theatre will end up as just theory, emptied of any real content, cowardly, utterly lost, psychotic. Like a captain who hasn't a ship any more. Theatre must be a ceremony that confronts the heart. An alien can sell newspapers or win the lottery. Art addresses the heart concerning the heart. Theatre is a gold frame around the pulse of feelings, around the sense of truth, around the taboo of serene instructions. The soul of man calls out in the theatre, knows she is alive and breathing, like a body—though she has no body. The body is the alien."

One night, after a year of peace along the Elat shore, Beatrice came out of the water in a fascinating green bikini. The beach was empty, blank. The moonlight skipped on the water. A ship sailed in the distance, and as it approached, its image was doubled in the sea. And green-bikinied Beatrice, wrapped up beside the fire, suddenly seemed to him a pallid demoness. Her gracious face, beside the flames, was the face of a spook. He knew the truth now, and the truth was bitter. The coals exploded and every once in a while Beatrice was concealed by a reddish veil of sparks, by the devious paths of a flashing snake. And when the fire rose to its full strength and you could hear the terrible snapping of the wooden logs, his face convulsed. He suffered, knowing that he suffered, and pitied himself, and suddenly he could no longer bear it and he started to push the spook into the fire. The bikini tore and she was naked. Charred by the fire. Her eyes aghast. Her white face shrieking. And then he was all alone by the fire. He sat and, in his seated position, urinated. He urinated on the fire and the flames would not go out. His daughter danced inside the fire. Beatrice danced inside the fire. He urinated on her bikini and fell asleep sitting.

And she slipped out of my hands for always, forever. I searched for her in Elat, in Beer-Sheva, in Tel Aviv. She disappeared, my beauty. That Dutch spook. With whom I drank Arak and ate olives and Bedouin goat cheese. Sweetheart, do you remember my martinis? My ratio of seven to one, eight to one? And the olive which was the only sane thing in that tall white glass? Vanished as though she never existed. In Tel Aviv he slept in public parks. He went to the Dutch Consulate and told the girl at the information desk: "I'm looking for a woman I love. Her name is Beatrice Grauchart. She deserted me. I wanted to sanctify her, but she didn't understand and fled, not knowing how much I loved her. If she had known, she would have sung in the fire." Two officials, flaxen-haired and blue-eyed, with a pinkish down of hair on their cheeks despite all their shaving, these two stuffed-shirts despised him in their hearts. To them he was somebody who ate from garbage cans and slept in public parks. They didn't believe, they refused to believe, that a man of this sort, who looked as if he was ready to produce Shakespeare before an audience of mentally disturbed field mice, was in search of a woman. That a man like this was able to love. Love was a thing of high fashion, they thought to themselves. One secretary took pity on him and informed him that Beatrice Grauchart had indeed been there, but had returned to Holland. Her address? No. She had left no address.

And then he recalled his house which had been taken from him. He knew that his former wife, his daughter's mother, was working in a city. He knew that his daughter was a student in an educational institute at a kibbutz for the destitute. How old was she today? Eight? Nine? Time had lost all meaning in his head.

The moment his daughter caught sight of him she burst into screams. She climbed onto the table and shrieked. Nothing would stop her. She howled, and then fled from him. He sobbed, pleaded in front of her. Out of shame for himself and for her. He wanted to touch her hair, to embrace her—if only for a moment, if just for the last time. To die in that memory. Her face was black from fear. She screamed. Then he went berserk. Broke furniture. Struck the women teachers, and afterward escaped. He reached Tel Aviv, put on his demonstration outfit, hung the drum from his neck, beat it, and went out on his demonstration against City Hall. He shouted at the window behind which—as he was told by an old man who had no teeth but gave him looks of great affection—sat the mayor. He screamed at the mayor: "There's no point in loving! Nobody understands love! And so nobody understands fire! Disinfection is a new thing. I'm a refugee. You're a Nazi. Give me back my Beatrice. Give me back my daughter. You're hiding them. Why have you abandoned me . . . all of you?"

And some nights—some nights Arthur wakes and finds owls pecking at his eyes. He hears voices. And each voice has a joyful color: greenish, rosy, violet, orange-yellow, olive-yellow, whitish-mauve. The owls are pecking the white flowers off his eyes. And other events, many others. He recalls a certain street, the street on which those words forsook him, the words for houses,

trees, flower pots, a silver-haired woman, a gold tooth in the
mouth of a bagel vendor.

Arthur would sometimes wake in the night and write. And
what would Arthur write? Arthur would write in ancient Egyptian and not know why. Adam mocked him. "Are you an Egyptian, Arthur? Are you the transmigrated soul of one of Poti-
phar's eunuchs?" But down deep in his heart Adam was jealous
of him. Arthur was a swindler, Adam was certain of that. Such
an impostor that he didn't know to what extent he was an impostor.

One day Dr. Gross invited Dr. Jonathan Sternshuss, the expert on Egyptology from the Hebrew University. The expert
stayed at the Institute for a few days. He took away with him the
latest note which Arthur had written in one of his moments of
great depression. When lost in the abyss of his agony, he wanted
to sanctify the entire building, and almost burned Dr. Gross's
chair. Dr. Sternshuss translated the ancient Egyptian script and
this, word for word, is what he came up with:

1. Herman Von Schichrach. Montevideo. 37 Independence Street. Married. Pseudonym. An eight-year-old who
answers to the name of Alfonso. Has grown a mustache.
Aged somewhat. At present the director of an automobile
factory. Writes professional articles on the problem of anti-
freeze in engine motors. The articles appear regularly in
seven journals published in Germany.

2. Dr. Ernest Schloss. Bonn. Foreign Office, Middle
East Department. Room 29. Candidate for the office of
senior consul. Each morning goes fishing alone in the
Rhine. Drives a gray Opel. Father of two daughters. The
older studies law in Cologne. Her name is Gertrude; a
blonde; she dreams about a modeling career. Her legs are
too fat.

3. Willy Brown. Syracuse, U.S.A. 274 Main Street.
Dentist. Forged diploma. In Auschwitz was in charge of
removing gold from teeth. Occupation before the war: a

nurse in a Dresden hospital. Has a son and a daughter. Every Thursday he drives in his Chevrolet convertible to a country club. An excellent bridge player.

4. Robert Laufer. Formerly Robert Darius. Chancellor's Office in Bonn. Lives in a country villa by the Rhine. Known as someone who, before the war, taught Roman literature in Leipzig. Falsification: in Meidank was known as the Red Dog (his hair was red, now it's white). Details about him are in the hands of Dr. Weiss, formerly Klein, who dwells at 33 Himmelstrasse, West Berlin.

5. Robert Darius (formerly Robert Laufer). Prime Minister's Office in Bonn. Two daughters. Crippled wife, diabetes victim. Pale, shaking hands. Details in Gestapo dossier number 428/MS10, Office of Justice, Bonn.

6. Stefan Zingfeld (formerly Stefan Zingfeld). Foreign Office, Bonn.

7. Adam Stein (formerly "Adam," the huge dog of Ilse Koch, a woman who was known as "The Beast of Buchenwald." She followed a very familiar system. At present she's free, released after a four-year prison term; her case is soon to be reopened). Adam Stein was a clown. Sent his wife and daughter to their deaths. He played his instrument and entertained while Jews were turning into smoke. At present a famous swindler, wealthy, lodged in the Institute for Rehabilitation and Therapy, Arad, Israel.

Jonathan Sternshuss, comparing this list with others found in Arthur's room, discovered that all the lists followed the same pattern; only the names and details were shifted around. Each list of names ended with the name of Adam Stein, identified always as "Adam," the famous dog of Ilse Koch, who was known to many as "The Beast of Buchenwald," and about whom Arthur used to say that she proved the rule that while a Jew was alive he was a pain in the ass, but once the Jew was dead he was a gold mine.

Some of the lists were handed over to an institute in Jerusalem which was researching the holocaust, and after a month came the following reply:

Dr. N. Gross
Institute for Rehabilitation and Therapy
Arad

Dear Sir:

We must turn your attention to the fact that out of thirty names which you sent us (accompanied by instructive details) twenty-five are names of men we have been after for many years. Just a superficial perusal showed us clearly that each and every person mentioned in your lists was located in the place designated by the lists you transferred to us. Legal proceedings against most of these monsters will soon be instigated, for the Jewish nation shall not rest in peace until "they" all, one after the other, come before the judge's bench. We are amazed by and shaken with respect for that man in your midst who holds in his heart a secret undeciphered map that can uncover our many enemies. We implore you respectfully to permit us to send to your institute two experts who have been toiling in this area for years, so they may gather and collect from that man the material whose proper and thorough use they know so well.

Yours, with great respect,
Dr. N. Yahel,
Director

Dr. Gross didn't postpone his answer. In a lengthy detailed letter Dr. Gross explained why it was impossible to receive at the Institute, at least at this stage, any unfamiliar researchers. Arthur Fine would not tolerate any investigations. If he knew what he was doing, he certainly would write his lists in Czech or German or Hebrew. But the reason he concealed his findings in an Egyptian disguise, in a strange weird script, was the very reason he was sick: you couldn't have the one without the other. He was damaged, so much damaged that, despite his phenomenal memory, several years had been totally erased from his mind, or, more precisely, their memory had been preserved only in these odd lists. An encounter with unfamiliar people would be bound to injure his therapy. But the Institute would continue to forward the lists and hope that the well wouldn't dry up.

Arthur Fine, Chief Hieroglyphist, stenographer for Adam Emanuel Adameus Adolf Wolfgang Stein, sits and takes notes. His mind wanders through his life, toward strange lists that keep popping up out of nowhere, but his hand takes notes: "Hamlet! Every act is perfect, complete in itself. The entire play creates a different perfection. A tragedy of madness, exactly the way, yes . . . the young prince escapes, but was he really so young? Go away, you madman. . . ." Adam is finished with the bottle. Just a drop remains. And this time, as the whiskey courses through his veins, he ceases speaking as a mere swindler and says something straight from his heart. Arthur notices the change in tone of voice and pays attention. Blood flows in Adam's words now; consequently, Arthur stops writing and listens. This isn't more chatter about "How to drink in a theatre." ("Watch, you lift the bottle, grabbing it by the neck—write that down, little Schwester!—and you gulp; and, of course, the bottle contains tea; but you have to twist your face, pretend, pretend with your whole head and heart, so the entire body is drinking; watch, my whole . . .") No, this time he has other words in his mouth. His eyes are looking down. Is Adam crying? Nonsense. Everybody writes. They don't sense any difference. Only Arthur. He alone senses it. "Two children," says Adam Stein, "two children were playing a game. One was a horse and the other a knight. The knight rode on the horse's back and shouted: 'Ooooooo!' and the horse neighed 'Eiiiiiii!' In the evening the knight tied the horse to a post. One end of the rope he wound around the post and the other end he put in the horse's mouth. Then the knight went home to have his supper and sleep and dream. The horse remained in the street. And wept, because it was late and dark. A man passed by in the street, saw the child, and asked him: 'Child, why don't you go home? It's late and they must be worried about you.'

" 'I can't,' said the child. 'I'm tied to the post.'

" 'So why don't you open your mouth and let the rope drop out and then you'll be free to go home?'

" 'Yes,' answered the hungry sad child, 'but then I wouldn't be a horse any more.' "

Adam's voice boomed: "How much better off we are on stage! Who doesn't believe me?" Nobody dares say a thing. They take notes. Each hand writes quickly. "We are acting in a play which both the playwright and the director have abandoned, and we are left to ourselves. There is nobody to turn to. To consult. To ask questions. Nonetheless, to close the curtain is against every rule in the book, is impossible. For then, though we would be free, we would no longer be horses . . . dogs . . . This way we can be madmen or princes, members of government or dogs. Theatre ripens in drunken hearts. There is just one outlet. Only one way to rescue yourself. To laugh. So I become a clown. If I had been unable to laugh there, at Klein's place, I couldn't have taken it, I would have died from it, and the same goes for everybody, for all of you. Men and women, him and her, you and you. Klein, too. The moment he ceased laughing, he became Weiss. And the rubber condom which I brought him only made him cry. You have to know how to laugh. There's no other way. You must tell yourself you're a blue kettle and subsequently act like a blue kettle, boiling and whistling like a blithering blue kettle. And laugh. And bury your face, wrap it in a mask, shriek, stick yourself in clay, pinch your own ass, try to behave like a dog, sell shares on the moon, and laugh. All the time, always. That's the objective."

"Stop it, Adam!" Arthur's face is as pale as ashes. He tries to rise from his chair. But Adam, tottering, empty bottle in hand, approaches him. His eyes blazing, Adam screams into the face of the hieroglyphist, choking him with a blast of alcohol: "Burning? Whom did you try to burn? Your daughter? Arthur, you are the king. King Arthur and the Knights of the Round Table. King and hero. And, like him, you shall be punished. Heroes are hopeless." And Adam pushes Arthur back into his seat. Arthur covers his eyes with his hands, and after a long silence that buzzes through the tense attentive breathless room, Adam says: "That's what's called a dramatic pause! The second law, after laughter: the pause. The crowning achievement of the theatre, of clowning. It's even in the Bible—the timing, the pause." And thirty pencils scribble feverishly. "The secret of stage dialogue is the pause!" Adam shouts, waving the empty bottle. "The way to happiness is strewn with pauses. Humor is all a question of timing. Just as tears create sadness, laughter creates joy. Just as speech creates a connection, the pause creates the deep awareness of that connection. Little Schwester, please get up . . ."

The younger Schwester rises, her face frozen.

"Nice little Schwester, please open your mouth. Squint your eyes." She does exactly as he bids. "Relax your neck muscles, tighten your cheek muscles, stretch your mouth, stiffen your lower lip, crumple up your nose, and—laugh. Try. It's coming. But you haven't created laughter yet, my little Schwester. We are lost people sitting on a remote island, my sweetheart. Where's your respect for the dead? Yes, now you're beginning, you're trying, good, little Schwester, you're laughing!" And from her throat escapes a dull *kh-kh-kh-kh* that gets louder and louder. A *kh-kh-kh* that fits the expression on her twisted face, the locked spasm of fear. And from the willingness to laugh (Adam commanded a laugh, so it must come, it must be released) her face grins against her own will and her tears are forced back and in their stead, transformed by the vigor of pain, by a mute incomprehensible force, emerges the gladness of fun, laughter. Her laughing increases till it fills her whole face, till it captures her entire being in a seizure of expectation, of sudden intoxicated joy. And the younger Schwester twin starts shaking like a branch in a storm and laughs with her face, her body, her woolen underwear, her flabby breasts, her loose stomach, even her shoes. Immediately the others join her paroxysm of laughter. Adam points with his empty bottle and the person indicated gets up and starts to laugh. Noses crumple, muscles tense, and out bursts laughter that cannot stop. *Kh-kh-kh-kh!*

Jenny storms into the room.

"What are they doing? Stop them!" Her face is red, her face is angry.

Adam laughs.

"Damn it, stop them! It's dangerous, such laughing!"

"What's so dangerous? You're a licked ice cube!" he shouts to her, but the others cannot hear a word, they are suffocating with laughter. "What's the matter? All you can do is catalogue my caresses and then come here and butt in like a goring bull, like a whore who's after her payment. Here it is. Your fee!"

"Adam, I don't know what you're talking about, I don't understand. Tell them to stop."

"You know very well." All of a sudden he calms down. He's stable. A member at a country club, a swimmer in a pool, an honorable member of the municipal museum, invited to cocktail parties at the Bolivian embassy, at the Philippine and Cuban embassies. "You know? If you were married I would have someone to betray, but who would take you, take you for a wife yet? You'd poison a man in his bed, knife him while he slept. Look," he raises his voice, "they're laughing, it's good for them, they can't stop."

"Make them stop, it's dangerous, make them stop."

"Jenny, don't ruin it!"

"You're drunk, Adam."

"No, I'm not."

"Then what's that bottle?"

"It's empty."

"You emptied it."

"I was teaching them how to act. Today they learned how to play a man drinking on stage."

"You're drunk."

"But you're not. That's the trouble. Klein used to say—and, to a great extent, rightly so—that he didn't trust anybody who didn't drink."

The laughing continues, choking, hysterical branches in a hurricane, staggering in the wind, shrieking, eyes squinting, crying from too much laughter.

"I'm free, Jenny. A free man. And I'm breathing. For the time being. Just listen to them. My philharmonic. No dog there, no Gross, no Klein, no Jenny. Only laughter in a phosphorescent Temple."

"You're behaving like a child, Adam."

An ominous finger protrudes in her direction and Adam says quietly: "Why are you jealous of them? Because they're laughing? Because they suddenly feel good?"

"Adam." Her voice is somewhat softened, pleading. Like "ketchup," thinks Adam to himself. Nothing more, nothing less. But now her presence seeps into the mind of the laughers. Once they have discovered her, they all—the Schwester twins, Miles, Wolfovitz the Circumciser, everybody—all of them feel like a gang of crooks in a police station, a gang of crooks captured with sneezing gas. They want to stop sneezing, but cannot. Jenny's hostile look, which wrestles with Adam, gradually overcomes their laughter. Fear of Jenny, of her starched uniform, of her cold proud expression, silences them. A helpless laugh hovers yet for a moment and then dies out. The reign of silence begins. The silence that follows every laugh. Their eyes, green from curiosity and fear, swivel, swivel, from Adam to Jenny, from Jenny to Adam. And Adam says in a loud voice: "Arthur! Arthur! You didn't laugh!"

"I laughed, Adam, I did."

"Arthur, do you know where our bananas are buried? Our clown's bananas? Here, in our souls. And you know that that's where we slip on these bananas, on the inside, in our hearts, in our souls. That's how!"

"Yes, Adam." Arthur the great arsonist thinks about his being humiliated in front of Jenny. Adam is yelling at him. What does he want from me? That Cicero Stein! But Arthur bursts into a short loud laugh. His face flushes with shame.

"Thanks, Arthur." Adam throws him a kiss in the air. Arthur's humiliation is complete. Adam approaches Arthur, totally oblivious of the presence of Jenny, removes his own hat and stands at Arthur's side. He extends his hat like a beggar in the street, like an organ grinder. He smiles the smile of the satisfied dramaturge. Arthur pulls out two dollars from his pocket and drops them into the hat. And looks around, disgraced. But everybody is doing the same thing; Adam begs from one person after another, hat in hand. This millionaire needs those pennies? says Arthur in his heart and envies him, envies him because he can be a pauper and a millionaire, a hero and a cry-baby, drunk and sober, dead and alive, loved and hated—and everybody drops coins and bills into the hat. Adam empties the money into his pocket, replaces the hat on his head, hooks his arm around the arm of his poisonous beauty, and steps off with her. He is drunk to the toes of his feet. He totters. "I taught them how to laugh and how to drink!" He gives her a loving wink and against her will she smiles. The music is playing "She was a young girl by a Galilee lake." They tread along the twisting turning corridor until Adam collapses. "Now I'm going to show you, dear students, how to buckle on the stage like a drunkard!" And he clings to the carpet, his eyes closed, his face in the black wool, and, involuntarily asleep, he sinks and sinks into a trance and onto the train he once took as the greatest clown of Germany, holding in his hand, with exaggerated confidence, his magnificent suitcase, on his way to the last station of his life and the first station of his death.

8

OLIVETTI

ADAM IS on his way to the dog-child. Ilse Koch is back in jail. They sentenced her to life imprisonment. A pleasant enough punishment, considering that the answer has not yet been given to the question: How can we punish the Ilse Kochs? But how to punish Adam Stein, that Adam Stein knows! That's the subtle difference between the chosen people and the choosing people. In other words, between the nation that thought God chose them and consequently chose God who abandoned them, and a nation that thought God would not choose them and consequently attempted to escape from God but God chose them as a scourge against the believers. Chosen? Choosing? It doesn't make too much of a difference to God. He seats himself on the blood and laughs. The butcher laughs last, thinks Adam, that was why Herr Commandant Klein was fond of him, though today his name is Weiss.

The dog, no longer covered, having abandoned his foul sheet somewhere in a corner of the room, opens his watery lake-blue eyes and crawls over to greet Adam. Adam senses much happiness in that greeting. The dog has heard how Adam wouldn't allow Jenny to come inside with him. Adam is certain that the dog's joy is partly due to that.

Nonetheless, instead of satisfaction, it is helplessness he feels before the child, before the kind expression facing him. He stretches out his hand, touches the dog's hair, its straggly hair. The greasiness and the filth disgust him, and the child senses it clearly, moves back, and howls. Adam, moved by the howl, clasps his hands behind his back and says: "Come, let's go out for a walk."

The dog turns his face away. Still standing on all fours, he turns his face toward the window, shamed.

"I understand!" Adam speaks quickly, swallows his words. Every moment is painful to him. "I know that you're a dog, I'll walk you the way they walk a dog. . . ." The dog's face is still averted. Adam feels the ground slipping from under him and he bites his words, in a hurry, in a dash, in a staccato: "Y'r 'fraid?"

The dog's head moves up and down, up and down.

"Dumbbell of mine. You have nothing to worry about, nothing to be ashamed of. I'm here. You know who I am? I'm a king. If I were you, do you know what I would do? I'll tell you. I'd crawl down those lousy corridors and bark at them all. They deserve it."

For some reason, he doesn't know why, the dog faces him with an expression that reveals a pinch of a smile. Adam continues: "Those carcasses! They aren't worth more than a bark. Listen to me, I'm experienced. Therapy? They try to cure the soul with pills. Somebody who has death's backyard lodged in his heart they inject with Mexican cactus juice. That's what that leper Seizling's millions are used for, while good people have to wring their hands and put on a smile, whereas all they want is Pierre Lotti's great soup. Listen to me, I know." The dog's azure eyes are fixed on Adam's face. Has he understood? Has he not understood? Adam is uncertain and the question isn't even important, not that important. The child comes closer now, stands right next to him, sprawls at his feet. For a moment, there is complete silence. For a moment, complete peace. For a moment, nothing matters. The child sticks out his wrinkled hand, his paw, and points to Adam's pocket. His finger is extended like a sword.

"What is it, child? I don't understand."

The finger dangles, pointing to the pocket. The dog then jumps on all fours, leaps here and there, hums, gnashes his teeth, wails. What does he want? Is something hurting my child? What's in my pocket? As a last-ditch effort, the dog leaps at him, stretches out his hand, and with amazing speed steals into Adam's pocket and springs backward. Adam puts his hand in his pocket and comes out with the tiny transistor radio.

The dog howls with delight, the dog without a sheet howls. Adam is concerned. Adam holds out the transistor and the dog grabs it in his hands. He fondles it a long while, delicately places it on the couch, jumps about the couch with the rhythmic ecstasy of a ritual, his face aglow, his expression joyous. He takes it again into his hands, tosses it from hand to hand, brings it to his mouth, licks the brown plastic ecstatically. With his teeth he scrapes the grooves and knobs as an act of caressing. "It's yours, yours forever," says Adam tenderly, and the dog comes near to him, growls in between his legs, and draws back.

Adam opens the door and waits. The dog gapes at the opened door and also waits. The dog's face is so white. He hasn't been out of his room for a whole year. But Adam has made up his mind and will force the dog to go out. How do you force a dog? He slams the door in anger, approaches the child, takes up the transistor, intending to smash it, but doesn't, then puts it down again. The trembling dog comes over and kisses the transistor. No, he doesn't kiss it. He barely touches it with his quivering lips, like a butterfly. Then Adam picks up the chain whose one end is tied to the child's neck and starts walking; at that very moment the dog calms down and starts following him, as though his whole security depended upon that chain. The door opens and shuts behind them, and they are already treading along the corridor, the singing corridor, the corridor with a black carpet and thousands of lightbulbs piercing its ceiling.

Jenny stands beside the bulletin board. The dog's eyes catch her shoes as he walks on all fours. He won't lift his head. Adam, with a pride that contains a gram of frivolity, pays no attention to her whatsoever. The dog suddenly halts and Adam, who keeps going, almost strangles him with the chain. He sniffs her shoes, the odor of her jealousy.

Outside, around the goldfish pond whose waters remain always blue, are sitting the students of Nurse Spitzer's nursery. About twelve men in their sixties or older, and ten old women.

"Nurse Spitzer's nursery is an unusual experiment," Dr. Gross once told him. "The nursery is under the supervision of Dr. Avramov, who's come to us from Switzerland; before working here he operated under the influence of, and along the lines of, the American John Watson, whose system isn't too different from the behaviorists!" Gross smiled, enjoying himself, and Adam boomed: "They're going to do experiments on me here!"

"After all," said Dr. Gross, "our Institute isn't an ordinary hospital. We do plenty of experiments here, we try out various systems. We're open to everything. We have a place to work, and we have the money. So we try, we try. We are groping in the dark, but we won't turn away from any ray of light, however misleading it may be. Science is not apathetic about daring ideas. You must break through to shores that have not been . . . you must turn your back on the . . . you must determine to be broad-minded so as to . . . you must . . . So our nursery has a goldfish pond, a sandbox, swings, two rust-eaten Chevrolet chassis, a paper skeleton, a Spitfire propeller, toys, dolls, tables painted blue, paper, plasticine, newspapers, glue. Every morning the aged nursery children trek from the dining

hall to the kindergarten and stay there until four in the afternoon, building houses from blocks and singing, making castles
and palaces, shooting pistols and dismantling toy machines, sobbing, and some even suck their thumbs."

At present they are seated around the pond and singing:

> *Purim is me, Purim is me,*
> *Joking and jolly,*
> *I'll be here, once a year,*
> *If I take a trolley,*
> *Jolly, jolly trolley!*

Nurse Spitzer nods a greeting to Adam and stares at the dog
in surprise, but says nothing about it. She turns to her attentive
class: "So, children, soon we will celebrate the holiday of
Purim! Do you know what we do on Purim?"

Naomi Cantorovitz, whose face looks like a raisin, and who
until a short while ago, in Jaffa, had sat for five years on a
bench, her head bowed, without stirring, without speaking, without lifting her face, now jumps up, wide awake, and mumbles
excitedly: "I know! We light candles." Her voice has the clear
ring of a child's voice. Adam and his dog cock their ears.

"No, Naomi." Nurse Spitzer has acquired the style of a kindergarten teacher: checked pathos, restrained childishness, nonsense pronounced clearly with punctuation in the proper places.
"No, Naomi. We light candles on Hanukah!"

"And at funerals too. Right, Sarah?" says a man about sixty,
his hair white as snow, his clothes threadbare, his voice nasal.

"Yes! At funerals too . . . But we light candles during the
holiday of Hanukah in order to commemorate the miracle of the
oil that burned in the Temple without being used up. And what
do we do on Purim?"

"We masquerade. Right, Sarah?"

"Correct, Nathan."

And immediately they all speak at once. They shout, butt into
each other's words. They're all going to put on costumes. "I'll be

a cowboy . . . I'll be Queen Esther . . . I'll be Napoleon
. . . I'll be Ben-Gurion . . . I'll be God . . . I'll be a cat
. . . I'll be Mickey Mouse . . . I'll be a house . . . A newspaper . . . A statistics table . . . A publishing house . . . A
committee . . . Bluebeard . . . Peacenik . . . A well . . . A
priest . . ."

Adam and his child pass by the herb garden of Pierre Lotti,
by two tiny cypress trees that were planted not long ago, and
reach the chess corner.

Here are heavy concrete tables planted in the ground, and
surrounding them wooden chairs set on a concrete base. And in
between the tables, in the middle, a small fountain. Each table
has a chessboard drawn on it, with huge solid pieces arranged on
the board, each piece in its proper place. The players sit on
either side and study the board, but neither one moves a piece.
Neither man dares. They ponder, in silence, they concentrate,
yet they will not shift the pieces from their spots. Day after day,
they sit there petrified. Still undecided. The pieces wait until the
bell rings, when the players get up and go to eat. Adam wants to
move them around, but he understands his comrades, he pities
them—they haven't decided yet. Nearby, some individuals are
holding strings attached to balloons. Balloons filled with helium
that hang in the air without stirring, like lovely flowers. Red,
violet, yellow. Each balloon has the figure of Mickey Mouse on
it, except for one that has the face of Ben-Gurion.

"They're afraid of the sky," says Adam. "They're afraid the
sky will drop on them, so they try to hold it up." The dog nods
his head as though he understood. He's tired. Adam senses the
dog's sadness, his exhaustion, his fear. He pulls a pocket-knife
from his wallet and punctures one of the balloons; Ben-Gurion
crash-dives onto the head of a man. The torn strips cover his
forehead, but the man doesn't budge. He looks straight ahead,
one hand stretched upward to the sky.

The man continues on his way through the big courtyard with
the dog zigzagging behind him. He starts to dance. He lifts his

right leg, jumps up and kicks it with his left leg, like Nijinsky in the "Dance of Fire." This evening Diaghilev will come and take him to the castle of Wilvitz and his charming wife. The dog shivers and Adam Stein is in a good mood; the weather actually improves his good spirits, bringing lovely odors from afar. He spreads his feet wide apart, turns them outward, and they, on their own, hop farther and farther apart. A head pops out of a window on the second floor, a head with a face, a face with eyes, eyes with binoculars. Dr. Gross is observing from a distance. Arthur Fine, sitting on a bench beside the fountain, watches Charlie Chaplin and his dog move deep into the yard. He even sees Dr. Gross's binoculars. The plot is clear to him now. Freedom? In a detention camp there is no freedom. Whatever freedom is given is for the sake of appearances. "Adam, you're not such a big revolutionary as you think," he says to himself. There's a hand behind the curtain, following, outwitting, moderating, knowing, pulling the strings. Jenny would kill herself if she knew. Arthur laughs to himself. The figure of Jenny hanging from a rope and swinging in the wind amuses him for the moment. He recalls what Adam's neck looked like once when they stood watching the sea, back in the Jaffa days in the old hospital. His face was young and proud, but his neck was an old man's. Whereas Jenny's neck was young, but her soul was an old woman's. Adam is killing himself. What majesty and pride Adam had to hoard in himself in order to rise from the dog's bowl of Commandant Klein, who was listening to his Schubert, and to make his wife laugh on her way to the furnace. How did I get this blue number on my arm? Where was I? The camps are empty now, they're just museums. You can dance on the tile floors now. I was in Buchenwald as a tourist. That was in '54. It made no impression on me. I felt nothing. Somebody else was there, not me. I thought I'd recollect something, but I didn't. A small child asked his father if this was the place where he sat in his pajamas, as in the picture, and his father said yes. And here, my child, were the showers, and here's where they assembled us before calling the roll. And what's that tree, Daddy? Oh, that's where they had bonfires. The smoke is gone now, evaporated. Adam dances, walks duck-footed like Chaplin. The dog toddles after him. Adam has a dog, has Jenny, while I have nothing. My daughter shrieked when she saw me. What will Adam Stein, Adam Charlie Stein, tell dear Schwester's God? Wolfovitz holds that if Adam were a German, an Englishman, an American, a Persian, an Indian, he'd be able to find some way to calm himself down. These noble nations who have benefited from the absence of law, these victors, have something to say. But the question is, according to Wolfovitz, what can Adam say? You've offended, sinned, robbed, insulted, cursed, killed, strangled, destroyed, punished, blocked, interfered, fooled around, fornicated, looted, whored, mocked, pillaged, buried, shot, fleeced, slaughtered? Is there anything else he can add?

Charlie Chaplin's skipping rope
Charlie Chaplin slips on soap

As old Leibowitz quotes somebody somewhere, God has died from an overdose of shame, or an overdose of compassion for his creatures. Both opinions hold water. Isn't that downright hypocrisy? No? I'm losing my mind. My veins. My body's finished. I want to cry. I'll go to my room. And he gets up. Now he will slowly amble, enter his room, burn some papers, put on his army outfit, chirp with his children's trumpet, and write his list of names in ancient Egyptian script. He'll write names and not know what he is writing. He'll tattoo Adam's flesh with an iron. Arthur runs toward his room, sick. Today, once again, very sick. As though he had cave malaria, which comes and goes, goes and comes.

They enter Adam's room: the dog, who is merely making a courtesy visit, is nervous, but Adam pays no attention to his mute plea for help. He has plans. The dog crawls all around, growls, and Adam hangs his coat up and yells at the dog: "That's enough, stop it, cut it out!" And the dog obeys. The dog looks at the chest and as he looks, his face glows. What does he want in the chest? Memories? "Stop looking over there!" Again the dog obeys.

In the chest is his pride and joy, his Hebrew books, standing in a row. How, in less than two years, did he learn the Hebrew language to perfection, linguistics and all? He had a system. He is a master of languages. He always knew how to pick them up very easily. That's how he learned French, English, Spanish, Russian, Yiddish. *Correct Hebrew, Hebrew Thesaurus, Hebrew Exercises, Manual of Hebrew Style,* Hebrew, Hebrew—occasionally he actually dreams in Hebrew. Why is it that nobody can detect any foreign accent in him today? He has his system. And one day perhaps he'll lecture about it before his colleagues at the Institute.

Into the room now storms Handsome Rube — after having knocked several times and received the answer "Go away!" Rube throws himself on the bed, and the dog, hiding under it, sniffs his shoes. "Adam, they're after me . . . the general! They hypnotized Gross, they're going to put him in jail, you got to do something."

Adam wants to be rid of him, for he has an important guest today. "It's all right, Rube. Wait a second and I'll fix everything." He dashes over to his chest, takes out a small typewriter, his lovely Olivetti, rolls a piece of paper into it, and types quickly:

To Each & Every Plotter & Attacker
    (CONFIDENTIAL)
The bearer of this letter, Reuben Kritz, also known as Handsome Rube, is employed by the State of Israel. He works in the Information and Security Department which is attached to Division 69/907 of the Prime Minister's Office. Any harm to the bearer of this letter will be considered an attack upon the security of the country, and appropriate retaliation will follow. Any aid or succor to the bearer will be looked upon with favor.

*The bearer is active now in the tracking down of a gang of war
criminals hiding in Arad, Mitzpah-Rimon, Beer-Sheva, and the
surrounding area, and for that reason has set himself up in the
Institute for Rehabilitation and Therapy. His identity and his
mission are known only to the Head of the Security Services
(70 Moriah Street, Ramat Gan), his Aide, the Prime Minister,
and the undersigned. Kindly show the bearer of this letter the
proper respect.*

Adam Klein
Cmdt.

Adam pulls the paper out of the machine, reads it aloud to
Handsome Rube in a confident voice, adding: "This'll teach Arthur to stop scaring you! Keep the letter in your pocket and
nothing bad can happen to you. It's like a charm."

"B't Arthur'spy!" Reuben jumbles his words, frightened. "His
un'form, trump't, writing in's sleep . . . He signals at night
from th'roof, I know't!"

"He burned his daughter, burned his library, his office,
burned the ladder of officialdom from rung seven to one. He
burned flags. Portraits of the President. The map of Israel. The
Golden Book of the Jewish National Fund."

"Wasn't his daughter Jewish?"

"Rube, you're trying to be funny. The dog smells your shoes.
Handsome Rube, where did you get your sense of humor?"

"Me? A sense o' humor? I flunked third grade three times. I
was in the same class with my older brother and my younger
sister. I haven't any sense of humor. I named myself Handsome
Rube. Doesn't that prove it? No?"

"Yes, that proves it."

Adam relaxes, takes it easy, but actually his patience has already snapped (*the dog, the dog, the dog*). Arthur will definitely
not take the letter literally. Yet he is too wise to inquire into the
depths of these simple words, for the day-to-day limits upon his
soul have been torn and burned and he is remote from his own

life. "You're too stupid to understand how difficult it will be for a man so wise to follow such a letter. But everything will turn out for the best. Arthur will see in the letter only the hints unpleasant to him or pleasant to me. For example, the "gang." This word hints at something. It's a common word—all words are common until you see them in a new light. For instance, *Adam*. Adam was the first to forestall the near extinction of the human race, and Adam was a great saint, and Adam was the dog of Ilse Koch. Adam is a word; illuminate that word with the proper light and it takes on a completely different meaning, containing all human possibilities. And whoever doesn't do this—and nobody will do it—will simply see the letter as a correct, wise, impenetrable measure against poison and murder. Don't be afraid. Listen to me, Rube. Everybody here is a porcelain general, Mrs. Seizling has castrated them. Muzak music is the soda they put in army tea. Porcelain generals are the acme of innocence in a counterfeit world, and you symbolize the acme of stupidity in a clever and criminal world. So there is always a balance. And me, my heart goes out to you with love. Now go and don't worry, everything will turn out all right. Try to love all dumbbells, because they were created in your image. Thus spake Adam, the large silver-haired dog. You, I promise you, Handsome Rube, *you* will be the pillar of salt that Lot's wife, made of tin jewels and stinking from perfume concocted from sewage, shall gaze at with her own eyes just before the world expires. Listen to me. And if you haven't understood, it makes no difference. I too don't always understand exactly what I'm saying. Sometimes the mouth talks while the mind still sleeps. Now go, I'm busy. I'm in a bad situation, so go, and I'll love you for that."

The moment Handsome Rube left with the letter in his pocket, the moment he went through the doorway and into the corridor, his body straight and strong, his shoulders stiffly held, looking like a scarecrow with a motor inside, at that very moment the dog crept out from under the bed and, without turning

right or left, crawled straight to the typewriter, the small Olivetti, embraced it with both hands (feet?), forgetting everything
else in the world, squirming not just into the machine but—and
Adam truly and perfectly sensed this—into the future, the past,
into vague intimations of the days when his body was still walking about, when his voice was still talking, when he once belonged to the human race. A *miracle?* There are no *miracles*
when it comes to love. Adam was angry with himself for having
dared introduce this word *miracle* into such a simple and regular
situation. A child and a machine. In every kindergarten there are
machines, in every closet of toys there are dismantled machines,
tiny pianos missing keys, dolls with their eyes pecked out and
their straw insides ripped open, teddy bears without limbs,
squashed . . . do you remember? The electric shaver? The
transistor radio? And I somehow remember still more; Herbert
the Heidelberg philosopher also remembers.

The dog jumped onto the chair and his wrinkled paw petted,
with shocking ecstasy, the typewriter keys. His eyes flashed.
What sort of encounter was it? Was this his forgotten mother?
Perhaps he was nothing but a cross between a man and a typewriter? Adam almost smiled. The nonsense which he told Handsome Rube he won't tell the dog. The dog is holy, a tormented
saint. Look at the wreath of thorns about his head, the crown of
atrocity. The child pats the keys, pokes his fingers into the area
of the levers, fondles the metal, the softly shining plastic, strikes
the keys, strikes the carriage return, shifts it right and left,
presses the capitalization key and lifts the carriage, which drops
with a loud click, click. The dog's eyes stream with tears, real
tears. The tears pour across the white letters etched on the shiny
black heads. Ruthie, the golden-eyed blue-haired landlady of the
pension, the woman with the lovely flat ass and the mysterious
old body that never aged but preserved itself like frozen meat till
the very moment he tried to choke her, she was the one who
bought him that compact Olivetti. What was left from that relationship? The Olivetti. The dog's fingers stretch, his tears flow.

The dog is a prisoner in a world of paradise, the machine world
of Olivetti. Mr. Olivetti, do you know that a certain dog in the
Institute for Rehabilitation and Therapy in Arad is playing
Satan's Requiem on you? Mr. Olivetti, do you know that on
your little piano somebody, a dog, with a human stylus, is in-
scribing a letter of love? Mr. Olivetti, I salute you from far
away, from Arad, from the outdoors, from the desert. By the
way, do I have a face? I'm looking at the dog now, is his face
mine? Is my face the portion of suffering which explodes in his
face of sunshine? What a fantastic match, like the old days: Rex
and Adam, the dogs of Ilse Koch and Commandant Klein. One
dish. One piece of meat. Pure Jew meet Pure Pig. And here
before you, in life size and in natural color, the Jew of Jews.
He's handling that machine. What passion! I once saw a woman
like that, Klein's wife, in bed. She too was that lustful. Why was
she so hungry? Because of the odor of burned bones? Because of
the white powder that was like a carpet, that turned the entire
camp into one white carpet? And she wanted to believe that
everything would change after dedicating one night to a dog. I
shall die, but she—she's already dead. And he? My Klein? He's
alive and will yet live. Germany is new, its recovery a miracle. I
shall die to atone for the sins of Mr. Weiss, who became a Jew.
There is no justice in the world. Only my child is just. My dog.
His fingers hover. Almost but do not make contact. Extended,
craving, like birds flying toward summer. After my death, give
the following eulogy: He was a dog and lo! he is no more; he
lived the life of a man and became a dog; he died like a man but
was buried like a dog; buried and inherited Hell like a dog.
Child, child, don't cry. Mommy is coming and she'll bring you
candies. The sight of those fingers worshipping that cold Olivetti
is somewhat endearing and human, perhaps also noble and warm.
Who made this Olivetti? Other Olivettis, foreign Olivettis, made
this Olivetti. Olivetti begat Olivetti who begat Olivetti who begat
Olivetti. This Olivetti was born from the successful cohabitation
of two workdays in a Milan factory, three machines, and a slide-

rule. And this Olivetti is worshipped by the hands of my saint. There's a certain irony here, but what it is, what exactly it is, I don't know, I can't catch. Not yet. One minute before the end I'll understand. That, and everything else.

The simple mechanical symmetry is worshipped now as a wonder. The precise arms spread out like a fan, like a peacock's tail. The letters stamped in lead. The red-black ribbon. The levers that go up and down. Black, gray, brown, white. The functional ugliness of the frame that extends on either side. The round carriage, the cylinder that rumbles and rings at the end of each trip—*tsik!* The great ring of discharge of the carriage's crossbar. And the child wants, wants so badly to strike the keys! His eyes sing, his ears sing, his whole being is concentrated on the song of the typewriter, striking gaily, stooped over the face of the machine, unable to straighten up because he's a dog, and he's already managed to conquer the machine or, perhaps, the machine has already conquered him.

Olivetti, you are the Revelation. Whoever cohabits with you will beget a dog. Adam laughs, but the dog doesn't hear, doesn't see, doesn't smell, doesn't know. The machine, that's all. What stubbornness, what love at first sight.

Adam smiles to himself with satisfaction. In order to defend himself against the devotion in front of him, he entertains himself. He inserts a sheet of paper into the machine and the dog strikes: a.3.5.1. % = ×/?; dlgkh khlgchdfshchgkhah kh ndchglhkh gldkhsh kdhglkhch ckhgldchsh fdckhbalhakh

It didn't take long before time itself was keeping pace with the machine. Time jogged with the dog, Olivetti time spilled enthusiastically. The child moves the carriage and Adam says: "Dog, a day ago you lay under a sheet and barked. Do you know what has happened to you? You've passed through a million years of evolution. Consequently, necessarily, I am God. There is no other explanation, there cannot be." And the child, the child strikes: gggdddhhhh88888timzor kinior.

Sweat flows, time flies, the hands strike, a back bends, another sheet of paper is rolled in. The dog doesn't lift his head, his feet are crossed, a stooped dog, a dog writing writing writing, untiringly. Adam tires. Slowly the evening descends on the desert, the evening that always comes early. In a short while rain will bang the window. Here inside it's warm and pleasant and terrifying. A small light shines above the table. The wild eyes of the dog are fixed upon the machine. A little child is taking a hopeless journey toward the blocked past, and Adam, suddenly, truly and completely, is frightened. As in that story which Dr. Gross told him about the amateur hypnotist who appeared one day at the Jaffa hospital, hypnotized one of the patients, didn't know how to rouse the man from his trance, and panicked. Adam takes out his guitar case and drums on it. In time with the beat of the machine, the beat of the dog's strokes. They breathe in unison, as in the act of love.

On the windowsill between the lattices sits Herbert. "That's the song of victory, Adam, that's the song of victory."

"Why have you come? I don't need you." Adam is weary. He wants silence. Both Herbert and the dog can go to Hell. What do they want from me? They suck my blood. "I'm laughing!" Adam gets bold. The child drums the machine, Adam drums his guitar case.

"You're not laughing, Adam, I recognize the rhythm, you're crying. The way you cried when the goldfish died, the time we came back from the cemetery, just the two of us, me and you, two orphans."

"I'm crying? Me?"

"You."

"Why?"

"Because the dog isn't a dog."

"He's a dog." Adam raises his voice, suddenly concerned. "He's a dog!"

"Look at him, Adam, look, observe, see for yourself, because once you were in fact clever, before you withdrew, before you went bad."

"I'm looking. What I see depends upon me, everything's blurred, the guitar is a train, the train is you, Heidelberg is eternity, Jerusalem is a cemetery, Ruthie is a clown, and the dog is a child."

"You're looking, but you're afraid to see."

"I'm looking. As hard as I can. You have no right. You are me. I am you. We are both the two of us. I. You. Look, he's writing. A letter. A song. To God. I see that God's come home."

"He's a dog. A dog doesn't write. A dog barks, ar-ar-ar. A dog is Ilse Koch's man. A dog is Rex. A dog is me when I wasn't paying attention."

"Some dogs write. Some dogs make people laugh."

"Like you?"

"Like me. In other words, like you!"

"Like you?"

"Like me!"

"You're not a dog."

"I *am* a dog!" Adam screams. "That's what you never understood. Herbert, my brother, my dearest, despite all your studies and enlightenment and doctorates and comprehensives and Spinoza and Fichte and your *Introduction to Ethical Theory* and Hobbes with his dog-eat-dogism, man-be-wolfism, and Rousseau and Leibniz and your Hegel and Kant in Königsberg, the new Polish city which will last a thousand years, and Plato and Anaximenes and Anaxagoras, those Greeks, all of them, every single one, all the Nietzsches and the Master Ringleader Schopenhauer and his dog, despite all of them, you never understood that you were—that is, I was—a dog."

"The child is a dog."

"And me?"

"Not you, you're a swindler who didn't make it. You failed, Adam." And Herbert laughs and escapes out the lattice.

WOLFOVITZ THE CIRCUMCISER

WOLFOVITZ THE CIRCUMCISER isn't a circumciser, he never was, at least as far as he knows. Only the "infantile cruelty"—to use Dr. Nachwalter's term—of his fellows at the Institute could have caused a man as dear as Wolfovitz to be labeled "The Circumciser." Like everyone else who has dealings with Adam Stein, he appears one day in Adam's room. Some come for selfish reasons. (How's my investment doing? When will you teach again? When do we play our instruments again? When are you going to report to us about your research? And what's up between you and that dog?) Unlike these others, Wolfovitz comes to Adam on a high mission. As soon as he is inside and sitting on the bed and nervously drumming his own knee, he asks if Adam will arrange his funeral which is to take place on a Tuesday, two weeks from now.

"Exactly?"

"Exactly."

The dog is crumpled up on the chair, the dog's chair. Adam has been bringing him here to the machine every day for several weeks now. The child types, the child types real words already: *water, dog, wind, Gross, Jenny, bastard,* and now—*funeral.*

After Wolfovitz's little speech, Adam bursts out laughing, takes his friend's lean bony hand, strokes it, closes his eyes as if in devout prayer, and says: "In my opinion you will live at least another fifteen years. At least!"

"Nonsense, Adam!" He resents Adam's disbelief. "I'll be dead in two weeks, on Monday, and in my grave by Tuesday, and you don't believe me, and if *you* won't, *nobody* will, so where can I turn? Has faith in Adam ceased? I mean Adam in general, not necessarily the first Adam, not necessarily Adam Stein, but all Adamkind—that is, mankind."

Adam rises from his seat and mumbles: "What faith? Who has friends who all of a sudden cease to have faith? And who is a child of man anyway? I have no children, so there are no children of man to be found. The children of the first Adam were swallowed in the Flood, and all the rest became smoke. Who should know that better than you? There are no friends, only people, like ants. And lots of wicked Hamans in the weave. In fact, they're all Hamans. They don't even let us die in peace. Look what the dog's written: *funeral, funeral; mother, father, a funeral.* Good child of mine! Listen to me, Wolfovitz, I'm experienced. Nobody will let you die in peace like a dog. They'll let you have your death agony as long as you want, but they won't allow you a last moment of peace. Child, I'm going out and I'll be right back." The child, as though mesmerized, doesn't interrupt his typing. Wolfovitz and Adam leave the room together.

The music machine plays "Somewhere over the Rainbow," Skitch Henderson and his orchestra of geese schmaltz up the corridor. Adam pulls a bottle out from behind a radiator and gulps a drink. Jack Daniel's. "My God, what great bourbon!" He wipes his lips. "You understand, Wolfovitz? Jack Daniel's?

To die in two weeks without ever having understood or experienced the magnificent taste . . . Wolfovitz, taste!"

No, he doesn't drink alcohol, not to mention bourbon. Once
he almost died from bourbon. Bourbon and beer. And as he says
this, Wolfovitz is wrapping himself in his shroud; in his mind's
eye he is already shrouded. Though today is Monday and he has
another two weeks.

In the courtyard hangs a bright cold wintry day. A few clouds
are skating across the sky. "It's going to rain!" says Adam. The
desert will drink the rain and nettles will grow. Wolfovitz smiles
and shows his two teeth, which are very far apart. It is that
distance between his two upper front teeth that graces him with
the expression of a child and endears him to everyone. Shyness
is stamped on his open round face with that potato stuck in its
middle and above it, far apart, matching his two teeth, a pair of
big brown eyes set in worn-out sockets. Whenever that sweet
smile opens his face, a flush floods across his cheeks. "Ah!" he
says and flings a swollen white finger at the blue sky where some
gray clouds are gathering. "Soon the rain will drop and the
ground will loosen and the gravediggers won't be obliged to
work too hard."

Adam laughs. "Don't give Satan ideas!"

"Satan?" Wolfovitz smiles a hopeless smile. "You, Adam?
This is the only place on earth where Satan has no power. How
can anybody seduce and tempt the mentally ill?"

"Don't say mentally ill!" Adam says, trying to be kind. "Just
ill! Not mentally ill. Isn't influence a mental illness? And what
about a stomachache? What's the difference? What's a stomach.
What are stomach muscles? And here . . ." For a moment he
sounds like Dr. Gross, like Frau Dr. Gross, thinks Wolfovitz.
The Frau once told him things along this line. Gross's Frau loves
grapefruit juice. He brought her some grapefruit juice once and
she said: "God bless you." What a phrase. I was blessed already
in Dachau, there even the bread was blessed, the bread of
ravens.

"Look, Adam, I'm dying and I know that I'm about to die, and your words are a prophecy based on nothing but dust. I realize I sound fancy, but that's the way I am. I don't have to tell you that. Last night I saw the angel of death, he was so close I could have touched him, he touched me. I am not afraid of him, I am prepared."

And, in truth, Adam does know. He tries to take his mind off it, but he knows very well that Wolfovitz saw death. He wasn't fabricating the whole story. Only the end was ad-libbed. The conclusion wasn't just right, for nobody is more afraid than Wolfovitz of extermination, gravediggers, shrouds, and not living forever.

At night Wolfovitz senses that death is coming closer and closer. Babies and children grow at night like trees and plants. And at night Wolfovitz realizes how much closer and more substantial his death is. But with a difference. Infants and trees and vegetables and flowers do not know that they are growing in the night. Night is opaque. They sleep through it. They rest. They die for a few hours. Wolfovitz doesn't die at night, he stays awake in the knowledge of his coming death.

But Naomi, his daughter. His daughter, Naomi. Adam met her several times while he was still in Jaffa. Naomi was her father's comfort, his life, and his disgrace. One time, after he had nearly swooned from fear and they brought him to the Institute in a cab from Tel Aviv, he composed a letter to God that very night. Adam has this letter.

God! [begins the letter, in ornate script, without a single erasure, a perfect copy]

My daughter Naomi took me to the hospital today and went back to Tel Aviv. I don't like Tel Aviv, they built it too fast. I want to tell you about Naomi. You've forgotten her. I'm writing you from outdoors, in the air. God forbid, of course, that you should come out and take a look. I'm going to write

*to you about Naomi, whom you have forgotten. She was a dear
child, not pretty but dear. She had, actually, a round nose, like
me. If my nose is a potato, then you could call her nose a berry.
In those days, I mean, long ago. In Poland, Poland which was
once Jewish and is now, as Adam Stein says, "Jüdenrein." In
this Poland they burned down all your houses of worship one
day, but even this you didn't notice. Whereas your angels all
came down from heaven and saved the curtains hanging in front
of your Ark and made prayer shawls out of them, because after
they had seen what they had seen, they wanted to pray. And
they stood inside the ruins, wrapped in grief and your holy
curtains, and prayed. They wept: "Master of the World, you
are the only One, unique, for there is nobody like you or alongside you, you are without a partner or helper, for you have
long since manufactured this world, all by yourself, all for
yourself, to the greatest glory of your name!" And they concluded, still wrapped in those bejeweled curtains that were somewhat scorched at the bottom but nonetheless as perfect as you,
they ended with a threefold shriek: "Master of the World, how
could you? How could you? How could you?" At this point,
obviously, you wrung your hands and said: "Yes, really, how
could I?"*

*And there, in that Poland, before the curtains became prayer
shawls, I had a daughter and her name was Naomi. Naomi
Wolfovitz was her full name. She was five years old and called
out to me, Daddy, why? Daddy, when? And one day—the exact
date I don't remember, I actually refuse to remember, because
it could have happened any time, before or after—one day your
messengers came, your boys, and they began assembling us in
pens. Little Naomi found favor in the eyes of a certain Polish
woman named Mrs. Maroshak, and Mrs. Maroshak took Naomi away to the cellar under her house. In other words: What
you didn't do, Mrs. Maroshak did do. Whose way was better,
yours or Mrs. Maroshak's? The house was old, they built it in
1819, and the cellar underneath was damp and low-ceilinged*

and Naomi sat in this cellar for seven months, which are 210 days, which are 5,040 hours, which are 302,400 minutes, which are 18,144,000 seconds. Take your Omega, your Doxa, that must be marked with Hebrew letters, or perhaps instead of numbers you use the symbols of each of the twelve tribes? Roll up your sleeve, watch your watch, and count: a lot of tick-tick-ticks, quite a lot. And the ceiling of the old cellar was low, or maybe the floor was high? Anyway, Naomi sat seven months with her head stuck in the ceiling. She couldn't lie down on account of the dampness. The day she entered that cellar, her head, when she was seated, reached the ceiling. Her head stuck in the ceiling! Do you understand what I am trying to tell you?

And there in that cellar, at night, not during the day—though it was difficult to distinguish day from night—at night she would feel how she was developing, how she was growing. But how was she developing, how was she growing? She was growing into the ceiling, into the damp stone ceiling. Her head was rising into the ceiling, lifting itself into the ceiling, but the ceiling wouldn't move an inch. Pale, wet, solid, eternal. And her head stuck in the ceiling, tried to screw through the ceiling, and was squashed by it, in it. That ceiling, Master of the Universe, sculpted her skull according to its own shape. From one month to the next, her head was squashed more and more. Her spine curved, her spine buckled, and she sensed as clearly as could be, while her head was squeezed into the ceiling, how much— so she told me later (much later)—how much she was growing there, just how much she was developing. Once a day Mrs. Maroshak would open the door enough to insert her little finger, to insert some food and water; except for this tiny spray of light, she saw nothing during the entire seven months. Her head was growing into the ceiling and she was thinking about, feeling, her own growth. Weren't those angels wrapped in curtains weeping over her? Naomi's head petrified, became callous, and its growth was perverted, crushed, and what patience, what helplessness! Her body kept growing, developing, it had to, one centimeter (0.3937 inches) a month? two millimeters (.0786 inches) a week? The exact amount is impossible to determine. Her head wanted to escape, to get out, but the ceiling was solid mass!

Signed: Wolfovitz

Nicknamed: "The Circumciser"

Wolfovitz, the man with the childlike face and the bashful smile who composed a letter to God, senses at night that he is dying, that he is growing and developing toward his conclusion, his end. Slowly, confidently, dreadfully. He dreams and his dream ceases being a dream, his dreams are daydreams that extend into the night, merging with his fantasies, his imaginings in which he feels death coming, his arteries hardening, his blood congealing, his stomach turning to stone. Look, the muscles of his heart have stopped functioning, his liver is eaten away, the kidney defunct . . . his entire anatomy is clear to him, in colors. As though he were examining a diagram at some medical school, Wolfovitz sees his hands, his stomach, his heart, his chest, his legs. He sees his muscles, his tissues, his bones, his blood corpuscles as though X-rayed. And, furthermore, he sees the struggle between his spirit—his soul, whose image is hazy but whose existence is assured—and his body. He feels that his body is a battlefield. A desperate war is raging, terrible encounters, tanks and cannon, bombs and shells, and even songs of victory and raising of flags, tearing of clothes and dark despair and severe defeats and shattered and abandoned cities and wrecked streets. Only the final battle remains. Two weeks from now, on Monday. And on Tuesday will be the burial. The earth will be loosened on account of the rain. Wolfovitz is certain that the end, his end, which he is so afraid of, yet is doing nothing to prevent, that this death of his is stamped inside him, deriving its instructions from the blood in his veins. Just as his daughter, Naomi, was a sort of bridge between the damp floor and the ceiling that would not budge, so too is he, Wolfovitz, a bridge. A bridge between the impossible and the possible, between his mother's warm forgotten womb and that refrigerator in the main hospital of Beer-Sheva where his corpse will be taken on Monday two weeks from now. And is he, Wolfovitz, at all able to outwit his fate, to trick it, to forestall his end that is about to swoop down upon him like an eagle? Or would it have been possible to raise the ceiling, even for just one night? Or postpone Naomi's growth for one night?

Maybe it is possible? Maybe if he could stay awake all night, awake at the time death gallops across his sick shattered body . . . maybe? Yet how could a man or a dog or a little girl in a cellar or even Dr. Gross stay awake while sleeping? While dreaming? If it were possible to keep awake while dreaming, there would then be a chance of staying alive forever, without a stop. Definitely. "But I shall die," he says to Adam Stein, "because at the zero hour, at the set and decisive hour, at the hour of hours, I shall be sleeping and dreaming my death."

"I'm busy with the child!" Adam is furious. "God? Let's leave God to the Schwester twin. I'm too busy and the child is maturing, progressing. No, I don't know what draws me to him. Or maybe I do, yes. The child. I once had two daughters. Did you ever meet Joseph Graetz, Ruth's husband? No, obviously you never met him. But you met Ruthie the pension keeper when she came to visit me. She has a body of marble. I'd gaze at her body and see my face reflected there, as in a mirror. Perhaps she preserved it in a hermetically sealed container for many years? The child types all day."

"The child?"

"The child." Adam squints his face into a stern, harsh expression and says: "It'll rain soon, there's no question that it'll rain."

"Child? Your child is a dog." Wolfovitz is startled by his own words, his innocent face flushes. He drops his eyes and notices his polished shoes, polished to perfection, polished for a funeral, his own funeral.

"My child."

"You really want, maybe—I mean, are you going to try to turn him into a human being?"

"I'm not attempting anything, I'm just having fun."

"You're drawn to him, Adam, you're not just having fun. You give him everything. I don't understand why."

"I don't either. No, that's a lie! I am having fun, he growls at me, but he's a child, the thing puzzles me, brings me closer to myself, like a man who meets a monkey that was once, a long time ago, his great-great-grandfather. Do you know the bachelor's prayer? I don't remember where I read it. *'I pray to you, God, let me remain unmarried.* (I'm not married now and I won't ever be again.) *But if I must marry, let me not be the husband of an unfaithful wife.* (Plain and simple! I was ruined by her betrayals. I used to cause her betrayals with my own hands, and laugh.) *And if I am married to an unfaithful wife, let me not know about it.* (The knowledge is the only enjoyment, the fun.) *But if I must know of it, then let it make no difference to me.* (If I knew, only if I knew, would it make a difference to me, but not the difference you expect, so the marriage would succeed. At one and the same moment I would be the murderer and the victim.)' And that's how I feel about the dog."

Dog? Child? Dog, dog. An unfaithful woman. Ruthie. Dog. Dogruthie Daddywhy Daddywhen . . . simultaneously two events occur at this point, Wolfovitz jumps back, in fright, and screams: "Scat!" And the child, crouched on all fours, smells Adam's shoes. The child has crawled to him, seeking him out, and now nods his head up and down, up and down.

A wave of love surges through Adam's heart. "He missed me!" he says, then holds his tongue at once. I must arrest shallow feelings, I have no permission and no right. But his words come from his mouth, not his heart. His legs leap and he is running to the house. Wolfovitz follows. Adam isn't running, he's flying. Wolfovitz huffs and puffs. And the dog, the dog crawls after them, howling.

Once they have reached the room and bolted the door, Adam places the cross-legged, hump-backed, nose-quivering, hand-trembling dog on his chair, points to the typewriter, and says: "What are we going to call you? We have to give you a name. The only name you have now is the one in Gross's books. But that name doesn't interest me. You were born because I gave you candies. Don't forget it. I'm not concerned with Mommy-Daddy. I had two daughters, you a mother-father. These are questions of semantics. The problem before us is the selection of a name. Without a name there is no existence. Without a label, without a number, without some nomenclature, without a dossier, life cannot go on. Therefore, child, it is a time-worn custom —every creature has a name, and you are nameless, and that's arrogance." The dog is confused, shivering. He doesn't understand yet. He shifts a canine perplexed look from Adam to Wolfovitz and back again. Then his blue eyes sink and his face wears a pitiable expression. Adam despises the plea in his face, he is insulted. When he returned to Berlin, he saw such pleading looks in every corner, in eyes that begged in every direction. It was cold, the first winter after the war. And he had a nice house and a heating system and a car. A car he bought from a Wehrmacht officer named Wolf, Wolfgang Wolf. A whole year the car had remained in the garage, since Wolfgang had no money for gas. Everything was rationed, with coupons. Russian soldiers went around the city arm in arm with American blacks while the children of the thousand years of glory were selling matches. The blue-eyed children of the thousand-year Reich sold American cigarettes. Two Chesterfields were worth a night in a warm bed with a woman, her daughter, and her mother. Adam purchased the car and tossed the money on the floor of the garage, but the officer Wolf didn't stoop to pick it up. His wife stood in a corner of the garage and stared at him with gaping eyes. Pale and trembling she was, like a leaf. He, a proud officer, a tattered one, with tattered eyes. He, who knew himself destined to share a thousand years of glory, was obliged to sell his lovely old polished black Mercedes for pennies. Without any gas in it. His wife, who was starving, just watched. Her face ashen. They had to push the car out of the garage to start it. The house had been demolished by a bomb and just the garage was left standing. Like a scarecrow. Like justice, which has no color and no odor. Erect like a penis. Adam laughed then at the calamitous ruin of justice erect as a penis, proud and amorphous and colorless, and he laughed at the erect officer who wouldn't stoop to pick up the money. But in his heart he said, This erect German officer has self-respect. And with that same heart that laughed, in that very heart he respected him. For his own training dictated the same thing. For he knew that he had no place to go. Ruth hadn't been born yet a second time. He was an orphan, a widower, and wealthy. Looks of pleading. These looks offended him. The victors bore a mournful countenance, like the defeated who did not know that they had a share in the future. And, in fact, then they didn't know. Weiss, is he still Weiss? No doubt he returned and became Klein. For who will bring him coins in a rubber condom? Inmate number 20187? The dog? Rex? Adam?

"If you're going to give him a name, I think you should give him a dog's name," says Wolfovitz. He swallows the word *him,* afraid to utter it clearly. What *him* is there to talk about? Who is he, this *him?* Let's choose a dog's name.

"Wolfovitz, you amaze me. What are you saying? Say something."

"It's forbidden to give him another name, a human name. People are a holy thing, man is the chosen creature, even after the betrayal." Wolfovitz the old mystic, the saint whose father (Rabbi Zalman from Schurkov) refused to mourn on the ninth of Av, the day the Messiah would be born, Wolfovitz to whom the dog was nothing but the aide and ally of Satan, it is he who says these words. Approaching the dog, Wolfovitz roars at him: "Monster! Ashmodai! Scat, scat, scat!" Stooping, he tries to peek at the typewriter; the page is still empty, virgin. But the dog's fingers drum now on the keys, soon he shall play for us the

old melody. He knows. That a secret is packaged here. *Finis*.
Scat. The dog turns his pretty face, fixes on Wolfovitz his lake-
blue eyes that express evil and hatred, and barks into his face.
Wolfovitz is frightened by that look and sinks onto Adam's bed.

"He almost bit you!" says Adam. In his voice there is a grain
of belittlement. "And now—the name. What will his name be?"

"Adam's kid!" shouts Wolfovitz. "Isn't he your kid? Ilse
Koch had a dog, its name was Adam."

"Adam!" Adam paces back and forth, folds his arms. Suddenly it's important to him that he explain everything to the dog,
that Naomi's father also hear his reasons, the father of that
mangled skull. "When I emerged from my mother's womb, I had
an option," he screams through an almost locked mouth, "I had
the holy option, sir, the once-in-a-lifetime option of naming myself. I might have been Moses, Abraham, Isaac, I might have
been Boaz, Bar-Atid, Yoram, Yehoram, Ahab, Jezebel, Asuel.
But I chose the name Adam, and Mother smiled. Father was
angry. In his mind's eye he saw me sitting in the Garden of Eden
and ruining the future of mankind. He forgot, or maybe on account of his relations with his wife he refused to recall, that
Adam was the victim. Eve was the sinner. And who was the
seducer? The apple! And there came a man from the tribe of
Judah, desperate, handsome, rich, orphaned and widowed, and
his name was—what? I laughed and said: Adam. I wanted to
call myself God-Adam, or Brother-Adam or Father-Adam or
Master-Adam, and I became Brother-Herbert, Brother-Klein,
Father-Dog. And, actually, Father-Dog made the most sense.
But at that time I hadn't the ears for such things, I didn't know
yet. Child, write!"

The child raises his eyes to him, are they smiling? What's he
waiting for, what does he want? "Do you understand?" He nods.
"I could almost kiss his disgusting face! And there came a certain desperate man, not innocent or straightforward, a swindler
in Israel, a companion of Satan, and it was in the reign of Dr.
Nathan Gross, and lo! it's going to rain! It's definitely going to
rain! The desert will get a good bath, it'll blossom, the wasteland

will gasp its last, and on all sides Jews will arrive with baskets on their heads, and they will ascend the mountain of God, the mountain of man, the Seizling Institute, and here they'll all be jailed."

Wolfovitz bursts out laughing.

The dog has a smile on his face. Have you ever seen a dog laugh?

"Adam," says Stein, "Adam is a nice name. The Indians called the first man *Manu,* which means the master of intentions and great and occult ideas. The Greeks, who invented logic, who invented democracy with the help of slaves, and the modern sewage system and the drama, they called man *anthropos:* in other words, the observer from above. The Romans called him *homo,* the talking animal. The Hebrew called him *Adam,* after the material—the earth or *adamah*—out of which he was fashioned, in the name of his inherited fault or infirmity, the blood coursing through him toward life and death, and they called him also *Enosh,* for in the days of the man Enosh, as it is written in the Bible, people put God into their names. That means, not only is man *Adam,* made of earth and blood and mire, but also *Enosh,* with God inside him. The man created in God's image was part angel, part muck. The criminal and the savior, the Messiah. According to the Hebrews. And, after all, when was man created? On the last day! As the sages say, whenever man begins to feel haughty, the angels improvise a tune and laugh: Why is your head up in the clouds?—the mosquito was created before you! But Adam—Adam was made in God's image and formed by God Himself and, though last, not least, because he was closest to the final act of creation: Adam, the created Adam, the crown of creation. Adam the best product. Adam. Adam is judged every minute. There was an Adam who was a great saint, and an Adam who was a preacher in Livorno, and an Adam who was the Prince of Württemberg whose father, Prince Ludwig, was the brother of the King of Prussia. And what about the great hunter Albrecht Adam? And the writer Adam de la Halle, and Adamus Bremenis, who was a Bremen

man, a man of Saxony. And Jean Louis Adam, and the lauded
printer John Victor Adam, whose business was lithography in
the year 1728 in Edinburgh, and Adamuah in Sudan, and . . .
I chose that name because it has a deep significance. And if that
isn't the case, it ought to be. Now that I am and have been
Adam. Don't say a thing, Wolfovitz, you were given your name.
At some silly unnecessary moment they gave you a name. I pilfered my name from eternity and therefore I must eternalize that
name. Adam. Dog. Ilse Koch. Son of man. Man. Son of God.
Close to a flop. Son of understanding. A thinking animal. A man
of reason. A man of blood. Mortal. His life an ordeal. On account of Paradise. On account of the woman formed from his
rib. On account of his folly. Man is the son of man. And Adam
had no father except God. And subsequently where did He go
to? He went to buy a Havana cigar and forgot to come back.
The best cigar, maybe some coffee, maybe Jack Daniel's? Life is
so sad without God! Still, man is left. I am here, and I have a
child, and he barks and is Adam's son, Adam's own child. Here
is the proof that the child of man is a dog. And you must give it
a name. A Hebrew name, child!"

The child looks up, his eyes flashing.

"Child, you must write on your typewriter a name that you
choose for yourself. Like me. The way I named myself, so you
shall name yourself! What are you waiting for?"

It's forbidden to postpone. Time is flying. Time flies and you
don't know what the moment will bring.

"Write, child, write . . ."

He gapes at him. The skies darken outside; in the window, the
clouds press into each other, black lambs. A flash of sun splits
suddenly through the dark clouds and illuminates the gray desert. A sandstorm is gathering strength somewhere, a gigantic
whirlwind is approaching.

"Child, write! You thought you could rely on me?"

The voice of Adam, of God-Adam, Father-Adam, Son-Adam,
Enosh-Adam, quakes.

"I'm sick, child, you hear? Sicker than you. I'm standing at

the end of the road. In a storm. Outside. In space. Among the
angels of Wolfovitz, I am a miserable cog. I slaughtered hens all
my life, all the years of my life. I am Dr. Gross's rag, a medical
guinea pig, a psychoanalytic hothouse. They hypnotized me.
Write! What will you write? Adolf? Herbert? Weiss?"

Wolfovitz's eyes are streaming with tears. Wolfovitz is up
against the ceiling, up against the sky, and they won't raise the
heavens for him. The sky outdoors is getting darker and darker.
A wild wind blows. You can only see it through the window—
the heating system and the air-conditioning and the music machine smother the wind's shrieking. But a storm is something to
hear, not just see.

"That's enough, Adam," sobs Wolfovitz. "Leave him alone.
What's the rush? Who needs a name?"

The child matches the coming storm with his drumming: his
fingers, which are the extremities of man, the extremities of man
in a dog's body, strike now with a murderous rage. He types, he
writes: *bastarde, Gross, bone, Jenni, gote.*

"You bark, yet you are not a dog. You cannot stand erect, yet
you are not a dog! Write, the name will create you, the name will
establish everything, a good name is better than a good body, a
name is better than posture, better than anything, every creature
has a name, even a cockroach, Adolf Cockroach, creation's
diadem, crown, wreath, wreath about the cockroach's head.
Write a name!"

The dog writes: *clowds, undernith, Jenni.*

Suddenly the dog remembers something which floats at him
from the fogs of his past. Once he was a child—

> *The almond tree's in blume,*
> *Hitler's bald as a spune,*
> *Burds atop the cypress trees*
> *Befowl him head to knees.*

Adam laughs. Adam laughs from far away. And as though
coming from another remote world, the bell rings, announcing
the meal. Pierre Lotti's voice cries from the corridor—he stands

on the other side of the door and calls out: "Adam, I have a surprise for you today. You have to taste it, and I've also brought out the special Beaujolais de Beaujolais de Bourgogne '56, the cork was as red as a monkey's ass, what fragrance!"

"What's your name, then, child?"

The child types. Why does he type names that a dog would never recognize or know? Because—and Adam laughs through the tears which are pouring down Wolfovitz's face—because once, some time, any time, he was a child and heard them. He writes: Jesus!

No. Adam told him that story! Adam spoke—or maybe it was Herbert?—and the child cocked his ear and listened. Adam spoke about that Messiah because it was important for him to talk about him. *He was a child of this land, flesh of its flesh, while I was a refugee from the world of Klein.*

To Wolfovitz the argument is amazing: "No need to mix up issues, you are a refugee from the world of Jesus. That Messiah! Don't forget! Never!"

"Okay, you father of skull-clapped Naomi, another name."

The child strikes, writes, screams through his fingers, his mouth going at the same time like a dog's: David! Then Adam Stein applauds merrily. "David, King of Israel, the husband of Bathsheba, the murderer of Uriah the Hittite, noble of Judah, conqueror of the city of Yevus, architect of Jerusalem, confidence man who fooled everybody, who carved out an empire for himself, skipped around the Ark of God and brought God into Jerusalem in an Ark. Whoever can bring God into Jerusalem in an Ark, kill Uriah the Hittite and marry his wife, compose the Psalms and commit adultery, beget a son as wise as Solomon —to make up his mind and be able to beget a son exactly as smart as Solomon!—who made a contract with Hiram the smart-aleck merchant and begged God to allow him to build a lovely house for Him, a man like that is after my own spirit. Particularly here, here in Arad, which was his fortress. A fortress on the border of the desert, in which he imposed his will, and out of which he took to his palace hashish and spices and salt and wine and servants and beautiful women and camels and God in an Ark."

The child's head sinks suddenly onto the machine and the keys respond with a metallic whacky sound.

Adam embraces the child. The child swings his face toward Adam; the murderous rage with which he previously has written is destroyed, as it were, by that embrace. His face is calm for the moment, the shutters of his blue eyes open and tears flow.

Adam, his cheek against David's face, feels those tears. He stares at them, and all of a sudden something terrible, something monstrous, becomes clear to him, something he no longer has any control over. He realizes that these tears are not the tears of an animal. That his notion was right. That the dog, now he has a child's name, is in fact a child. That the tears are human, that the dog who composed a song about Hitler will never be a dog again, will never bark, never chew bones. Adam is alarmed. The realization stuns him. The awareness that he has once again failed seeps into the depths of his soul. Adam Stein was never a dog, and the child of Adam was never a dog. What a disgrace! God, again you have led me to bewilderment. You are a greater swindler than I am. You're awesome. At this point Adam is struck by terrific pains that split his back, that contort his body. The child is frightened by the sight, dumfounded, his tears dry up from fear, and Adam screams: "I told you that it was impossible to rely on me, I'm sick!" And he rises, bursts through the door, and escapes from the room.

He escapes from the child. He escapes from Wolfovitz. The child bundles himself up in a corner, pulling Adam's blanket to him and wrapping it around himself, howling into it. Wolfovitz leaves the room. He toddles, limps. . . .

They found Adam a few hours later in the courtyard. In the midst of the desert storm, the heavy sandstorm, the raging rains pouring-gushing-jetting down from God, from heaven, from the ceiling of Naomi Wolfovitz. The tears of the angels clad in curtains were spilling from tremendous barrels. The entire desert had been upheaved by the gale, and Adam was standing and beating his lovely head against the wall of the building. All the while screaming: "God damn David, King of Israel . . ."

The Hebrew month of Adar is around the corner, and with it the holiday of Purim. The dog shrinks in his chair and types on his machine. The transistor radio plays. The dog listens to the music. "His master's voice."

Adam converses with the dog. Having left the infirmary, he is now a few inches closer to his end, which is as certain as Lloyd's. The child types his replies. And now the passing time announces on the bulletin board that this evening at exactly eight o'clock a Purim celebration will take place in the dining hall, an obligatory masquerade, a Purim performance in Nurse Spitzer's nursery, as much refreshments as you wish, with wine —Dr. Gross has opened the wine cellar. Wolfovitz claims that nobody should bypass the custom of celebrating "until you don't know the difference between cursed Haman and blessed Mordecai."

Before going to the dining hall, Adam pets the child awhile. The child is sprawled on the floor, breathing heavily. Both he and the child are at peace. Each feels the existence of the other. Man to man, man to dog, man to manchild. That's how they sit. In the window the evening hangs black, though the skies are distinct and, in the distance, a light is moving—perhaps a military jeep on its way to the ridges—and the other side of the Dead Sea is radiant. The sea illuminates the portion of heaven above it. This Dead Sea which Adam Stein didn't kill, which died on its own, before his time, its dead waters would flow with that same graveyard hush, with that primordial beauty of pre-creation chaos, till the Day of Judgment. As the new moon rises, the wadi between the white mountains shows itself for a moment, bathed in light, like a breach into a mystery. When Adam leaves the room, however, the peace which filled him while he was there, his mind empty, his eyes watching the star-studded desert sky in the window, that peace is gone. The corridor is clattering with music, and his spirit also is in turmoil for some reason. Adam doesn't know why. He slaps a mustache under his nose and rolls up the cuffs of his pants and, in his judgment, is properly dressed and disguised for the party. As he makes his hair wild, he says to himself: I am not Adam Stein, I am Herbert Stein! Herbert Stein, mustachioed and trousers rolled.

A light is on in the laboratory. All glory to the Jews, laughs the swindler in his heart. He knocks on the door and enters. Dr. Uriel Slonim is sitting at a gigantic wall-to-wall table, wrapped in a flashing white oilcloth, and cataloguing medicines that have just arrived from Haifa. By the time the goods were delivered here, with all the taxes paid, evening had fallen. But Uriel has to complete his catalogue. Tomorrow the doctors will be asking for certain amounts of drugs and pills and serums for injections, and everything has to be catalogued and numbered. Uriel gives Adam a smile and Adam says hello and sits opposite him. Then they don't say a word. Uriel continues his catalogue work, building towers of medicines like a child with his blocks, and he doesn't notice the exhaustion, the depression, on Adam's face. Uriel Slonim is not interested in the faces of patients, he builds towers. The only thing that interests Uriel Slonim is the nature of the medicines, the contents of the capsules, the chemistry of their activity. The neo-mysticism of pharmacology: peyote, mescalin, LSD, heroin, amphetamine, opium, permodin, cocaine . . . all kinds of cocaine, hashish. Uriel does research on how these drugs affect not people but white mice, rabbits, cats, even bees. It never once occurred to him to check the face of white mouse #191, red marking insulin file arranged into A, B, C, to determine whether this mouse was in any way depressed, exhausted, or happy. Adam studies him, him and his blocks. He wants to join the game, he must get the new drug that arrived today, Dr. Gross praised it to the skies in their conversation this afternoon.

He has forgotten the name of the drug for the moment, but he knows they are going to test it this week on some of the patients. It is something very powerful, hallucinatory, and they have to measure its hallucinatory effect, make comparisons, compile statistics. Oh, they want so badly to turn psychiatry into a science of controlled experiments, to investigate heartache with a microscope, to file away the spell of death. . . . A wonder drug. But what's the effect of this wonder? Drunkenness is not enough, neither are pills or smoke. Something new is needed. He craves for some escape. The child is getting on his nerves, driving him crazy. *He is my pill, my baby pill. He'll tie me down with chains. I hate being tied down, it kills any possibility of a true rivalry with life. Once when I was still a child, my goldfish died. We called him Franz. It was as if my friend had died, my father had died. When we buried him in the yard, I cried. Afterward, Mother died, and Father, and Lotta, and Gretchen, and Daddywhen-Daddywhy, and I didn't cry as hard. Ilse Koch did not die, she will live forever.* And Adam? Adam is alive, but a child is tying him down and the child is bound to die and then he'll be very sad. Something is needed, Slonim, a wonder drug!

Adam takes a fifty-cent piece out of his pocket and starts rolling it from finger to finger with fantastic speed. He knows, he understands his Slonim. What his dejected face can't accomplish, the nimble fingers of Germany's greatest clown can. Slonim's eyes are fixed on the coin, mesmerized, flabbergasted. Adam keeps them spellbound to his hand. Overcomes any resistance. His mouth babbles, doesn't stop talking, now you see the coin, now you don't. Where is it? Guess. Slonim doesn't know, it's a game. Adam pulls the coin out of his ear, flips it as a further proof of its existence, and next it's in Slonim's clenched fist, and again Adam is rolling it along his fingers and at the same time talking about the circus, how he used to steal the show from the animals, from the trapeze artists, from the great conjurors, from the fattest woman in the world, from the man with six fingers. He talks about W. C. Fields, in his opinion the

greatest American comic, not of the circus but of the cinema,
the man he admires most. He had a potato for a nose, a face of
total apathy, and a superb sense of humor. Adam once met
Jimmy Durante, who told him: "There are plenty of handsome
guys. I'm something different, something new." His mouth keeps
prattling, his hands keep flipping that coin, and then, with the
professional adroitness of a circus man, he sticks out his right
hand and, under the very nose of Slonim, rummages up and
down the towers, picking out the new wonder drug whose name
he doesn't know but which he recognizes at once, as an expert
on every single kind of medicine in this house. This one is different, new, like Jimmy Durante. Others are lovelier, but there's
nothing quite like this. When he leaves Slonim the cataloguer, he
returns to his room, swallows the capsule, and heads to the dining hall, to Purim, to the great celebration. Mustachioed, hair
wild, trousers rolled, a clown.

Nurse Spitzer's nursery performed a Purim play, but they
weren't the only ones taking part. The elder Schwester twin, like
many of the old kindergarteners, was dressed up as Queen
Esther. Arthur was in the costume of wicked Haman. None of
the kindergarteners was willing to masquerade as wicked
Haman; they were afraid they'd be tossed into the furnace and
burned alive. Arthur wasn't afraid of fire. Arthur loved fire. The
great arsonist was not scared of playing Haman and being hung
over a fire with his daughter, whose names were Parshandotha
and Dalfon and Aspotha and Aridi and Veizotha. How were
these children guilty? Adam wondered and Arthur wondered.
The Schwester twin was never bothered by such questions; God
was beyond her comprehension, she said, and when He appeared He would explain everything.

Wolfovitz argued that because King David made a census of
Israel, which was against Biblical law, God punished him and
struck seventy thousand souls off the nation. "A cruel God!"
concluded Wolfovitz, who had recognized God's cruelty long

ago when Naomi was in the cellar. The Schwester twin was not of this opinion. God's logic is not our logic, therefore we do not understand; for two thousand years we have been standing opposite each other, the nation and God, and that, she said, was an amazing story, not easily understood. Nobody can match God, in the whole universe. Scripture is one continuous dialogue, a compassionate and a forceful dialogue, brutal and kind, sublime and insane, between a nation and a God who chose each other and, consequently, are responsible to each other.

"Until he turned tail and sicked Adam Koch on his nation," said Wolfovitz.

"Right," said she, "but you don't understand why. There are reasons, but you don't know them. Just as you don't know why the Holy-One-Blessed-Be-He allows you to talk heresy. Only a believer—and every Jew is a believer, whether he calls his belief religion or atheism, righteousness, socialism, nature, positivism, science—only a believer who suffers on account of his belief, on account of the Covenant, can break out into slander. The man who guards his tongue too much probably hates too much. On Dr. Gross's couch lie hundreds of people prating about hatred, hatred for mother and father, yet all their words are nothing but a manifesto of trust, and trust is love. You are laughable, like every Jew who casts stones at God for being cruel and jealous, because He chose you and you chose Him, the two of you are in the same boat, and the waters of death swirl around it, until, in distress, you cry out, God!"

"God, God, God," screamed the kindergarteners.

"Go, go, go!" shouted Miles in the background, and finally Nurse Spitzer silenced them all and began final preparations for the performance, the *Purimspiel,* the Purim play. Everybody was arranged in lines: three Ahasueruses, two King Davids, King George III with a lovely paper crown on his head, Napoleon III, Louis XIV (Pierre Lotti with a drawn sword), Queen Esther, Madame Pompadour dolled up to the point of monstrosity, Madame Bovary, Ilse Koch, Madame Pasteur, Greta Garbo, and Marlene Dietrich. Wicked Haman, alias Arthur, tried to imitate the gait of Adam when he was walking with the dog in the yard like Charlie Chaplin the Dictator, alias you know who. There were other costumes too: Hess and Himmler and Heydrich. And the Rabbi from Tchortkov and two Hassids and three Israeli army officers, and a pilot, and a bulletin board, an evening newspaper, a ram's horn, Mickey Mouse with too long a tail, a rabbit, two dogs, an automatic central telephone exchange (young Mrs. Elmug with two telephone receivers on her breasts so that it was possible to dial directly, so she said, to the place where it was worthwhile to rest, namely, down there between her you know what, ring up and get an answer—and some even phoned, but most received *Sorry, wrong number!*).

Jenny wasn't there, nobody knew why. Maybe she was afraid. She longed for Adam, but was afraid he would pay no attention to her because of the crowd. Some were dressed as cowboys, political slogans, traffic lights, racing cars. They raced into the big hall and made a great tumult, screaming *Whoooooooppppp-peeee!* In the background Miles played his *yeah, yeah* symphony, and Himmler shouted *Jawohl,* and the others answered: *Go, God, go!* Then the children of the nursery began their first song:

> *Purim's a big holiday for the Jews,*
> *Masks, songs, dances and booze.*

Off in the wings sat Arthur, fat Manny, and bearded Davidovitz disguised as a bulletin board, and they sang:

> *Adam-Shmadam in the store*
> *Bought a juglet and no more,*
> *Came a cop and came a crook,*
> *Pulled his tail with a fishing hook.*

On the other side, across from the poetic face of Miles, rose the hoarse bass voice of the old man dressed up as Ahasuerus, his clothes tattered and his eyes muddied:

Man was born to die,
Cows to give birth.
If you climb too high
You'll flop to the earth.

Then another Ahasuerus stood up, but everybody burst out laughing. The kindergarteners clapped their hands with glee until Nurse Spitzer quieted them all and gave the second Ahasuerus a signal for his recitation.

"Honored and distinguished guests, why do we celebrate Purim? . . ."

Having finished his recitation, the child sat and another stood up instead who bashfully carried on the speech: "The Jews were in a terrible situation. Wicked Haman wanted their blood. He sent agents throughout the world in order to exterminate all the Jews. . . ."

Nurse Spitzer gave another signal at this point and everyone stamped three times, swung a noise-maker, and screamed:

Where is Haman now?
Any child can tell you how
It turned out in the end.

And Miles did his thing in the background, "Yeah, yeah, when the saints come marchin' in . . ."

"Ssshhh, children! Miles, don't interrupt! Please! Naomi, it's your turn," said Nurse Spitzer.

The old woman with the furrow of wrinkles straightened and said, without any expression whatsoever: "And in Shushan the capital there was a king, a great and awful king. What was his name?"

"Ahasuerus!" they all shouted with joy.

Nurse Spitzer: "And what did Ahasuerus do?"

Shrieking chorus: "He sought a queen."

Old child: "The queen he had was sick and ugly, and her name was Vashti."

Chorus: "Shti, shti, shti . . ."

Old child: "The King's in Israel, the Queen's in Hell, the King plays ball, the Queen's in the can."

Nurse Spitzer: "Ssshh . . . And whom did Ahasuerus find?"

Queen Esther rose, bewildered, looking around everywhere. Her eyes met Adam's eyes. Adam was depressed. Gradually the capsule was beginning to take effect inside him, to dissolve in his blood. His eyes stared mute and secluded, at the old-woman-of-a-child dressed in mats, an ugly miserable creature with a forced smile, who said: "Me! Queen Esther, Mordecai's niece. Me he sought, me he wanted, me he found, me he saw, in me he heard the steps of salvation."

Everybody: "Salvation for the Jews. A light and a candle for the Jews. For the scattered Jews everywhere, with their knapsacks and their sticks."

A child who was an old man with a mustache, bald, and dressed as a ship, mumbled:

> Hoo, hoo, hoo,
> Who are you?
> A smokestacked ship!
> What's your trip,
> And your cargo?
> Far away, not long ago,
> Are Jews with bag and stick in hand
> Waiting to climb to the Holy Land.

Chorus: "Israel is the land of ours, David is a king of ours, Mordecai is a salvation of ours, and Esther is a beauty of ours."

Their faces shone, glowed. An old woman who was a child recited in a whisper: "The cold wind blows, Hitler to bed goes, his wife gives him a glass of juice, and Hitler's bowels are loo—" They all burst out laughing. Laughing hysterically:

> Dad found Ma in the street
> Hanging from a telephone wire

And turned off the electricity.
Vive la compagnie!

Nurse Spitzer, patient, smiling: "No, you've mixed up the holidays. It's a nice song, but out of place. Children, please, what happened in Shushan?"

An old woman, a child, in rags, a beggar in the capital Shushan, mumbled through her closed mouth, her eyes terrified: "Esther made a feast and invited wicked Haman and Ahasuerus and there she related the terrible news . . ."

An old man, a child, dressed as a cowboy:

Well, Haman, who had one Hell of a Mom,
Wanted to give all the Jews napalm
And hang Mordecai from a tree,
But as he was writing his evil decree . . .

Nurse Spitzer: "And what was Ahasuerus' question?"

Naomi: "What should be done to the man whom the King wants to honor?"

Nurse Spitzer: "And who was that man?"

Chorus: "Not wicked Haman who set up the block, but Mordecai the Jew whom he'd mocked. Haman they strung in the air, his cronies too—which was only fair. Mordecai was second to the King, Haman a fine dead thing. Esther remained the Queen, Ahasuerus still loved her mien." In a frightful, jarring chorus they all sang: "Jacob the lily shouted for joy at the sight of Mordecai in blue."

At this point Queen Esther, plus another Queen Esther, plus the elder Schwester, who also was Esther, all sat down next to four Ahasueruses, and the others marched past them in an impressive procession, singing nonsense like *yo, yo, yi, ye, ya, jawohl, ya, ju, yo,* while Miles deafened everybody with his tambourines, drums, and assorted noise-makers.

Adam stopped his ears. He screamed, not knowing that his mouth was dumb, that his voice made no sound. The crowd of people gradually receded from his vision. Somewhere, down there, at the bottom of the mountain, had stood Arthur-Haman and Ahasuerus and Esther and they had sung, marched in a procession, intoxicated and screaming. He no longer heard them now. They were gone. He was alone, above. Suddenly he witnessed his entire life, years, months, days, filing past him in a pitiful parade, and deep in the background Purim was being celebrated without a drop of noise.

Nurse Spitzer looks like the wife of the grocer we bought our Sabbath loafs from, Mr. Loitler, who went from Munich to Berlin and from Berlin to Heaven and the God of smokestacks —thanks to the fascinating chemical process invented and perfected by the laboratories of I. G. Farben factories in the years of glory, during the thousand-year stretch of victory. Do you remember, dog? Hoo, hoo, my Rex. "My boy," said the American colonel who stamped the contract which entitled Adam Stein to Baron Von Hamdung's mansion, "my boy . . ." The years pass by his face. A dizzying procession. Via Dolorosa. Will saintly Helen emerge and wipe my face? There, in the streets of my Jerusalem? Will the handkerchief then be cloistered in some out-of-the-way church, with my face yet imprinted in the cloth? A thousand years later Naomi Wolfovitz's head shall be swathed in it. It's the 5th of May, 1939. A dreary, rainy morning. He buys a newspaper at a streetcorner. It's October 7, '41. As horses neigh in the background, somebody with a smile says softly—and his softness is poisonous: "The circus cannot belong to a person who is not of the Aryan race! Here is the historical, philological, and legal authority kindly supplied to us by Dr. Joachim Hess, Dean of the Law Faculty of the University of . . ." Cologne? Heidelberg? Dresden? Berlin? He has forgotten. Forgotten. All deans look alike, Mother Germany gave birth to millions, trillions, all with identical features. They all wrote similar books, authorizations, millions of authorizations; obviously it was the national sport of intellectuals in the years of glory. The thousand years of splendor which the world shall never forget. Writing authoritative books, proofs, concerning race, blood, sweat, Aryanism, *Jüdenreinism,* in those pyromaniacal years of dread. The days crawl by. And he along with them, transforming, contorting. Contracting and expanding, image by image, without order, without sequence, without the logic of time. In October '22 he was a young boy; in October '46 he was an old man. He's both persons, marching and saluting himself. Once Herbert, once Adam. They pass by. Laughing. Next "The Rhinoceros." That's what they called Hans Deutsch, who died in '39, died because he couldn't understand how what was happening could happen, that his nation, that his culture . . . When he looked out his window in Cologne and saw a dark Cologne and flags and banners and youths, his youths, screaming *Sieg Heil,* he dropped dead from sorrow. If Goethe, or Schiller, or Von Hamdung, or Goering, or Jean Paul, or Thomas Mann, or Bach, or Ilse Koch, if any one of these people had been standing at a window and seen all this, he would have understood certainly, but Hans the Rhinoceros was the great-grandchild of Mendelssohn, of the Emancipation, and he didn't understand. So he died. Adam fixes a look of scorn upon him. He, Adam, understood. And Commandant Klein, now Weiss, can testify to that, for he admired Adam accordingly and said: "You understand, Adam, that you are me, because I am you, both of us dogs, but I have a whip and you don't." Next, Mrs. Elsa Kurz, the English teacher, a ridiculous old woman, wearing the straw hat she bought in London on the single occasion when she managed to reach London and nobody in London could make out her English, the English teacher's English. And next, little Ginztag, and Louey and Paul and Josef and Father and Mother. Uncle Franz-Josef, named after Emperor Franz-Josef. Would *he* have understood? There he is, and everybody with him. Any minute Adam will start sobbing. It's sad here. Down below, at the bottom of the mountain, some celebration is going on, Purim. In another thirty years Jenny will be Nurse Spitzer, praised be her name. There is no future to life, life's an invention that didn't succeed.

At this point he screams. Hysterical screams. Everybody recognizes the sound and goes silent with horrifying suddenness.
With looks of guilt on their speechless faces. As though they
suddenly realize that a Purim party is a luxury. They vaguely
sense it, at the sight of Adam's contorted face. Each and every
one of them begins running his hands over his clothes, his costume. Even Nurse Spitzer, who isn't a stranger to these screams,
changes the tone of her voice and no longer speaks like a kindergarten teacher. The shrieks penetrate deeply into them. How can
Adam shriek like that today? In Arad? In Israel? Is Adam
dreaming? All eyes are on him. Him and his screams whose melody cannot be matched. And then—for Adam, incomprehen-
sibly—everybody is there, his cries have brought them all back,
with their procession; the Esthers and Ahasueruses and military
police and bulletin boards and a woman with telephones resting
on her breasts and Madame Pompadour and Madame Bovary
and Madame Pasteur and Ilse Koch. The parade and the people
are back. Adam stops screaming and says, "Wolfovitz, stand
here." And he obeys. Adam's mustache slips off, but he doesn't
pick it up. His eyes are as wide as they can go. "Schwester, over
here!" And she steps as commanded.

They all whisper: "They're coming. They've come. They're
here."

Adam: *"There* is *here. Here* is *there.* There's no escape. No
rest. . . . Wolfovitz, who are you?"

Wolfovitz: "I am Wolfovitz. My daughter Naomi was in a
cellar."

Adam: "No. Raise your hand, roll up your sleeve. Look,
what's written there?"

Wolfovitz reads slowly, "8 . . . 1 . . . 9 . . . 8 . . .
7 . . ."

"Well, then, who are you?"

Wolfovitz: "Yes, I am not Wolfovitz. I never was and never
will be. I am 81987."

"And you, Queen Esther? My old dear Schwester? Who are you?"

She rolls up her sleeve. "6 . . . 1 . . . 3 . . . 4 . . . 5." The whisper from her lips sounds like a prayer.

And Adam says in a low hoarse voice: "Who are you? Who are we? Subtract Schwester from Wolfovitz. 81987 less 61345 equals 20642. Will that year be the year of redemption? Well, in what *anno domini* are we now living? 1965? Then let's try subtracting the elder Schwester twin from Arthur, Esther from wicked Haman. That's my guess for today. Arthur, raise your arm. See? 63310. And dear Schwester—61345. The difference: 1965. In other words, today." Everyone roars, *"Ja, ja, ja,"* and Miles plays his agreement in the background. He has no number on his arm. He's a stranger.

"Now let everybody roll up his sleeve," screams Adam, and they all obey. Each numbered arm is stretched up high. "Yes, that's the way. Strain your muscles. I want to see a smile on your faces. No tears. It doesn't hurt. It hurt once, but not any more. Yes, lovely, I see that you are all smiling." Miles keeps playing, that bastard. Miles lived in Palestine, expelled Arabs, conquered, smashed, built a crazy democracy with faulty telephones. We came to you, my friend, and you accepted us with open arms, like a fool. That was a fatal error, the Law of Return will beget the end, we shall cause the soil to rot, pollute the atmosphere. We shall remember. We shall be like frontlets between your eyes. Play, Miles. You who escaped to New York and played with Charlie Parker, who died young and beautiful and a genius because he no longer wished to suffer.

"Smile, children. Hands high. Head up, shoulders back, feet together. Like in the army. Like soldiers, good." Smiles, everywhere teeth. Gold teeth, silver teeth, false teeth, dentures, bridges, young teeth, old teeth, hundreds and thousands of teeth, all smiling at him. Hands raised, a sea of antennas. That's what the butcher city looks like today, Berlin, the city of a thousand years of glory. On every roof, antennas. What are they after in the skies, these antennas that look like the hands of witches from Grimm fairy tales? Grimm fairy tales and Luther's essays and the inner thoughts of every proper German were fulfilled in Auchhausen. Arms, a sea of antennas, and on these arms, in blue: 5343121586742 316578011436799 992045602192753-1976432100916431869 43588119100706051019 87431100-7552344109765. There's no end to the numbers. He stops. And calculates the sea of antennas staring at him with fear, the fear of a dog, of a child sprawled by his Olivetti, of insulted Jenny, of Dr. Gross who is unable to baffle the wheel of misfortune, of Naomi Wolfovitz whose head could not budge the ceiling. Adam concludes: "Eight trillion, five hundred billion, seven hundred and fifty million, four hundred thousand—in other words, eight trillion tears, teeth, soapsuds, taut skins, ground bones, schools without children, wrecked houses, dreams, unused sperm, unripened old men, unwritten books, unrealized inventions, unfulfilled loves, unslept-in beds, empty walls, unlit lamps, miles of sky without God, angels dead from the plague. According to the facts at my disposal, there are now, or there once were, three hundred and one million, six hundred and fifty-five thousand, seven hundred and twenty-two angels. Where are they? Did they too die? Or maybe they are sitting in the heavenly amphitheater and watching the great drama of their Lord? Burned High Holiday prayerbooks, songs, melodies, stories from father to son, uneaten apples, tears, trillions of tears. Lick those numbers. You are beaten. Lick. Don't hide them. You're celebrating Purim? For what reason? On account of one Haman? How does that repay my calculation of numbers, the trillions of tears? Will God do the paying? That very God that punished the ten sons of Haman? Some hero. In his neighborhood he's the bully, but among the other nations he's hidden in the crowd, scared stiff. When he's with you he shows off his strength, flexes his muscles, screams, curses, smashes, kills, but among the children of Adam Koch he trembles like a leaf, keeps quiet, enjoys himself, hires murderers behind your back, pays them overtime, brings their brains up to date so they can invent the best inventions, gas, zyklon B, modern HCN. Whom are you singing to? You want another Schwester, another Wolfovitz, another Adam Stein, another Herbert, another Arthur, another Naomi, another, another, another . . ."

Everybody pays attention. Tense. All arms are stretched high. Toward the ceiling. Toward the sky. Adam shuts his eyes and sees himself. A child. A child. A young boy. A young boy becoming an adult. A young man. A man. A clown. A student. A philosopher. A violinist. A joker. A comedian. A thinker. A charmer. A husband. A father. A dog. God. He commands: "Right arm extended. The blue one, up. Up and down, up and down." Morning exercises. The music ceases. Everybody obeys as though stunned. In this building it's possible to get away with it, Adam knows. "Right arm to the right, right arm up, up and down and around." A forest of trees. In the wind. Tossing. Praying.

Who was the first to laugh? Nobody knows. But someone began. "We are memorial candles," he screams, and they laugh. *"We* didn't die, *they* did!" And they laugh, still swinging their arms in all directions. Their faces twist with laughter. Adam is a mirror in which they see themselves and laugh. The kindergarteners come to life. Old Naomi with the furrowed cheeks bursts out screaming:

> *Haman, Haman, Haman,*
> *Run quickly through the grass,*
> *A tiger's going to eat you,*
> *And then you'll get a mass.*

The palsied old man with the murky eyes, the prince of paupers, poor Ahasuerus, laughs. His hand shivers and he thunders:

> *The almond tree's in bloom,*
> *Hitler's bald as a spoon,*
> *Birds atop the cypress trees*
> *Befoul him head to knees.*

And somebody else, in back, shouts between the lines: "Hitler's dead, his wife is sick, a German submarine, one two three four." The others, in a chorus:

> *Hitler in Germany couldn't be found,*
> *The devils took him underground.*

> *Doctor Gross has a hole in his head,*
> *A hole in his head, a hole in his head,*
> *And we have a hole in our ass.*

Adam stands, his face concealed in fog, and sees Goering and Goebbels. He sees Goebbels in a public gathering, in the days before he was imprisoned. Goebbels spoke then with the voice of his nation, the voice of his culture. Two thousand years of that culture blurted from his throat: "It's true that the Jew is human, but the flea is also a living being, not too pleasant a one. . . ." And he sees Lotta and Gretchen and Ruth as unlovable fleas. While the others are laughing, he sees himself, his violin, his circus. The hands tumble in the fog. 659711031178-9134456198176. A ballet of old hands, young hands, hairy, smooth. The laughing increases, gets bolder and bolder.

> *They stuffed her mouth, they stuffed her mouth,*
> *They stuffed her mouth with a broom.*
> *But I am Purim, with a mouthful of jokes,*
> *Though I come once a year, dear folks.*

Laughter. And time flies. Backward. Toward the past, toward there. Where they all are frozen. The laughter stops. And Adam, Adam buckles, eyes ripped open, muddy, his brain a mixture of fog, his eyes a mixture of tears, Adam buckles and falls. Doctors burst into the room. The male nurses force their way in, frightened. Pierre Lotti removes his costume, ashamed, not knowing what is happening. The nurses try to lower the arms of the patients to their proper places, but cannot. The muscles have gone stiff. With all their efforts, the nurses cannot put a single arm into a sleeve. Adam hemorrhages, spits blood, screams. They tie him to a stretcher and carry him out. Four nurses bearing a hemorrhaging dog.

10

DAVID, KING OF ISRAEL

THE STILLNESS of the infirmary is bathed in the smell of iodine and the fumes of alcohol. The walls are green, pale green. Nobody knows why the walls of the infirmary are painted green. Opinions vary among the patients. Green is the color of the dollar, green is the color of anemia, green is the color of a sick man's stool, the color of neutrality, the color of insecurity. Adam awakens into a world of white aprons, pale greenness, and doctors hesitating to give an opinion one way or the other. He vaguely realizes that the night of the Passover Seder has already passed. That the elder Schwester is looking for, longing for, her God and is afraid that Adam—no, he couldn't, he wouldn't disappoint her. The bed opposite him is empty, whoever was there has recovered and gone. In the window above the bed sits Herbert.

Herbert is conducting a seminar which he calls satirical—the bastard does have humor—on "The Monster or the Dog," and Adam recalls, with a painful pang, his David, King of Israel. Does he need me? To Hell with him. Herbert says: "It is characteristic of dogs that they develop definite human traits, they acquire the ways of their masters, a man and his dog are alike, the dog notices everything and understands much more than you imagine. The dog hears the word 'Eat' and jumps, hears 'Let's go out' and wags his tail—even though the dog in this particular case does not have a tail, since it's a member of a tailless family, which is a phenomenon that demands an explanation. In the dog's presence you have to talk in a secret language so the dog won't understand. But if you should so much as mutter, 'Who's going to put the monster out?' you'll see how quicky that monster will wag the tail he doesn't have." Adam smiles. His twin is a bastard's bastard, therefore all his life he's been dealing in philosophical matters. He never mingled with the common man, never got the cuffs of his pants wet, never clowned around, so he never became a dog. He never married, so he never forfeited his children. Conclusion: He is healthy and I am sick. But when I die, he'll die too, and that's a smudge at least of vengeance.

A small girl at the end of the infirmary recites:

> *How pretty you are, Spring!*
> *In the field and in the meadow!*

Accordingly, he knows that spring is here, spring has come to the desert, perhaps flowers are already flourishing in places among the wadis, in the ravines, and the air is clear, the sun is blazing, the fragrance intoxicating, a reminder of perfumed blossoms far away, not here.

Jenny comes to visit him every day, sits by his bed and knits. Listens to the news blaring from the small transistor radio, stares frozen-faced at the living corpse, waits, wonders. Vaguely he recalls that once he woke up for a moment, stretched out his hand, grabbed the ball of green wool she had placed on his bed, and tossed it away. The ball of wool rolled along the floor, the yarn unwinding and tangling. Jenny neither got up nor even looked at the disappearing ball, she just smiled at him and he went back to sleep.

At the end of April he returns to his room. Jenny has renovated it. She has cleaned, scrubbed, scraped. When he comes in, she tells him that the child—and her eyes suddenly are tender—that the child misses him. He shut himself up in his room, she says, with the typewriter "which you said I could lend him," and he types all day.

"I never said you could lend him the typewriter." Adam wants to be furious, but he is unable to.

"You didn't?" She plays innocent. "You must have said so."

"You won't get anywhere, Jenny. The child won't be yours. We won't be sharing the booty, the child's mine."

She gives him a look of astonishment. Her eyes are no longer tender but harsh. She imagines her own voice grumbling: I scrubbed your room, cleaned up for you, every day I came to visit you at the infirmary, I worried about you, I knitted you a sweater, I took care of the child, I lent him the typewriter, I washed your shirts, ironed them. And now you yell at me? Is that your way of saying thank you? I made sacrifices for you . . . She recognizes her mother's voice trembling in her own throat, her mother with the furrowed forehead, and she is seized with amazement and also shame, real shame.

"But it makes no difference," he says. "Let the child write."

"Oh, no. From the time you fell ill, something happened to him. He became paler. It's hard to grow paler than very pale, yet he became paler than very pale. He used to sleep in the bed— you remember he began to sleep in the bed? Like a human being? But after a few days, after he realized that you weren't coming back, he went back to sleeping on the floor. Without his filthy sheet, though. He just held on to the end of the sheet and squeezed it. Hours on end he would squeeze the end of that sheet and sometimes suck it. He tied himself to the chain and that's how he lay all day. Later on he untied himself. But he wouldn't respond. We tried, Shapiro and I, and Dr. Nachwalter, we tried speaking to him, but it was like the old days, before you . . . in other words, like before, and he didn't understand us, didn't react. We speak, and he howls like a dog. He doesn't bark any more, just howls. A sort of half-bark, a bark that isn't a bark and yet is."

Adam is wearing his best suit, the dull blue one, its gold buttons with the insignia of Van Hamdung adorning the jacket. He even has a perfectly ironed handkerchief sticking out of the breast pocket, as he steps toward the child. He is amazed by the sweat dripping from his hands, by the irregularity and speed of his own pulse.

The dog, the child, David, King of Israel, is sprawled in a corner of the room and purring. He sees Adam close the door after him, and he growls like a beast of the jungle. He squints at Adam, but his expression lacks the liveliness that Adam had got used to.

Adam thinks with a pinch of disgust: The light has gone out of the animal. And the moment he thinks this he feels that in the interval he has recovered, that he is stronger than he has been in a long while. He feels his blood circulating. His life coursing through his veins.

The child, all bundled up, hops toward the couch, leaps onto it, hugs the Olivetti, and types as quickly as he can: *U didunt cum, u war saposed too cum, and u didunt cum.*

"You type nicely, child. Very nicely. You've improved. Look, I've brought you a present."

He takes from his pocket his electric shaver and holds it out to the dog. The child creeps close to Adam, hesitates, but brings his mouth to his hand. The child doesn't open his mouth. His lips, dismal as they are, cleave to the back of his hand and then snap apart. He examines the shaver, handles it, turns it over and over, his eyes become foggy, their blueness dissolves in water.

"Do you know why I didn't come?"

The child goes back to the couch. A few seconds pass, the

room is perfectly still, in the corridor you can hear a food trolley clanking along the black carpet. The child crawls to the Olivetti and types feverishly with one finger while his left hand embraces the machine.

He writes: *Dont wunt too kno. Pippy in bedd. Not rane.*

"Oh." Adam smiles as he reads. "Yes, you do, you do want to know. You're lying, dog."

The child types fast. The bastard has learned quickly. He looks ridiculous. His fingers recall the beak of a cuckoo-clock bird. The child writes: *Jenni! Pippy wid Jenni.*

Adam raises his voice, thunders: "No, I wasn't with Jenny!" The child types: *Evribuddy runz away.*

Adam paces in the room. Heavy steps. He clasps his hands behind his back, gives the child a sly look, and shouts: "Know why I didn't come?"

The child goes on typing, his face inside the machine so as not to see Adam, he is frightened, his disappointment crawls all over him, he knows the answer, he feels it.

The child types: *U didunt wunt too, didunt wunt, didunt wunt . . .*

Adam stops him. Pulls his head away from the machine and for a moment almost hugs him, but at once releases his head and it bangs down against the machine. "So what if *I* didn't want. *You* did want. Now listen to me. The question is why I didn't die, not why I didn't come, why I didn't die! I didn't die because I wanted to come back and see you again, I stopped the angel of death at the very gate, I wrestled with him, you must believe me, you're the only one in this entire idiotic building who is capable of understanding. I could have died, but not yet, because I had to come back again to see you. The truth is that, according to the program, I should have died right there at the Purim celebration, during the ballet of numbers, then and there, when I fell, I should have come to my end. But instead, in order to see your face again, you, the dog, and the Olivetti, I came back. That's why I didn't die. But I haven't too much time left, so don't get your hopes up too high, and now I want to piss."

Before the child can answer, Adam is already inside the bathroom, the door locked, and Adam pissing. Adam feels somewhat relieved and doesn't bother to wipe the tears from his eyes.
He returns to the dog, and the child writes: *U couda died. U
didunt cum. I didunt wate.*

"I could have died, I could have." Adam speaks in a whisper.
"But I wanted to see you, to find out, maybe, perhaps, you and
I . . . to find out if you ate, slept, if your face had lost its
wonder."

The child types: *Pippy in bedd. U didunt cum. I made pippy
on de flore.*

"I was sick, child, I imagined I saw everybody, everybody,
everybody I ever met, anywhere, anytime, the whole bunch.
They passed before my eyes in a line, even Franz, the goldfish
that died when I was still a boy, the biggest loss of my life, he
too showed up. I saw my father, who was younger than I am,
and my twin, Herbert. They all went by. Years, specific dates,
the first of May, 1917, toward the end of World War I. Exactly
at four in the afternoon I lost my first tooth. I actually saw that
too, and placed the tooth under my pillow. At night the fairies
came and put fifty *pfennig* beneath the pillow and took the tooth
away with them. With that money I bought a book about sexual
education. I read it to my whole class. Before my eyes I saw the
stretch of grass at the foot of the cruel black statue of Hinden-
burg. I read to them about insertion and ovulation, and they
laughed in bewilderment, and scratched in their pockets and
swayed as though they were praying. Afterward the principal
grabbed me and for the first time in my life I found out that I
wasn't a German. His hair was as white as mine is now, and
nights he used to listen to his phonograph playing Wagner. He
loved Wagner. After I found out that I wasn't a German I broke
into his room and smashed the first three records of that album.
I remember the label. Grammophon Berlin. The title was *Götterdämmerung.* I smashed them and the gods didn't protest.

They didn't catch me—the principal suspected me, but said nothing because he had no proof. I was a genius. I read his thoughts. I knew dozens of books by heart. I read them right through the binding and the teachers were afraid of me. Much later, when I was appearing in the circus, he came to ask for my help. He wanted me to help him get a higher pension. I took him to the first record store we came across and bought him *Götterdämmerung,* and then I chased him away. I wanted to die and couldn't, on account of you, so you'd know the facts: I'm not writing a research paper on the Institute for Rehabilitation and Therapy. I'm a patient, like you. They're all whores. Everybody hates everybody, the smart man is the evil man, when they operated on me I fought off the angel of death and he panicked. You have no right to wait for me. My teacher was David Richter Frank, whose brother became famous later on."

The child types: *Badd, peepul ar badd unkels. I made pippy in bedd.* The child's hands tremble. Adam wonders, Is he offended? Whenever I bring my feelings out in the open, he's offended. So why did I come to him? In order to talk to somebody. And he's insulted. *Perpetuum mobile,* no exit. But he's waiting, oh and how! He's waiting for some words.

The child types: *De plane haz a redd ass, El-Al cen landd onn glass, a donkkey blynd inn won ei will soon kiss my fly, my plezure's anal, yourz iz jenital, you make pippy inn yore handd, try a bottel if you cann.*

Adam laughs. The child doesn't laugh, he's a dog, but the corners of his mouth quiver. Adam reads the words aloud. The child is frightened on hearing them for the first time. What memories popped into his canine mind? Was this his revenge? Against whom? Because he managed to become a dog and he could have remained a dog. But I came along and ruined everything? Hocus-pocus, now I'm going to interrupt and halt the process so he'll be stuck in the middle, neither dog nor child. The child is scared. For he was a child once and had parents, uncles, friends, bears, a red ass, blocks, rags, tattered papers, books with garish pictures, maybe a sea and a beach and shells?

The child yanks the paper out of the Olivetti in anger. Tears it into tiny pieces and chews them eagerly. He swallows the words and the paper. Adam tries to stop him. He attempts to pull the paper out of the child's hands, but the child jumps up and bites his hand. The very hand that fed! Adam brings his hand to his face and examines it carefully, his face pale. The child lies in a corner and breathes deeply, his terrified eyes bulging. He sounds like a weary locomotive. But Adam discovers immediately that the bite is no simple bite. A dog hasn't bit him, neither has a child, but something in between. The two of them sense this. The imprint of teeth in his flesh isn't deep enough for a dog or minor enough for a child.

"You're not a dog!" Adam swallows his words, unaware that he's spoken them. The child still quakes in the corner, his eyes weeping without tears. His mouth shivers, but no saliva comes. Adam's hand hangs as if it had no life. The child keeps chewing the pieces of paper and swallowing them.

"You can't bark!" A terrible insult!

The child nods, ashamed, chewing, swallowing. Adam sits, picks up the electric shaver and passes it from hand to hand absent-mindedly, as though his hands were there but he himself were far away. A painful silence. You can almost make out the buzzing music in the corridor. The child lowers his eyes and fixes his gaze on Adam's shoes.

When Adam notices the downcast eyes, knowing that Rex would wrestle for a meager portion of meat and that he himself is rolling his own eyes and is nothing but a shadow, a miserable shadow, a useless shadow, he whispers: "But I love you, child. This is bad, this is maybe even monstrous. Why? What do you want from me? I'm a broken reed. We'll both collapse. Your revenge is not sweet. You'll fall and so will I."

Instead of any unexpected answer, instead of the expected silence, there is a knock on the door that frightens them both. Into the room, with measured steps, comes Miles Davis, wearing dark sunglasses, a pink shirt with too many buttons on it, black pants and orange shoes. Miles is carrying a tremendous package which almost topples him, but with great difficulty he manages to set it up in the middle of the room. He breathes heavily, obviously excited. The child and Adam stare at him and then at the package, back and forth. Miles is impatient. He starts undoing the package, pulling off the strings, tearing first the wrapping paper and then the carton underneath, and what emerges is an average-size xylophone, pretty as a picture, pretty enough to make you want to cry—glowing wooden rungs attached with wooden nails to two yellow metallic slats. Adam has never seen a nicer xylophone in his whole life. Miles holds in his hands the sticks with the rubber balls at the ends and flaps his arms in his excitement.

The child's azure eyes gape. Those lovely Swiss lakes, those eyes as blue as hope, stare at the xylophone. What do you see, child? Does the xylophone look like a God to him? Like a superior creature? Like a thousand and one Olivettis? This dog's Olympus is strewn with little machines, man-made. Cigarette lighters, electric shavers, transistor radios. And the God of Gods, without a doubt, must be this xylophone.

"This is for David," says Miles, smiling. "Let him get a little peace, let him deaden his nerves, do you know what it's like to go from the kennel to the throne? Despair, man! So here's a gift for you, and let's all play together, a quartet, the Four Lost Souls, Lullaby of Arad, Lullaby of Mrs. Seizling's. Man, I am sick, this pad will swing, baby, swing . . ."

"But why?" Adam is dumfounded. The child sprawls in a corner and keeps quiet. He doesn't even approach his gift. He half understands, half doesn't.

"Two days ago, in the evening," Miles says as though to himself, "I went out into the yard. I was pretty sad, I wanted to go back to New York, but they would never let me. The government won't let me leave. They drafted me into the army. I'm an American citizen, man. They fabricated documents, forged papers and locked me up here, in this transient station until the American Embassy gets me out. They won't let me return to New York, they're scared of my success. I'm the author of 'Take the A Train,' not Billy Strayhorn. I've written a lot. I wrote something called 'Israel' which some bastard Italian swiped.

"It was so quiet all around, spring was everywhere and spring has such a fragrance, I once actually made music to the odor of spring, so I walked through the yard longing to meet somebody I knew, a friend, a comrade, someone who really knew me and I knew him, somebody I was together with in some real place, not just here, not here with those bastards. I was pretty confused, man. I wouldn't say I wanted to cry, I just cried—without wanting to. Tony Scott, Gerry Mulligan, Dizzy Gillespie, Lou Jackson, those were the guys I wanted to meet up with, be with. But I was here, and by myself. Suddenly I heard a voice. The voice was so familiar. I didn't quite hear what he said, but I recognized the speaker. I tried to locate where he was, but couldn't. The voice was caught up in the air, coming from afar. I stood by the Institute bridge, at the very edge, and actually thought about breaking through and escaping, but I couldn't. I didn't care.

"Did I say this was a transient station? Well, it isn't! It's a prison. With armed guards on the bridges. And they shoot, man. They don't fool around. The desert swallows the corpses. No cemeteries here. Bang, sand, ravens! In the distance I could see the lights of Arad. In one house, far off, a window was open and lit. I could see a woman in the window wearing just a bra, no dress, just a bra and panties. Her husband was stretched out in the armchair, or maybe it wasn't her husband, I don't know. The phonograph was playing something of Charlie Parker's—I knew the record, a collection of assorted pieces, a posthumous release. I recognized his voice. He was speaking, speaking on that record and it was an act of friendship.

"He told me the most important things, about New York, about my city, about people I loved, about Canal Street. I know the neighborhood. A bit gloomy. There's an abandoned movie house around there. And an ice-cream stand in front of it, and a used-clothing store beside it, plus a store selling Hebrew books. A pale Jew used to sit inside wearing a poetic old hat. From your window you could see the Pepsi-Cola sign across the river, right? And that's near the editorial office of the Yiddish paper *Forward*. The information lady is a woman about fifty, always dressed in black, always smiling. Yes, I know the whole vicinity. We used to have jam sessions there. There was Dizzy, Perez used to come sometimes, Max Roach, and Lenny Tristano, the blind guy—I remember him, he came and played. And Charlie Parker.

"I was in a turmoil because the woman had stripped and was already in bed. From where I was standing, she looked like a beetle in the distance. Her husband poured something into a glass and turned the record over, and the sounds from their stereo traveled miraculously across the desert and reached me. Once, after I heard him play, I wanted to die. And he knew it and burst out laughing. He had a great laugh, Charlie Parker, and a high forehead, and his face was the face of a sad child. And what did Parker do?

"He went back to death. That's why he laughed when I said I wanted to die. Because jazz began as a musical accompaniment for funerals, black funerals, since a few conscienceless Arabs had hunted down their ancestors in Chad and Tanganyika and brought them in little boats to Zanzibar and from there to the New World. Funerals for men who even in Heaven—so Parker told me—had nothing to look forward to, because God was white. Because their black little Jesus was ridiculous. His father was white and cruel, his mother a Hebrew woman, a Jewess, and he black as coal. And innocent? How could anybody be as innocent, as pure, as Parker? Parker was the genius of the music of the defeated. He was beautiful and he was black, even on the inside, deep inside, where the soul is usually white. Mister Jazz, Mister Bebop, Mister God of Rot and Roaches. He cracked the world like an almond and took out the seed of music like a Hassid devoutly praying. And he knew he was going to die, and he died with a clear head, and the world went on its merry way. Back to business as usual. They quarreled about the rights to the corpse, fought over the will, his legal wife came and claimed her share and his real wife was pushed aside, friends forgot that it was Bird who had played and they remembered just the face and mouth and the arm hungry for an injection. I know, I was there. . . . He used to get up in the morning, drink a little bit, take the agony that covered him like sweat and put it in the refrigerator and freeze it there. And then, at night, he would take out his frozen pain and melt it gradually, and suddenly, inside the note blaring from the saxophone, you could hear the black man's story in a megalopolis. Inside, in his soul, he was black. Like his grandfather who was once a slave. He is the alchemical wonder which magicians and wizards seek in the muck. I'm white, inside and out. And I belong to a God who has fallen asleep from laughing too much, to quote Wolfovitz the Circumciser.

"And I heard him talking to me the way the Schwester twin hopes to hear God talking to her, or the Prophet Samuel, or Isaiah. It's a different century. God screams now through the dying jaw of Billie Holiday, from the saxophone of Parker, from the coughing and groaning of Wolfovitz, from the head of his daughter Naomi. No? Obviously so."

"Who knows?" says Adam. "We don't ask questions. We don't understand, we don't even *not* understand. We accept everything. We keep quiet. We gnash our teeth. We study hard. We discover dogs in the Institute. Let's see what God says. Who are we to ask, to gape?" And thinks: Anybody who's come to this place has good reasons. We dream when we're awake, therefore we'll die more fulfilled. Adam knows perfectly what shame was, and what precisely it cost. To the last drop of blood. Yes!

"Thank you for the xylophone."

And then the dog crawls over to the xylophone. The lovely, shiny, modern xylophone. Where did Miles buy it? Miles doesn't lack for money, his father would be glad to pay him off with

huge compensations if he'd just sit there quietly in the Institute
and not disturb the father's peace or his new marriage. For
Miles's father doesn't like unexpected disturbances, and Miles,
as he is, is an unexpected disturbance. Consequently, on good
days and on days that are just so-so, Miles's wallet is always fat.
He ordered the xylophone from Tel Aviv and it came, all packaged, for David.

The dog stares at the xylophone for a long while, slowly sticks
out his hand and begins to pat the radiant varnished wooden
strips. Forgetting Adam, forgetting Miles, forgetting everything.
And while the dog is studying and handling the xylophone, Miles
sings a song, stumbling over the words, and then bursts out into
an uncontrolled laugh. "There's nothing like children's songs.
The Purim party was a sensation," he says.

"It was terrible," says Adam and observes the child, who
gapes at his big new toy.

"No, you don't get me. If it were possible to play with dolls to
the last day, if it were permitted, don't you think that would be
the best thing to do? And the songs. I once wrote a jazz piece to
a song I used to sing as a kid of ten:

> There are kids in this world
> Whose parents have deserted them.
> They have nothing to eat
> Because an Oriental meal in Tel Aviv
> Costs two cents more than
> An Oriental meal in Jerusalem.

I made up a melody for this song. I used to sing it to myself, and
any time I wanted to cry I'd think about the child who had nothing to eat, the kid who was hungry because an Oriental meal in
Tel Aviv costs two cents more, and to travel to Jerusalem was
out of the question. I can sing dozens of children's songs. I try to
liven up the flat tunes. I want to take some songs along with me
to New York, for my friends, and maybe show them a new di-

rection for jazz, so jazz can move forward."

The child picks up the two sticks in his eager hands and starts striking the glowing wood strips of the xylophone, first hesitantly and then with more force. And Miles ponders about the pearl on which he composed a jazz fugue once and realizes, yes, now he realizes why he bought the xylophone for David, King of Israel. Charlie Parker had told him: Remember the pearl, she's as delicate as you are and she mocks, she despises the divers that search for her. That's the way of all mysteries, to laugh at the mire that surrounds them, that always tries to analyze them, that claims that these secrets owe their existence to it, the hunting, dredging, fishing, investigating, conquering muck.

After half an hour the child can play tunes. Adam is flabbergasted, and furious. Adam is jealous! says Herbert from the windowsill. Adam answers, Adam is *not* jealous! Herbert replies, Adam is jealous and angry. The child's already playing in half an hour.

Miles takes his trumpet out of the bag hanging from his shoulder and joins the child, goes along with him, following his steps without even knowing it, without the child's knowing it, keeping in line with him, though he wouldn't admit it, marching together with him. The music repeats the rhythm of their hearts. They're talking to each other through music. How can a dog that only a few months ago was tied to a chain, that never spoke, never stood, that lay sprawled in a sheet in a dark smelly room, how can such a dog be stooping now over a modern, up-to-date, radiant xylophone and, with his canine hands, strike the strips of wood with two sticks and make lovely subtle music? How is that possible? Adam has no idea. It's incomprehensible to him. Herbert, that eternal mocker, disappears. Miles has no thought in his head now but the music. Let Adam take out his guitar and strum on it and try to overtake the other two, and if he cannot, let him drum on the back of his guitar with his fingers, according to the beat, the heartbeat, and stop ruminating and beating his brains and just accept things as they are.

And for the first time the word "recovery" is used to describe the turn of affairs. It is Dr. Gross who says the word, and in his heart a little celebration is going on. Not a noisy one—as slight as a puncture.

It was Sunday. Time, in its flight, had brought us summer. The first fruits of summer, summer in its early stages, not yet unbearable, still without its bite. And even here at the Institute it was as if its teeth had been dulled. A pleasant dry breeze. In the Institute everything was still, sterilized, and chilled. Soon it would be a year since Adam Bluebeard Stein had returned to the Institute. A year since he had tried to throttle Ruthie. A year— almost a year—since he had encountered the dog. Now Adam and Pierre Lotti sat and discussed a matter dear to their hearts.

Today, Sunday, was Pierre Lotti's Sabbath. His wife and daughter had gone to Beer-Sheva to pray in the mission of Mrs. Samit on Trompeldour Street in the old city. The American woman and her eight children and her white-haired husband had been living in that city for several years and hadn't yet managed to convert a single Jew. Perhaps they hadn't tried. They simply awaited the Day of Judgment, and prayed for the souls of the lost and erring. Pierre's wife, who adored Mrs. Samit, would bring a cake and some biscuits for the children, and a meat pie, and after the prayers they would gather in the enclosed court-yard of the ancient Turkish house, a courtyard paved with river pebbles and overgrown with vines and shrubs, and they'd discuss world affairs, the future of Beer-Sheva, the future of the mission in the land of the Messiah, and the fact that the Jews behaved as though they were unable and would always be unable to see the light.

Now that Pierre Lotti was without his wife and it was Sunday and he was off work and his underling, Jonathan Treyvish, was substituting for him, he was able to sit at his ease and consider with Adam the matter of the sacred waters of the Jordan. The scheme, apparently, was quite simple. Adam had conceived it a few months earlier and discussed it with Pierre Lotti; since then they had met each Sunday to go over the details of the idea and discuss the best ways of implementing it.

All that they had to do was collect a certain amount of water from the river Jordan, since, as everybody knew, the Jordan was a sacred river (or at least a sacred stream, to anybody who had seen it—and Adam had seen the Jordan in his travels through the country before going up to Jerusalem and meeting Joseph Graetz). The Children of Israel had crossed it on their way to the Promised Land. Jesus had been baptized in it. And therein lay the seed of the idea. There were close to a billion Christians in the world, many of whom were strongly attached to the holy places. For example, Pierre Lotti himself had wept profusely when he first saw the waters of Jordan. "Therefore," Adam picks up his theme, "what do we require? Holy water, or water that we can make holy and package in tiny plastic flasks and sell throughout the world." Moreover, Adam has a further scheme. They must contact some artist, not a modern artist but an artist who knows his stuff, a good craftsman, who can come and paint the holy places, stereotypically, with nice olive trees, towers, and churchbells. These pictures would be printed on cardboard cards which fold into a spring. Adam knows this method, which is very popular in German department stores. You open up a children's book, and actual houses, in three dimensions, jump out: like jack-in-the-boxes. And on these pictures they could glue a thin sliver of olive wood from Nazareth. A flask of sacred water from the Jordan. Genuine sand from Jerusalem. But not to be sold in some silly haphazard fashion, like ashtrays! "No, we'll get in touch with some priests in Jerusalem or Nazareth and together we'll put out a prospectus for the entire world, so that all the buyer will have to do is send a letter accompanied by a check to the address 'Birthday Greetings, Nazareth, Israel,' specifying what friend he wants us to send these cards to. Once we receive the buyer's letter we'll pick out one printed picture card, a jack-in-the-box card with the Jordan water and the olive-tree sliver and greetings and a prayer selection in Latin, English, French, Spanish and Hebrew, and mail it to him, or his friend, or his relative." In this way the world would gorge itself on cards from the Holy Land. Who could resist such a temptation?

Pierre Lotti, who had come to Israel by pure chance, was a man of ideas. One of his dreams was to establish a factory for the manufacture and export of frozen falafel. Frozen falafel is a superb product. And he already had a fantastic recipe. Frozen falafel from the Holy Land for cocktail parties in Europe and America. But now he was convinced that three-dimensional springing birthday cards with holy water in them were his road to wealth and worldwide renown. Big business. Travels. Financial transactions. Public relations. And yet he wouldn't abandon the Institute. He had it good here. His wife felt at home, his daughter was already in every way an Israeli, with a Hebrew name even, and she was studying in Beer-Sheva and perhaps would go to live on a kibbutz.

Jenny Grey. ("My Jenny, Jenny mine, my dear Jenny," Dr. Gross once sang to her at a party when he was drunk and suggesting that he escort her to his home. She laughed then: "What would Sarah say?" "Oh, that's really a problem," he answered, and that was the end of that.) Jenny is looking for Adam, she wants to talk to him. In her pocket she has a list of insults; she wants to pay him back or get an explanation.

This morning she woke frightfully depressed. She swallowed a pill, her head still aching, and after she showered and combed her hair she looked into the mirror. She found there a face that was despicable, and she longed for somebody who would tell her something compassionate and kind, or insert his flaming tongue into her. "In other words, I need you, Adam," she said and smiled at the face which, to her eyes, was disgusting.

Not finding Adam in his room, she opens a window and sees the summer stretched across the white mountains and inside the grooves of the wadis. Soon the sun will blaze deeply and powerfully, showering upon everything. As yet it is in its swaddling clothes. Far off she sees smoke rising from the smokestack of the new ceramics factory in the young developing city. And she ruminates for a moment about the landlady of the pension and about Adam's wife and his daughters, whom, if she could, she would have liked to know. She knows where they came from and is filled with affection for them. *Gretchen became smoke,* she says to herself, *and I am embracing shadows.* She opens the cabinet, wipes a fine layer of dust from the Hebrew grammar books and dictionaries that stand in a row above some German books she can't understand at all. She sees the electric shaver. *I thought he gave it to the child! Apparently he has two. He must have two.* She had forgotten that he was wealthy. *Look what he has here.* Cameras, slide-rules, pipes, a set of tortoise-shell brushes and combs, medicines, after-shave lotion, Pelican and Montblanc fountain pens, cigars in a very thin wood humidor, and assorted strange items. She picks up the electric shaver and absent-mindedly begins cleaning it. She takes a tiny brush from the brown case and brushes the small blades. The sound of the brush against the minute steel fibers is pleasant to her ears. Her spine tingles. With diligent patience she removes the white bristles from the machine and wonders why this mechanical concentration lifts her spirits and makes her forget everything. She collects the bristles in a paper bag she finds, and tells herself: *I'm ostracized here, all alone, among all these objects. It's my fate to be here in Adam's room. Why? If my fate is to love, to know and to love, the white hairs brushed out of an electric shaver, then my life's purpose is destruction. My soul is uplifted now, but that amounts to destruction.* Yet she cannot fathom her own thoughts. She remembers that once, in Jaffa, when she was sharing a room with Sarah Avidom, Sarah's lover came to visit. As he emerged from the bathroom after taking a shower, the fragrance of powder and perfume wafted from him. Sarah smiled and Jenny despised her in her heart: how could anybody love a powdered man?

In the typewriter is a paper with an enumerated list. She assumes that the child has answered Adam's questions.

1. I wett my bedd. You wont eet.
2. Dont evver kry. I meen it.
3. U ar to blame for itt. I dont kno how oldd I am. Jenni de hore has a glass ass. A glass ass is lyke a mirrer. In de mirrer iz evry Daddi.
4. Dey have no names. Doktor Gross haz a dirty vace.
5. U screw Jenni. U wont die.

And she wants to inherit the place of his wife Gretchen! He has told her many a time how much he loved her, but Jenny knew he was lying, that he had never loved anybody. That he was incapable of loving. And now—and it isn't the first time—the fear seizes her that perhaps he will come to love the dog. That would be the first time in *his* life that he had actually loved, and she would be left out in the cold. She wants to cry. It's not right, it doesn't look right, to cry, it's simply not right. Gretchen, according to him, was a tiny person, a toy in the ocean of passion and pleasure. The beauty of her mouth was perfect, designed by God Himself. She had the slight figure of a bird, her breasts like two lemons. She worked in the circus and became, as he said, a comma in the jokebook of history. On the day that Gretchen gave birth to Ruth, on that very day Adam Stein sprained his foot. Jenny smiles to herself, closes the shaver and puts it back in the case. His oh-so-beloved wife whose body was the body of a bird, whose breasts were lemons, whose mouth was perfect, was brought to the hospital to give birth to their daughter Ruth, to become queen for a day, to be admired as the one whose womb had performed a miracle, and Adam sprained his ankle precisely on that day, at that very hour, and was admitted to the hospital for treatment, so that everybody could visit him. A coincidence? No. She knew it wasn't. He wanted to be comforted. He wanted to be able to talk about and cry about his pain, to exaggerate, to lie . . . A few hours after Gretchen gave birth she came to visit him in his room in the hospital, to comfort her clown.

Jenny cleans up everything. Arranges, dusts. *A Key to the Language.* How did he learn Hebrew? How did he learn to make his venomous retorts in such good Hebrew? She can't figure it out. All she knows is that since Gretchen is dead, the relationship between him and her should be a simple matter. But the child, the child has become a person, in every way, on both sides of the coin. What idiocy, what arrogance!

Outside, the desert sky is clear. Not a single cloud. A blue sky stretches like a roof over the entire world, like a *yarmulka.* She takes a deep breath of the good desert air, as deep as she can. Arad is visible in the distance. Clouds of dust billow from a large building still under construction. Adam argued that they ought to establish a soap factory here: "Fight Air Pollution! Use Arad Soap!" He was always making fun of himself, mocking himself. . . .

Adam, back from his meeting with Pierre, faces Jenny. She was looking for him when he appeared. They head toward the secret corner behind Pierre Lotti's herb garden, sit down on the tarpaulin canvas whose function is to protect the plants in case of rain. Adam pulls a flat bottle of brandy out of his pocket and takes a long swig.

"You've been thinking about Gretchen today," he says, "and that's not nice. You've been thinking about her and me. About the child, the dog. He succeeded, I didn't. But I gave him a good beating. It was terrible. I had no choice, he's bound to recover, and then I'll be all alone. He's the only one that has any value. Pierre Lotti flatters me, wants to get rich from the holy Jordan waters."

"And I thought it was your idea!"

"Yes, but I don't need the money, I'm rich. They expect me to be dazzling. Pierre Lotti is anti-Semitic. Do you know what he wrote about the Jews when he visited the Old City of Jerusalem? I'm prepared to quote him for your benefit: 'Perhaps a visit here is the best proof for the incontestable fact that a special sign is stamped on their foreheads—the Jews—that a mark of shame is printed on this entire race.' And in another place he writes: 'After numerous frightful sufferings, after hundreds of years of exile and dispersion, an unbreakable tie exists between this nation and its lost homeland! And you almost weep for them, except you realize they are Jews and you gape with a frozen heart at their loathsome faces.' "

Jenny, who hasn't drunk any brandy, is stunned for the moment. "When was he in the Old City?"

"Oh, at the end of the last century!"

"But he's . . . I mean, how can that be? He wasn't born yet! I think—"

"Every Pierre Lotti is an anti-Semite. Believe me."

"You're babbling, Adam." She smiles with relief. She recognizes this mockery, this pride, when he gets silly, clowns around, quoting books he read thirty years ago, in an attempt to astonish, to be extraordinary, to be alien to her and to himself as an act of self-abasement.

"You have no right to brood about Gretchen," he yells at her. "I didn't give you permission to meditate about her. You have a lot of nerve! If you had been there and watched me clown around as they took their last steps, would you have been afraid?"

"Of course I would have been scared."

"That's the difference! Gretchen trusted me, I was everything to her, she was delicate and feminine and all mine. You make me think of a sergeant-major. You've come into the world in order to torment me, in order to deter me from my path. She had faith in me, you have faith in nobody."

"I have faith in you, Adam."

"You're lying." He sets the bottle down beside him. "The King's drink, it goes down the throat like a caress, it plays with your insides—Hennessy! I dreamed a dream a few days ago. I saw a bottle of cognac, hundreds of bottles. Napoleon, Remy Martin, Hennessy, Martell, Courvoisier, Mateksa, Stock, Baron,

Seven Seven Seven, Lord of Carmel—hundreds of bottles chasing after me. Finally they managed to catch me, and put me in a gigantic sink, right in the middle, and turned on the faucets until I was drowning. I was lapping and dying, lapping and dying. Suddenly a terrifying brothel madam appeared and rescued me, only to sell me in the market. I was sold to a whorehouse, the customers quarreled over me, and I had the image of your pretty face plastered onto me. I wrestled with the customers."

"And who won?" She reclines comfortably, looking up at the bright desert sky, at the magic of the Judean hills. And yet her eyes are also fixed on the patch of stomach peeking out from Adam's shirt where a button has somehow come undone.

"Guess."

She refuses to guess. She knows. He'll say, Guess, you snake! And indeed he says: "Guess, you snake. Seduce me." At this point she knows that his look of boredom and mockery will fade and he will be hers again. As in the old days. For a moment his deceit will be unnecessary, for a moment he will calm down, and she will love him and he will make her feel better. She never asked to fall in love with him, it just happened, there is no way to undermine the logic of the heart, for the heart is always mined. She takes a comb and a pair of scissors from her uniform pocket, squats on her heels, keeping her back straight, and asks:

"Now?"

"Now, Jenny. See, I'm vanquished."

He gets down on all fours, her Adam Stein, the hero of her life, his head resting on her lap. Her body rises erect above him and she begins to cut his hair with spectacular expertise, with passion, with joy. The scissors sing out like swords clashing. His face clings to her narrow, pleasant knees. Her white uniform is rough against his face. The sharp intoxicating odor of rosemary swings upon them from Pierre Lotti's herb garden.

In the distance a siren sounds. Has a fire broken out? Are they rushing somebody to the hospital? To her? To the infirmary? There isn't a hospital yet in Arad and maybe it's an emergency. Somebody has been mortally wounded, electrocuted, shot by infiltraters? Those Bedouins. They won't give up their ways. In the murky nights they go on their donkeys and camels. Sometimes he imagines that he hears them at night. When birds fly south, to the sun, they cross seas that have no islands to afford them rest, and the paths they take are at times much longer than more direct routes. The fact is—so Adam read somewhere—that they preserve in the inherited memory of their kind the routes which their ancestors took. At that time, a million years ago, there was an island on this path where they could stop and recuperate. And such was the case with these Bedouins. Romans, Nabateans, Byzantines, Mamelukes and Persians, Arabs and Turks, English and Jews, century after century, one power succeeding another, wars, struggles, murder, the desert swallowing seats of government, the loess soil and the dust covering gorgeous palaces and houses, irrigation ditches and vines, but the Bedouins, they alone do not alter their ways. From east to west, from banditry to trade, from trade to banditry, they continue to follow the same routes, they cross and recross the same sun-scorched cleft landscape of the desert. At night he imagines he hears them, hears some Bedouin singing a drawn-out nasal chant, an invocation to the wind, the sand, and the black skies: "From here to Beirut, from here to Beirut." And the voice protracts until it merges into the desert and is lost. She cuts hair marvelously, this Jenny. Her hands are so professional. My Delilah. Bitch Delilah combing and cutting, destroying my strength. And for what reason? Woman, snake, one and the same.

The haircut is over. Jenny gathers the white scraps of hair, rises and shakes her apron. Some of the hair flies into her face and she smiles as though to a friend. He is waiting now, for her to take a small mirror from her apron pocket, blow on it with her hot Ashmedai breath, wipe it with a handkerchief she keeps attached always to her belt, for her to hold the mirror before his

face and allow him to gaze in astonishment at *her* handiwork
and *his* beauty. She will praise his beauty rapturously and he will
enjoy that. His hand will pat her leg, climb along her thigh and
up to the boat of her appetite, and he will say: "Gale warnings
today! The Mediterranean is shaking." And she'll laugh, as usual,
her face glowing. A hospital nurse, he'll say to himself, a watch-
dog and a prison officer. And then his desire will double, he'll
want both to kill her and to resurrect her again, out of her inner
self. His hand will grope inside her apron, her modest additional
covering. His hand will reach her two oranges and squeeze them
gently. And then, at a specific moment, very specific, as in a
ceremony, as in a cult whose traditions are fixed and must be
conformed to, while his hands are massaging her erotic zones,
Jenny's hand will start placing crowns on his head.

Out of the box concealed in the dog's hut, Jenny takes rolls of
colored paper: gold, silver, red, blue, yellow, white, orange. She
cuts with her scissors, criss-cross, folds the papers and again
cuts, in reverse. He is patient and waits, his hands still inside
her, permeating her erotica, and her face is pale, excited, yet her
hands remain nimble, cutting and joining together without a
stop, until the crowns are ready, lovely and grandiose. Praise be
the paper and Jenny Grey's talent, the whore of his courtyard.
Now he will again be the king in the dog kennel.

Her white face smiles at his head with its golden crown. He
looks into the mirror she holds up to his serious face. His white
hair flashes under the gold crown. Now she will take off the
golden crown and dress him in a blue crown and smile and remove that one too and put a yellow crown on his head and a red
one and an orange, many, many crowns.

He's on all fours, a red crown on his head. She dons a silver
crown and she too is on all fours. Two dogs, face to face, rubbing noses, solemn. The sun hangs above them. They sweat.
Jenny embraces him and undoes his buttons till he is naked.
Then she takes a small crown, golden, and rings his penis. He
gapes at her. He is no longer playing a game. He barks at her
fiercely, barks and barks, while she admires the trembling

crownlet. His sex is rising in her honor, clad in a crown of gold.

Later on, when the crowns are all trampled and crumpled and the sun has wandered to the western horizon and the supper bell is ringing in the distance, later on she says: "You're wasting a lot of time with the child, you could be with me much more. He writes nicely, I see, intelligently. I looked at the page in the typewriter. But you live just for him and that's not good for you. What do you want from him? He's a child, he'll break. And this time it will be once and for all. No hope left. I mean it, leave him alone, Adam! He's weak. He needs love. Devotion. And you yourself need somebody to lean on."

"You nut! You idiot!" He stands up and stares at her with open hatred. "Dog, Jenny. Dog!"

"What?"

"He's a dog. Not a child. He is not a child. Don't say child."

She bursts out laughing. "He types on a typewriter, no? He understands when you talk to him, no? He doesn't bark any more. You made him into a child, God. He was non-human and now he's human." Her voice softens. "It's been such a long time since we've seen each other . . ."

"You're jealous?" He smiles and arches his body backward. His back is leaning against the fence in front of the herb garden, his eyes fixed on the dog kennel. In the middle of the garden stands a scarecrow, a scarecrow in children's clothes. A French sailor's outfit with a white collar, gold buttons with anchors crawling all over them, a small sailor's hat that looks like a crown of narcissus. Adam points to the blue sailor wearing the crown of narcissus, and Jenny grumbles:

"What's the matter? Am I forbidden to be jealous? Don't I have the right?" A childlike expression covers her face.

"I would nurse you now, child—" he yells and cuts himself short. His eyes stick to the scarecrow that sparkles in the sun. "Those gold buttons are signaling to the enemy."

She doesn't hear, doesn't see. "I'm jealous. Yes, yes, yes, yes, yes."

"That's good." He pauses for a moment and smiles. "Good,

good, good, good."

"We used to be together a lot, remember? We did things. I used to cut your hair almost once a week and adorn your head with crowns." She giggles, then is serious again. "Now months go by, Wolfovitz says moons, moons is prettier than months, no?"

"Months or moons, you're exaggerating. People are busy, Jenny."

"Once you used to think differently. It was important to you. I was yours, always."

"You scarecrow!" he shouts at her in a loud voice. "You know he has nobody but me. He's alone, without parents, family, brothers, sisters." And screams, shattering his features into a contorted image which terrifies her. "No, he has nobody, no family, no brothers, no sisters. And if he has any—" his voice softening for a second—"I don't want to know a thing about them. They neglected him, betrayed him." And Adam grabs a fistful of sand and tosses the sand at her.

She doesn't shake off the sand. Her gaze is fixed on his face. "His parents? Did they ever come to visit him? Not even once! And why was he a dog? I'm no fool. I know. I'm the only one here, Gross is out, and his parents, and Nachwalter, and Shapiro, and you. There's only the two of us, him and me. Him and me against the world. You won't understand that. You tried to bark before, was it fun?"

"You know that I love to bark, that I know how to bark." She's up in arms. "You remember how you taught me to bark? You remember that I could do it? I bark nicely, you said so yourself, you faker, you . . ."

"To bark in a world of furnaces." He pays no attention to her. "The eastern border of Prussia, the Mediterranean border, greater Germany, Morgenthau desired to reverse them and they reversed Morgenthau. Churchill was right, Germany is a wedge, and I and David, King of Israel, bark against wedges. Our bark is considerably innocent. Like my Dr. Weiss, like this scarecrow that has to stand here and exist without laughing, in innocence. Like flying a kite on a battlefield, or picking flowers among the corpses. I don't give a hoot what they say about him, that he used to bite, that he used to lie under a sheet and growl. We are two dogs in the middle of nowhere, two shrieks in the center of the desert, two tears on a face of marble, two prayers in a synagogue where there is no God, yet he succeeded where even I failed. And I took off his mask for him. The bastard. The clown. What nerve. You won't come between us. I'll smash him, I can't be a true dog. No. Neither can he. He won't be. You hear? My failure will seal his fate. That's how it'll be. There's no other way."

She pats his sweating head. The crown slips to the tarpaulin. Jenny Grey lays his gray and weary head on her lap. The scarecrow is an army of enemies, she is Sancho Panza, he is Don Quixote, together they will rescue the world from evil. But evil, she knows, is fixed deep in the heart, and that is why her Adam is dying, slowly dying. That is why he is winning and she losing badly. And nobody is there to pity her. Because didn't she pretend she was a monster? So she could choose her own life for herself, without anybody to interfere? A blue sky stretches above them. Far off, the desert moans. She smiles at the enemy's extra-large white old fingers, undoes the buttons of her uniform and shows her soft round breast. Her breast falls from her brassière like copper sparkling in the sun, and Adam presses his mouth into her nipple. She pours brandy onto her chest from the flat bottle and Adam licks the brandy off her breasts. She says in a sad voice, "My baby, my sweet baby," and Adam sucks the barren chill of that lovely nipple drowned in sour-sweet cognac. He realizes that he is chained and that he will never be able to unlock the chains which he chained himself with. "Not everyone who laughs at his chains is free of them," said Schiller. He squeezes Jenny, Jenny the Jewess, ridiculous irrelevant Jenny with her many deep hates and her one deep love, uncompromising Jenny. He presses into Jenny in order to escape Schiller and the Prince from Weimar who imposed sufferings on him and who gave him the most sacred moments of his life. For a second he loves Jenny, and is afraid of that second, for in that same second he knows that he hates his child with a homicidal hate.

11

THE MIRACLE

THE MATTER of the sacred water is still being discussed in back rooms—for good or bad, let's issue some springed greeting cards. Wolfovitz the Circumciser didn't die. But in the course of a time a black raven did die, in the courtyard. Two children in Nurse Spitzer's nursery gave it a funeral ceremony that was touching. In Adam's judgment, these ravens fly above the Institute because they sense lots of slaughtered flesh around. But their timing is off and they don't know how to make their coming coincide with the coming of death. Wolfovitz the Circumciser revealed that the name Adam, in Hebrew, added up to forty-five. In '45 Adam was saved from the dog bowl of Commandant Klein and returned to Berlin. Man is an inferior creature—according to Wolfovitz—because God didn't say, after He created Adam, that Adam was good. Instead, the option of choosing between good and evil was given to man, and Adam

Stein, as everybody knows, chose evil. Miles Davis holds that
David, King of Israel, is a born great xylophone player: he's
progressing nicely and this keeps Miles busy. Adam is concerned
with many things important only to himself. He is fundamentally
depressed. Jenny came down with the flu. Adam didn't visit her
and she sent him a vexed letter. Gross claims that Adam, if he
wanted, could help himself, but Adam completely and irration-
ally refuses. The elder Schwester twin is waiting for God, and
every day she comes to Adam, her face looking to him like a
question mark in the shape of a mustache, a baby mustache. He
throws up his hands in great sadness: "What can I do? Not yet."
Another day lacking God falls into the far-off sea, there across
the desert. In the news there was a report on infiltrators at the
northern border, the prime minister of Ireland announced that,
in America the blacks attacked the, and opened fire hydrants,
rioted, children looted, police wearing helmets fired on them,
one ruler said that, the president could not because, popularity
dropped two tenths of a percent, in Tel-Arad an archeological
dig is discovering the past, the past, the past, whereas the future,
on the contrary, is gaining strength every day. Mrs. Seizling is
still in the morgue freezer, the court will soon give its ruling,
lawyers by the dozens are craving for her corpse like ravens.
David, King of Israel, and Commandant Klein's dog are having
lengthy discussions. One speaks and the other types. Something
mysterious and strange is going on between them. Doctors are
gnashing their teeth, there is no explanation whatsoever. The
hundreds of pages in their books offer no answers. Nonetheless
the labs have discovered a new drug which Adam will try out. A
new delivery of Hennessy, Jack Daniels, Dewar's, Beefeater gin,
J&B, White Horse, Chivas Regal that had soaked for more than
ten years, into a barrel made of oak has arrived hugger-mugger.
Pierre Lotti transfers everything to Adam, Adam thanks him,
converses with him again about the matter of the sacred water
and in the meantime hides the more or less holy water behind
the radiators, in the generator house, in the ventilation ducts,

everyplace. In short, time flies. It's the month of July, the Hebrew month of Av. On the 9th of Av they didn't have any
mourning ceremonies here; something might have been done,
but the date was apparently forgotten. They remembered Madame Seizling in the refrigerator and wept by the waters of whiskey.

"Air-conditioning is divine," says Wolfovitz, forgetting for
the moment his opinion about God. "There's no doubt about it,"
confesses an air-conditioning engineer named Yashka Weinstein
from the atomic team in Dimona, who was invited for an evening of fantastic mind-blowing Beef Stroganoff, "there's no doubt
about it, no other place in the country, the entire country, has a
system of air-conditioning as up-to-date as the one in the Institute." And the man knows what he's talking about, for he's built
dozens of these systems throughout the land, whereas this one
was built by an expert from Cleveland. "And he's not even Jewish," says Gross a bit sadly. After all, when all is said and done,
a Jew, you know, is smarter. Like Rockefeller, like Shakespeare,
and Dante, and Pasteur, and Napoleon, and Dostoevsky, and
Kant, and Jung. At the funeral of the black raven they chanted
dirges as the raven lay on the stretcher borne by two old children. They sang:

> *Raven, raven, why did you die?*
> *Soon we'll all be down.*

Jenny has recovered. Adam too is better again, after some
special treatment over the space of a month. He returned to his
room and even gave a lesson in the history of the French Revolution. Arthur participated, naturally, and left depressed, blowing his bugle in the corridor and marching in his one-man parade
dressed in an old Boy Scout hat. And on a blazing day in September when the skin feels as though it's been sliced up and fried,
three figures are seen slipping out of the air-conditioned house,
away from the murky chill of the singing corridors, into the sun-
struck courtyard. It is midday, with the sun in the middle of the

sky. No shadows, no shade, no shelter. The burning sand and the white hills and the yellow loess soil stretch to the very horizon.

The figures stop by the big concrete ashtray. In it is sand, and around it is sand, sand wherever your eye takes you, sand to the ends of the world and inside your mouth and your soul. Adam stops walking and signals to the child to stop crawling. Jenny, following them, also stops. In such terrific heat—102 degrees according to the forecaster, who most likely didn't know the half of it—in this heat Adam Stein is dressed like the Adam Stein who went to the opening of the opera: white shirt and custom-made suit. Elegant, almost classical lines. A red carnation in the jacket lapel, black patent-leather shoes made in Italy. Opera patron Stein, the child, and Jenny. By an ashtray. Sand and sun. The weather man is crazy. A hundred and two degrees? A thousand and two degrees!

They stand. Adam looks at Jenny. The child turns around and also looks at her. Her face is harsh. She doesn't want pity, she wants only her rights. Nobody says anything. Adam starts walking. The child crawls after him in the sand. The sun, no pity in it, strikes. Creating a world that has no colors, no shadows, no compromises, no corners.

"She has no self-respect, that's what she hasn't got." He talks to the child and the child smiles into the desert which is so close to his nose. Jenny, at this moment, isn't going to say anything. Her mind isn't made up yet, it keeps turning, and she is just one of three. She smiles inwardly: *It won't help him.* And Adam says, "The holy trio, Father, Son and Holy Ghost." And he bursts into laughter. "Father and son I can understand, but Jenny as the Holy Ghost? Jenny? *Jenny?*"

Father and Holy Ghost step together. Son crawls on all fours. Already they've passed out of the big courtyard, passed the neglected chess tables, the goldfish pond that is scalded by the sun, the row of cypresses and tamarisks that were planted not long ago so their tops reach only to your belt, and they come to the tall fence separating the desert from the Institute, a fence that seems to say, *The wasteland is for the wasteland!* Adam sweats. The Holy Ghost is drenched. The child, the Son, is prostrate. From afar, the three of them look like three beetles on a gigantic white tablecloth. Or on a sheet of ice. They stand motionless. In such fierce heat any movement is a burden to the lungs. The muscles weaken, the body fatigues.

The child, the Son, pulls a piece of paper out of his pocket and holds it up to Adam. Adam stoops and takes it, reads, and says: "Of course. Absolutely."

"What did he say?" asks Jenny.

"It's none of your business!" The child smiles at him, proud of his strong wise father. "You should be ashamed of yourself," whispers Herbert from a distance, though clearly. "Whom are you trying to impress?"

Jenny casts her eyes down. "Adam?"

"What is it, Jenny?" His voice is somewhat softer, reconciled. "All right, he wrote that I shouldn't forget who he is."

She nods. Streams of salt water gush down the fancy suit of the patron of the arts. He barks: "March, hound!"

The child turns his face. His azure eyes with the two trenches under them stare for a long while at Adam, and then he lowers his eyes and crawls toward the fence. On the way he cannot control his confusion; he casts a longing look at Adam, but Adam refuses to return his glance, so the child goes on crawling. Adam paces around, his hands clasped behind him. He is busy with his business of pretense. Jenny is far behind, silent. The child reaches the fence and lies there. Doesn't budge. Adam raises his voice. "What's the matter with you?" The child stretches out a hand limp from the heat, pats the fence, the iron wires with the spaces between them looking like honeycombs, and tries to get up. He sweats, his eyes weep tears of sweat, his body swims in sweat and quakes. Quiet is Jenny, white as the desert. The canine body of the child who already has typed on an Olivetti, played the xylophone and discovered that a whore has an ass of glass, refuses to get up.

"Try, David. You can do it, you'll see." The words jump out of her mouth.

"Don't talk. Shut up. You don't belong!"

"Adam . . ." She is on fire. "Stop that. Give, be a friend for a moment. What's wrong?"

"You don't understand anything!" His eyes like two perilous arrows.

The child hears nothing, sees nothing. The heat is blinding. Mouth screwed up, he tries again. His right hand closes on the fence and he tries to hoist his body upward. By sheer force. But it doesn't work. He drops down and lies sprawled. His face in the sand. Adam witnesses the total failure.

"It's all your fault," he says. She keeps quiet. He goes to the child lying prone in the boiling sand and says softly, "Lousy dog! I did everything for you! What haven't I done? And now, when I ask you to do something that's important to me, you can't do it? No! Go ask favors from a dog. Why did I give you all those presents, why did I starve myself, why did I sacrifice myself? Shitty dog. Get up!" And he shouts with his last drop of spirit: "Get up, you dog!"

But the Son cannot. He tries, he tries with superhuman effort, yet is unable, is unsuccessful. "A geometrical tragedy in a tamed desert," says Herbert far off and laughs. Adam is terrified by the sound of that laughter. Now he sees just how ridiculous he is, as though he has come in party dress to view a tasteless melodrama.

Adam shrieks, but his shrieks are swallowed by the scalding desert. "What's so difficult about standing up? Any fool can stand. Any idiot. Jenny Grey can stand. Dr. Gross can stand, Wolfovitz, Arthur—any *shmuck* can stand. But you, David, King of Israel, you can't stand?"

Once more the child tries. His hands are taut. All his power, body-and-will, is concentrated on this net in front of him and on his hands that clasp it, yet the metamorphosis that occurred a million years ago, that altered the map of the universe, that upset the course of creation, the prehistoric phenomenon of standing up, refuses to happen now. And Adam, as a man, as a patron of the opera, is offended to the core of his soul. He is offended in the name of mankind, for at this moment, in this foolish circumstance, he is its representative. He is insulted because of the gifts he gave, because of the hopes he held. He approaches the dog, stoops over him, slaps him across the face. The slap rings into the distance. The dog, heartbroken, panics and starts howling. He wraps his slapped face in his hands. The odor of sweat rises from him, the sweat of fear, the sweat of pain.

Jenny comes over to the child, but Adam forces her back. Now he is his usual boastful, confident self. He adjusts the carnation in his lapel, smiles, and shouts at Jenny: "I told you not to interfere, I warned you! Didn't I warn you? I told you not to stick your pretty nose . . . See, I'm here, he's there. You're a stranger. I allowed you to come along, that's all. Don't forget that he's mine, not yours!" He turns and faces the child with a proud expression. The child is still bundled up, hiding his cheek in his hand. Jenny looks at Adam, at the back of his neck. His collar is disheveled now, his suit sweaty and wrinkled, sand all over his pants. She feels somewhat relieved, as though she has had her revenge for his harshness, for the cruelty of his smile. But the child starts wailing again and drives away her thoughts.

"You're no longer a dog and you're not yet a child, so what are you? A lizard? A leech? A rag?"

The child digs his face into the sand and starts eating the sand, his mouth kneading the dry burning sand. He chews it the way, a few months ago, he chewed the piece of paper.

"The puppy is chewing, that leech, that's how he gets his confidence! The poor thing, he's ludicrous!"

"Like a child," says Jenny, her mouth twisted, but he doesn't reply. He approaches the child, drops on all fours, and hugs him. His clothes are crumpled now, filthy. The carnation has fallen from his coat lapel. The clown's face opens and tears flow from his eyes. The child feels the tears caressing his face, sees the tears dropping into the sand. And the child cries too. They drink each other's tears, stick out their tongues without any shame whatsoever and lick each other's tears, embracing like friends, like brothers.

David, King of Israel, squints up at the sky and the sky blinds him. He crawls to the fence, drenched in tears and sweat, puts out a hand, tries once more, once more, and once more. He rises a bit and again slips down. Straightens a bit and again drops. Drops and stretches flat on the sand under the sun. Gone to rot.

Jenny is nailed to the place where she stands, paralyzed by fear. Adam gets up. He says nothing, his attention is riveted on the child. Dead midday of summer. 1,323 degrees. Far off the noon dinner bell sounds. Titmice stuffed with liver, diamond juice, potatoes roasted in gold, green beans glazed with marble, Beaujolais 1956, white Ashkelon, red Avdat, chocolate mousse with whipped cream.

"Don't despair, child," whispers Adam. "It'll happen. You'll see!"

The child straightens again. His hands grasp the fence and this time he doesn't stumble. His body creaks. Every muscle is taut as a bowstring. Each bone seeks its position. His body gets taller and taller, each inch an inch of fear. Each inch of height a million years of evolution. The dog will become a man while Adam, who was once a dog, stares in amazement. The circle is complete. Is that the meaning of squaring the circle? Adam lowers his eyes. The dog's hands clutch the fence as though it were his salvation. They ooze blood. They are everywhere scratched. His face is somber, drenched with sweat and tears. His pants are torn, his shirt ripped. He continues to rise.

Adam lowers his eyes more and more, closes up his face, shouts: "Okay!" His voice is hoarse and frozen with fear. "Okay, child."

"Adam, he's doing it! Leave him alone. Let him. He's doing it!"

"Whore!" he screams. "Leave *me* alone, leave *me* alone! David, that's enough for one day, enough!" His voice begs. "Enough for today, you hear me? We'll try again another time. I can't take it, I'm dying, yes, me. Enough, you're scratched, the sun will burn us up."

Shocked she looks at him.

The child doesn't listen. Won't listen. His ears are shut. For the first time in years his head is aloft, between heaven and earth. He is almost erect, on two feet, close to the sun and the sky.

"I beg you, David, stop, you're bleeding. That's enough! It's all her fault. That whore. The child wants to lie down and she makes him stand up. She wants to make everything stand. The whore. The idiot. I'm sick, my body aches. These clothes hurt too. I'm ridiculous. I'll go to Klein. I'll lick his boots. Child, enough!"

The Holy Son's body is at its sacred height. The Holy Ghost mumbles something about a miracle. And the Father? They betrayed the Father. He shouts without a voice, exhausted, lost.

The child frees his hands, lets go of the fence. His legs are almost straight, his body almost erect. Blood pours from his hands. He stands like this for a moment, with everything shifting at his feet. The world flies around him, the earth slides, dances, escapes, retreats, and consequently he stumbles and his body falls heavily. Adam turns and flees toward the house. Jenny bends over the child, his child. And his child pushes her away from him. His eyes gape; she sees his humiliation in his pupils. She whispers in his ears: "You're a hero, David, you're a man!" But he knocks his head in the sand and weeps. She whispers: "You made it! You're a man. Our man. His and mine. I'm proud of you." Her face glows. But he grabs a fistful of sand and with his last strength tosses the sand at her. Two beetles drinking sand.

* * *

Dr. Nathan Gross, who through the vision of Mrs. Rebecca Seizling, may she rest in peace, rose from the category of run-of-the-mill doctor in the mental asylum at Jaffa to the level of director of the splendid Institute at Arad, leaves his small villa and arrives at the Institute at 7:40 in the morning. If not for his wife, who makes his life bitter, he would live in the Institute and save himself the extra journey. But she absolutely refuses. Because she can still telephone directly to the Institute kitchen and order from Pierre Lotti "something special" for supper. Every day toward evening one of the help brings the food to her house, in thermoses and special pots. Dr. Gross won't argue with her as though he were a lawyer in a courtroom. It is enough that he has taken her away from Tel Aviv, from the lovely apartment on Dubnow Street, enough that he has brought her to the Negev, to the desert—"to the ravens" as she generally expresses it in her fury—to an Inferno, to these nuts, enough that there is no proper hairdresser here, no proper school, no department store, no veterinarian, no theater, no concerts.

She is frightened of her husband's maniacs, of the building, of the doctors. Of their hyper-seriousness. She loves to sit hidden in her house (which was also built by Mrs. Seizling, designed by Ilon, Tamir, Gat, & Shoshan, and lacks nothing) and play cards with her two girlfriends Zelda and Deborah, those lucky dogs who are blessed with a nicer life than hers—one is married to an official and the other to a bus driver. "Only I had to marry a nut doctor! To tell the truth, he's just as nutty as his patients," she confesses to her friends. "Sometimes he talks really weird. Once he looked for flies in my nose. Sometimes he'll scream for no reason, just like that, 'Avalanche!' And if I ask 'Where, what avalanche?' he points to the sky and makes a sad face. Once he cried in his sleep, and afterward burst out laughing."

The morning is still chilly. Dr. Gross parks his gray Plymouth in the shady garage and enters the Institute. He passes the nurse Shapiro, says hello, and goes into his office. He sits down at a desk, reads the reports that have accumulated overnight, pulls a cigarette from a container made of pure silver which plays, when opened, *Havah Nagillah,* lights it and inhales deeply. An ordinary morning, ordinary day.

On the desk is a telegram that arrived this morning from a lawyer named Ayib Steiner in Cleveland: COURT DECISION ON CORPSE ABOUT TO COME STOP CHANCES GOOD FOR CORPSE IN INSTITUTE STOP IF SO WILL FLY CORPSE STOP SPECTACULAR FUNERAL APPROPRIATE STOP FINAL EXPENSES WILL BE TELEGRAPHED STOP. Dr. Gross examines the telegram and wonders about Mrs. Seizling's corpse lying in the refrigerator. Are her eyes open or shut? Once, many years ago, a lovely young woman loved Dr. Gross, but he, who was not as yet Dr. Gross, married somebody else—that was the bed he made, that was the bed he would have to sleep in! He married "Xanthippe" Gross. Heavy with hysterical complaints, card games for comfort, luckier friends, ambitions. She prays in her heart that he'll win some prize or other. The Nobel Prize, for instance, would compensate her for her sufferings—she would go to Sweden and meet the King.

Jenny knocks on the office door and enters carrying a silver tray which contains a steaming coffeepot, a pitcher of milk, sugar, cup-and-saucer, fresh hot rolls covered with a white napkin, jam, butter, and, as an expression of friendship on Pierre Lotti's part, some fragrant pickled herring.

Jenny smiles at him. Down deep in her heart, she is fond of him, mainly because he is the Director of the Institute. Jenny knows she functions according to very simple rules, but she cannot help herself. Though her smile is somewhat unsatisfactory—the product, as it were, of a command—Dr. Gross loves that unsatisfactory smile of Jenny's. It arouses wild instincts in him. At the sight of her smile he is able, and apt, to think about stormy orgies—or about what he imagines to be stormy orgies, for he has never in his life participated in a stormy orgy. Nor has he partaken of any orgy, stormy or not. Jenny's melodramatic (as he calls it) smile rescues him every morning. Without explicit words spoken, they have managed to establish a procedure which has turned into a ritual. She, not one of the kitchen help, is to bring him his breakfast. She is to smile, and her smile is to save him from suddenly falling in love and save her from the necessity of devoting herself to somebody she doesn't love. He asked her once, laughing, if she would respond to such a request, and she answered immediately: "Yes, of course," and smiled, while he instantly began imagining stormy orgies and was rescued.

Dr. Gross raised the telephone receiver, gave Jenny a mischievous look while she was pouring the steaming coffee into his cup, and dialed. "Hello? Wifey? My wifey?" He waits, listens, knits his brow. "I miss you!" Another pause. "Yes, at eight in the morning! See you." The receiver slams back to its former position. He is furious. Morning morning Jenny Jenny his wife his wife coffee coffee.

Stout, gigantic Dr. Gross, a native of Jerusalem, sips his excellent coffee, bites into a roll, and spreads out the morning paper. He leafs through the pages, but the news doesn't interest him very much. Though what could be as interesting as his visit last night, before driving home, to Adam Stein in the infirmary? They talked about the film that was shown in the infirmary the previous night. Adam said: "The movie was average. The photography boring, far too static, considering the action of the story. As for the framing of the shots, we've seen them in thirty-one other films. But the interesting thing was that the hero, James Cagney, spoke 4,222 words in the course of the movie, whereas the heroine, whose name I forget, spoke 2,050 words, yet she gave a much more convincing performance than he did." After such a conversation how could the morning paper interest Dr. Gross? A strike in the port of Haifa (again!), a stubble field was burned in the area of Tel Katsir (that's far away, in Galilee), the Prime Minister of Syria announced that his country would destroy Israel (we've heard that before! he won't make it!), Russia was sending, America declared, the popularity of the President of the Philippines was declining, democracy in Greece was in danger, a Turkish citizen was killed in Cyprus, in Tel Aviv a tourist was robbed of a pair of earrings. . . . He turns to the classified ads. These he reads carefully, with fascination. Jenny arranges everything on the desk. Straightens the papers, opens the blinds, wipes the dust off several thick folders. Somebody announces through the pages of the newspaper that he is handsome and rich, experienced, has a car, and now seeks a good, beautiful woman for the purpose of matrimony—happy matrimony, naturally. A young engineer compliments himself in public. Jeeps for sale, public auction. Last chance to see *My Fair Lady*. In Beer-Sheva you can buy an office building three stories high. Dr. Gross completes his examination of the paper, and his breakfast, and goes out on his daily rounds. Jenny and her unsatisfactory smile stay in the room. She must finish arranging his desk.

Dr. Gross passes the turned-off radiators behind which Adam Stein hides his various bottles of liquor. He doesn't notice them. The music machine is playing *Persian Market;* then it'll play *Scheherazade* and afterward *Havah Nagillah*. The bulletin board is illuminated by a dim fluorescent light. From a distance, the bulletin board looks like a church altar. Next to it lives the "astronomer" Sohnman, and Dr. Gross now enters his room. Sohnman is sitting by the window, behind a table with a telescope on it. He has dreamed all his life of becoming an astronomer! Galileo Sohnman. But instead he worked in a Jerusalem post office. He came to Israel in '47, on the *Shabtai Lodjinski*. The ship managed to penetrate the British blockade and Sohnman was carried to the shore on the broad shoulders of a man whose name he didn't know, though he kissed him wildly. He spent some time on a kibbutz, then went up to Jerusalem, rented a small room in the Bucharest section and tried to become an astronomer, but didn't have enough money to acquire a telescope. So he got a job in the post office, where he filed letters. He was promoted to the category of second-class filer. After a few years the elder Schwester twin bumped into him in Tel Aviv, on Allenby Street, opposite Whiteman's ice-cream place. He had been standing in front of a public lavatory, staring at the steps descending into the earth, thinking that this was the entrance to the famous Tel Aviv subway. He was weary, worn out. In the war a finger on his right hand had been lopped off and one eye had almost been blinded. He wanted to travel to somewhere and use the stinking lavatory. When he was up on the sidewalk again he was dressed in a white robe and sandals. He had left his clothes in the doorway of the lavatory. He wore white gloves and held a rubber tube in his hand. He surveyed the heavens through his hollow tube and talked to himself. The passers-by paid practically no attention to him. Somebody tossed him a ten-cent piece, laughed, and went on his way. A small child tried to trip him. In the nearby Carmel market a hulking butcher, his apron splashed with blood and grease stains, stood sluggishly watching Sohnman. He shouted: "Hey, you there! What are you? Crazy?" and returned to his shop, raised a cleaver, and hacked a dead chicken.

"I am Galileo Galilei," he told the Schwester twin as she approached him and examined him with interest. "I wanted to take the subway to somewhere, but there wasn't another train. The robe I got from my mother, of blessed memory. I am an astronomer."

His eyes glowed when he delivered his message to the Schwester twin, whose baby mustache quivered. In Sohnman, in his white uniform, the Schwester twin saw a sign. His figure constituted, in her eyes, a chapter in her book of revelation: somebody seeking to tickle the heavens. "You come with me," she said to Sohnman. "You'll sit and study the anatomy of the sky, and if you see a chariot flying across the heavens, you'll inform me and we'll all go out, prepared." He didn't understand the gist of her words nor did she understand the gist of his, but their destinies were bound together.

And so, in the Institute, for the first time in his life he was able to be a real astronomer. He took a toy rifle from Nurse Spitzer's nursery, removed the barrel, and stopped each end with two blackened disks of glass that he had patiently prepared in the workshop on the ground floor—according to the astronomy book of a certain Rabbi Juda Basilki from Salonika. He attached the barrel to a swivel which he made with his own hands out of two strips of wood joined to a tin can of American Quaker Oats (Dutch-made), and sat at the window searching for secret stars. He hadn't discovered the Divine Chariot yet, but the Schwester twin wasn't putting too much pressure on him.

As far as he was concerned, daytime was a barren stretch between nights, a shocking waste. He hated day, despised light and the sun. They embittered his life, ruined his future. "I've lived fifty years," he said. "Twenty of them I've spent in sleep. Now I sleep during the day, because the day is useless. At ten in the morning I go to sleep. I get up at five, go to the therapist, the analyst, my agony. If only the day was one long night! Twenty-four hours of night, as in Alaska. But I'm sitting here in the desert, and the stars are clear and beautiful, and the nights poetic and still, and I, at last, am able to do my thing. I no longer have to file letters. I wasn't an astronomer in the Warsaw ghetto. My father had a small store, and then came the Germans."

Dr. Gross asks how he is. Does he have complaints? Problems? Requests? No, he has none, everything's fine, more or less, why should he complain? What's wrong with his situation? Should he be filing letters? No, thank you! Let me sit in the window till the day I die. A portion of his observations have already been filed and classified. Over there, in those gray folders, in the cabinet. Someday he'll publish his results and they are bound to cause a storm in the world of science. He'll be hunted down, he knows, but this time Galileo won't submit! No, and again no!

Dr. Gross parts from him and continues his rounds. He makes notes, figures out certain improvements that might be made here

and there. He visits Nurse Spitzer's nursery, where you can sense
the preparations for the coming Days of Awe. These days won't
be here for a month, yet they've begun to sing songs and discuss
the nature of the holidays. He peeks into the rooms of Arthur
Fine, Adam Stein, Miles Davis, Wolfovitz, and the Schwester
sisters. He criticizes Mrs. Tamir for not calming down the melancholic boy, he talks with Mr. Leunstein, with Mrs. Dovdov-
ani, with Yashka Peretz, with Dov Nahmani. He looks in on the
new patient who was committed this week.

An ordinary day at the Institute, the end of summer. Dr.
Gross returns to his office, which has been cleaned, dusted, and
put in order. Outside, the sun boils fiercely. He shuts the orange
shade and takes a look at the papers that have been brought in
and left on his table. The weekly report of costs, of medicines.
Pierre Lotti drops in for a moment to discuss various kitchen
matters, and they go over the menus that Pierre has planned for
the coming week. He picks up the telephone receiver and dials
and hires two additional nurses from the Health Department in
Jerusalem. Assures them of salary raises, apartments, other ben-
efits. There's no problem. There are many who will jump for the
jobs. He discusses details of sanitation with the man in charge of
it, particularly the matter of the new garbage-disposal equip-
ment that recently arrived from America. He decides with the
gardener what to plant on the western side—cypresses, tamarisks. He writes a memo for himself to contact the Negev Institute in Beer-Sheva and ask them what's worth planting, maybe it
would be a good idea to try out a new variety.

Later, close to midday, a few doctors enter, therapists and
analysts who have problems. Every day, at this hour, they come.
They pour out their hearts. Day after day they sit with their
bottles of orange or grapefruit juice, pumpkin seeds, peanuts,
sometimes black coffee. And, as always, the conversation finally
shifts to the problem called Adam Stein. Adam Stein and the
child. Adam Stein and Uriel Bloch. Many of the doctors find it
difficult to play the bystander, the spectator, and accept the ab-

solute authority of Dr. Gross. Zevi Erd, a doctor with a considerable reputation who has published an interesting study of the
new methods of treating schizophrenic children, complains:
"Where is the limit, Nathan? You permit him to hide bottles of
liquor behind every radiator, to give unintelligible lectures to the
other patients, to have a love affair with a responsible nurse
whose work is important to the Institute, to accept money from
patients and invest it in dubious ventures, and all this only a
year after he attempted to strangle a woman, and when his sickness is extremely dangerous. Wouldn't a strict, severe frame-
work be more helpful in this case than the present total license?
And, to top it all, there's this business with the child Uriel
Bloch. You permit Adam to abuse an unfortunate child whom
we have been trying to cure for the past few years, whom . . ."

"Whom what? Please, Zevi, finish your sentence!" Dr. Gross
lights a cigarette, inhales the smoke, and straightens up a bit.
"What about the child? Had we seen any hope of improvement?
A drop of hope? Today this child walks erect! He types on a
typewriter, he responds, he has removed his sheet, he pays attention, he carries on a conversation—not yet through speech, but
he types. Is that what you call abuse?"

"Yes . . . *Who* is bringing about these miracles?" Dr. Erd is
stubborn. His voice rings cynical. "Who, Adam Stein? I'll tell
you a story, Nathan—with your permission. A certain individual
once complained about terrific stomach pains that attacked him
after he drank a glass of tea! They asked him when that glass of
tea caused him a stomachache. And he told them that he went to
the cafeteria and ordered two portions of chopped liver, ate, and
felt fine—no bellyache! He had vegetable soup with dumplings,
no problem, had a schnitzel with potatoes, noodles, eggplant
salad, tomato salad, some sesame paste, and a little liver—still
no stomach pains! Even the wine caused no trouble, he drank
two glasses of red wine and actually felt terrific, a stomach of
iron. And bread, you name it! Hot, white! He ate at least half a
loaf. And at the end he ordered ice cream with whipped cream,

and no pains in his stomach occurred. Then he drank a single glass of tea, one glass of tea and a little lemon, and bang! His stomach exploded with pain. You get it? For years we've been trying everything, doing our job untiringly to find some cure, then along comes this glass of tea in the form of Adam Stein, praised be his name, who offers the child two candies, barks at him, and the child jumps to attention all cured? Let's be realistic. It's hard to believe, it's simply hard to accept the progress that's occurred in the child, but just because we despaired of saving him and Adam Stein stepped into the picture, we have no right to give the credit entirely to Adam Stein and relinquish our share, just because we despaired."

Dr. Gross extinguishes the cigarette in the ashtray, rises from his chair, and paces back and forth. "Tell me, Zevi. Are you jealous of the child?"

"Jealous?"

"No, you aren't jealous of him, and that's the trouble. Adam Stein *is* jealous of him. In this fact lies the difference. That's the subtle difference. What you said has no basis in reality. Adam Stein entered the picture at the point where we failed, so we had better call a spade a spade. What is more amazing is that Adam himself, in the process, has improved—without wanting it to happen, either for himself or for the child. Two serious cases, and they are curing each other. One dog is healing another dog. Isn't that fascinating? And you, instead of kneeling down and thanking God, you stick your noses in the air. Your diplomas are scraping against your deflated chests, you regurgitate the books that you've read. You're offended. Don't be afraid, let the miracle happen, it's permissible. Applaud it, watch closely, but don't interfere. We are Mars men—with your distinguished permission—Mars men who are trying to understand what is hurting the miserable ant crawling in the sand, far off, on the surface of the Earth, or maybe it would be more correct to say that we are ants on the surface of the Earth trying to understand the pains of Mars men. A miracle has occurred. A swindler has met a dog, and we must keep quiet, we must listen to what's going on, we may not understand, but we must wait. You cannot compare this situation to any other case. What's good for these two patients may be bad for others. But we must listen, learn, pray for success."

"But what does that have to do with it?" Dr. Nachwalter, who has been silent till now, wipes his glasses and replaces them on his nose. "If that's the case, why don't you let all the patients cure one another and we'll sit on the sidelines playing cards."

"Not a bad idea!" Dr. Gross laughs, but his face remains very serious.

"You're retreating again to your defeatism, Nathan." Zevi Erd is burning, his face aflame. "We progress slowly, heel toe, heel toe. Mrs. Altshuler, who a few years ago was a hopeless case, is today almost cured. Contact has been established, a connection, you can point to some significant achievements even here. You are a hopeless sentimentalist, Nathan."

"Zevi, wait a minute. No, that's not the truth."

"Yes, yes. Hopeless. Even so, I admire you, and you know that. Because of you I came to the Institute. Not because of the great working conditions. I don't doubt your strength, your accomplishments, but here, in this case, you've let go of the reins. You've fallen into a trap that you've hidden from yourself. The two of them are *not* curing each other. The cure that has occurred is *our* handiwork. The relationship between the child and the man is a miracle *only in their eyes,* and perhaps also in yours —and that's what pains me, because in *our* eyes this miracle is a disaster and you will soon regret it. Listen to me! It's dangerous."

"You know, Zevi, I agree with you." Dr. Gross smiles. His big black dreamy eyes stare at the vigorous young man. "Everything you say is right, and yet not right. We didn't help them, we gave up hope, and rightly, because we had no other choice. They are progressing, in each other's presence. I don't know the reason why, but I am not going to stop them. Even if the end is

bitter, so that I will regret it and have to resign, still I am the one
now who makes the rules! We are able to cure the colds of
people who are suffering from cancer—that's as far as we can
go, no more! These two have penetrated beyond colds, into the
rusty tissues of the soul. I will take off my hat to them, I will
stand like an excited child and wait. And when the day comes, I
will step up and pin gold medals on their chests. The pins will
stick into the whole bunch of us, but the medals will adorn
proud chests. I have faith because I do not understand. You'll
grow old yet, Zevi, like me. Adam plowed the fields of Hell inside his body, from the exit to the entrance. And at the entrance
stands a barking dog. What will happen? What, exactly what?
We aren't any smarter than they, we're just healthier, and even
that is questionable. Inside them they hold the secrets which we
want to uncover, and they are suffering, not us."

Dr. Gross sinks into his armchair, browses through the papers
on his desk, and lifts one sheet in order to mask the pallor of his
face. Nachwalter remembers that they are waiting for him. Zevi
Erd keeps his eye on the diagram hanging on the wall. The
others rise and leave one after another. Dr. Gross mutters between his teeth: "Hopeless sentimentalist!" And young, talented, ambitious Zevi Erd, who is obviously going places and
will one day get very far, laughs through the tears that have
collected in his eyes.

12

DESERT NIGHT

FROM THE MOMENT David, King of Israel, stood on his feet, Adam Stein was critically ill. So Adam Stein lay in the infirmary and the child was shut up in his room. Between them, the Institute held its breath. The kindergarteners of Nurse Spitzer sang: "Happy New Year, Mom. Happy New Year, Dad." Adam wouldn't listen to them. *What child? What dog? I have no child whatsoever, David, King of Israel, was buried in Jerusalem, his son Solomon ruled after him.* The child was shut up in his room, and everyone sat waiting. Arthur tried to run a lottery. Fifty argued that Adam would go to the child, sixty-two said that it was all over.

One night, at a time when Adam was already much better and walking in the infirmary though David, King of Israel, was still stuck in his room, the elder Schwester twin lay in her bed fast asleep. And suddenly a winged angel appeared at the edge of her bed and whispered to her: "Dear Schwester, the longed-for day is at hand." He repeated the sentence seven times, and then said: "My little Schwester, beloved pure one of mine, the Day of Judgment is approaching, prepare for the great day, the trumpets of the Messiah will soon blow, my good lovely Schwester. . . ."

That same night, at that very same hour, the astronomer Sohnman was sitting at the window looking through his telescope. He saw a comet glowing in the sky. In the Milky Way, stars erupted and skipped for a while like goats.

That night and at that hour Dr. Gross, on his way home to Arad, had a flat tire. Pierre Lotti woke at that time from a nightmare, panicked and vomited for a long while, stooped over from the pain that shot through his head like lightning, but fell asleep again and forgot what had happened to him.

Other amazing things occurred (as became clear later on) at that fateful hour. Wolfovitz woke from a nap and for a moment imagined that he could escape from the net of Satan which was spread across his feet—he felt certain that he was now actually baffling death. He looked at his watch. It was five past eleven. An hour later it was still five past eleven. At the hour of five past eleven the elevator got stuck in between the second and third floors, and the big refrigerator in Pierre Lotti's kitchen stopped working.

The elder Schwester sister concluded that all these facts were clear signs pointing to just one meaning. The great day was at hand! Therefore she declared a day of fasting. She sat in her bed and meditated on God. And at night she slept and the angel again appeared. He stood at the end of the bed, which was suddenly larger and wider and alone in a desert whose walls were water and whose ceiling was the sky, and he whispered in a pleasant and enticing voice: "Schwester, Schwester mine . . ." And she answered with the sadness of an old woman whose body had been loved by insects and whose upper lip was topped by a delicate black mustache: "Last night you called me *dear*

Schwester, and now you call me *Schwester mine.* I see portents, but do not understand. My body aches, I haven't eaten all day." The angel smiled at her. She saw that sweet smile spreading over his face and regretted her words. He whispered: "On Tuesday night, in the desert, over a flat hill with a furrow on top and a dry thorn bush, beyond a hill that looks like a ram and beside it a shrub, on the long way to Elat, a hundred steps to the right in the direction of Gaza."

The elder Schwester sister awoke totally shaken; she fell on her knees and prayed. If only Mrs. Seizling were with her now! But Mrs. Seizling was in a refrigerator in Cleveland, Ohio.

The Schwester sister completed her prayer and at once set about organizing, planning, putting everybody to work. It all had to be finished by Tuesday. The Creator doesn't choose an hour of destiny randomly. He has his reasons. She herself was nothing but a messenger, she knew that. And she also knew that the true go-between, the Prophet, would refuse to come along and she would have to force him to arise and go, for the fate of the nation and the world was in his hands. The burden of this fate was so heavy that the Schwester sister felt every day a kind of vertigo which didn't leave her until they were out the back gate of the Institute and entering the desert.

Though Wolfovitz tended to have faith one minute and no faith the next, he attempted to minimize the significance of the signs. "It was a coincidence merely. A coincidence is not a miracle and not even a sign. Prophecy was given to fools, and God is dead. And if He isn't dead, then He's certainly busy, or playing some game. Do you know what game He's playing, Schwester? A whale of a game! As the Bible says, God created the Leviathan to play with! He sits there in Heaven and plays with His toy whale. Pulls its tail, opens its jaws— He's busy."

Arthur Fine was excited. He argued before Handsome Rube and Mrs. Tamir that although everybody was convinced that God would elect to speak with Adam Stein, they would soon find out that, on account of Arthur's sufferings being greater than

Adam's, seeing that he hadn't betrayed anybody the way Adam
had, he hadn't killed his wife and two daughters, hadn't fooled
around and played the clown in the house of death, God would
therefore speak with him! Thus spake Arthur Fine the great arsonist, the honest man, the chocolate soldier, and laughed.

The Schwester twin was a new person. Her face shone, her
entire being was younger by ten, by twenty, years. She walked
along the paths outside, down the corridors, inside all the rooms,
singing:

> If I were a baby and you a nurse
> I'd suck your lovely breast and break my thirst.
> If I were a tent and you lodged inside,
> I'd dally with love and strengthen with age.
> If I were a tongue and you my words,
> My silence would burn for you with desire and song.

On Tuesday night, at ten in the evening, about twenty men
and women have gathered beside the big refrigerator in Pierre
Lotti's kitchen and the signal is given. The rear entrance facing
the herb garden is forced open, and stealthily, slipping into the
night, the "nation" leaves the courtyard of the synthetic sanctuary of Mrs. Seizling and is swallowed by the darkness of the
great desert that closes in on all sides. The night is lovely, clear.
The sky stretches out like copper. Stars sparkle by the thousands. At the head of the nation steps the elder Schwester sister
in a white dress that comes down to her ankles, a white wedding
dress of silk and lace. On her head she has tied a wreath of
plastic flowers. Everybody wears white, save Pierre Lotti and
Adam Stein. Since Pierre Lotti knows that he is a stranger,
though he longs to be a part of the nation, he wears the corduroy
pants of a mountain climber and a green Austrian hat with a
feather stuck in it. To the hat he has sewed a white label with the
word *Jerusalem* embroidered on it. In his hand is a carved
walking-stick.

Adam Stein wears a broad-brimmed black hat made by A. N.

Fischer, Berlin, a dark suit, and a white shirt whose every button is buttoned. Around his neck he has a tie the color of Bordeaux. But the others, the others wear white. They hold one another by the hand and step into the desert without a word.

Miles has brought his trumpet along, Arthur his drum.

Locusts marching into a wasteland, and the sound of their steps smothered by the sand. Nobody says anything, nobody raises his voice. They are scared. They hold hands. In a single file. The elder Schwester is in the lead, her eyes gouging out the darkness of the night. A certain malaise exists in the stretched heavens. Nothing is stirring inside them. At last a star shoots; a plane flies in the distance, its lights going on and off, though its engines stay inaudible. The desert night is a silence that mutters, or perhaps a muttering that is silent. Adam knows that it's the dust of bones being ground secretly, the dust which the angels, wrapped in curtains, brought from "there" and cast down over here as a proof of the conservation of matter.

The Institute gets pinched smaller and smaller. Its many-colored lights are blocked by the hills. Any minute it will be invisible, it will vanish into the darkness which tightens and clamps all around them. Every person holds a hand. A slight quake travels from hand to hand. Storms were here, in Edom, in Moav, in the Negev, in Paran, the Amon deserts. Great kings fought in this murky desert. King Kadralomer of Elem, King Tidal of the nations, Amrafel, King of Shinar. Arioch, King of Alosar. The king of Sodom and Gomorrah. Lo and behold, Abraham, Lot and his wife. The crossroads of nations: Greeks, Romans, Mamelukes, Egyptians, Arabs, Chaldeans, Babylonians, Assyrians, Christians, Hebrews and Jews . . . the land of salt, broom and copper. The land of mountains, of birds of prey, eagles and kites, the land of Melchizedek, the priest of the god called the One Above. They trek hand in hand, the elder Schwester sister in front. Adam is smoking a cigarette. Someone's teeth begin to chatter, then someone else's. Soon everyone's teeth are chattering. White teeth, black teeth, gold teeth, bridges, crowns, they all chatter. The desert night wind is cold, chilling. Their bodies shrink, quake, freeze. The chatter begets moaning and the moaning begets groaning and the groaning begets coughing and grumbling and a soft hum. God! Where are you? Where? "He could be a she!" announces Arthur all of a sudden. But nobody hears him. The first words spoken go unheard. He could be a she! Or a microorganism, or a male eel, or a female eel? Nobody responds. It's cold.

Their feet no longer hurry. Somebody breaks off from the chain. Then another, and another. And they are no more a long line stepping into glory. Their feet are heavy, the cold penetrates to their bones, the grumbles increase. Adam Vasco da Gama Stein pays no heed to the grumbling. Small fry grumble, heroes weep. His broad-brimmed hat perfectly suits him in this great hour, and he would be the first to admit it. His gait is firm, his body strong. This is not the sick Adam Stein from the infirmary. This is a different Adam Stein, a new Adam Stein, surprising— that's what he tells himself. The dawn of a new era has commenced. Arthur's drum dances on his thigh and his mouth sighs. His face glows from the cold, his legs swell. "I must have smallpox, one pock for each step I take." Suddenly Arthur is convinced that he's been deceived. Jackals howl, an owl hoots from a hidden crevice, far away. The new moon rises, the sand turns pallid. The pale moonlight instills a certain tenderness and warmth into the cold earth.

Arthur's shriek plows through the desert: "Schwester! How long must we wait?"

"It will be very soon, my child." Her eyes stare at the darkness extending in front of her. She feels neither the cold nor the wind, hears neither the grumbling nor the chattering. She sees Adam and is proud of him. She and he are two of a kind. They both knew, and know. The rest form a flock. And a flock you must lead with an iron hand, she knows. They grumble, their teeth chatter, and what's worse—they are beginning to doubt her.

The journey, which began as a procession, one person following another, each eye containing a vision, now seems to Adam to
be the retreat of a beaten army, an army that has lost its faith,
its direction, its loyalty, and its shoes. Every man for himself,
solitary, in the desert each person is trapped inside his own
fears, inside his own soul.

The cold is terrific, and they begin to be thirsty too. The walking exhausts them, and they don't know where they are walking
to. They've already forgotten. They want to go back. But how
do they get back? Everywhere is dark, monotonously, frighten-
ingly dark. Terrifying shapes enclose them. Mountains look like
monsters. Cold wind and thirst. The small canteen that Pierre
Lotti has brought is already empty. Their lips, parched from the
cold, crave water. Adam sees a procession of Johnny Walkers
wearing hats, good beer—Amstel or Tuborg . . . green bottles, huge glasses with clowns painted on them, draft beer from
cellars.

"I trust in God," sings the Schwester twin. "To God I call."
The wreath of plastic flowers flutters proudly on her head. "And
He shall reply from his sacred Mount . . . I have lain down to
sleep and waked, for the Lord is my support." No, she need not
suffer on account of these petty souls. She hasn't waited all those
years for that, her hope is not for a drink of water. If they're
thirsty, let them be thirsty! The pangs of redemption are painful.
They want juice and "the Lord rideth upon a swift cloud." The
dark desert excites her. She visualizes the intensity of creation.
In every location, every crevice, every breeze of wind, she sees
signals.

Time passes, hour by hour. Some faint, sinking into the cold
soil. Exhausted, wrung dry, stunned. They cry, but no tears
come. Miles trembles. Arthur beats the earth with his hand and
raises a burst of thick dust that blocks his breathing.

Even the Schwester sister collapses all of a sudden. When she
tries to get up, she finds out that her legs will not obey her. The
cold has begun to gnaw her with its sharp teeth. Her white dress

feels like a sheath of ice that is about to split.

Adam approaches her, scans the horizon, and says quietly: "Don't despair, Schwester."

She raises her eyes and stares at him.

"It's a test, Schwester. Your God is a hard nut, he has no pity, like his daughter: look at the desert—pitiless. We must go on, there's no other choice."

"You're right, Adam. I stumbled, but see, I'm getting up." He extends a hand to her, against the background of the mountains of Moav, a clown dressed in the clothes of Von Hamdung. God is bound to burst out laughing. She grabs his hand, folds her legs—swollen and blue from the cold—under her, and rises. Now she will storm the mountain. "I slipped, I stumbled, and now, God, I am coming to You. My song will be played on Your violin." The vision seizes her again. "I was bird dung in the desert, and will still be bird dung, but a light of honor and worth will illuminate my face. I shall be Your servant, my Lord God. Do with me what You want. Punish me! Punish, punish!"

Her lips whisper. She barely catches what Adam is saying: "I'll go on alone. I'll look around, check things out and be right back." She swings a gaze of wonder at him and continues to pray. "Yes, yes. My Lord, who shall dwell in Your tents, who shall lodge on Your sacred mount? Someone who speaks the truth, to himself and to others, who walks with truth and acts with truth."

Adam listens. That's not the God they've come out here to find, but there's no turning back. She is innocent, Schwester is, and the world is packed with surprises. Who knows? He casts a glance at his comrades outstretched on the cold earth, shuts his ears to their pleadings, to their beaten faces, to their trampled bodies, and turns off on his own track. He walks. The desert imitates itself, repeats itself. The hills differ, yet all resemble one another. As soon as you reach one, you forget what the previous hill looked like. It's a sort of organized chaos, or existence organized by the corporation Chaos, Inc. God's chewing gum. He chews the mountains and the hills and kneads them, and then spits out rosy buttocks; he pushes them around, tosses them around, and they stick together, one beside another, mountain by mountain, desert by crevice, owl by eagle. Adam walks on. Treks. His heart pumping. Where does he get his strength. What source is he drawing on? Isn't he thirsty? He has a canteen concealed in his pocket. No, he is not thirsty. What about his feet? Two weeks after an operation? Those small-fry believers, they don't understand. . . .

He owes them this. He doesn't know why, he is not afraid for himself. He is willing, desirous. If he only could, and if only for this one time, do something for others, whoever they might be. This is the chance he has been given. For a moment he feels that he is no longer a fraud. And immediately he interprets his feelings as an indication of an even higher level of imposture, and that relieves him, as it were. He walks farther on, scanning the desert, and after a while returns to his flock of fellow humans. Everyone is sprawled out, except for the Schwester sister, who is standing. They are gazing at him, not in accusation but in entreaty.

They wait. If he were to scream now: *We made a mistake! There's no way!* they would give up their ghosts and die. In the desert. There is a power in him. He smiles: "Schwester, follow me!" And they all rise, as though on command. Once more they have a leader. There is a path, there is a direction, somebody knows the way. They walk through the frozen desert and the Schwester sister sings in a nasal voice: "How long will You forget me, O Lord. Forever? How long will You conceal Your countenance from me?" And they all repeat after her: "How long will You forget me. O Lord. Forever?" They are close together, almost touching one another. They sway in a tortured, intoxicated rhythm. Adam out in front. His hand holding the hand of the Schwester sister, whose face is flooded with a holy splendor which alarms—so thinks Miles Davis—the dozens of un-believers in her midst. "The hyena will come and finish you off," her Auntie used to tell her, the hyena would hypnotize her and lug her to a cave in the desert and eat her without salt—dear Auntie, it wasn't for nothing she always talked about hyenas; she herself was one—living, on principle, at the border, in the last house, among the exploding hand grenades. The Arabs claimed she was like Rashid Abu Aljaji, "the father of hens," who would sneak into the coop and mesmerize the chickens so that they all followed him. Adam mesmerizes Schwester, Schwester mesmerizes us, we mesmerize the bear, Auntie mesmerizes her husband till he dies.

By a misty hill Adam halts and orders the others to remain standing. He pulls a flat bottle from his pocket and waves it in their faces. He smiles, all of a sudden he's enjoying himself. All eyes stare at the bottle as though it were their last salvation. Arthur bursts into shrieking sobs. "That's vodka! He's tricking us, that's vodka!" His eyes burn, in spite of the night, in spite of the complete darkness.

"No, it's water! One after the other, please. Just wet the lips," says Adam, victorious, and they come, kneel beside him, and each one sucks the bottle until Adam pulls it away for the next wild-eyed customer.

"Now wait for me here! I'll be right back." The bitterness in his voice is something they expect. They drop down where they are, pull their thin shirts and blouses closer around them— wrapping themselves in coldness. But the Schwester sister, on her knees, begins an endless song of gratitude in a gasping voice: "My God, my God, my God, my God . . ."

Miles's trumpet feebly states the beat. Arthur must join in on his drum, but his fingers thump soundlessly, numb from cold. The Schwester sister whispers: "Your deeds are miracles, God, and my soul knows it well. . . . I cannot conceal from You the things I've done in hiding. I plotted underground." And Miles blows "Take the A Train," "Lullaby of Birdland," and "Tzena, Tzena." A certain rankness hangs in the cold air. Adam walks on. The others, all bundled up, shiver. They do not want to die.

The desert engulfs them; its lions, leopards, kites, eagles will devour them in the ravines. God will not show his face. Dr. Gross will lock them in solitary confinement. If only Adam would come back! The old gigolo has gone to God, his inamorata is praying, Arthur is gnashing his teeth. Schwester is going to give birth to a son, the Holy Ghost's son. All is lost. "Take the A Train." Sometimes, when Arthur feels that everything is over, he examines his number. This number is a document of identification issued by a superior authority and therefore has immense significance, and the moment Arthur examines his blue number his act is repeated by somebody else who has no idea why he is doing it. If Arthur scrutinizes, so must the others. There is nothing else they can do at that moment. It doesn't take ten minutes before seventeen numbered arms recall the Purim celebration and begin swaying in time to the music. That way the world becomes warmer, clearer. The numbers skip in the desert and Adam, the absent conductor of this numerical symphony, is bound to sense what's going on here and do something so that they can all get out of this desert alive.

At the sight of these raised arms, these faces, Pierre Lotti is dumfounded.

The little water that they drank has only served to excite their thirst. The Schwester sister mumbles: "My God, my God." She is still dreaming her vision. Soon the great and mighty dawn will break, and we shall be saved. Has everything been smashed to pieces only a moment before redemption? Pierre Lotti feels as though they are sitting in a jungle and telling jokes to a lion on the prowl who is simply waiting for them to finish their jokes so he can stop laughing and then . . . Miles and Arthur are playing jazz to the desert: if, after this tense journey toward a brutal God, God does not reveal Himself this time, He never will.

Adam, in fact, is walking toward God. Trekking across hills by himself. He is mocking himself because something pushes him, driving all his senses crazy, forcing him to re-interpret his hidden past. It tells him: "You are a messenger! Go on!" He, the former dog, the former clown, the former student, the former man of the world, he, abetted by the conjunction of weird elements in a complicated nightmare of an old woman whose mustache was loved by mosquitoes, whose body was loved by fleas—he, *he* is the prophet, *he* the messenger. It is hard to believe. He wants to believe just the opposite, that he must return and smack the truth in their faces like stones from a slingshot: that no, He will not show up, it's a lie, a joke, their seriousness was Adam's jest.

It's idiocy, only a lunatic would have faith. But as he goes, he sheds bit by bit his last comic routine and he believes, the child of craving and forgetfulness, and Herbert disappears, and Jenny is nothing but a remote dream, and he, yes, *he* shall stand face to face with God, he believes it through and through. The sun will shine and I will be there.

And at that very moment he hears the Voice address him. From the desert comes the playful, commanding, familiar, warning, tricky Voice. Is that you, Herbert? No! He wouldn't allow Herbert to confuse or soil or trample the great moment. Who are you? The Voice chuckles, such a familiar yet strange sound. Desert irony. And Adam, the believing child, whispers: "I am Adam Stein the suicide." He chuckles for a moment himself. For a fraction of a second the swindler is himself again. The Voice bursts into laughter, and the whole desert laughs as though it were being tickled, and Adam thinks to himself: "What a pity." Then, more bold, Adam pierces the darkness with his eyes and sees Him standing on a mount with a thorn bush, beside another hill, just as the angel had instructed the Schwester sister, and he kneels immediately without any amazement and stares straight ahead and watches and wants to laugh while the voice of Commandant Klein engages him. The Schwester sister was right after all.

Yes, he cannot stand, he has to kneel. His Klein is smiling, dressed in a gorgeous beige suit with a jaunty three-cornered handkerchief in the jacket pocket, and a cork hat on his head, like a British officer's. Commandant Klein smiles. "Now sit, my Adam, and tell me why you ran away from me. I looked all over for you." Adam sits and pulls a pack of cigarettes from his pocket. He lights one and smokes. He doesn't offer God a cigarette. Nor does Klein ask for one. Klein gazes at him with a look of boundless sadness. "Sacrificial victims die nicely, Adam," he says in a fatherly, compassionate voice, "and you too could have died nicely. But you ran away from me, you bolted, came here? Why? You don't belong here! You're like me, a nobody, you're part and parcel of the ashes, you can't be a flower in the desert. You were shit once and will always be, the manure that matures trees for gallows. But you chickened out, you were afraid to keep the thing going right to the end, afraid to bring me the bridal price, the hush money, the dowry, the harlot's fee. I was starving without you—boy, was I thirsty! You had no right, Adam. I could have told you plenty of stories—lovely, sad tales. Let me choose one. Many years ago a young man was walking in the streets of Berlin one day, looking for a way to kill himself. His love had deserted him and married another. The unfaithful girl had asked him to attend the wedding ceremony, and he had gone to it. So the young man was wandering through the streets of Berlin, incredibly depressed, when he came upon a circus and watched a famous clown. The clown was clever, wise, and funny, the clown played the guitar and the violin, the clown divined the stupid past history of two old women who both wore hats with feathers protruding like cock's combs, the clown clowned, and the clown was truly a wonder drug and the young man was salvaged. He no longer paid any attention to the tablets of poison in his pocket which he had earlier decided to take. Years later the young man met the clown again, and the clown wore a fine suit, had a lovely suitcase in his hand, and was standing in a line. The young man, seated by a table, was no more the young man who had gone to the circus. He was an official: he pointed to the right and to the left. When he saw the clown, he burst out laughing and the clown returned a smile involuntarily.

The clown didn't recognize him. How was he to know that ten years ago he had saved this man from death? The order was given and the clown was taken aside, not sent to the right or to the left. The clown was saved. And who was the one who saved the clown? The young man who hadn't swallowed the poison pills.

"More years passed and the young man aged some more and returned home a complete pauper, wounded, hungry, miserable. His wife had died in a bomb explosion, his son was missing and couldn't be traced. In order to live, he had to eat, and the clown was willing to come to the rescue. Life for life. The clown brought him coins packed in a rubber condom, and the young man who had aged changed his name. He sat hidden in his room and studied Semitic languages, composed the dictionary of a new language which he himself had invented so as to isolate himself. He lacked nothing. Until one day the clown disappeared and he was left all alone, hungry and lost. Then he had a choice: to become an alley dog, steal, bark, or to become one of the boys, go downstairs and greet the American Johnnie smiling in the street and open a small shop, buy and sell stolen goods, open a gift shop, marry a young woman who was a young woman no longer, Klopfer by name, who had once sat on his knees and kept a file of the rings of smoke undulating from the stacks: Jacob, Rachel, Leah, Abraham, Hirsch, Mottel. Ring after ring, date of birth, place of birth, cause of death. He refused to get married, though. Refused to become a dog, refused to sell goods. If he wanted, he could have been an alley dog in the streets of Berlin, could have barked, fallen ill from self-hate, made a public confession, borne the picture of Anne Frank in a procession, screamed, sobbed. He could have admitted everything and gone to Argentina, or been shrewd and entered the Foreign Office, fitting into the miracle of recovery, purchasing a sparkling Opel, driving to the woods on Sunday, fishing, hunting, begetting blond children, contributing to the United Jewish Fund.

"Instead, he became God. Came here, to the desert, and now asks: What do you want, Adam? Isn't Klein standing at the end of the road waiting for you? Why won't you surrender and understand? Why won't you—out of your own good will? Don't stir up the best of mankind against you! Come on! Once and for all! I'm waiting, and I'll always be waiting for you at the end of the road. Nothing else can help you, not rubber condoms with coins inside, not pistols, faith, rifles, atomic bombs, socialism, oral polio vaccine, Nobel Prizes for physics, and the best will in the world. History is a mournful story, it has neither logic nor meaning. The future is wrapped in mist. Everything depends on you, you alone."

Adam squints. Klein hasn't changed. His hair may be a bit grayer on the sides, but the same nose, the same sensual lips, the same smile. Adam wants to speak, yet the words escape him. He who always knows the right words for the right occasion! What's right? What's not right? God crosses his legs and sits there. In front of him. They gaze at each other. Such a simple matter to be in God's presence! And he could ask questions, about suffering, about the illogical logic, about the small children, about what is about to happen or not happen. Klein, for his part, recollects the time Adam asked for permission to brush his teeth and he, Klein, refused. "What else could I do? Could I have written to Berlin and requested permission to grant the entreaty of a certain dog who wanted to brush his teeth? But you yourself must admit that I made believe I didn't know what you did, made believe I was blind. Once, when I was gone, you stole the toothbrush and brushed your teeth above the sink with my yellow deluxe. For a long while I stood there behind you and I didn't have the heart to interrupt you." Adam ponders these words. He has a heart, I would never have got back to Berlin if he didn't have a heart. But there were others besides Adam, and how will He understand? Will He ask? "Jewish history is over," says Adam, "or maybe it's just beginning. You are superfluous. We are living in a cemetery. There is nothing to rescue." God examines him at length. They peer into each other's eyes.

Klein recalls that day at the circus, they were selling hot dogs
at the entrance and he ate two or three, and also some terrific
ice cream. . . . Adam doesn't remember. He is sorry about
Mrs. Klein's death. Her thighs were warm and her breasts gener-
ous. He remembers the way God snored at the edge of the bed.
"*Mein lieber,* my sweet Klein, today I slept with a dog. I was
tired and sad. Smoke was rising outside the window, I wasn't
used to the smoke yet, to the odor. The idea, I admit, was
strange and appealing: smoke. All our neighbors! Do you remember the time, while we were living on Wilhelmstrasse, when
Mrs. Seligman used to give piano lessons to little Adolf? There
she is now, billowing. A smoke ring. Hard to take. And suddenly
I'm with a funny dog, and I wanted a little . . . well, it was
exciting too . . . a dog in bed, my heart beating passionately.
I'm very sorry, *mein lieber,* but you drank so much vermouth
you were as impotent as a cucumber." Klein must have heard
and nodded. "Of course, of course, my sweetheart." Then he
came back from the war. What a disgrace. He had gone out to
save the world and all that he had accomplished was the extermination of a tiny portion of sub-humanity from the face of the
globe. Where was the New Order? He returned starving and solitary, he didn't even have me yet! Where did we meet for the first
time after all those years? Yes, he was begging then in the streets,
or looked like a beggar in the street. Ragged, tattered, wretched.
Camp Director of Auchhausen for four years and honest to the
very end: he never stole a penny for himself. Two chairs from
Warsaw and a toothbrush, that's all. The smoke was his single
contribution to the nation, to tradition, to eternity. He sent all
the teeth to the warehouse and kept a complete record of what
was in that warehouse. Honest, loyal, obedient. An unfortunate
man. And he was picking up from the gutter the cigarette butts
that the American soldiers had proudly tossed away. When I
found him, we wept. The two of us wept at the well of Frau
Glanz. She wanted me to marry her, that worn-out old woman.

Her husband, she said, had been called away to arrange things for her in Paradise, but in the meantime there were a few good years left. So why not? And, really, why not? I was wealthy, the Mercedes knocked their eyes out. What looks of envy! That's how I got rid of much of the defeatist attitude which had begun to attack some of them. That constant regret, that mournfulness, that sneaking away from guilt. Guilt was lovely in my eyes. I wanted to see a celebration in its honor. The new exchange rate and the miracle of recovery were things that came in the nick of time. The victor should not allow himself to get too sad. Whatever you, God, have permitted and commanded must, in the nature of things, be ethical and aesthetic. And you know that I didn't blame anyone. Klein bursts out laughing. The way he did then, at the well of Frau Glanz, when Adam pulled out a rubber condom from his pocket, a nice white balloon, and stuffed it with jingling coins. A few seconds of astonishment pass. What more can they say to each other?

"Why have you come?"

"I came so you could kill me."

"I can't."

"Yes, you can, and must." And he laughs. There is nothing worse than a laughing God.

"I can't. I haven't the right or the strength. If I could, Weiss—"

Klein barks: "I'm not Weiss here, forget him! Here I'm Klein, understand?"

"I can't do it," repeats Adam, in a whisper. "That wouldn't solve anything. Besides, I love you. I know that you're a bastard, but I love you. I'll curse you, yet come to the desert to look for you. We are both lost, we have both perished. Our voices are the voices of ghosts. Jew to Jew, God to Son of God, man to father of man. In these synthetic, beheaded days, that is the only dialogue that makes sense. You, my God, shall wait for me at the end of the road. I won't murder you. I can't, and it's a shame, such a shame."

* * *

Arthur has stopped beating his drum. Arthur wants to sleep, dream, write strange names in ancient Egyptian script. Miles has dropped to the frozen, freezing sand. Frozen, freezing, he freezes, she freezes, we freeze, they freeze, he will freeze, you will freeze, we will freeze. If an eagle were to swoop down now from the sky and lick me, he'd certainly think I was a brick of ice cream. "Yesterday an eagle ate a brick of ice cream in the Paran Desert." The eagle will return tomorrow. The eagle will overcome his stomachache. There's nothing like the ice cream in the Paran Desert. Four in the morning. Soon dawn will break. Where are we? Why doesn't Adam come back? It isn't because he's lost, because he's led himself astray and us astray. We are going crazy, swooning from the cold. What will become of us? We will perish and nobody will know. The sand will bury us, black ravens will pluck out our eyes. God is in hiding. Schwester and her vain dreams. That liar. She and her swindler, she and her clown are making fools of us. All is lost. Arthur's blood rushes to his head. Look at that Schwester with her mumbling lips. "Liar!" he shrieks. "Those bugs never made love to your body, your husband died from shame, your husband got sick at heart, that mustache of yours is an aesthetic crime! Listen to me, those bugs attacked you because you hadn't taken a bath in a month!" And he rouses into a man of action and strength. They all gape at him, those wretches, wrapped up in the soil, freezing along with the soil, upon it and already inside it, part of it. But he rouses, runs off, fathers some broom shrubs, and feels warmer already. He makes a pyramid of the sprigs he's collected. He rummages in his pocket, takes out a pack of matches and lights the twigs. And nothing in the whole desert, from the sources of the Persian Gulf to Santa Katarina and Jebel Moussa, is a more heart-warming sight, more endearing and more distressing.

Arthur stands above the fire and fans it, and the flames catch. The sprigs burn quickly, Broom brush is good for kindling. And he screams into the fire, out of the fire, his own face as red as the fire: "Adam Stein will not come back. We will die in the desert. There's no way out of here. We have to fumigate everything. Liquidate the devils. Because of them we are here, because of them we are going to die. . . ." And with clipped step the chocolate soldier (who from 1939 to 1945, during that closed chapter, lived in a labyrinth, lived in tunnels and emerged finally into the light and became the master of conflagrations, the fumigator of crimes) approaches the Schwester sister, who, still sunk in her illusions, notices nothing and doesn't resist. She turns to stone as he drags her across the frozen soil. Her dress catches and rips. A demoness in white. With plastic flowers on your head, woman. Into the fire. Into the fire! The devils will then go mute and flee. Her mouth mumbles sentences of prayer. Her body gives in to him. Arthur lugs her and lo! Twenty people do not come to life. It's amazing. The fire burns, the Schwester twin is being dragged, Arthur screams, Adam is still away. The moment her body—or, more correctly, her dress—touches the fire, only then does the woman inside the frozen sister, the body which is the soul's package, begin to struggle with the angel of destruction. She has no idea who it is she is wrestling with. But she realizes her danger and, while there is still time, screams for help. Nobody heeds her cry. A frozen congregation. Her dress rips and is scorched, and Arthur's face flickers in the light. He tosses her belt and the torn pieces of her dress into the fire. He is in a state of complete frenzy. The Schwester sister, naked, whispers: "I forgive you, I forgive you. . . ." And she trembles. Her breasts sag, her thighs are blue, her stomach slack, and on her head sits a wreath of plastic flowers. She doesn't know that she is naked. Her mouth babbles on, she is so close to her soul's longing, so close to the realization of her dream, and Arthur Fine—the flaming demon—is preventing her from seeing the fulfillment about to take place before her, the revelation that will bring with it a total victory over the dark desert that strangles everything.

A cold sweat covers her. She wants to cry, from the fear that shakes her. In her dream she and the desert gave birth to children and they became rocks and boulders, and once even an eagle emerged from her womb, and the eagle studied her with its glass eye and smiled at her, though it was still attached to her by the umbilical cord. Her mouth mumbles. She is in a tunnel, a place where a fantastic truth is hidden. She is moving, moving from the cold to the heat, from darkness to a halo of light; but to Arthur she is a female demon dancing by a sacred fire. He is amazed. He contemplates his Beatrice. Didn't he once love her? Nobody rises. Nobody will rise.

What saves the Schwester twin is Pierre Lotti's newspapers. He has brought with him the newspapers and magazines in which his triumphs as a cook are described. They were to be his credentials before God. He wanted to offer them on the altar if and when the Revelation took place: the *New York Times,* the *Philadelphia Bulletin, Le Monde, La Notte,* the *Observer, Gourmet.*

Now he snatches the Schwester sister out of the fire, rolls her in the sand and wraps her in his newspapers.

At this point, while the Schwester is wrapped in the newspapers of Pierre Lotti, while the fire is still going and shooting sparks on all sides, Adam Stein reappears and stands among them. Everybody turns to him, in longing and entreaty. His mouth is screwed tight, and their eyes are riveted on that tight mouth. Finally he consents to speak: "The golden calf!" And she, packaged in the newspapers of the world, mutters in her pain: "And all the people broke off the golden earrings . . ." Adam stands in front of her, not like a man returning from God but like a student who has just flunked. Arthur's voice declares: "There's no calf here, no false prophet, it was cold, the clothes were used to make a bonfire, she is not a golden calf, we are thirsty, where is God?"

"What faithless creatures!" says Adam. He wasn't talking to them, but to the elder Schwester. Adam smiles at her. He is

exhausted. His head is splitting. *Sturmführer* Arthur is getting
on his nerves. But within his pain and weariness, in their core,
he senses a new being. He has no words in his mouth to express
himself, but a change has occurred inside him. Words were ordained to describe comprehensible sights. Man shall address
man and the speaker be a telegraph wire and his signals, his
flashes, clear letters, intelligible, standard symbols. But how is it
possible to define a vision? How can he indicate the vision he
saw? Would they believe that Commandant Klein was . . .
Would they understand? And if they understood, could they go
on living? Dr. Gross obviously will examine him. Adam had
taken the long route. You can take the short route, by chewing
mescalin, and thereby witness the gates of heaven opening. You
can smoke a little grass and everything seems simple. Doors
open, Paradise drops in your lap and you're there, within each
other. The awareness of an experience is not necessarily an experience, and the experience of an awareness is not necessarily
an awareness. To reach Commandant Klein in the desert, totally
sane and sound, that is a true experience. Adam feels uplifted,
yet cannot bring them to partake of that experience. They must
remain standing on the other side of the entrance, on the other
side of the wall. He will pity them. Every face is pinned on him,
every eye, every expectation. Now he shall say: "It was all a
lie," and they shall remain silent, mournful, lost. He continues
to speak, but they do not believe him. All the former sacrifices
are no more sacrifices. It was the last chance and, as always, it
went sour. "Out of consideration for the depressed state of
the Jew in our midst, I was forced—though it saddened me
boundlessly—to postpone my revelation to a later date. The
time will be set at the general tricentennial meeting on earth,
which will take place on the thirteenth day of the third millen-
nium, in the ninety-sixth year of splendor, in the woods border-
ing the national river Mein. . . . I am sorry, really very
sorry. . . ." They do not believe him. He screams at them, he
yells at them in anger: "Lunatics, there is nothing, no, *nicht,*

rien! The balloon is burst and there's nothing left but air, nothing, but nothing, but nothing! Look at our Schwester, that's the
realization of sorrow for you! Look, concentrate, on Schwesterism, the general idea, the holy idea, of Schwesterism. There's
nothing more to look forward to. You've built a house for nothing. Waited for nothing. He won't come."

Sadness covers the desert like the dew. It causes the sun to
shine, dries up the coldness, warms the sand and the loess soil,
illuminates the horizon. Adam laughs. He came, yes, actually
came. And now they no longer believe in Him. That's Hell: one
man shouts in the ear of another, but nobody hears. The desert
arouses into life. The dawn wakens in the east. The sadness
which begets the new day begets also the heat, the heat begets a
new hunger and a new thirst. The wilderness stretches on all
sides. Treeless, houseless, cityless, villageless. A hot wind begins
to blow. We are going to die, very soon we are going to die.

Five military command cars, three jeeps, and one search
plane are scanning the desert for the escapees. They've been at it
for several hours, scouting up and down. "Twenty mental patients from the Seizling Institute for Rehabilitation and Therapy
in Arad ran away into the desert last night."

The morning paper has an article by a correspondent who
handles mental-health problems: "The ultra-modern Institute,
which makes a startling contrast, on the one hand, with the
barren Judean hills that encircle it and, on the other hand, with
the type of patients lodging inside, was built by the widow of the
late Jewish American industrialist Joseph Seizling, who in his
youth founded a business empire which he managed from his
home in Cleveland. After his demise, his wife inherited the business and developed it even further, turning the Seizling Corporation into one of the largest industrial enterprises in America.
Last year alone the corporation profits were a sound $420 mil-
lion net, based on a business turnover of more than $2.5 billion.
The Institute, which is unrivaled the world over, is populated

mainly by holocaust refugees who have not recovered from the horrors of that period, and who now receive the best scientific treatment. Dozens of doctors, nurses and therapists attempt to benefit them and improve their mental situation."

After a description of the building, its architecture and procedures, the article continues with the strange fact that "Last night twenty patients, went out into the darkness of the desert—so goes the report—in order to find God. In the small hours of the night, as soon as the directors of the Institute learned of the escape, desperate efforts were made to locate the fugitives, but in vain. Apparently they were wandering through the desert among the many wadis. It seemed likely, however, that after daybreak they would be found." The article goes on to deal with the case histories of Adam Stein and the Schwester sister and Miles Davis, giving many details gleaned from publicity-hungry female nurses and a few male nurses craving some distinction. Adam Stein and Miles Davis and the Schwester sister and Wolfovitz the Circumciser and Mrs. Naomi Merimovitz—they become heroes of the day. Children ask each other: "Hey, did they catch the nuts yet?" Mrs. Shapiro shouts from her porch in Beer-Sheva: "Dalia, Joni, come home! The lunatics are coming home too!" A red-haired street boy in Ashdod runs through the street, yelling: "Latest news! The crackpots are dying of thirst," and the radio newscaster, in his monotonous voice, makes Jenny Grey's heart shiver: "At nine-thirty this morning four of the escapees were located at the edge of the Paran Desert. Their condition was . . ."

Adam Stein, who didn't act wisely, who didn't tell it like it was and, as a result, caused them all to evade one another, to scatter in the desert and disappear, each one to his own devices and with his own secrets—Adam is left by himself. He is unafraid. The sun beats down mercilessly. Adam and the desert, a song of thanksgiving—"You and me." Is the Hebrew word for desert male or female? He forgets for the moment. His eye fills with nothing but rocks, mountains, wadis, loess soil, dust, and broom shrubs. The shrubs suck the grains of sand like scorpions, with the stubbornness of a zealot. A sycamore tree in the distance which supports the sky with its multi-branched head of foliage looks to him like an Indian goddess with many arms— the goddess of wisdom or the goddess of folly? He doesn't remember. Her breasts were exposed and her face was the face of a mask. Berlin, 1919. Remember, Weiss? Weiss isn't around. He's disappeared. Weissboy, Weissmine, where are you? Weissgod, Weissführer.

Neither Weiss nor Klein answers. Where's the limit to this desert? He'll reach Egypt soon and show Nasser his mistakes. He'll cross the Nile and survey the pyramids. To see the Nile and die! To be alive here, that means to be a Japanese soldier, to be a fortified scorpion. Do you remember, Weissie boy, that scorpion we saw? In the zoological gardens, in a glass cage, rolling into a ball like Nijinsky and sticking his stinger into his own head and killing himself? From excessive self-love, biological hari-kari. Japanese chivalry is anthropological hari-kari. In the camps the buildings were made of red brick. There I understood everything. Even the smokestacks I understood. Klein claimed: "Good smokestacks. Hans Pashmil designed them. Remember him? Bremen? 1931? The Bremen prize for architecture. The papers printed his picture then. You must remember. His face was full of freckles and his wife ran off with that actor, what's his name? The Englishman. I once met Hans in the street and made the following proposition: 'Hans, design some smokestacks for me that will filter the smoke so the stench won't spread!' And Hans thought for a moment and said: 'Okay, but on one condition. You control the practical end, I control the aesthetic. In other words, the smokestacks should be lovely for the satisfaction of my soul and efficient for the satisfaction of yours.' We agreed. We shook hands." Nightingales are in Paradise. Here in the desert are eagles. There the gods designed Hell, but here, in Hell itself, God Himself was designed. The owner of the red bricks is comprehensible to me, whereas the owner of the desert is a stranger. I am a stranger, you are a stranger, we are all unfamiliar. Let's go back, come on. Klein was right. I am losing the sound of a sane mind. I no longer have a clear head. The desert has no meaning, no associations, no future and no past.

He staggers, but goes on. Sun-struck, sun-worn. Sweating, the dust covering his eyes, penetrating his throat, his nose, his stomach, and he continues. Where to? He doesn't know, yet must go on. It's hot enough to die sitting. I have to pee. He tries, but there's no water in him. Suddenly, like a dream that hides from you as soon as you try to trace it, a certain movement, a certain stirring far off, plays with the retina of his eye. Two figures emerge in the distance and at once hide. And again they lurk in the fog of his weary mind. A tent, a smoking fire, a man waving his arms. Nonsense, a dream. Next, a woman, growing, decreasing, growing again, and again decreasing and disappearing. The sun blinds him. His skin is burned and peeling, his clothes ripped and threadbare, his hat awry. Next, a hilltop, and in the distance hands are swaying. Fata Morgana! He runs, he'll reach them, he'll make it. The two figures stare at him. He gazes back, and the world wheels. He sees two smoking logs. For a fraction of a second they glow, they burn, and immediately are transposed into negatives which are substanceless. They tremble, as in a silent film. On his side, the back of the screen, Gretchen appears. My sweetheart, let me play Bach for you on my violin. . . .

When he wakes from his faint, darkness is everywhere. He opens his eyes and gradually gets accustomed to the dark. He is lying inside a tent on a soft woolen blanket. He is wearing clothes that aren't his own. The starry sky peers through the entrances of the tent. He hears a woman's voice. The woman is speaking German, a lovely German, the old-fashioned German of Ruthie. She says: "He was dehydrated. I sat there letting water drip into his mouth from a watering can. He was lucky, another hour in the desert and he would have been dead."

Where am I? Who are they? Cave bandits. Spies. Have I actually reached Egypt? SS men guarding the training camps of Gamal Abdel Nasser. Who would ever think of looking for him in Israel? Is it any wonder that Klein is no longer Weiss?

Herbert Stein, Heidelberg 1923, crawls out of the tent and looks around, investigating. Three figures at a fire. A tripod stands over the fire and a pot hanging from it gives off a marvelous odor. By the fire a small lamp emits a strong clear light. A man wearing khaki clothes and a sweater, a woman in khaki and a black scarf, and with them is Joseph Graetz, who gazes at Adam and nods like David, King of Israel, with a certain restrained joy. Herbert Stein feels a bit uneasy, disturbed. Joseph Graetz will think that I am Adam. How can I correct his error? He approaches them, squats beside the fire, and introduces himself: "Herbert Stein, pleased to meet you." The two strangers are Gunther Shalom and his wife, Ruth, archeologists from the Hebrew University in Jerusalem who, temporarily, have been dragged into a project researching the Negev. Joseph Graetz has joined them. No, he hasn't become an archeologist all of a sudden, of course not! He chuckles a bit and Herbert Stein's back tingles. Gunther Shalom puts down the book of Psalms he was studying before Herbert came outside, and explains: "A few weeks ago the base of an ancient building was discovered here and we are mapping out the entire site. The dig itself will begin, God willing, in two months. Some think this was an ancient hideaway. Others, that the place was a Roman fortress, constructed in the Byzantine period, which served the Nabateans and later was converted into a border fortress of the Crusaders and finally became a Turkish inn. We found some interesting coins here and clay pitchers. Two sarcophagi in a cave not far from here prove conclusively that there was a Jewish settlement in this place some time or other in the deep past." Gunther Shalom speaks softly, and Herbert, sipping the coffee which Ruth served him, listens and studies the starry sky and the mountains whose silhouettes stand out in the distance. The theory is that the grave of a holy Arab named Omri is close by, at the source of the wadi Al-abid. The Arab name rings so precisely in Gunther's mouth, and yet so oddly Germanic. "Legend has it," continues Gunther in his monotonous voice, "that once when the Bedouins went to the grave of this saint to fulfill their oaths, a wild wind burst from the desert, uprooted their tents, and scattered the sheep and cattle. The Bedouins, from the tribe of Ti-aha, fought against the wind and brought their sheep and cattle into safety while they could still catch their breath. And from that time on, Omri was in disgrace, regarded with abhorrence because he paid no heed to the entreaties of his descendants and followers and didn't halt the winds. To this very day they curse each other with, 'May Allah take you together with Omri.' Isn't that fascinating, the direct relationship between the saint and his descendants? The saint is assigned a specific role, and if he doesn't fulfill it, he turns into an abhorrence."

Herbert smiles and Ruth says: "He's just been rescued and you cram him with stories about saints who have betrayed their followers! Let him eat first. We heard about the escape on the transistor radio and Joseph Graetz told us about you. A command car will be here in the morning with supplies and it can take you to Arad." Across the mountains you can make out now very clearly a fierce electrical storm. Herbert partakes of the meal. He announces forcibly: "I am not Adam. I am Herbert. We are twins." Nobody replies. They study him closely, as though they understood. He knows they do not understand, but it seems best not to prolong the discussion on this topic, there's no point to it. And immediately he laughs and says: "Thanks. I would certainly have been dead otherwise." And Ruth answers: "You lost all your body liquids, you were as dry as old wood, I dripped water into your mouth with a watering can. For hours and hours and hours. Drop by drop, drop by drop. I watered you. And you swallowed and choked and vomited. But slowly, drop by drop, you came to life."

The atmosphere here is cultured, relaxed, alien to their surroundings, and Herbert feels at home. Dr. Franz Sturheim is about to begin a series of lectures on the profound difference between morality and ethics. Abraham sacrificing Isaac is ethics; Agamemnon sacrificing his daughter, morality. The group investigating the question of Pure Reason started long ago. Heidelberg, the green trees, the raspberry blossoms, the rosebushes, the ancient wall, and the church belfry. Children with scarred cheeks, a bald professor, debates, a Hebrew study group. The three of them are serious types. Gunther Shalom peruses his small book of Psalms. Soon he'll put it aside and pick up Goethe's *Faust, Part Two*. Ruth is sewing buttons on a coat. By the tent is a pair of shoes polished to perfection, with shoe trees in them to preserve their shape. When was the last time Herbert saw a shoe tree? And who shaves nowadays with a barber's razor?

"It's idiotic to look for God in this desert, Adam," says Joseph Graetz.

"Herbert."

"Herbert Stein?" Herbert says yes with his head. "Yes, Herbert, it's idiotic. Forgive me, but I couldn't refrain from saying so. There's something atavistic in this search. God alone is not Judaism. Judaism is a total faith, and you cannot find this faith, this Judaism, in the desert, in a cave, among rocks."

"The Jew doesn't have to take things on faith," says Gunther, quoting Franz Rosenzweig, "because the Jew is himself the faith."

"No!" Joseph complains with some resentment. "That's not what I meant."

Herbert puts down his cup of coffee and says: "You are distinguished men, and each of you has a degree. You are distinguished men with degrees in the presence of a desert, and that puzzles me. The Judaism of Hillel is not Judaism itself but a part of Judaism, and a part won't help you at all. Judaism is a totality. A jealous God, a delinquent God, a God who ran away, who betrayed, a God of ethics and a God of un-ethics, a God of murder and of compassion. Judaism terrifies as well as comforts. To believe in it is to believe in a meaningless command, and that is why we went out to search for God. Moses also went out, and Samuel and Elijah and Saul. Your Judaism went up in smoke. But that you won't understand. Never. Ask Mr. Graetz, he saw Judaism in its disgrace and its glory: the time when somebody who shall remain nameless made his daughter's corpse laugh. Your Judaism is the Judaism that only looks in the mirror. And that is just part of the disgrace. To understand the miracle of Judaism you have to look at the smoke on both sides. Smoke goes up to heaven in order to ask forgiveness for itself."

Ruth Shalom tries to change the subject. "Gunther, you and your philosophy! Here in the desert, everywhere, philosophy!"

Herbert examines Gunther. He wears slippers of brown and yellow wool. The transistor is playing the Sixth Symphony of Bruckner. A desert night. Bruckner. *Faust, Part Two.* Psalms. Smoke rings. They smile at one another, sip coffee that Ruth has prepared Bedouin style. Converse. Won't they tire of their great Emanuel, from that Königsberg of theirs?

Joseph Graetz dozes off. These things are too remote. Gunther and Herbert look into each other's eyes. Here, in between Um-el-Fatakh and Ras-el-Omri, they sit together and each tries to fish out a past that is hidden in the other man's eye. Herbert is looking for Heidelberg-Herbert in Gunther's eyes, and Gunther seeks in Herbert's eyes the image of Heidelberg-Gunther. Gunther sees two Gunthers, in the desert and in his old-fashioned German. Herbert sees two Adams hunting down *Gottführer* Klein in the desert. "Lost," he hears himself say. "Lost forever."

13

OLD ARAB

A lame pitiful old Arab man
Married a lame pitiful old Arab woman
And they had a lame pitiful son
Who married a lame pitiful old woman
And they had a lame . . .

THE SEEKERS after God have scattered in all directions. Tomorrow morning Adam will come home in a pickup truck. Joseph Graetz will part from him without a smile. A few other patients will be picked up. "By nine o'clock this morning, fifteen out of the twenty patients who escaped yesterday from the Institute for Rehabilitation and Therapy in Arad had been found in various parts of the desert. Search operations are still going on for the missing five." Handsome Rube has hitchhiked as far as Elat. He appears in the nightclub "The End of the World" and presents the letter of credit which Adam Stein wrote for him. The next day he is taken to the Institute. Miles Davis got a truck ride to Beer-Sheva with an Arab from Nazareth who was delivering clay soil to the north. In Beer-Sheva Miles enters a small coffeehouse, sits down at a corner table, and orders from a waitress with a creased apron and bleary eyes two hard-boiled eggs and a cup of coffee. At the next table an Australian "giraffe" is smiling at him. She sees the trumpet in his hand and hears him order in English two boiled eggs and coffee, notices that his hair is entangled in his sunglasses, and at once knows that a man after her own heart has dropped into her life. The giraffe moves over to his table and tells him without hesitation that her name is Anne but in Israel he can call her Hannah, and he informs her immediately, with amazing frankness, that he's hoping now to put his papers and documents in order so that he can finally return to New York. She is glad to hear it. Maybe they can travel together. She has a fantastic apartment there. He tells her about a certain poet named Pierre Lotti with whom he got lost in the desert. A Jew-hater who came to Israel on a secret Arab mission. He tells Hannah-Anne, the Australian giraffe with green eyes, straw-colored hair, and a gold star of David around her long neck, with her dress pulled up above her lovely knees, and her legs crossed so that the toenails of one foot can scratch the other foot, he tells her about the spies he caught in the Negev. He says he was born in New York and played in Elat. He says he was arrested for selling LSD to minors. On her way home Hannah wants to travel to India and from there to Japan. She has already been through Europe and America, around the world, she even went into Jordan with a forged passport. Now she is on her way to Elat to catch a boat for Iran, but she is willing to go with him to New York. She has a great place there.

Birds of a feather. When he rises to get the salt-shaker from the next table, he realizes that she is as tall sitting as he is standing. If that's the case, how can we go together? That would be a crippled affair all right! Some woman! Over seven feet! Miles Davis makes a private forecast: It's a visual disaster!

But Hannah-Anne wants to step out into the street. Miles submits. They walk. The second floor calls out to the fourth floor: "How are things up there?" The fourth floor replies: "Fine, the weather up here is great." She is proud of him. Two small Yemenites say: "Look how tall she is!" And the Polish woman who sells ties and jeans on a street corner smiles through the pure silver teeth sparkling in her mouth, opens and shuts her hand, and says: "It makes no difference, in bed everything will get straightened out!" Miles wants to take a bus. Sitting in a bus, their heights will be equal. The giraffe will be level with the trumpet player, according to the law of intercourse. But she wants to walk, to window-shop, to wander through the stores, to go into the market, to go down a wadi, visit Father Abraham's Well, the woods, an Ulpan, drink an apéritif in the Oasis Hotel. She has money—"Don't worry, loads of money. Daddy is crazy about me. Take, he said, travel, do what you want, just love your father always." Miles laughs. At a kiosk at the end of the street, next to a wadi that passes by the market district with its tin shacks and filthy dens, there is a little place that he's wanted to visit for a long while. For a small amount of cash and a slight percentage of future compensations, papers can be arranged, documents, and a number on your arm. The place is known. Any haberdasher can tell you the address. Miles heads there. The name of the owner is Naftali Klein, formerly Dr. Weiss. Now he calls himself Naftali Klein and he has a small kiosk in the Old City, among the tin shacks in the market place.

Hannah-Anne the giraffe sits and waits. Miles sits in the dentist's chair in Naftali Klein's kiosk and Klein tattoos his arm. The number selected is a Meidanek number. In addition he receives a map of the camp, a list of the officers, the name of the commander, a description of the place, its routines, certain unusual features, etc. He receives a document identifying him as Abraham, the son of Solomon Cohen, and Hannah-Anne pays. Her dear father gave her plenty of money, and she saves money by hitchhiking through the world, so she gives Miles two hundred Israeli pounds. Now he is entitled to receive a compensation of ten thousand marks, five percent of which he must hand over to Naftali Klein, formerly Dr. Weiss. The agreement is signed in red ink. But Miles has no intention of applying for compensations. All he wanted was to have some blue numbers tattooed on his arm, nothing more. As for the two hundred pounds which the giraffe Hannah-Anne gave him, those he deserves for the agony he endured while accompanying that telephone pole from one end of Beer-Sheva to the other, exposing himself to mockery wherever he went. Naftali Klein, alias Weiss, was the only one who didn't laugh. He has a big dog in his kiosk named Rex. Miles hears him call to Rex: "Adam, sit!" and Adam sits. Miles laughs. Naftali asks: "Vhy does de gentleman luff?" and Miles tells him that he was imprisoned in a detention camp where they wouldn't let him return to America because they suspected him of being a spy, and in that detention camp there was a man named Adam and this Adam had a dog named David, King of Israel. At this point Naftali Klein laughs.

Hannah-Anne sees a halo around the head of Naftali Klein. For a moment she thinks that Jesus has come and in excitement she opens her legs wide. But nothing happens. Miles receives his number and the opportunity of collecting ten thousand marks, less five percent that goes to the man whose dog is named Rex or Adam. Naftali Klein studies the number. He enjoys his handi-work. Hannah-Anne also thinks that he did a superb job. A short woman who works in the next kiosk comes over to exam-ine the number. According to her, the figure 7 should be more faded. In Meidanek the figure 7 always came out a little faded. Naftali Klein takes down a small bottle from the shelf, dips cotton in the yellow liquid, and wipes the 7. The woman nods yes. Miles Davis has gained a homeland, a house, a past, a gene-alogical tree. Everybody whacks him on the back, congratulates him. Hannah-Anne the giraffe pulls him to her room in the small hotel opposite the Bedouin market that will be open tomorrow, on Thursday. In her little room they can sit and wait for the Bedouins, Miles can play for her, tell her about Lester Young and Miles Davis. And she'll listen, sigh, sip arrack, eat green pickled olives and memorize the number tattooed on his arm. He'll make love to her and together they'll wait for the Bedouins to come tomorrow.

The Bedouins expected in Beer-Sheva on the morrow are now trekking through the desert. And in the desert, wrapped in one of Pierre Lotti's newspapers, walks the elder Schwester sister. She wanders aimlessly through the desert, the desert she has had great dreams about, the desert in which God refused to show Himself. The hot desert that wails in its cruel, clifflike, desolate wadis. She is thirsty, exhausted, in pain from her burns. She wants some shade. But in the entire vast stretch of copper made by Ashmodai and his associates there isn't a ghost of a shadow. The little strip above her upper lip is the only shaded place in the whole gigantic wasteland. She can budge no further. Her legs no longer obey her. As she stands chained to her place, dehydrated, a scarecrow a moment before its death, she sees that caravan of Bedouins heading toward Beer-Sheva. Out in front walks a black youngster wrapped in rags who has a stick in his hand. Behind him walk a gray ass and its gray lovely-eyed offspring. Next come two camels, stepping peacefully and quietly and slowly, and behind the camels are five Bedouins in cloaks, with sticks in their hands, and they are as black as can be. When they come near the woman clad only in newspapers and weeping heavy tears, they stop. The ass and its young one gaze at her lazily and the Bedouins say nothing.

Her heart flutters, but she is already beyond fear. She had only one thought when she saw the black figures: Men. Human beings. Mankind. Fellow creatures. She is no longer a lost soul in the wasteland. She is among people. And people, be they Bedouins or savages from the moon, will not let her die. She stares at them through silent tears, the last bits of liquid in her system. Suddenly, as if by some vague instinct or recollection, she embraces her body with her two arms, for protection.

The old man who has stepped out of the group gazes at her with lustful eyes. His glance traces her whole body, her bare legs, her bulging veins, her mustache. The old man says: "Greetings, woman. You must be a demoness." The Bedouins agree with nods, and one of them howls wildly and beats his lips with

his finger. The old man fixes him with an angry look and the
Schwester sister says: "I am truly a demoness." She knows that
she has to say something, she must keep talking, no matter what.
"I lost my way to Arad, I must reach Arad."

One of the Bedouins, wearing a pistol, chews gum voraci-
ously. His tiny eyes, the color of olives, flash. He wears yellow
sandals. Through his cloak you can see watches hanging on a
string, fountain pens, cigarette lighters. His whole body is
wrapped in shiny merchandise. She is dazed by the sight of this
walking, gum-chewing, tar-black, five-and-dime store. The man's
mouth gapes and a single gold tooth peeks out. The Bedouin
says: "We gonna slaughter ya, lady demon. You seen the
watches, the fountain pens. . . ."

The old man smiles and comes up to her, staring at the one
newspaper she has kept to cover herself. His eyes rest on the
blackprint and blink. "No need to scare her, why scare her?"

"Right, why?" laughs the Bedouin with the watches, exposing
his single gold tooth, and he spits angrily.

"You speak Hebrew?" Unconsciously she tries to give her
voice the sound of entreaty, of childhood, in order to prevent
any atrocity. Notwithstanding her age and her disgraceful situation, she imagines for a moment in her sun-baked brain that her
voice sounded equal to the sixty years of her life.

The Bedouin wrapped in watches smiles at the old man. "We
Bedouins of Israeli state, we can to speak a little Hebrew every
weeks at market in Beer-Sheva." And he laughs. "Also in
market at Hebron, and market at Gaza. We have no borders. We
men of spirit. You know what we are to doing?"

"Shepherds," she says with enthusiasm. "Shepherds, you're
obviously shepherds."

He bursts into laughter again. "Shepherds . . ." Her hands
still embrace her dehydrated body. Her mouth is parched, any
minute she won't be able to speak at all. "We smugglers, lady!
Smugglers! We saw army trucks before, and hid. Us they don't
catch."

The old man prattles, rubs his fingers together, he must show off in front of the white lady demon. He points to the black print which pecks at his eyes, wanting to be certain that the words are not terrible ones, that they are not some devil's prayer or oath. "You read?"

"Ah, the newspaper! My clothes were burned," she says.

"White demons die in desert!" declares the young Bedouin with the watches slung around him. "Can read or not can read, no difference. They die in desert!" His eyes lust, fondle, sneak off.

She is more confused than frightened. Demons die in the desert. Doesn't she herself know that she is going to die? From hunger, thirst, heat, Bedouins, what difference does it make? Yet in this stinking place, in the middle of a boiling afternoon, in front of Bedouins whose eyes are pulling off the one torn newspaper from her almost naked body, the old woman who was a fugitive from everything, who sought God and found such pain and heartache that she gave up all hope of life and dreams, this old woman drops to her knees and begins to beg for her life. The intense heat rising from the sand and the stones scorches her body. She spreads out her arms and pleads, and the newspaper slips down. She no longer knows what she is asking for, to die, to be burned, cast out, or given a piece of cloth to cover her nakedness. The camel chewing its cud in peace is laden with all kinds of material.

The Bedouin with the watches is shaken. The smile abandons his face. He kneels and begins to massage her scorched back. The old man stands above him and laughs. The gold teeth sparkle and everything goes blurred. The old man over her is a laughing piece of burnt wood. The black youngster drags a cloak from one of the saddles and spreads it out on the sand. The Schwester sister, her eyes dumb, is lugged onto the cloak. Her white body flashes in the sun. The Bedouin wrapped in watches takes off his pants. The old man laughs again. The boy says: "Ya ya ya!" then hides behind the old man's back and lowers his eyes. The Schwester sister doesn't emit a sound. As though she were dead, as though the heat and the shame had erased her existence. An old woman like me! Actually, she herself couldn't ever believe that the insects loved her with an honest passion. Now she catches sight of the Bedouin laden with watches. His face is riveted upon hers, his eyes do not stir from her white old body. She sees his leg muscles, his huge hands, his eyes that sow fire. If he were to tell her that he was God, she would believe him. His blemished smile, his gold tooth, his leching body, his tortured features impose on her mind the memory of thoughts of ascent, the memory of distant dreams. She will now get her revenge for the humiliation of her empty life, revenge against her idiotic sister, against her failure, her husband, her mustache, against shaving razors, forests, the camp, Cyprus, barbed-wire fences, against the wretched boat, against hostile Israel, against the children who eat bananas and sour cream and chant patriotic songs.

The old man talks to her, the boy hides and breaks into a short loud laugh. The other Bedouins sit in the shade of the camels and seem to be sleeping. The odor of strong tobacco emerges from their mouths. The old man sticks out his hand, caresses her breast, and lets it go. The dropped breast arouses him. He says something in Arabic and gets up. The young watch-laden man lies down on top of her. The old man covers his face with both his hands and moans. The boy runs and hides behind a camel. The camel lifts its head and chews its cud. The sun burns and burns.

The old man now says: "No sabers! She a man! She a hero! She not scream!" The dark God stands up and gazes at her. He sees an old woman. The desire for murder glows in his eyes. He returns his saber to its scabbard and goes behind a camel.

That very moment one of the napping Bedouins rises, approaches the Schwester sister, and stretches on top of her. She lies there, eyes wide open, eyes watching the dark God who is pissing now behind a camel. Her complete attention is on the powerful stream penetrating the dry sand. She wants to vomit, to cry, but her tears no longer exist and her eyes gape at the tumult of water. And then the miracle occurs, the miracle which rescues her, the miracle on whose account she will get up and continue to live and hope and believe. A ray of sunshine strikes the stream and colors it for the moment with all the colors of the rainbow. The colors of the rainbow hang in the horizon and through them she sees the pale figure of an angel. He wants to come to her, yet does not approach. He stands far off and watches her through the rainbow. He is fond of her. He gives her some sort of sign, but she doesn't understand. This fact, however, does not depress her spirits very much. Many injustices have been done her in the course of her lifetime, and now, as always, some rescue merges, a signal is given. God is not dead.

She kisses her blued arm, she kisses the hand of the Bedouin who jostles on top of her and makes deep noises as though he were talking from the depths of his stomach. She smiles at the old man, who is quick to toss her a cloak even as he laughs. His golden teeth sparkle and obliterate the angel and she whispers: "Like frontlets between thine eyes," and the old man says: "What?" And she says: "Thanks," and the old man says, "She said thanks," and the young man spits and the youngster bursts into sobs and runs and conceals himself behind the old man's cloak. She wraps herself in the cloak and sits up and drinks from the foul water which the watch-carrier offers her with the submission of a young man who knows that God has caught him with his pants down. Did he see the angel too? she wonders, and drinks. And she gets up to go, fortified, yet pure and even happy. The Bedouins wave to her with their dark hands until she drops out of sight.

The helicopter pilot who discovered her telegraphs: "We found an old crazy woman. Wrapped in an Arab cloak. She keeps on laughing. Calls herself the Schwester sister. Claims she saw an angel in the desert. Somebody pissed behind a camel. Sorry, I'm just quoting her."

14

CHILD AND DOG

BACK AT THE INSTITUTE, he asks after the child. He doesn't ask Jenny, but she is glad he's back. As soon as she saw him, she opened her mouth and screamed. Her full agony was captured by that scream. He slapped her face to quiet her and then kissed her on her mouth to calm her down. And then she told him: "Your David sat riveted to the transistor all day and listened to the news. He can sit erect and can stand up now, it's really amazing. The doctors peek through the window and don't believe their eyes. He refused to see anybody. He just listened to the news. When it announced that you were found with those archeologists, he smashed the transistor against the wall."

A mournful man named Herbert God-Discovering Stein drops his face into this hands and totters toward the infirmary to destroy, in a week's time, one of the two kidneys which the Creator had honored him with.

A thorough probe was made. Dr. Gross assembled everybody in the dining hall, except for Herbert, who lay critically ill in the infirmary. Herbert sent a letter in which he said: "The responsibility for the escape falls solely upon me. I went out to seek God and didn't find him, or perhaps I am unprepared to divulge what I found. All those who participated in the trip through the desert were under my exclusive influence, consequently I would like to acquit them of any blame."

On the other hand, the elder Schwester sister claimed that she was the guilty party, though for reasons of security she cited an authority named Mrs. Seizling, may she rest in peace, and she then related what everyone knew quite well, how she had kindled in Mrs. Seizling the desire to build the Institute so that we might be able, when the day came, to go to God and hear His word. "Not counting Mrs. Seizling," argued the Schwester twin, the joy in her eyes confusing the stern-faced doctors, *"I* was the crucial guilty party. Not Adam or anybody else. I saw an angel among the hills. And I know now that God will not appear. And it's better that way."

"The number engraved on your arm is God!" screamed Wolfovitz in a fury and at once broke into laughter. At the sound of these words everyone laughed, though the doctors despaired of figuring out their meaning. As always, no matter what was done to prevent it, a gap existed between the careful and partial intelligence of the doctors and the capacity of these others to unite in a secret society rooted in unintelligible truths. Again the group laughed and the doctors cleared their throats and took notes in blue notebooks that had the seal of the Institute stamped on their covers. When Miles heard Wolfovitz's words, he raised his arm and exposed and displayed his number to everybody. Arthur squeezed the arm. The Schwester sister sucked her lips. "Good job," said Wolfovitz, "you too now have a share in Paradise!" Once more they laughed.

After a promise was made not to repeat the incident, the investigation concluded with a general amnesty and with a bitter argument among the doctors. Dr. Gross, however, came out victorious. As far as he was concerned, the fact that the Schwester sister could smile was reason enough to approve of the entire venture. Handsome Rube told tall tales of his doings in Elat. Miles had found a home. And Adam—Adam was critically sick again, but when wasn't he so? Even Pierre Lotti was granted amnesty. A military command car found Pierre Lotti in a remote wadi after he had fainted from the heat. The morning following the investigation, Pierre drove to Beer-Sheva and for the first time in many years prayed in a church and thanked God. The church—the miserable lodgings of the missionary Mrs. Samit and her pale children—was decked out in celebration of the event.

Most hours of the day, Adam—who no longer can play Herbert and has to play himself—is in absolute darkness. Jenny comes every day and sits beside him. He pays no attention to her. She talks to him, but he simply doesn't listen. He can hear her in the distance, yet he is not listening. He carries in his heart a faded negative of a dog, a dog he hates. That dog tried to depend on him, tried to reconstruct himself out of Adam's ruins, consequently Adam hates him in his heart. The poison of hatred soaking inside him is the one positive thing that keeps him alive. That child wouldn't dare come here.

Yet he comes. Jenny sees him sprawled on the floor in his room. The window is shut and the stench of the room is unbearable. She enters and he howls. She says to him: "A miserable man is lying over there and you don't go visit him." The child barks and curls up in a corner. The bark makes her laugh. "Purim is over, child, and you are not a dog. Don't pretend." He clears his throat and leaps at her, but doesn't bite. Her face pale, she stares at him with hate, straight into his eyes. He jumps back and grinds his teeth. He is a disappointing sight now. Resigned, submissive. The moment he was unable to bite, his pride was trampled.

"Listen to me! The man is sick, very sick. He's going to die. He did everything for you, and you sit here and type on his typewriter the curses of a retarded child. You should be ashamed of yourself. So what if he went out to the desert and left you here? Does he owe you anything? A man who loves you is about to die, child. And you keep quiet. It's shameful of you, disgraceful!"

The words bounce off him like bullets off bullet-proof armor. Without a doubt he would stay there alone and desperate, he would not get up or dare to get up, except for one expression that penetrates every inch of armor: *a man who loves you.* When she speaks those words she sees him flush, sees his resistance break, sees that he is devastated. The words enter him and shine in him like a traffic light, and when the lights change she rejoices in the amazing phenomenon of a soul wearing a body right before her eyes.

He lowers his eyes and begins crawling toward the door. Crawling from the door into the hall, slowly, for the act of crawling is already difficult for him. People pass him and he smells their shoes and continues on toward Adam's door. Adam already expects him. Commandant Stein prepares his dog's bowl. Guests are coming today, Adam! Adam, why not bark a little? The next thing you know, Adam is barking.

Herr Sturmführer Schwein, look, the situation is simple and workable enough. My two dogs, Rex and Adam, will stage a play in honor of the Committee for the Advancement of the Ethics of Work in the Liberated Territories, and I can positively assure you that we will get the desired contract. There is no doubt about it. Work is cheaper with us. We're closer to Berlin. We solved the problem of the midday meal and we function on a three-week cycle of work, whereas at Auschwitz they cremate them only after two weeks. If you ask my opinion, I think that's foolish. The third week, my friend *Herr Sturmführer* Schwein, is the crucial one! If Heinrich were to hear me out to the very end, he'd be convinced that my system is immeasurably better than

Hess's or Frank's and many others. I checked with a statistics expert from the University of Dresden and he clearly established that a work day in our place was equal to a day and a half in any other camp. Consequently, it is my opinion, my friend *Herr Sturmführer* Schwein, that we will enjoy the show, that my dogs will entertain the members of the committee and make their stay in the camp most pleasant. You know—that odor! Adam, today I want you to smell Rex. Rub noses and then let him have the extra piece of meat I'm going to toss to you. Is that clear? Afterward you'll bark at each other. That'll be so amusing. The dog is approaching. I know. I can smell a dog from a distance of a million light years. The dog is approaching. In the monastery at Latron where the monks have sworn to keep silent for the rest of their lives, they speak just one sentence to each other: as they pass a fellow monk, they say: "Remember death!" That's all. And that's what I'll tell the dog. Remember death! Let me die, leave me alone, render to Caesar what is Caesar's and render to Adam Stein his death.

The moment the child enters, Adam is overwhelmed with terrible pains until he falls asleep and dreams something which escapes him when he opens his eyes and sees, through the blurred room, the dog's eyes gazing at him.

"Child, what do you want? Who are you? What do you want here?" His voice shakes with anger. The child, perplexed and astonished, pouts. Poor dog. His legs shrink under him and he drops on his knees at the foot of the white bed in the green room.

"You don't belong in this place. What do you want from me?"

The child opens his mouth to answer, but no sound comes out. The machine, the Olivetti, is not with him. How will he speak? All he can do is clear his throat. He leaps up onto the bureau beside the the bed, takes a worn wallet from one of the pockets of Adam's pants. From the wallet he removes some bills, a penknife, and a small fountain pen. The child rummages through the bureau with increasing nervousness. Adam's eyes follow his every movement. The child finds a pad of paper, grabs the pen, and draws. He draws a dog, and the dog is ridiculous. Its head is too big, its eyes are outside its body. The child hands Adam the sketch. Adam gives it a quick look and immediately tears it into tiny pieces and tosses the pieces away. They float and land by the window, behind the radiator. "Rags!" says Adam. The child doesn't give up; his hands quiver, but he doesn't submit. He draws on another piece of paper: a fat man with a Chaplin hat and a cane. The fat man is chasing the dog. The picture is a joke. The dog is too big, the man too ugly, his nose itty-bitty, his ears gigantic, his belly bare, and inside it a fish. Adam takes the drawing and, with a venomous smile, rips it. The pieces he flips over to the closed window. "A synthetic world!" he says. "Mrs. Seizling has ruined us all, she has pissed on us three times over, she has desiccated our brains." He almost laughs. On his lips is a sort of forced smile, as though they were about to burst. His body burns. The child continues drawing. Page after page he draws, yanks off the pad, and hands to Adam, who rips and tosses each one to the shut window. Adam knows who the child is, but doesn't know who he himself is. He half wants to know, half doesn't. As the pictures keep coming, he accepts them without even examining them, and rips.

The child finishes the entire pad. He glances at the floor covered with torn pieces of paper, approaches the bed, straightens himself, and suddenly kisses Adam Stein's face, and from his eyes tears drop on the face of the old man. The tears remind Adam of something. What? He concentrates. What, God damn it, do those tears remind him of? He recalls a kiss gritty with sand. And then all at once understands. His daughter Ruth. Suddenly she has a face, he sees her before him, he can almost touch her. He wants to escape—but it is too late. He cannot ask forgiveness.

He wrestles with angels. He wrestles with witches and wizards. But a smile escapes from his heart, the smile he refused to smile, the smile that will again be stuck, like a wedge, in the wheels of death. The smile swerves toward the child for a moment, drops to the floor and rests on a quarter of a dog drawn by a dog and torn by a dog. The dog's face—a Boxer?—has one tooth and is circled by a ring of smoke. Adam's smile shifts now from the picture to the puffing dog who came to visit him despite everything. Four eyes: one pair is glad, the other confused. A connection is made. In the middle of a filthy world. It's a marvelous world and one ought to sing a song of praise in its honor. Smile begets smile. "Listen, child, the next time you draw a dog, look in the mirror! And when you draw me, look at me and then you'll discover something fantastic: each drawing will come out opposite. The man will be a dog, the dog will be a child. And you will take your old father out for a leak beside one of the trees along the avenue." Adam laughs and the child laughs. And beyond the window the sun sinks into the desert like a red ball which has been crammed into some terrible inferno.

15

GUILLOTINE

AFTER READING ONE DAY in the newspaper the following ad, Wolfovitz the Circumciser (who was never a circumciser) bought a used guillotine.

USED GUILLOTINE

Good condition. Width: 75/100 centimeters. Works automatically (or foot pedal too). A spare blades kit, no extra charge. For cutting.
Kindly send offers to "Mehiran," Guillotine Division, P.O. Box 7594, Tel Aviv.

He purchased it immediately. For what bugged him most, as he claimed to Adam, was what he called "the pretense of fate." "I was supposed to die a long time ago, but didn't. Big sister Schwester was stung by African bugs and discovered love, after she discovered love she also found God and longed for his appearance, but in the end he turned out to be a dark Bedouin who raped her. And you? You announced publicly that you were about to die and nobody had the slightest doubt that you were going to die, but here you are, walking around like a young goat, healthy as a wild ox, and planning more projects. And what about those curtains? I want to tell you about those curtains. You remember the curtains the angels took from the synagogues throughout Poland—a country that, thanks to the good nature of the Poles and the deep psychological insight of the Germans, became *Jüdenrein*—and made into prayer shawls for Heaven?" They sat opposite one another, Wolfovitz playing with the guillotine which he had just bought, and Adam scratching his forehead.

"I was a refugee then," said the father of Naomi Wolfovitz. "At the end of the war I somehow got to Paris. My deceased mother had a brother who hid in the woods during the war, living off carpentry, and right after the war ended he went to Paris and opened a small shop, manufacturing antique furniture which he used to sell in the flea market to American soldiers and later on, in '48–'49, to the tourists who had begun to come in hordes. I joined him. I had no other place to go to. I hadn't found Naomi yet, I thought she was dead. Once when I was sitting there in his little cellar, a tiny stooped Jew entered who looked like a raisin with his terrifically wrinkled red face. He had a shabby leather bag strapped to his body. His clothes were threadbare. From head to toe he was totally crumpled and worn out, yet his eyes emitted a brightness which filled our hearts, mine and my uncle's, with wonder. His eyes seemed to be exploding in his face, they had such a wild sublime look, as though the man were an early Hebrew prophet. He didn't speak. He just pointed to his mouth as if to say, *I cannot talk*. He sat down on a Damascus cushion that my uncle found somewhere, took out of his ragged sack a rolled-up sheet of paper, handed it to us, and bowed his head, waiting, with a courtesy mixed with despondency, for us to finish reading. The rolled sheet of paper was old and stained. On it was written:

To whom it may concern:

The bearer of this letter is a flea, not a man, a despicable outcast, a world-wanderer exiled by the edict of his own mouth. Show him no sympathy, show him rather your full anger. On the first intermediate day of the holiday of Succoth in the year 1929, in the small town of Tchortkov in Galicia, the bearer of this letter was a light-headed young man who had a wonderful wife and two daughters: Regina and Tamima. On that day, the first intermediate day of the holiday of Succoth, his daughter Tamima, the most pure girl of the town, was playing with the articles in her mother's sewing kit and, in childish mischief, almost swallowed the thimble. At the sight of this innocent game, the bearer of this document burst into a rage and yelled at his daughter and even attacked his delicate and good-natured wife for allowing her daughters to do whatever they damn pleased. He was the victim of a seizure of hate, a malice deep inside him, and the issue of the thimble was merely a pretext. In a huge voice he cursed: "You are making my short life ugly, you don't let your father alone. You are driving him crazy. I wish you'd all go up in flames!" After this disgusting creature finished screaming and cursing, he left the house, and the moment he was outside and heading toward the bathhouse at the end of the street, a fire from the stove on which the afternoon meal was cooking suddenly jumped out and set fire to the small wooden house with its three angels. In a jiffy, as if Satan wanted to take advantage of the curse immediately, the entire house was eaten up.

For seven days the bearer of this document sat stunned and petrified and then, with his head down and his soul all jumbled up, he went to that great genius, and "light of Israel," the holy Rabbi of Tchortkov. As the Rabbi listened to the story, the bearer of this document saw with his own eyes, right before his every face, how two hairs of the Rabbi's holy black beard went white, while the glory of the Creator Himself shone through the holy Rabbi's eyes.

When the holy Rabbi concluded his reflections, he said: "If that mouth has such power, the only thing to do is condemn it to silence." And the bearer of this document accepted this judgment and from that day on, in 1929, he didn't let a single word out of his mouth.

When the bearer of this letter was hiding in the woods around Tchortkov, the Nazis caught him and ordered him to sing the Jewish prayer "The Lord of the World" with his pants down, standing naked in the snow. He refused, so they gave him a murderous beating, but with the help of God (bless Him) he managed to escape and, as testimony of blind Fate's strong sense of humor, he didn't die. (Let Fate be damned for it.) The great majority of the people living in this holy town were slaughtered, yet the bearer of this document, whose accursed mouth set his sacred wife and his two angels on fire, remained alive.

The bearer of this document has pronounced upon himself the decree of everlasting wandering. In his knapsack he carries beautiful, delicate curtains, soaked in love for Israel and endless sorrow, curtains which were rescued by angels dressed up as Jews from the many synagogues throughout Europe. And the money collected from the sale of these curtains—discounting a few pennies for the bare necessities of bread and water—are delivered by the bearer of this document to the Word Research Foundation, which was established at the close of the war by several scholars rescued from the Inferno, and directed by Rabbi Meir ben-Moshe, the brilliant grandson of the holy Rabbi of Tchortkov. The aim of this foundation is to investigate and understand the profound and mysterious influence which the word has over action, the decree has over Fate, God's "Let there be light!" has upon Creation, and the command "Demolish!" has upon the history of our oppressed nation, To explore the essence of the sacred Hebrew language, its authenticity, its relation to heavenly forces, its influence on the patterns of existence. To get to the bottom of the matter, and pick out all the secrets hidden in Scripture and in all the later writings of the Rabbis, the books of Rambam and the holy Ari. For, as any schoolboy knows, there exists a basic and deep connection between the Hebrew word and great events, holocausts and miracles alike. The study of these words is bound to redeem a nation that has forgotten the true meaning of its own words and trampled these very words with awful crimes and immense sins.

> *Signed:*
> *The most despicable man,*
> *Joseph Kaufman*

P.S. I herein confirm every word written in this document as true as true can be, and therefore, in order to give further force and confirmation to these words, I now sign my name.

Tuesday, 8th of the Hebrew month of Av, in the year 1945

> *Signed:*
> *Rabbi Meir Nathan of Tchortkov (may he be remembered as a saint), the son of Rabbi Sheshot, of blessed memory, Israel's diadem. Alas, now the earth covers the best!*

Wolfovitz gazed at Adam. Adam swallowed from a bottle hidden in a pocket of his suit, Old Crow. Wolfovitz smiled.

"Of course, of course." Adam pondered. "He belongs to our order, an honorable member! Everything is foreseen, yet we have free will. Free to destroy ourselves!"

"When I finished reading the letter," said Wolfovitz, "I lifted my eyes and examined the Hebrew raisin standing opposite me and I swelled with compassion for him. The faith of this Jew . . . The Jew took some curtains from his sack and my Uncle Hershel, who, when it came to religious articles, was a connoisseur and an expert even in Poland, bought two of them. One from the sixteenth century, which adorned the Holy Ark of the synagogue named after the Saint Rabbi Lemech Malmalin from the town of Troike, which is near Trenopol, and the other an eighteenth-century curtain from the synagogue of the followers of the Holy Baal-Shem-Tov in Lvov.

"The Jewish raisin took back his document and the money, hid them in his bag, and began to prepare himself for his journey. He refused to eat or drink. Before leaving, he approached me. Felt my sleeve, rolled it up with one quick gesture, and kissed the blue number on my arm, and went out crying. I heard him crying as he walked down the Paris street in the pouring rain, and I saw him bump into an English tourist dressed in a beige tweed suit who managed to take a picture of him with the camera that was hanging from his neck.

"A few weeks later the famous Jewish painter Manny Zion entered my Uncle Hershel's store and bought the ancient curtain from the synogogue named after Rabbi Lemech from Troike. He was a short man and his gray hair tossed in the wind. During the war he had escaped to London and settled there, and now, wealthy and rich, he had come back to Paris, purchased a magnificent atelier, and in his atelier, so we heard—and what Jew of Paris in those days didn't follow with excitement each and every doing of our distinguished artist?—he gave small parties, and the big shots of the country came to drink wine next to the great artist, to buy his paintings and listen to the words of his mouth, so in his case the Scripture was fulfilled 'For out of Zion shall go forth the Law.'

"One day, about a month after our distinguished artist purchased the curtain, a rich American tourist happened to visit my uncle's store and bought from us a complete set of furniture in Baroque style, all made by my Uncle Hershel. The tourist asked me to take him to the house of the great Zion so he could have the 'honor,' as he said, of purchasing two or three paintings. After I telephoned the artist and explained the matter, we were all invited to his house that very evening.

"I won't bother you with unnecessary descriptions. It was a

beautiful house. The furniture, the paintings, the decorations, the carpets—everything was in the best taste. His gracious wife, who was a head taller than he, served us superb Calvados.

"Following our drinks, the artist led us into his studio, the place where his paintings were woven out of what he himself earlier called 'a starvation for Judiasm.' 'Through libations from God's own hands, I am filled with a terrific hunger for Judaism, its symbols, its sacred tongue, its past, my grandmother Miriam who died a martyr's death, God's own spirit unlifts me and sanctifies my hand and paints for me, while I, who studied the techniques of painting from the French, assist God with great modesty and try to bring into realization and focus His ideas.' Those were his own words, and I won't say, Adam, that these words did not make an indelible impression upon me. I was no less agitated than the tourist, who was shaking already like a blown leaf in the presence of such sanctity which in a few minutes would be his own exclusive property.

"In the middle of the studio, on a lovely couch covered with silk and muslin, sat a model whose fat nakedness was being sketched by two students of our distinguished artist. I admit that a certain excitement seized me at the sight of the woman, at the sight of her white and rosy flesh, at the sight of her erect breasts, between which danced a small golden crucifix. The tourist paced back and forth in the room and paid no attention to the woman. He studied the artist's paintings, whereas I couldn't take my eyes off her—off her wonderful thighs, her flat stomach, her magnificent black hair that spilled across her back in waves upon waves. She was bored and was chewing gum. She stared at me with her laughing eyes. She smiled at me. And then, with a kind of vague fear and confusion, I lowered my eyes and saw, underneath her, the curtain from the sixteenth century. All at once I saw the angels wrapped in these curtains and praying, I saw the demolished synagogue, German soldiers pissing on the remaining hot ashes, I saw one Ukrainian with thick eyebrows pick up a scroll of the Torah and toss its ornamental crown into the river. I saw

Naomi, I heard the footsteps of the Creator and laughter, the laughter of the victors, and sobs splitting out of the rings of smoke. I saw the silent, suffering, world-wandering raisin. The blood and Naomi and the Rabbi from Tchortkov and the golden crucifix dancing between the woman's breasts and the artist with the white hair and his tall and erect wife. Do you understand? I fell upon the white cow and pulled the curtain out from under her, and she leaped up in horror, chewing gum, stunned, lovely, human. I fled as far as my breath could take me. To the Métro, to the street, to a friend's house. Until I was caught.

"I have bought a guillotine that is able to cut plastic. If Naomi's head had been made of plastic, she would have been saved and God acquitted. I bought it so that I might be reminded of the atrocity which here, in this house, sometimes starts to disappear. Dr. Gross calls this the beginning of recovery—in other words, forgetting. It will stand here and I, whenever I want, can lay down my head and bring to a close the agony of dying, what I call fate's game of pretense. The curtains may be found on the shoulders of angels and under the asses of loose women. The Schwester sister sees an angel of God in the stream of a Bedouin's piss. Thank God for giving me life so that I would be able to die!

16

WATERMELON,
WATERMELON!

SUNDAY, THE DAY OF REST for the uncircumcised laborer. The little church in Beer-Sheva constitutes a symbol of the stubbornness of the Jews, for it is as small now as it always was. Mrs. Lotti, whose asthma has been almost completely defeated, is nibbling on some tasty brittle cookies and talking with her friend Mrs. Samit. Since Pierre's rescue in the desert, she's got into the habit of adding a chapter of Psalms to her devotions. No, they won't be leaving. Actually, to tell the truth, their situation is good here in Arad. Pierre is happy, it's as if he'd found his life's cause. As for her, she has no complaints. This isn't Paris, you know, but the conditions here . . . the air-conditioning, the heating, the apartment, the car, the holidays and all.

Sunday at the Institute is visitors' day. Ruthie sometimes comes to visit Adam, but he has refused to see her. His grandchild, Ruth's son, is too young; Joseph Graetz won't bring him to the Institute. Nobody will come. That's why Adam doesn't usually look forward to visitors' day.

Sunday at the end of September. The sun outdoors has reached the boiling point. In the air-conditioned Institute, people are smiling on black carpets. Adam Stein and David, King of Israel, are treading down the corridor, and the hidden loud-speakers are playing *South Pacific,* sung by Mary Martin and Ezio Pinza. Adam pulls out a bottle of Remy Martin and takes a swig. "Look, child, I have proof that God is brutal. Take, for example, the song on Passover, about the 'kid' and the 'butcher.' It says that the cat ate the kid. Yes? So, if the cat ate the kid, then the cat is nothing but a killer, right? That's why the dog bit the cat, which was a good deed, a punishment for the sinner. But, then, why did the stick hit him? The answer is that the stick was a criminal and a bastard. But if the stick was a lousy crook, then the fire did the right thing when it burned it. Why, though, did the water put out the fire? The water sinned grievously. And the ox that drank the water was a saint, but the butcher who slaugh-tered the ox a notorious sinner. And the angel of death who slaughtered the butcher did the right thing. The conclusion, therefore, is that the Holy-One-Blessed-Be-He who murdered the angel of death had no right to do what he did."

David lifts his eyes and stares at Adam's lips as they swallow the Remy Martin. He knows Mr. Stein, and waits. Adam puts the bottle back and feels greatly relieved. He has drunk some Remy Martin, proved God's folly, and now they may proceed on their way, on Sunday, the day of rest for the Christians and visitors' day for the Institute of Mrs. Seizling, may she freeze in peace. "As for Remy Martin, here's a right answer for you. Remy Martin goes down the throat like oil. Regular Israeli brandy saws the throat like a file. The best liquor is worthy of somebody who has waved goodbye to clowning, my young friend, and has begun to smoke Havana cigars and relate to life as though it were a pretty bad joke which it's best to simply go through with, with as much courtesy as possible toward others and as many real pleasures for yourself." Thus spake Adam Stein on Sunday.

Now that the child's hair has finally been cut, his face is unrecognizable. He walks erect. The orbs of his blue eyes, those circles of sorrow, have softened, and his face has been rosy since the time he saw sunlight. But, though his face is no longer pale, there is an inexplicable sadness, an incomprehensible regret, in his eyes.

Adam carries the xylophone and talks nonsense. His spirits are high. The Remy Martin has had a good effect on him. He is about to meet people, he has plans. And not holy-water plans! This time he has really important matters up his sleeve. Dressed in a bright suit and a wine-colored shirt which gives him the appearance of a rebellious poet, Adam carries the xylophone and leads David, King of Israel, thinking about what is to happen today, visitors' day. He has dressed the child with great care and foresight. Short pants to emphasize his thin long legs that only two months ago straightened for the first time, an open tricot shirt, and the red sandals of a girl in order to "evoke laughter and compassion." That is the plan.

The lecture hall is buzzing with people. The air-conditioning is working at its glorious best. The festive soft music is winding its way through everything. The delicacies of Pierre Lotti soften the atmosphere even further, alleviating the usual tiresomeness and confusion of the encounters. For this day Pierre Lotti has prepared meat cut into small pieces and soaked in a sauce of onion, eggplant, aniseed and wine. Small fish in orange juice mixed with white horseradish and whipped egg yoke. Halvah pastry filled with nuts and dipped in fragrant Cointreau. And many other tidbits. The music dulls the voices and the noise. Smiles, handshakes, the tasting of dainties, the drinking of coffee with closed eyes.

Adam Stein signals to the child to stand in the corner, and the child obeys. He places the xylophone beside the child. Smiles at his fellow creatures, says hello to his friends, studies the faces of the visitors closely, the visitors he has never seen before. David, King of Israel, cleaves to the xylophone in the corner of the hall. David David David David, we will overcome, Adam says in his heart. Wait and see! I'll show you a spectacular swindle.

Adam approaches Mrs. Barrenbaum, who only two months ago was totally mute. In Jaffa she used to sit in the corner of a room, her eyes open but empty, without stirring, as though she were circled by rings upon rings of sponges. When she was living on Levinsky Street in Tel Aviv, the children in the street would torment her, howling by her window and imitating the sounds of dogs and cats and leopards and horses and she would come to the window, her eyes stretched wide open in the expectation of seeing terrible lions out to tear her to pieces. For when she was a girl of nineteen she married Bruno Barrenbaum, who used to travel to Africa and buy from hunters in Chad and the Congo wild animals for the zoos of Europe. Mrs. Barrenbaum knew Adam from the time when he would purchase elephants and bears and owls and other animals from Bruno for his circus. Once Hitler came to power, Bruno sold the owls and rare birds and took his wife to Israel.

When she met Adam more than twenty years later, she didn't recognize him. She had lost her memory completely. Her face was wrinkled and a vacant expression was stamped on it. Her eyes were blank and her hands trembled as she embraced her own body, so as to cut off any possibility of contact, any physical approach.

After Bruno died, wild beasts enveloped her on all sides, the children and grandchildren of all the captured animals Bruno had caged, come to seek their revenge against her for their forebears' loss of freedom. She shut herself up in her apartment on Levinsky Street, and the lions and elephants surrounded the house, so poor Mrs. Barrenbaum lived in a frightful and perpetual siege. Once, late at night, a black cat climbed onto the porch and scratched at her window. When Mrs. Barrenbaum turned to the window, she saw what looked just like a panther.

She smashed the window with a butt of her head, seized the cat in her quick hands, and strangled it. The unfortunate animal died in her apron. She burst out in triumphant laughter because she had throttled the panther that would have torn her to pieces.

The moment Adam nears Mrs. Barrenbaum, "the woman who is recovering," she climbs onto a chair—in accordance with Adam's prior instructions—straightens her orange dress, which she put on in honor of the great occasion, claps her hands, and when they all are watching her, begins her address. This is what Mrs. Barrenbaum says: "Ladies and gentlemen, kindly forgive me for disturbing your get-together, but there is no doubt that sometimes, for various reasons, we must turn aside from whatever surrounds us and pay attention to what is pushed off in a corner. I am referring to *that* boy!"—and at this point she lifts her narrow, bony, weak-muscled hand and points to David, King of Israel, who was wringing his own hands in anguish, his eyes riveted upon the plight of a fly that has got trapped in the synthetic air-conditioned sanctuary of Mrs. Seizling. "Yes, that boy. Kindly look at him! Perhaps you never had the privilege of meeting him, but his reputation must have reached your ears. Shut up in his room, chained, wrapped in a foul sheet, doubled up . . . Ladies and gentlemen, this lovely and tender boy, whose mild blue eyes you see now, was a dog. Yes, a dog. Simple as that. He barked, ate from a dog bowl, was chained to the wall, and was heading for death as a dog." She pauses for a moment. She learned her lesson well from Adam. Now that everyone is silent and the stillness is heavy and oppressive, she says: "Do you know who cured him? Did the doctors cure him? Was it Dr. Gross? Science? The male nurses, the female ones? No! Adam Stein cured him! And today, eleven months after Adam Stein and the dog met, the dog who has returned to his boyhood wishes to honor his teacher and savior with an offering. Ladies and gentlemen, would you please be so kind as to sit down a few minutes and thereby enable this boy, David, King of Israel, who has been resurrected from the oblivion of doggish-ness, to play, in honor of his teacher-savior, some melodies on his xylophone?"

A grumble of agreement. Heads nod, gaze in astonishment, and guilt freezes into a curtsy. They recall the dog. They have talked about him and now he is right before them. His pants short, his legs stilts. The crowd finds chairs and sits down. Adam, standing behind Pierre Lotti, signals to David with his hand, but no visitor catches that quick half-gesture. David, like an obedient puppet, responds. His hands have not yet been tamed; his long gaunt fingers, ten bones bound with skin, grope sadly and pick up the sticks. Adam hums, "Now!" Yet to himself, as he takes a swig behind Pierre Lotti's back from a flat bottle yanked out of his pocket quickly (Johnny Walker, Black Label), he says: "You're shit, child, you're a dog's grave, today I'm going to wipe you off the map once and for all!"

The puppet's hands feel the varnished surface of the wooden keys that sparkle in the fluorescent light of the hall. He sticks his elbows into his body and his hands swing smoothly. He starts striking the keys. Says Adam, half in anger, half in pride: *My genealogical tree, sir: fish eggs, frogs, a one-eyed donkey, and a dog. Art has no future if any dog can play an instrument! Where there's a will, there's a way!* The hall is hushed. The child's face glows, while the faces of the crowd redden with a certain embarrassment. The hands keep playing. The notes chase each other. Miles has taught him to play "Every man has a woman." A network of swindlers is discovered by the music at this point. The swindlers are caught and stuck in bottles. Once there was a sheriff who murdered the children of Scottsboro, lowered the ceiling on Wolfovitz's daughter, and killed Ruth Stein. A dog-child is playing jazz in the Arad desert.

Adam laughs to himself. *My wretched embryo is entertaining the Philistines, but soon the full man, Adam, will handle the real task.* Applause interrupts his thoughts. Happy visitors whack the boy on his back, embrace him with their eyes. However, as soon as they see his doggish fingers quivering, they flee as though they just remembered something important; they return—some to their relatives, some to their wives, some to their husbands, some to their children. Adam pulls David to the buffet of liquor and delicacies, feeds him and pours him a drink, and asks him to wait there. "I'll be right back!" he says. Adam steps past Sohnman the Astronomer, who is crawling on all fours and neighing like a horse while his three-year-old daughter rides on his back.

A tall woman is standing with her back to the Schwester sisters, who are conversing with two men dressed in dark suits. The tall woman kisses her thirty-year-old melancholic son, who once tried to join Miles's jam session but bolted as fast as he could from the noise. He loves cotton and quiet, flowers, the color red, and soft slippers. The woman, dressed to kill, kisses the young man, who suffers in silence. His face manifests revulsion. He doesn't open his mouth. With one hand he rummages through the purse hanging from her arm and takes out a shiny metallic lipstick, a black eyebrow pencil, a brush for eyelashes, a small pair of scissors, and a delicate round mirror framed in gold which resembles an early Babylonian piece of jewelry. He rests these items on the cheek that is free of his mother's kisses, and for a moment, as his cheek is touched by these objects, his face turns peaceful. At night he'll place the stolen goods on the chair beside his bed, he'll get undressed, turn on the radio and listen to the soft night music, and, gazing at the chair, he'll smile with joy.

Adam walks right past him, past the guests. He knows that every once in a while they will sneak a quick glance at the child. He knows that they are already, basically, sold on his idea, though they may not know it yet. The child has conferred hope on them. His strong appearance and his lovely playing have awakened their best instincts.

He halts in front of Wolfovitz the Circumciser, who is standing now by his daughter, Naomi. Naomi's head is wrapped, as always, in a black scarf. A few people are standing around them, including the very well-dressed old woman whose son has stolen her lipstick, eyebrow pencil, and brush. "It's a miracle, it's really hard to believe," says Naomi Wolfovitz. "I can still remember how he used to crawl like . . . how he used to . . ."

"Bark!" shouts the young man, all excited, his face flushed. "I remember how he would bark and scare everybody. Once he bit Shapiro and once he made shit in the middle of the dining hall in Jaffa. He tore the dress of one of the nurses, I forget her name, and one time he barked at me and I went berserk."

"The truth is," says Adam, pushing into the group, "I'll tell you what the real truth is, so they won't stuff you with fairy tales. Between you and me . . ." They listen eagerly. "They!" —and everybody knows who "they" are: Dr. Gross, Nachwalter, Jenny, Dr. Erd, Watson, Freud, Jung, Adler, Pavlov, Harlop the hypnotist—they, the establishment, the lawmakers, the muscle men. "They tried to cure him. Ten years they tried and failed. Then I came on the scene. Let me reveal a secret to you. It bugs them, it drives them crazy, it boils their blue blood, it mucks up their minds. They are jealous of me and therefore plot against him. Not me, they cannot touch me. They are cruel to *him*. They avenge their helplessness on him."

"Who?" Sarah Brody, a tiny woman with a melancholy face, raises her eyebrows. Her voice is a bit grating, verging on a shriek. "Who, who is cruel to that lovely boy?"

"They are, those bastards," Adam answers with fierce feeling. "They gave him insulin, electric shocks. They bound him, tortured him, but nothing worked. The secrets of the heart are unintelligible to them, and will always be. Air-conditioning, yes! But tears, no! But I, *I* taught him to stand, to write. He is an intelligent, talented boy. You heard him play? So they're jealous of me. And what do they do? They take it out on the poor child. But I'll take the wind out of their sails, I'll show them what has to be done. Those bastards! I am stronger than any fate, and they cannot forgive me that. The world loves the average doctor and hates the magician, the world loves the singer and hates the seer. That's how it is."

Adam designs his speech like an architect. Each word, each sentence, is well thought out. Their ears are cocked, their hearts are cocked. The circle of listeners increases. Glances swerve toward the child in the corner. Adam knows that the visitors have a hidden resentment against this gorgeous prison. In the depths of their hearts they would like to see here a snake pit, a Turkish jail, a Nazi detention camp, something brutal and inhuman, in order to have true feelings of compassion. But here everything is lovely, clean, sparkling. Now, suddenly, Adam Stein informs them that underneath the sterile covering, on the other side of the smiles and the excellent food, beyond the air-conditioning and the heating system, the music and the wine cellars of Pierre Lotti, are concealed cruelty, wickedness. In other words, everything they came here in search of. They can have their feelings of guilt and compassion to the full.

"And their jealousy! Their jealousy!" Adam continues, and the circle of listeners increases even more. "Their jealousy is hatred, and in their hatred, they abuse this unfortunate boy. The xylophone? The xylophone which you have seen here today was broken six times this week. And who do you think broke the xylophone? And who locked the door in the face of the crying child? Ah, why add and multiply words! It's all clear already. A patient whose cure they consider an impossibility cannot play a xylophone while they're around, not in their establishment! They withhold food from him, they lock him in a foul-smelling room so that he'll go back to being a dog. His parents refuse to visit him, the doctors and nurses all conspire against him. But the worst thing of all—yes, the very worst thing, though it may seem unimportant in your eyes—is that they refuse to give him what they know he loves most: watermelon!"

Mutterings of astonishment rise and fall. The woman with the gloomy face chuckles. A middle-aged man, dressed severely, repeats the word in a whisper: "Watermelon? Watermelon?"

"Yes, watermelon," says Adam Stein. "It's funny, but very simple! This child is crazy about watermelon. What can you do?

In everybody lurks some special craving. What's the problem?
Who is to decide what is significant and what insignificant? The
child wants watermelon. He wrote letters to the directors of the
Institute, but they refused. I brought him some watermelon, they
pilfered it from him. *Now* they wouldn't dare do that! But how
can I get hold of watermelon in this Institute? The minute I step
into the kitchen they hide all the watermelons. They've set up a
watchman whose single and only function is to prevent me from
reaching the refrigerator where the watermelons are kept. And
that is a direct violation of Mrs. Seizling's will. Boy, would she
turn over in her grave if she were ever buried! But who can stop
them? Here they are the supermen. If you asked them about this,
they'd deny it, of course, yet it's a fact. They get their revenge
against me by being cruel to him. It's nauseating. If I could just
get him a watermelon! Even one waterm—"

Adam doesn't complete his sentence. He escapes from the
group on some pretext and is immediately swallowed up inside
another group. He tells his story all over again. He spices it up
or tones it down, lengthens or shortens it, according to the reactions on the faces of his listeners. He circulates from group to
group, telling the same terrible story of the watermelon.

David, King of Israel, wants to run for his life. The glances of
curiosity sting him like arrows. But Adam ordered him not to
budge from his spot and he's afraid to disobey. The visiting
hours have ended. People make their farewells. Adam leaves the
last group, grabs David, King of Israel, and drags him away.
The xylophone remains standing in the corner. They step down
the corridor. Adam, in good spirits, whistles "Mack the Knife."
When he was a young man, the great Lotte Lenya sang that song
in his exclusive honor, at a party which the famous Ludwig
Meyer gave to honor the Jewish "stars" in Berlin.

The child weeps, but Adam pays no attention to his tears.
They won't spoil today's victory, they won't becloud his joy. No,
good people, don't cry. We will rescue our dear child, the darling
of the universe, we will name him David Asshole, Masshole,

Shmasshole, Casserole, Israel! Look at that, ladies and gentlemen, did you notice the association? He begins as David Asshole and ends up as David Israel. Doesn't that testify to something? Ah, we will save Asshole, we will give him watermelons
by the hundreds! Ladies and gentlemen, let me divulge a certain
secret! I never even asked him if he liked watermelon! It's very
likely, in fact most likely, that our dear child Asshole loathes
watermelon. After all, have you ever seen a dog eating watermelon?

The child is frightened now, and emits a bark. Not a dog-like
bark, not a human cry. Something in between. And Adam's
face whitens all of a sudden. They stand before the door to
Adam's room, and, terrified, Adam pulls open the door, enters
his room, and slams the door in the child's face.

A week passes, and Sunday comes again. Visitors' day at
Mrs. Seizling's Institute for Rehabilitation and Therapy. Along
the road leading to the Institute comes a green 1958-model
Chevrolet, its antenna broken and one windshield wiper missing.
The brakes shriek, the car stops. Adam Stein approaches and
smiles. The window opens, a big green ball is handed to him. He
mumbles something, the car drives off. Adam transfers the ball
to Jenny. Jenny runs to Arthur Fine, who is hidden behind a
pillar. Arthur takes the ball and runs into the yard. Transfers it
to Phyllis, Pierre's wife, who gives it to her daughter, who takes
the ball and runs to the kitchen. Pierre grabs the ball, lays it
down beside the large refrigerator. Arthur returns to his hiding
place. A red Simca, license-plate number 208842, stops. Jenny
approaches the window and receives a package from the driver:
a green ball. Adam stands by a cypress sapling that was planted
not long ago and waves his hand. Two cars are nearing the curve
up above! Jenny hurries, thanks the driver, signals with her
hand as if to say: *You can go now!* She takes the ball and runs
with it to Handsome Rube, who is standing by a wheelbarrow
covered with a tarpaulin. Rube removes the canvas, Jenny

places the ball in the wheelbarrow, and at that very moment two cars appear, one after the other. Rube snatches up the canvas, runs in between the two cars, and conceals from the passengers of one what's happening to the second. Jenny laughs and, pointing to Handsome Rube, says to the driver, "He's from the Meteorological Institute. He's checking wind frequencies!" The canvas flaps in the wind. The driver smiles, takes out a big green ball and hands it to Jenny. At the same time Adam accepts a green ball from the driver of the second car. Adam runs and drops out of sight, Rube steps aside. The two cars move off. The balls are inserted in the wheelbarrow, and Rube wheels them to Phyllis. Phyllis wheels them to Arthur, Arthur to Pierre's daughter, and Pierre's daughter to the kitchen. Pierre takes the balls out and lays them down by the huge refrigerator. Pierre's daughter brings back the wheelbarrow. Another car approaches and Adam halts it. A man hands him a green ball.

"For the poor child. A watermelon! I'm sure the others didn't think of doing this."

"They didn't. You're the only one," says Adam.

The man starts up his car and drives away happy.

Another car erupts around the curve. Adam hurls the watermelon to Arthur, Arthur is struck hard and falls, but crawls with the watermelon to Jenny, and Jenny transfers it to Rube, who puts it in the wheelbarrow while Jenny covers it with the tarpaulin. The car that had burst upon them stops, Jenny comes running back to the path and gives the driver a charming smile. She wants to gain time and enable Arthur to disappear. She doesn't want the driver to see Arthur crawling. No, he didn't notice. Another watermelon. A bus comes puffing from the top of the hill and screeches to a stop. The driver takes out a Bedouin wicker basket with about ten watermelons in it. The passengers smile good-heartedly behind the windows, closed on account of the air-conditioning. Adam thanks them with a wild wave of his hand. A Deux Chevaux car is almost there. The bus drives off. Adam hauls the heavy basket to the cypress sapling. Handsome

Rube and Arthur leap to the path and drag the basket away.

The Deux Chevaux arrives. Jenny swoons in the road. The driver bursts out of his car and tries to revive her. Arthur and Handsome Rube rush toe-to-heel toward the wheelbarrow (her one eye sees everything, her other is closed, a trick she learned from the swindler), they empty the basket into the wheelbarrow, and wheel it to Pierre's wife. Pierre's wife wheels to her daughter, her daughter to Pierre, Pierre removes all the watermelons and his daughter returns the barrow to her mother, her mother to Handsome Rube. Jenny now wakes from her swoon. Adam arrives and takes the watermelon from the driver. They roll the watermelon to the tarpaulin and cover it. A hot wind blows. Another car approaches. The Deux Chevaux has gone. Adam accepts the watermelon, conveys it to Arthur, Arthur to Jenny. Jenny dashes to Handsome Rube. Handsome Rube, his feet going like scissors, carries it to Pierre's daughter. Pierre's daughter to her mother, the mother to Pierre. Another car halts, a black Ford. At its heels, a white Triumph. Adam pulls a balloon out of his pocket and blows it up quickly. The driver's eyes are caught by the inflating balloon. Jenny approaches the window of the Triumph and gets the watermelon from the driver. Delivers it to Rube, Rube to Arthur, Arthur to Pierre's daughter. Adam flies the balloon, the woman next to the driver laughs. The balloon has the shape of Mickey Mouse with black ears. Adam accepts another watermelon and rolls it to Arthur, who jumps over it and then falls on top of it. Rube brings the wheelbarrow. Jenny lugs the watermelon to Pierre, Pierre's daughter and the mother push the barrow. It's hot. Three cars appear, one after another. Adam flies another balloon. Arthur blows his trumpet. Jenny adjusts her stocking, exposing a gorgeous leg. Each driver watches something different. Handsome Rube runs handsomely with the tarpaulin. "He's from the Meteorological Institute," says Jenny and smooths her calf. The driver tosses her both a watermelon and a kiss. Jenny to Arthur, Arthur to Adam, Adam to Phyllis, Phyllis to Pierre. Arthur blows his trumpet some more, Jenny faints again. The driver and his wife burst from the car and try to revive her.

Adam grabs two watermelons and rolls them. Rube is back with the barrow. Pierre's wife and daughter rush over to assist him. They roll the watermelon to the barrow. Arthur lugs the canvas and they cover the watermelon. Jenny concludes her faint. The driver starts his engine, but his wife wants to photograph the desert. Adam shouts: "Military area! No pictures!" The woman is taken by surprise and returns to the car. They drive off. Another car arrives. Arthur runs, transfers to Adam, Adam to Rube, Rube to Jenny, Jenny to Phyllis, Phyllis to her daughter, the daughter to the father, the father to the refrigerator. It's hot. The operation was a success.

While the guests are all conversing among themselves in the recreation room, drinking coffee, eating biscuits and delicacies fit for a king, Adam stands in the kitchen examining the pyramid of watermelons. Pierre stands beside him. In his hand he holds a small notebook and a pencil, and together they count and re-count. They still haven't reached an agreement. Adam claims there are 320 watermelons and Pierre counts 308. The argument ends in a compromise: 315. Actually, Adam knows very well that there are just 300. Pierre also knows it. But they pretend, Adam for the sake of swindling and Pierre for the sake of Adam.

Pierre: "Okay! Three hundred and fifteen watermelon! That means nine hundred liras."

Adam (scratching his forehead): "Eleven hundred."

Pierre (hesitating): "Nine hundred and fifty?"

Adam (quickly): "A thousand and sixty. Not a grush less."

Pierre (begging): "Nine hundred and ninety-five?"

Adam (shooting his words): "We made a deal. A thousand and ten."

Pierre: "A thousand?"

Adam: "A thousand and five."

Pierre: "Five!?"

And Pierre Lotti opens the cash box and takes out twenty fifty-lira bills. With a gay gesture he extends them to Adam. Adam waits for another five. Pierre was going to forget about that, but not Adam.

Adam is happy today. He hasn't been so happy in a long time, a very long time. He has organized the operation from start to finish and everything worked like clockwork, without a single mishap. What a brilliant idea, perfectly planned and executed! He flatters himself and doesn't blush. His mind recalls each of the visitors, the red Simca, the Deux Chevaux, the woman who laughed in the black Ford, the air-conditioned bus, all of them. Now they are sipping coffee, nibbling cookies, in good spirits. He knows that every person there is experiencing a sense of sweetness in his throat, as though he has accomplished some great task.

They won't reveal to one another the secret of that sweetness. Each one will think that he and he alone was considerate enough to remember the child.

At night, in his room, Adam sits opposite Jenny and explains to her in a soft monotone: "You go to Tel Aviv and approach Mr. Selegman, 72 Montefiore Street. You deliver the money to him and instruct him to purchase shares in the corporation Futurities. You wait a day and return to him at eleven the following morning, after there's been some activity and the value of the shares has risen five percent. Don't worry, I'll take care of that. You call Ziskind then, telephone number 324511, and inform him that Adam wants Plan 100 to go into operation immediately, without any delays. He'll trust you and call the municipal office and receive the information that it has been decided to build a bridge across the river and the value of the property across the river will rise today in reckless leaps and bounds. Ziskind will take the money from you, which you will get from Selegman after the five percent has been added, and will invest it in short-term loans linked to the Index."

She takes it all down. She will carry out every instruction. Jenny goes to Tel Aviv for three days. And after three days she returns to the Institute with a receipt in her purse from the Israeli Bank Leumi, in the name of David, King of Israel, which states that the bearer has invested in short-term loans the amount of 3,210 liras and if the bearer will maintain these loans and not withdraw a penny from the bank over the span of half a year, the above sum will be increased by 650 liras. Adam will invest this sum in shares, buy vacant lots, sell something else, buy again. In one year alone, as in the days of the miracle of recovery, the old dog will transform the young dog into a tycoon.

"He'll piss on them all," says Adam Stein. "On them all."

"And on you?" she laughs. She feels good because she's done something.

"On me too. On everyone. A king! Every dog is a king."

17

THE LAST LETTER

DEAR JOSEPH,

In this continuation of my previous letter which I was forced
to interrupt in the middle, let me try to be straight with myself
and, if possible, also brave, and finish the story that I tried, as
best I could, to tell you in that letter which you claim was "the
longest single sentence you ever read in your whole life."

I owe you, at least you, an explanation—or, more correctly,
an attempt at an explanation as what we call here an epilogue.
And I must perform it in a manner suitable for a clown like
myself and yet intelligible to a man of science like yourself.
Have you ever once asked yourself whether a true understanding, both theoretical and actual, could exist between a clown and
a chemist? The one mocks himself, the other wishes to explore
the nature of nature. In my opinion, no bridge exists that can
span the abyss separating chemistry from humor, for they are

opposites that cannot be altered. That is the case between you and me. Between us, between you and me, Ruth's grave will stand forever. I brought her into the world and you loved her—I didn't even have that privilege.

I will try, therefore, in simple words and in sentences with simple rhythms—for your jibes against my involuted style have clouded my spirit—to explain to you what exactly happened following the watermelon incident. Jenny, you remember, returned to the Institute with a nice enough bank account in her purse, and since there were a few other such incidents, the child left the Institute a wealthy youngster. But I am getting ahead of myself.

Yes, immediately afterward I fell ill again. Operation follows operation, the illness becomes more critical and nobody sees any outcome but death. Adam Stein fixes the date of his expiration plus the share of his sufferings, and he treks toward his death. Short and sweet. Yes, I was sick again and refused to see the child's face. Jenny pleaded, but I plugged up my compassion. I didn't want to see him again. I was afraid he would become more and more dependent upon me. I wanted to be free, to die unattached, I wanted to torment myself with the same freedom with which I had hastened my death. My skies were opaque. Herbert was mocking me, and in this last attack—for, no matter how strange it may appear, this was in fact the final attack—I sank into an absolute coma, and the passionate clamor of my twin Herbert and the mutterings of Jenny, my mad Jenny, were of no avail.

The day they decided to operate on me once again, a magnificent sun shone through the window in my room. I recall that I was thinking about Mrs. Seizling, who, just a few days earlier, had been brought to her final rest in the courtyard of the Institute. I didn't go to the funeral. I was of the insane opinion that a woman whose corpse had been frozen so long did not deserve my presence. That's what I told Jenny, who became very sad when she heard my words. She was smoking a cigarette, sitting at the head of my bed, and massaging my scalp. I was afraid of those fingers because they loved me. I hated love. I was scared of Mrs. Seizling's corpse. With her burial, something had come to an end. I even refused to initiate Herbert into the core of these matters. In my conversations with him, I held back any reference to the good-hearted American woman. As part of the funeral service, the Schwester sisters, I hear, sang sad and lovely songs. And Dr. Gross gave a splendid sermon. It was quite a ceremony! Pierre Lotti told me that the family representatives calmed down only after they had tasted his special Beef Stroganoff. Now they were back in Cleveland and Dr. Gross had ordered that I be operated on.

That dear man Dr. Gross. Sometimes when I think of him, I know for certain that I will miss him. A man who was destined to be a poet but became a doctor. His entire life is a search, an unflinching unflagging search for the answer to the riddle of sanity, and to this day he doesn't have complete faith in the superiority of sanity.

On the way to the operation, on the way to my last operation (that's what the doctors called it and Dr. Gross, after a bitter controversy, came around to their opinion), Jenny and the child stopped the cart I was being wheeled on. Fate, it seems, ordained that meeting. The child wept. How I loved his lovely blue eyes. He wept and Jenny spoke in clipped sentences. I remember her words. The way a needle digs into the flesh of a record, her words cut into my body and have not left me. At this very moment, as I sit in the pension of my old Ruthie beside the window looking out on the thick-trunked eucalyptus trees that canopy the Yarkon River, I sense how my body spins and her words slip out of the grooves of my skin, as though I were a record that Jenny had cut at that time. I don't know why I came back to Tel Aviv. Perhaps it reminded me of the white shapeless suburb in Berlin where I fathered the person who was later to become—a gold cross tied around her neck—your wife.

My child cried. You see, I call him "my child," and you knew him as a dog. No, he was no longer a dog, and as he stood there beside my operating table which the two nurses were about to wheel into the operating room, I understood that he wasn't a dog and would never be a dog again. The moment I saw him I called for Herbert, but Herbert refused to come. Jenny said: "You made him rich, you put him on his feet, you turned him into a human being, and now you pretend you're a stranger. You're cruel, you're hopeless, you're going to die. You don't know how to love. You hate not only yourself but also your daughters, your wife, this child, and me."

Her words didn't astound me. She was beautiful as she spoke. Her face was pale and not a muscle stirred. Her eyes pointed at me like daggers. And when I called for Herbert and Herbert wouldn't come, I saw the child's tears and realized that I had compassion for him. And, what was worse, that I had compassion for myself, that I had compassion even for Jenny. But I attempted to defend myself with the stubbornness of despair. I said to her: "He doesn't understand a thing. Money doesn't make a dog a human being. I am a dog and that's how I was able to avenge myself against him. I remained a dog, but he is nothing but a hermaphrodite. He's neither a child nor a dog." My words sounded, even to them, senseless. The child actually smiled between his tears. Anybody who has spent so much time on all fours and been a canine is able to develop senses which the ordinary man doesn't have. In us, in him and me, there existed a secret sense which enabled us to make out what was hidden or omitted.

In the Institute for Rehabilitation and Therapy there never was such a marvelous lunatic as Jenny. Her, too, I miss. But to her I cannot return. Without my madness I am a *tabula mortua,* blank as death, zero. I've been out of the Institute for a whole year now and she still hasn't visited me. My letters she doesn't answer. Though every week she writes to Adam Stein, though week after week I receive letters addressed to Adam Stein, Dog, Inc., these letters are not for *me.* They are for the Adam Stein she knew at the Institute. *Me* she refuses to acknowledge, and I understand her. She loved only one man in her life, and that man I murdered. The moment I recovered, Adam Stein was buried. Jenny is still in mourning for him.

There I was, in the corridor, Adam Stein the dying patient. Above me a beautiful angry woman and a child who was crying and smiling through his tears. Then, dear Joseph—and I shall never forget the speed of that rash action—the child and Jenny grabbed the cart and fled with it toward my room. I screamed and tried to stop them, but my screams and efforts were useless. The two appalled nurses chased after us, but Jenny managed to outrun them and they lagged behind. I was miserable and angry. I shrieked. Jenny slammed the door with a bang and the nurses cursed and yelled on the other side of the door. Jenny turned on the radio and some army marching songs drowned their anger. The child approached me and kissed me. He kissed me on my lips and hid his face in my shoulder. The act was sweet to me. I called to Herbert and Herbert didn't come. Jenny undid the straps and, together with the child, she carried me from the table to my bed.

Jenny argued that these operations were stupid, that all I needed in order to be happy was love. And right here, she said, stood two persons who loved me. She and the child. And before I understood what was happening, she undressed and entered my bed. The child sat at the edge of the bed and bit his nails.

Dr. Gross called out to Jenny from the other side of the door. Jenny turned down the radio, camouflaged a smile that was already dancing in a corner of her mouth, and said: "Gross, don't disturb me. I know what I'm doing. Everything is okay, believe me. The child is here. Adam will be all right. I swear it." She spoke, she shouted, and I'll never understand how she did it, but the fact remains that she convinced Dr. Gross everything was all right, that it was possible to postpone the operation, and Dr. Gross and his nurses went away from the door. When the longed-for silence came, Jenny burst out laughing, and slowly we joined her, the child and I.

We made love. Though the child didn't watch, he sensed what was going on. Obviously, he will never forgive me. However, somewhere in the intricacies of my brain I knew, in doing what I was doing, that I was cutting myself off from him. Apparently that was what I wanted. And also what she wanted, that vulture. He wept quietly. His tears cascaded down his cheeks. Though he wouldn't turn his face toward me, and I saw only his straight back and his taut muscles, I experienced his tears.

That was the last time Adam Stein slept with Jenny. The following morning, after the child had been taken away for a checkup, Jenny came back to my room and found me in an unfamiliar, weird mood.

After one whole day I had managed to find Herbert, but realized suddenly that this would be our last encounter; I don't know how it occurred to me that I would never see Herbert again, for he was my twin brother and lived with me a very long time.

When Jenny entered, overflowing with love and poison like that famous snake in the Garden of Eden who, out of love for Adam, sealed his fate, I ordered her to make love to Herbert. But I must emphasize that the Adam Stein who commanded Jenny to lie with Herbert was not Herbert. I can guarantee that. Today I can frankly say that Adam Stein actually stood off in a corner and observed. Just the way I wanted to believe that the child had done the previous day while I lay with Jenny, though in fact he was biting his nails. Here, however, in Ruthie's quiet pension, it is difficult to even imagine such a terrifying scene.

Jenny undressed, for she never could withstand an order from Adam Stein. She cursed from agony and shame, and took Herbert's body on her with a dirge of grief. But Adam's hidden eyes commanded her; throughout their love-making Adam's voice dictated what had to be done. The voice demanded a smile, so the dirge ceased. The voice demanded that she kiss Herbert's body, the voice commanded that she scream when her final excitement came. And Jenny actually screamed, and as she screamed Adam laughed, and at the sound of that laugh and that scream Herbert got up and left, never to return.

My dear Joseph, some dreads can match the dread of death. At that time, when I had lost the last remnant of my family, when I had become a total orphan and had nobody in the world I could call my own, then I felt a terror of this sort, to its full. This terror pointed to the beginning of the end of a dream of death, a dream that Herbert knocked into my soul diligently for many days: If Herbert dies, Adam must continue to live. I felt I had to be a living tombstone for Herbert, the way your son will be a tombstone for me.

Jenny cried. I cried, too. We mourned for our kinsman, our loved one. Jenny forgot her shame. I was the only one left. I called to Herbert, I pleaded with him, and he refused to come.

When Dr. Gross found out that Herbert had vanished, a smile broke out in his black eyes. This Adamphile was so happy that that evening, as Jenny informed me afterward, he got drunk and returned home singing at the top of his lungs and tottering.

My dear Joseph Graetz, I am sitting now in the same lovely room which, a few years ago, I left in order to make my final visit to the Institute for Rehabilitation and Therapy. Ruthie is glad I'm back. Although I never answered her letters, her face beams with joy. Each evening we sit in the living room, Ruthie pours superb French brandy into beautiful goblets, and, by the light of an antique table lamp, we listen to music and converse. How I love her German, the melody of the words, her quiet manner of speaking, which is as old-fashioned as an antique rug, yet caresses me like an embrace. Sometimes we regress to the madness of youth and go up to her room. Her bed is soft and covered with a rather nice pink spread. I think that's the way I am going to die: old and exhausted and as free of worries as a child. Ruthie takes care of me. And, in return, I offer her boundless satisfaction. I am at her side and she needs me.

Let me return to the events which, in the end, brought me back to Ruthie.

My child recuperated and suddenly I didn't resent it any more, so Dr. Gross decided to run a little experiment. An experiment *à la* Adam Stein. The swindle involved in this test was something that, I imagine, he learned from his master—namely, yours truly.

One day Dr. Gross called me into his office and told me a long and wearisome tale about a certain man who came to the Institute with a piece of his brother's clothing. This brother, it seems, died in some mysterious way and the man wanted to know further details about it, and since he heard that Adam Stein, etc., and finally he—in other words, Dr. Nathan Gross—promised to do as the man asked. "So please, Adam, for my sake, for the sake of our friendship, do me this favor and feel this piece of cloth."

I felt it. For a long while my fingers vibrated across the material and then I hit the ceiling. Nobody had died! I said. The whole story is made up! It's a lie, I screamed, a disgrace! Dr. Gross sat sunk in his armchair, his eyes staring at me like two flashlights. Nobody has died, I repeated, and nobody is about to die. The owner of this piece of cloth is alive and will continue to live for many years. He is not sick. Or maybe he *was* sick, dangerously sick, but he has completely recovered now. I don't know, it's not altogether clear. The man should be told this, I shouted. Deception is a terrible sorrow. You must tell me if he has recovered, I yelled. Maybe he doesn't know about it and such ignorance is terrifying, I'm trembling, I'm frightened.

Then Adam Stein was informed that the cloth was his own. A piece of material cut from one of his own suits. Adam Stein enjoyed Dr. Gross's prank so much that he had to kiss the giant on both his cheeks, and when he returned to his room he lay down a long time, his eyes fixed on the ceiling, and smiled like a young boy who has been caught in some mischief.

Since I do not wish to elaborate any more than is necessary, my intention being, dear Joseph, to reach the conclusion of this matter—or perhaps its commencement, if we take as our final

point our beloved child—I now skip over a certain period that
was, in essence, a period of adjusting to the changes that had
obviously taken place. The adjustment amounted to a gradual
approach to the ultimate clarification. In this way, the final clarification did not come as a surprise. I recuperated. Bit by bit, the
nightmares stopped torturing me. It was a strange, amazing, un-
thinkable turn of events. In the past few years I had been released several times from one mental hospital or another and
sent out to the world. But those recoveries were of slight value.
We always knew, I and the doctors, that I would be back soon.
But this time, after a year and a half, I was to exit and not come
back. Dr. Gross knew it and I knew it, Jenny knew it and Ruthie
knew it. Ruthie, my old woman, that young girl, sensed that I
was returning, and without my writing her a letter, she cleared
out my old room, painted it (covering the old wallpaper with a
layer of lovely yellow), and waited for me. And, indeed, I did
come to her. How beautiful and peaceful and restrained was our
meeting!!

In those same days of adjustment to my last recovery, an incident occurred which shed light on my relationship to myself and
to the child.

One gorgeous day, as I was sitting in the courtyard not far
from Nurse Spitzer's nursery, and surveying the chess-players
and the flying balloons, the child appeared and sat down beside
me.

Before going out into the yard, I had said goodbye to Miles
Davis. Miles had been released and was about to head home.
His recovery wasn't exactly complete, but from the day he admitted to me that he had never been in New York he felt better.
And now, after a thorough treatment, the doctors felt that it was
not out of the question for him to have a certain kind of life
outside the walls of the Institute. I believe that he will yet return
here, but who knows? Maybe he won't. We parted with great
feeling. I don't think we'll ever meet again. I found out that
Miles traveled to New York, stayed there a few days, panicked,

and returned to his parents' home in Tel Aviv. I was also told that he is now playing in Jaffa, in some nightclub that opened recently, and I'm glad he has found his place, for the time being at least.

We sat on the bench, the child and I. It was a marvelous day. I shut my eyes and pretended I was asleep, but my eyes followed his every expression through my lids. He studied me carefully. I knew he wasn't sure that I was actually asleep. He stood up and began pacing back and forth. Near to where we were sitting was a huge bulletin board. The child stood with his back to me, staring at the bulletin board. From afar the bell sounded, announcing the meal. I didn't get up. I sat and watched the child, observed his straight back.

And then something strange happened. Out of the bulletin board a voice spoke. The voice, which trembled at first and afterward became firm, read an announcement which I had stuck up on the bulletin board a few months earlier. The voice was unfamiliar, I had never heard it before. The voice said: "To all interested parties, I am happy to declare that on the tenth of this month at eight in the evening I shall again conduct my seminar on the history of painting and sculpture. The syllabus covers art from early man to our day, including ancient Egyptian art, Assyrian, Greek, Roman, Byzantine, and Medieval, all in a new light and perspective, the Renaissance . . ."

The voice droned on. Who was it? For a moment I thought: Maybe Herbert is back? But Herbert didn't sound like that. Had I begun to hear voices again? It was the dog talking. With his back to me. The dog had opened his mouth and his voice was as lovely as his eyes, as his straight back. We had recovered, he and I. Why? To this very day I haven't the shadow of an answer. And neither has Dr. Gross. God has the explanation, obviously, but we are not on speaking terms since that terrible encounter in the desert.

The child didn't turn to face me. I knew he was crying. I barked softly and laughed. He still didn't turn around. He was shaking. His hands sought me out. I stretched my hand to him and he squeezed it in his fist, but still did not show me his face. We remained in no-man's-land. From then on, we were able to touch each other just with our fingertips, like all other human beings. Only in the dark days of madness were we able to make a contact of hearts, rubbing hearts like noses.

At the end of that month Arthur died. One day he ran away. They looked for him for several days, but he was already dead when they found him. He had reached Elat, gone to the beach, and sought his Beatrice. When he couldn't find her, he went back to the kibbutz school his daughter used to attend. However, he never went inside the school, apparently because of fear. He squeezed himself into the branches of a giant sycamore tree, and there he sat until they found him lifeless. Nobody knows how he died. In the post-mortem autopsy, they found his heart was defective. But even that didn't settle the matter. Before running away from the Institute, he had inscribed several names in his hieroglyphic script:

1. Adam Stein. Dog. Formerly in Camp Auchhausen. Today: Society for the Prevention of Cruelty to Animals, Bne-Brak. A bastard. He won't die! Never!

2. Dr. Gross. Formerly Klein. Camp Auchhausen.

3. David, King of Israel. Formerly a king, today a dog. A traitor.

4. Beatrice. Holland. Amsterdam. Stumped Dream Street, #1939–45. Dark abyss. No answer. Kill me! Please.

Following Arthur's burial, I knew that I was soon to leave, and also knew that David, King of Israel, would exit at the same time. I made final preparations. I said goodbye to many people. It is interesting how souls as lunatic as ours became so attached. Adam, who was stuck in many a hospital for the insane, will admit at once to the usual estrangement among the patients, the almost total separation. But in our Institute numerous ties were made, and people loved one another or needed one another, and for that reason alone (though there are many others) the methods of Dr. Gross are important and first-rate and the man deserves respect and praise.

I didn't know what to say to the Schwester sisters when I parted from them. We gazed at one another with enormous sadness. But we did not cry. We didn't mention what had happened. We didn't mention the desert and God's revelation. I held their hands in mine, the interlocked old hands of these sisters, and my eyes caressed their eyes. Pierre Lotti was forceful and stern. He was glad I was leaving. He was sure I'd be back. He wished me a complete recovery as well as a speedy return to the Institute. No, he wouldn't be going back to France. He enjoyed it here, even without Adam Stein. We ate a festive meal and drank excellent wine which Pierre brought from the cellar in my honor. No speeches were made, but the elder Schwester sister kept humming under her little mustache. Pierre Lotti informed me solemnly that, although I was forsaking the Institute, I would still remain a partner in Greeting Cards, Inc.; the moment things picked up, he would get in touch with me. I thanked him and promised not to break off the connection.

Parting from Dr. Gross was very painful and I couldn't possibly describe it to you. In our relationship there had developed a certain mystery which was beyond my capacities to fathom at the time of my departure from the hospital. Dr. Gross had absolute faith in my recovery, whereas I was not sure. My doubts are still many. At our parting he came to terms, in a sense, with both his inability to cure me and his certain knowledge that my recovery was made possible only through his assistance. I do not accept the notion that I cured the child. The child cured himself, with my help, though my help was not necessarily deliberate.

And Jenny. Jenny didn't come to say goodbye. Earlier, before I knew the exact date of my departure, she came by and we talked. She gazed at me with sorrowful eyes and I saw how torn she was between hate and love. Throughout the days of our love (or whatever you wish to call our relationship) I never saw so clearly that terrible shuddering rift. I had seen it before in its perfection, as a mixture of love and hatred, but now I was witnessing two separate faces, hatred here and love there. The sight was shocking, she was ugly and gorgeous at the same time. I wanted both to kiss and to kill her. I was polite and cold. We spoke of the lovely weather. It was as idiotic as a funeral service for a man who has not yet lost his consciousness.

As I already said, she has written to Adam Stein—not to me, but to the Adam Stein who remained behind. To me, the Adam Stein who has recovered, she refuses to write. She won't acknowledge his existence. May this beautiful woman be blessed. If not for her, my life would have been nothing but Hell. There was much goodness in her evil soul. She always craved for some lofty goal, for the impossible marriage of love and death, of the kiss and destruction. She said to me: "You think you have outwitted fire, now you'll get burned." And then smiled: "You loved me!" and didn't give me a chance to reply. I wanted to say yes, I loved her. Though, had I said it, she wouldn't have believed me.

Will I return to the Institute? Dear Joseph, Dr. Gross does not believe so. He thinks I have recovered. Jenny thinks that nobody ever gets better. That's her confirmed belief! And you? Do you think I've recovered? I simply don't know, I do not know. Ruthie wishes to believe that everything will be beautiful and good again. But were things ever beautiful and good? She cooks tasty meals for me. I read a lot, listen to the radio, to records. I listen to jazz, Miles Davis has infected me with a love for that marvelous music. I listen also to Bach and Monteverdi, and especially, and often, to Berlioz's Requiem. That is a powerful creation. It speaks to me directly, as though we shared some secret. Death is no longer in my hands, I cannot command it, it will come in its own time. I can no longer give myself diseases, I no longer am able to bring about my own end. I have shrunk, as it were. I have recovered and become an ordinary man. Sanity is pleasant, calm, amusing, but it lacks greatness, it lacks true joy as well as the awful sorrow which slashes the heart.

On my last day at the Institute, I took the child's hand and we left my room. I gave him the bundle of keys which I once promised him. He understood and smiled. He owed me that. He opened door after door, gate after gate, and we walked. He first, I second. We reached the edge of the yard and the old Kurdi. This gate, too, David, King of Israel, opened. I waited, because once—when he jumped back, wailed, and bit my hand—I had told him that he would cast the last key into the Institute and the Institute would go up in flames. And now he had the last key in his hands. He lifted his eyes, gazed at me, gazed at the key, and then looked back at me. I waited. We both waited. A moment of tension hung in the air, and afterward the child turned and delivered the key to the old Kurdi and squeezed my hand.

I approached him and embraced him. A white Vauxhall car was waiting for him. His parents were there to drive him away. We hugged and he stepped across to his parents. He turned his head once and I smiled at him. Then I turned to the car that was waiting for me on the other side of the Institute.

I do not know his name, I do not know the names of his parents, his family name, where he lives, in what bank the money I collected for him is hidden. And he does not know where I am now living. We were two dogs who knew each other.

Ruthie has just brought into my room a chocolate cake and a cup of steaming coffee. I sip the coffee and am about to conclude. Dear Joseph, that's the whole story, though it is missing a recognizable end. Sanity is sad. Nothing happens. I live today in a lovely, good valley. The heights are gone forever. There are no more frightful deserts, and I no longer leap into the fire, I'm afraid I'll get burned.

Will I ever see you and your son? I hope so. Will I return to the Institute? I do not know. What will I do during the years I have left? Even that I do not know. I shall meditate, reflect, die bit by bit. And the child? My child? What is he doing now? Where is he? I miss him. But it isn't proper to be thinking about him. He should live his life without me. He is a fine boy and I am sure he will succeed. Love, like death, has its dark side, its incomprehensible blocked portion. Have we been born, in actual honest fact, to love? Ruthie is crying downstairs in the living room. I can hear her dry, quiet, mournful sobs. Today is her birthday and she thinks that I have forgotten to wish her well. In my pocket is hiding, carefully wrapped, a magnificent gold watch which I bought for her. I'll present her with it later, when evening falls and the darkness thickens and we are sitting together and drinking French brandy by the red candles.

Joseph my dear, goodbye and good luck. Would that everything which has happened will never happen again, and that whatever will happen may, in fact, not happen, and may all dogs talk to one another.

YORAM KANIUK

Yoram Kaniuk was born in Tel Aviv in 1930 and took part in Israel's War of Independence. A painter, journalist, and theater critic, Kaniuk is best known as a novelist. His books have been translated to great acclaim into twenty languages and have earned him numerous international honors, including the 1997 *Prix de Droits de l'Homme* in Paris and the 1998 President's Prize in Israel. He lives in Tel Aviv.